Ben's Way Out

Ben's Way Out

Israel Chafetz

VANTAGE PRESS
New York

FIRST EDITION

Published by Vantage Press, Inc.
419 Park Ave. South, New York, NY 10016

Manufactured in the United States of America
ISBN: 978-0-533-15941-3

Library of Congress Catalog Card No.: 2007908721

0 9 8 7 6 5 4 3 2 1

To my parents, Phil and Ruby Chafetz,
who taught me to keep trying.
I deeply regret they did not live
to see this day.

Acknowledgments

I thank my family, friends, and partners who supported me throughout this five-year project. Their loyalty and encouragement is appreciated more than these words can express.

I thank the staff in my office who regularly were called upon to decipher the mysteries of my laptop computer.

I thank my editor, Myrna Riback, who pushed me to do the best work I possibly could do. She always believed in the story and the way I chose to tell it.

Finally, I thank everyone who will take the time to read *Ben's Way Out*. There is a little bit of Ben in many of us and it was not meant to offend.

Ben's Way Out

1

In every decade there is a profession *du jour*. In my decade, the 80s, it was the law. Like thousands of other aspiring law students, I rode this academic tsunami not knowing where this wave would leave me. On this, my last day of law school, I had no better insight into what would become of me than I had on my first day of law school. In fact, I was more confused than ever.

The wood-and-copper doors of the law school were the final barrier separating me from reality. I opened those doors and crossed the threshold into the prairie sunshine. Standing there and feeling the warm spring air blowing on my face was a liberating sensation. As I heard those doors slowly close behind me, I felt the burden of my years in school lifting from my shoulders. Also, I was relieved that my family and friends could finally identify me with a degree they could relate to. My prior academic achievements were somewhat more esoteric.

My first decision as a former student was what to do with myself that afternoon. I had no assignments to complete, no exams to study for and no summer job. I could do anything I wanted. The first item on the agenda was to tell my father that my formal schooling had ended, finally. I mounted my 1972 Datsun 510 steed, rolled down the window, turned up the radio and sped away through the university gates not looking back, not even through the rear-view mirror.

It was just before noon when I pulled up to my dad's office. He didn't know I was coming but Nathan Stein always found time for a visit from his son. As I walked into his office it struck me how little it had changed over the years. He had the same oversized, carved oak desk covered with papers in no apparent order, a shelf full of plaques recognizing a lifetime of philanthropic efforts and stacks of plumbing supply catalogues in file boxes on the floor behind his desk. I sat down across from him and as soon as he put down the phone he smiled, got up from behind his desk, and took the chair beside me.

He reached over and patted my knee as his way of saying hello, a gesture from my childhood. "And to what do I owe the pleasure of this unexpected visit? By the way, call your mother. She hasn't heard from you in two weeks."

"I'll call her today. I came to tell you that it's finally over."

My dad stared at me over his reading glasses. "Exactly what is it that is finally over?"

"School. I finished my exam this morning. My academic career is over." I looked down at my watch. "As of thirty minutes ago."

"No more exams?"

"No more exams. No more courses and no more degrees. All done. Finished. Over."

"Well, this is news." He glanced up at the clock on the wall behind me. "This calls for a celebration lunch. Are you free?"

"Am I free? I've never been freer in my life and I'm starving." We both stood up and walked out of his office. "I'll be back later," he announced loudly. "I'm taking my son out for lunch to celebrate his finishing law school." I knew my dad was proud and wanted to make sure all three secretaries in the outer office could hear.

In Nathan Stein's world, a celebration lunch could only mean one thing, delicatessen. His doctor had told him to stop eating high-fat food but he looked for any occasion to justify an exception to his diet. He usually found an occasion about three times a week, so the exception became the practice. He could not tolerate a restaurant that had taupe tablecloths, three different forks and a menu with a tassel attached.

By the time we arrived at the deli, there was the usual queue of customers. But, no matter how long the line, there was always a table for Nathan Stein. Once the owner noticed my dad, we were escorted past a line of envious onlookers and to our table. This place always took care of the regulars. As we sat down, a waiter appeared with a straw basket overflowing with dark rye bread and a plate of pickles.

"Menus, daily special or the usual?" he asked in a familiar way. I nodded to my dad and he ordered for both of us.

"The usual with two cherry sodas, no ice," he said. For the uninformed, the usual is a deli platter that is not listed on the menu. The waiter nodded and left. "Ben, are you really finished with school? I've heard this before from you and that was two degrees ago."

"No, this is it. I am not going back." I took my fork, stabbed a pickle and put it on my plate. "Last time I talked like this it didn't feel over but this time it's really over. I won't be going back to school in the Fall."

"Are you going to look for a job in a law firm?" My dad pushed the bread basket toward me, knowing I like the crusty ends.

"I haven't started looking but I'm not sure I'm cut out to work in a law firm. I didn't mind law school but working for a law firm is an entirely different matter. I'll decide by the time I graduate."

"And when will that be?"

"In about five weeks."

"Ben, you can't work by yourself in a cave and you can't be a student forever. There comes a time when you've got to go out and make a living."

"I'm through with being a student and I know it's time to move on. I'm just not sure if that means a job in a law firm." I started nervously playing with the cutlery and my fork did a triple flip onto the tile floor.

"The law is the only thing you ever studied that has the remotest chance of making you a living." At that moment the waiter brought two cans of cherry sodas and blue frosted plastic glasses to the table. He picked up the fork, left me a new one and put a straw in each glass.

"Don't worry it will all work out. I'll figure out what to do. It will come to me in good time. By the way, would it bother you if I passed on the graduation ceremony?"

"Yes it would bother both me and your mother. This will be our last chance to attend your graduation. In fact, don't be surprised if we have a little party to celebrate. Your mother has prepared a guest list, just in case."

I smiled at my dad. "Whatever you want."

"If you don't want to be a lawyer you could come and work with me. The plumbing supply business isn't so bad."

"I don't think it's bad at all. Actually, I always found it interesting but I couldn't. I must make my own way whatever that turns out to be. I won't be one of those sons who depend on their father for a living."

My dad put down his fork and looked at me. "If I was in your position, I would feel the same way. You've had a fine education and you should make your own way. But, the business is there if you change your mind." The waiter was back and put down two overflowing platters of delicatessen. "Enough, let's eat."

For the next thirty minutes, we ate, talked and laughed. My dad always told me the same jokes at lunch and I always found them funny no matter how many times I'd heard them. When we were finished, he paid the bill, as usual, and I drove him back to his office.

My next stop was a bookstore where I bought a book on how to write a résumé, just in case. I had them put the book in a plain brown bag as a precaution in case I met someone that I knew. There's no point emphasizing my unemployment or even worse, admitting that I wanted a job. I went home and spent the rest of the afternoon luxuriating in my apartment having nothing to do, nowhere to go and no one in particular to do it with. Then I remembered I promised to call my mother. She answered on the second ring.

"Hi, Mom, have you heard the news?"

"Your father just called. Why aren't you going to be a lawyer?"

"I might. I'll decide by graduation. It's only five weeks away."

"You'll do the right thing. Now that you've finished school and you'll have a career, maybe you should think about settling down. Most of your friends are married and it's not like you're too young." She always gets around to this subject.

"I still have single friends and the married ones don't seem that happy. Anyway, I'm only thirty-four."

"Nevermind, your father and I have been happy for almost forty years and it should only happen to you."

"Mom, I never met a girl like you and no one can match your brisket. One day, maybe, but my social life has not been very active lately."

"You don't try to meet a nice girl. You aren't going to find a girl sitting at those Italian coffee bars or at a restaurant that serves raw fish. You should go to singles night or the lectures at the Jewish Community Center. There you'll meet a nice girl."

"Mom, they're not for me. I don't want a nice girl. I don't like nice."

"Not all Gentile girls are perfect either," my mother reminded me.

"I'll see what I can do. But, my record with these nice girls is not good."

"You're everything a girl could want. And by the way, we're coming to your graduation and we're going to have a party to celebrate. It's a wonderful reason to bring the family together."

An extravagant family gathering was exactly what I wanted to avoid but I could not bring myself to deny them. These events meant so much to my parents. *It's only one night,* I told myself, *so what could go wrong?*

2

I had never been to a graduation ceremony, not even my own. I didn't need it, I knew I graduated. God knows I've had chances, since this was my fourth degree, excluding Sir Edmund Hillary Secondary. I am not the type who enjoys organized events. I don't like being the object of attention, especially if it is a pedestrian accomplishment. But, here I was, May 4, 1984, in this coliseum of academia seated amongst 1,253 other graduates from various disciplines and observed by hundreds of adoring friends and relatives waiting to capture this Kodak moment, 1,254 times. I was but one more flattop in a sea of mortarboards, sitting shoulder to shoulder, listening to a button tycoon who gave ten million of his fortune to the university in exchange for his name on a building and the privilege of making the convocation speech. The Button King was a true visionary who had bought the license for velcro just before the start of the arthritis epidemic. He foresaw the aging of baby boomers and invested in velcro. His words of wisdom to the graduating class were that our future lay ahead of us. Well, of course my future lay ahead of me. How could my future be behind me? But, if you give ten big ones to a Canadian university, anything you say are words of wisdom . . . after the check clears.

I never wanted this fourth degree. I already had degrees in actuary science, animal husbandry and contemporary philosophy. School was my way of avoiding a real job and anyway, I was good at it so why change? My strategy had worked for the last twelve years but lately, it had become embarrassingly apparent that my academic career was not getting me anywhere, although I had nowhere to go. But, I had to do something to pay off my student loans in spite of my ambivalence about a career in law. I became quite adept at filling out those loan forms and, over the years, I had managed to milk the system for over $40,000.00 in "I'll-pay-you-back-once-I-finished-school-and-get-a-job" loans. It was the student loan pyramid scam.

I figured that if I kept on going to school then I would never have to pay back the loans and I could cruise the lounges of academia forever. But then came the great betrayal. The student lounges, the center of my social life, went non-smoking. I could understand leaving the building to smoke a joint but going outside for a cigarette was not worth it. These new smoking rules disabled my social life. I lost my favorite venue for impressing the nubile first-year young ladies by smoking exotic cigarettes and talking academic nonsense. There was little point standing outside in the middle of a prairie winter to smoke a cigarette in the faint hope of getting laid. My academic pursuit had lost its focus and it was time to move on.

My parents were very concerned that the first Stein to go to university would end up working in inner-city transportation, which is the Semitic term for a taxi driver. So, with my mother's threat that she would self-induce a heart attack if I ended up as an apprentice in inner-city transportation hanging over my head, I went to law school. Besides, what self-respecting Jewish boy would take a job as an actuary or zookeeper? We all know those insurance companies only hire anti-Semites and zoos are cesspools of former Gestapo Rottweiler trainers. So what choice did I have? It was law school or inner-city transportation. Little did my parents understand that my entire academic career was simply a pathetic and clumsy attempt at getting laid and avoiding a job. The real skill I mastered in all those years of university was how to get a parking spot adjacent to my classes so I wouldn't freeze in the dead of winter. This skill would later prove to be invaluable in my professional development.

As I sat sweating in the hot auditorium waiting for my name to be called, I understood that this convocation was the ultimate affirmation for my family that they had woven themselves into the fabric of Canada. They had changed their name, lost their accent and taken up golf. But still the ultimate symbol of assimilation would be their son's graduation from a professional faculty of a university. It really didn't matter that these schools had degenerated into money sponges that required constant replenishment so desperately that they would compromise their reputation by awarding honorary doctorates to the likes of the Button King in exchange for ten million.

The University of Manitoba allocates two tickets per graduate for convocation ceremonies. This rule was completely unacceptable to my mother since at least six of our closest relatives had to witness

7

the coming out of the Steins. So, in true Stein fashion, my mother went down to the events office at the university and threatened them with anti-Semitic allegations for trying to restrict Jewish attendees if she was not given six tickets to the blessed event. She had lined up a group of ultra-orthodox Lubavitches to picket the graduation ceremony. She had managed to do that by telling them that the podium faced west, a subtle denigrating symbol suggesting that we should turn our backs on the Wailing Wall, hand Jerusalem over to the Palestinians and recruit Jews for Jesus. By threatening to disrupt this holiest of academic days and possibly offend the Button King, my mother was allocated the six tickets. So, there I was, sitting in the auditorium knowing that as soon as my name was called, the hum of six videos would start rolling and six disposable cameras would start flashing to capture this historic moment.

Lost in thought within the intimacy of the overpopulated auditorium, I was struck by a wave of apprehension about what was to become of me. I did not have a job and my desperate attempts to break away from my heritage were not going that well. My pursuit of eternal love with a Jewish girl always ended in clumsy failure. In the Jewish caste system, I was pretty low on the totem pole. My parents are first-generation Canadian. That is not socially appealing if it doesn't come with money. My law degree would either elevate me to a higher caste in the Semite pecking order or simply be a temporary diversion from my ultimate fate in inner-city transportation. *Well,* I rationalized, *at least it would say LLB on my taxi license.*

I awoke from my moment of reflection by the sound of my name ringing through the auditorium.

"BEN STEIN." Come on down and get that law degree.

In alphabetical order, my name was called just after Stadnyk and before Gilda Stein who was no relation but, after three beers, I could even take a shine to her. I marched up to the podium to get my scroll. As I stepped up to the stage, I could hear the cameras rolling and saw the flashing lights from the disposable cameras. It was a sight to behold and it was all over in little less than fifteen seconds. The Dean of Law congratulated me, except that he called me Mr. Stain, which I did not believe was an innocent error. It was his way of getting back at those liberal judges, Arthur Goldberg and Bora Laskin, in one single swipe. As I marched off the stage I smiled and nodded to my admiring relatives who reciprocated with the wave and yelled in Yiddish a phrase which loosely translates as "YO' THE MAN."

As I was about to sit down I noticed a piece of paper on my chair. It was folded in two and it had the initials "BS" on the front. These initials had always been a source of adolescent embarrassment to me but I had come to accept it as the cross I must bear. In any event, I picked up the small piece of paper, sat down and unfolded it. I was not sure if it was a treasure map or a reminder to pay my campus parking tickets. Inside, however, was a note which read, "Call me if you are interested (two rows back—two seats to the right). Julia Windsor. 450-5675." I turned around to look for that assigned seat and it was empty. I refolded the piece of paper, put it in my shirt pocket and held my hand to my chest as if it were Remembrance Day. This could be love.

3

That evening, my parents held a small reception to celebrate my graduation. They invited our entire extended family and friends to the synagogue library for a traditional Stein gathering. Needless to say this was not an occasion which I looked forward to. From my perspective, this was another unwanted organized event. As an only child I did not have siblings to lean on for support or act as a buffer from my loving family. The focus was always on me. With 225 guests, this party resembled my bar mitzvah except that there were fewer envelopes with checks in denominations of eighteen. I wore my only suit with the oversized inside pockets just in case a few envelopes come floating my way. With $40,000.00 in student loans, you don't look a gift horse in the mouth.

The party was called for 7:00 P.M. But the Stein family likes to come early. I would have liked to come fashionably late or not at all, but since I was the guest of honor, I had to be early. What I didn't realize until I picked up the newspaper in the synagogue foyer was that my parents had not only invited every known relative and friend but they had also placed a graduation announcement in the legal section of the *Winnipeg Free Press*. Staring back at me from the newspaper was my picture when I was thirteen years old with a headline that read, "Son of Stein Graduates." Imagine, 5,000 students graduate from law schools each year in this country and my family places an announcement that says something about my looking forward to a career in the law. The announcement did not mention that I did not have a job but it did say something about my three other unremarkable degrees. Maybe no one would notice the announcement, although the paper had a readership of 300,000 and the legal announcements were prominently displayed on the back page of the business section. I feared my parents had constructed the path to my legal demise before I had a chance to fail on my own merit.

Well, the cars started pulling up to the synagogue front door and the Mogen David Valet Service was out there in full force. It was one of those no-charge valet events where there are never a lack of customers. In fact, they lined up for the free valet service even with an entire row of empty parking spots right in front of the synagogue entrance. No one could resist the status of having a recent immigrant from Pakistan park their car.

There are three groups of vehicle owners who attend our family functions. There is the Mercedes-BMW group, who find a way of justifying buying German products based on reparation money and the proposed construction of a Holocaust museum in Berlin. There is the Buick faction who can't afford a Mercedes but defends their choice of automobile on the principle of what more do you really need? It has air conditioning. Finally, there is the Cadillac crowd who identify this automobile with the fulfillment of the American dream, except that they live in Canada. But what's the difference? Dreams have no borders. We all rely on American television for our news and we all share the same cold fronts which usually originate in northern Canada.

All 225 relatives and friends showed up within ten minutes of each other. It was the usual wedding-and-funeral crowd but I wasn't sure which category my graduation fell into. Both categories of events are held in the synagogue and there is always food afterward. But this was no chopped-herring-and-bagel event. Thus, it more closely resembled a wedding. That meant non-refundable presents and speeches.

Slowly and painfully, every one of the 225 guests swarmed to wish me the best in my legal career which they were confident would rise meteorically with stellar results. Every guest mentioned that they knew the animal husbandry degree was a passing adolescent phase and each one had assured my parents at one time or another that it would all work out and, of course, now it had. They also wanted me to know that they noticed I had put on a few pounds and it looked good on me. Their weighty comments prompted me to spend most of the evening sucking in my stomach each time someone came up to congratulate me. Slowly but surely I made my way through the crowd, trying to be as gracious as possible while being reminded that I was the first Stein since our family left White Russia to graduate from a professional faculty of a university. If I did not set an appropriate standard for generations of Steins to follow them they would meander aimlessly into the trash heap of academia. No pressure.

I knew most of the guests by name. But I could never quite figure out how those labeled as family were related to me. From years of observation and accompanying gossip, I knew that many of them were not on speaking terms with each other. I had considered handing out programs to clarify for everyone which relatives were not talking to each other. I was going to line up two major sponsors, a hearing aid company and a bank, to help defray the cost of publication. All family fights had elements touching on both those industries.

Most of our out-of-town relatives had come for the party. The only ones who did not show up were the ones who would not come because of some fight which had taken place forty years about some bill which was not paid having to do with funeral expenses for a great-uncle from Pinsk. Those who came never wanted to be known as the ones who were too cheap to show up. The relatives from Springfield, Massachusetts came for a piece of marble cake baked by my aunt Edie. "How could we miss such an event?" they said. "Who knows if we will live to see another?" The Springfield cousins had made a small fortune selling mail-order vitamins. The truth is their fortune in mail-order vitamins was based on taking payment in advance and then failing to ship the goods. It was all a big misunderstanding which was sorted out by the lawyers. There was some sort of settlement which included never using the U.S. postal service again.

The almost-worst part of the evening for me was when my dad got up to say more than a few words. First he thanked all our relatives and friends for coming to share in this great celebration of the first Stein out of White Russia to graduate from a professional school. Then he acknowledged all those people who came from so far away to celebrate with us. This included the relatives from Montreal who hated the "Goddamn" separatists; the family from Vancouver who channelled every conversation into the value of residential real estate on the West Coast; the cousins from Los Angeles who go to the same Chinese restaurant as Robert Schwartz who was once head of Universal Pictures short subject division; and, of course, my cousin Ruth from Washington, D.C. who had been married three times and once attended a party at the White House in honor of Apple Week. This was not your average crowd.

If that wasn't bad enough, then came the horrid moment. My parents had made the dreaded video. There it was, my life captured on eight mm and converted to video cassette and playing on the big-screen Sony. Yes, the film had it all. The first time I did this and the first time I did that. It was all there for everyone to see. The magic of technology had triumphed again. At age thirty-four, I was not too old to be mortified. I was only grateful that my parents did not provide complimentary copies of the video to anyone who sent in a self-addressed envelope. Although I did overhear some guests asking for a copy as a memento.

After my dad spoke and my mom cried, it was my turn to tell everyone how lucky I was. I didn't feel that lucky except for the fact that I still had that incredible note Julia Whatever-Her-Last-Name-Was left on my chair. As a matter of fact, I was still debating when the optimal strategic time would be to call her and what I would say. But I put that aside and concentrated on the task at hand. I knew I had to say something sappy like I could not have gotten this far without the love and support of my parents. Little did anyone understand that I had been hibernating in academia all these years to avoid the everyday tensions of work and wanting nothing more than to get laid. I did the usual ethnic thing by starting with a joke about the parrot who could speak Yiddish. Then I told everyone how much I appreciated them coming and giving me the sixteen copies of the biography of Louis Brandeis which any graduate embarking on a legal career must have for bedside reading and reflection. I even managed to make a joke about my checkered academic career.

The grand finale. My dad rose from his seat and walked back to the podium. He was only 5'8" but he always seemed so much larger than life with his confident demeanor, his striking tanned facial features and slicked-back grey hair, what was left of it. Now, as he stood in front of his relatives and friends I realized it doesn't matter how tall you are, but how you carry it. He asked me to come up and presented me with a small package which was a gift from the family. I opened the package and found a metal box which made a metallic sound when I did the obligatory shake before opening. When I did open it I found a key on a chain. It was the key to a security box at the Toronto Dominion Bank's main branch. In that security box was $25,000.00 in State of Israel bonds. Well, it wasn't like the

13

red sports car Dustin Hoffman got in *The Graduate* but it was one of those gifts which brings complete clarity to your circumstance in life. My parents loved me, and for them, those State of Israel bonds represented their loyalty to me, their cultural commitment and success in the New World. I kissed my parents and wiped the tear from my cheek.

4

Driving back from the synagogue, I felt a lot of conflicting emotions. As a victim of academia I had been trained to analyze and reason everything. The pursuit of logical reasoning is the Holy Grail of academic understanding. I was relieved that the embarrassment of the evening was over and I was pleased that I hadn't shown my impatience as the guest of honor in an overdone ethnic celebration. In another sense, I took a certain pride that I had graduated from law school and I no longer had to invent excuses or contrive explanations about my future. I had graduated from law school and no further explanation about my ambitions or goals was necessary. But I didn't have a clue what the hell I would do with a law degree. The thought of working in a downtown law firm and referring to customers as "clients" was not appealing to me. Still, mixed with these conflicting emotions about a law career was a sense of anticipation and curiosity. *Could I function outside the academic cocoon in which I had lived for the past twelve years?* I knew that somehow I would muddle my way through this vocational problem and achieve some semblance of success. But I didn't know what success looked like. It would be a shame if I achieved this elusive success but never recognized it.

Traditionally, on the evening after convocation, the graduating class gets together one last time before everyone goes their separate ways. My class was no exception. I decided to stop in at the Rae & Jerry Bar where my class was holding their final celebration. Since I was about ten years older than most of the others in my class, I did not have any close friends among the graduating class. Older students are accepted at school, but with an asterisk. The asterisk is that older students have a past.

The Rae & Jerry Bar has quite the decor. The place is dark and dominated by red tufted naughyde chairs which shine in the dark like the full moon. It is classic 1950s decor except it's 1984. The place has the feel of a venue for a third-rate mystery where the people who hang out there are part of some inner circle of something so secretive they themselves don't even know what it is. It has the perfect aura for the young professional or about-to-be professional who is desperately trying to break away from the pack. The problem is that everyone who goes there is trying to break away from the pack so they all end up part of the pack they're trying to break away from.

I walked into the restaurant and immediately the host directed me to the area adjacent to the open-bar. I hadn't realized that I looked so obvious, particularly at my age, and I took it as a compliment that even at age thirty-four I had the demeanor of a student. But everyone in the bar was from my class and the host made an educated guess about someone walking in alone at 10:30 P.M. and looking a bit lost.

I immediately made eye contact with some fellow graduates hanging out around the entrance to the bar, drinking imported beer. Once you graduate, it is a right of passage to abandon domestic beer and matriculate to the imports. I knew these people by sight but, for the life of me, I could not remember their names. These were the captains of the third quartile, destined to be personal injury lawyers hoping to get a quadriplegic case with a 40 percent contingency fee. I graciously acknowledged their presence and said something about the sense of relief at graduating. One of them asked me how my job search was coming. I ignored him.

The lounge was crowded and I decided the safest strategy was to make my way to the bar and get a drink so as not to look out of place. I do not flourish at these social events. I always feel like I've crashed a private party where everyone else is best friends and I am the intruder who was never shown the secret handshake. As I approached the bar, I saw a friendly face waiting for a drink. Her name was Sarah Gold something . . . Goldbloom, Goldberg, Goldblum or Goldigger. Anyway, what's the difference as long as you get the first name right. Sarah's starched white shirt looked terrific against her dark skin and her jeans showed off a great body. She was one of those women with a year-round tan that you just knew she did not get from a tanning salon. I had a certain curiosity about her ever since we met in evidence class during second year but I never did anything about it. I am basically shy and socially awkward. Sarah

16

had an engaging manner and she was stunning so I was sure she had quite a social life outside of law school.

We struck up a conversation and I explained to Sarah that I had not intended to be fashionably late. But, I was coming from a party my parents had thrown for me to celebrate the academic coming out of the Steins. I told her about the video and the announcement in the paper. She seemed genuinely amused and told me how her family had recognized the blessed event with a dinner for twelve at the Westin Hotel dining room. This restaurant had a harpist for background music who played "Tie a Yellow Ribbon." There is no accounting for taste. I sensed Sarah had the same ethnic ambivalence that I felt. We were not prepared to be the generation that turned our backs on 3,000 years of Judaism but I did not want to be responsible for defending it either.

The more we talked the less I noticed what was going on around me. We had established a common bond and spoke mostly about what we were going to do next. I was relieved that she did not ask me any personal questions. While we talked, other male members of our class came up to the bar and engaged us, mostly her, in conversation. She had a sharp wit and she could plunge the knife in so quickly the victim barely felt the mortal wound. With a body like hers, no insult would deter a male suitor.

We had reached that moment in our conversation when there was nothing left to say and it was unsociable to suggest leaving without implying something. At that uncomfortable moment, some Adonis-like creature approached who was obviously interested in Sarah and began to talk to her about a common experience which I was not privy to. In one sense, I felt she was casting me back in the water for a bigger fish but, in another sense, it was a relief that I didn't have to think of anymore things to say. I didn't want to make up some reason for leaving so I excused myself, implying that I was going to the bathroom and took my leave. I left the restaurant without anyone noticing except for the same three classmates who were still standing at the door when I came in. They made some comment about the party just getting started and asked whether I was going home to polish up on my interview skills. I acknowledged their cutting humor and I left having decided that I could never work with these people.

As I turned to walk out the door, I could see Sarah laughing among a group of graduates. I was convinced that I was the punchline of her story. I was a gate crasher at my own graduation party.

5

Sunday is a lonely day. The city has little to offer on the Lord's day and what there is isn't worth the effort. While I was going to school I could keep myself occupied by studying. In fact, I attribute much of my academic success to a non-existent social life. Everyone thought I was dedicated to my academic career, and I gladly accepted the label. In fact, my dedication to learning was nothing more than a diversion to overcome boredom and loneliness.

Sunday was a particularly awkward day for me because it is the day when families usually get together for brunch or a traditional Jewish Sunday night Chinese dinner. In fact, making the arrangements among siblings and parents was part of the dinner tradition. It was a way of keeping in touch. However, as an only child I was the arranger and the arrangee. Going out for Sunday brunch or dinner with my parents was always a quiet time compared to the large round tables of families where everyone was talking, laughing and arguing. We found the contrast so stark that eventually, we made excuses to avoid such outings.

Now with school finished, I needed a new plan for my Sunday routine. I watched a series of Sunday morning news programs where brilliant news analysts explained everything that happening in the past week but could not predict if tomorrow the sun would rise in the east. It couldn't be easy being both a retrospective genius and a prospective equivocator on national television. After a couple of hours of listening to these news analysts moan on and on, I decided that it was now late enough to call some of my friends to meet for cappuccino at the Italian Coffee Bar, affectionately known as the ICB. I prefer this bar to those new coffee houses where you can order drinks like a decaf vanilla nonfat latte with extra foam and not too hot. My coffee hangout restricts your choices to a single or double shot. There was no decaf. What's the point?

I looked forward to meeting my friends for cappuccino. These gatherings are how we have kept in touch over the years. I am the last one of my group of friends to be in school and talking to them always gives me a sense of another world . . . reality. My best friend, if I have one, is Gerry Smith. He is one of the Jewish Smiths whose grandfather came over on the boat from Romania and changed his name from Smokavitchsky. The Canadian immigration officer could not spell or pronounce any name originating from outside of the United Kingdom so he ended up a Smith on his naturalization papers. No one ever bothered to correct it. The Smokavitchskys of Romania were carpet merchants and they continued their traditional vocation when they migrated to Canada. Gerry's grandfather opened a carpet store and started the Canadian tradition of the constant going-out-of-business sale. He single-handedly paved the way for countless carpet merchants to follow in the footsteps of his marketing genius. If there is ever a hall of fame for carpet retailers, Mr. Smith will have a bronze bust in the front foyer.

Gerry and I met in grade two, 1957. Our class had a music hour three times a week which consisted largely of thirty unruly brats randomly banging various percussion instruments to no discernable beat. There were never enough instruments to go around so Gerry was assigned the right cymbal and I was assigned the left one which we coordinated to make the loudest possible noise at unpredictable times. It was my first experience in teamwork and was particularly important in molding my character since I never had anyone at home to play with. Although we took very different paths as the years passed, we have remained cymbalic friends to this day.

Gerry never went to university but, of all my friends, he has the most common sense. He doesn't have the need to logically understand everything and, in fact, he could care less. All he ever took a genuine interest in was making a lot of money selling used computer parts to Third World countries and procuring the best hashish in Western Canada. As long as he did not confuse these two marketing activities, he did just fine. Once in a while he bought a new car but he never took it to the office in case one of his employees figured out that he was making a fortune.

I always look forward to Sunday conversations with Gerry because we find something funny in most everything. We laugh about the news. We laugh about predicaments in which we find ourselves and we laugh about Paul, our friend. Paul's wife married him for his money only to discover later that he had less money than she was led to believe. It was the ultimate spousal betrayal. You can forgive your husband's sexual infidelity because that's just getting laid. But, exaggerating the size of the trust account is a heinous spousal deception of the highest order.

I called Gerry and he was ready, willing and able to meet for coffee. When I left the apartment a few minutes after talking to him, I stopped off first at Mr. Cohen's store to buy a Sunday paper and hear the latest gossip in the neighborhood. He had owned the store for more years than anyone could remember and the store smelled of old wood. All the flooring and shelves were made out of distressed wood that was at least as old as Mr. Cohen. It was one of those little corner grocery stores from another era which sold everything from milk to shoelaces. The store was always in a state of disorganization with goods piled everywhere.

You could always find Mr. Cohen leaning against the front counter wearing a white shirt and a solid black tie tucked into his pants. He looked to me as though he had been born 5'5″ tall, 175 lbs. and seventy years old. You had to be careful what you told Mr. Cohen because anything you said could be the latest gossip for the next customer. Also, Mr. Cohen had been known to sell you yesterday's newspaper if you didn't watch what he put in the bag. Once I caught him committing such a crime. His defense was that nothing had changed since the day before so what was the difference? I was willing to concede he was right about most things but what about the sports scores and weather report? He just shrugged his shoulders, shook my hand and told me that I was the spitting image of my father. How could you stay mad at a man who tells you that you resemble your father?

The usual Sunday morning crowd was at the coffee bar, including a group of Italian men who were sitting around talking about how proud they were of their kids while watching European soccer off the black market satellite feed. I could never figure that, if their families meant so much to them, why were they always at the coffee bar on Sunday morning rather than sitting at a big round table at the Pancake House with their families discussing how much money their neighbors really had?

I said hello to four regulars all named Tony. Not only were their names the same but they were all 5'9″ tall, all clean shaven and all had slicked-back, jet-black hair. They all wore black jeans and

21

cream-colored patent leather loafers with the Italian flag embroidered on the back of their left shoes in recognition of the Italian Socialist Party, currently in power in Italy. The only thing that distinguished one Tony from another was that each one wore a soccer shirt of their favorite team. There was Milan Tony, Naples Tony, Venice Tony and Rome Tony.

I sat at the corner table in the smoking section. Gerry smoked. One of the worst-kept secrets about the ICB is that the whole place is a smoking section. It was early enough that the ashtray was still empty. I ordered my first cappuccino of the day and started reading the paper. I didn't really read it, just glanced through the sections and reviewed the headlines. If I read the paper this early then I would have nothing to do later. Anyway, it was the usual Sunday news with a smattering of local color and a story about the provincial Minister of Agriculture who had a so-called escort and paid for her services with a Visa card. Discretion be damned in the face of late-night companionship.

As I looked up, Gerry was coming toward the table already smoking what must have been his fifth Players Light that morning.

"So, you graduate again?" he asked, sitting down and pulling the ashtray toward him.

"Yup, fourth time lucky and not going back."

"Are you serious this time or is this just a variation of the Cindy strategy?"

"Who's Cindy?"

"You remember that girl in grade seven with the gigantic head-lights. You were hypnotized like a deer."

"Her name was Sandy," I corrected him. "And don't you think it's time to update your vocabulary about the female anatomy?"

"No, breasts never worked for me. Headlights works for me. Anyway, what's the difference? You took up horseback riding so you could watch her bounce around on those horses. Can you picture a thirteen-year-old Stein on a horse hoping to sneak a peek or cop a feel from Cindy?"

"Sandy," I corrected him again.

"Were riding lessons at thirteen any different than going to law school? Except this time you didn't break your arm falling out of your desk."

22

"I admit that I have gone to certain lengths in pursuit of my own version of a social life."

"Isn't that why you went to law school? You haven't changed since you were thirteen with xenon Cindy," he said smugly.

"It's Sandy and it's changed. All the girls at law school have fully developed xenons."

"Has your social life at law school been any more successful than breaking your arm over Cindy?"

"Sandy. No, but at least I might get a job out of law school."

"Since when have you been interested in a job?" Gerry stubbed his cigarette in the tin ashtray and looked at me.

"I'm not sure that I am. The law firm interviews start tomorrow and, if my suit still fits, I might see if anyone wants to hire me. If I get an offer I can always turn it down."

"A real job would destroy your image. You're not cut out for actual work." Gerry lit another cigarette. "So what else is new besides graduating from law school?"

"At my graduation a woman left a note on my chair. She wants to meet me." This got Gerry's attention.

"Did you call her? What's her name? What's she look like?"

"No, I have not called her. Her name is Julia and I've never seen her."

"This sounds like the highlight of your academic career."

"It certainly has been the social highlight of three years at law school. This only happened to other people."

"Don't sell yourself so short, although you are."

As I drank my second cappuccino, I tried to explain to Gerry my strategy for making the call to Julia. "If I would have called yesterday, it would look like I was desperate for a date and had nothing to do on a Saturday night. Of course this is true, but I would never admit it. If I called her Sunday morning, then she would figure out that I had nothing going on from Saturday night which would again lead to the conclusion that I was desperate. I have to find the perfect time that would send a message that I am interested but not desperate. I've decided on Sunday 3:00 P.M. as my OTTC, optimal time to call." My reasoning was impeccable. Although I was afraid that no matter what time I called, I would still fuck up the conversation. "What do you think of my strategy?" I was hinting for some indication of affirmation from Gerry.

23

He looked at me as if I was afflicted with some new strain of psychotic disease and told me I was full of shit, which was true. When pushed, I admitted that I was just too nervous to pick up the phone that minute and make the call. Gerry needled me to find the nearest pay phone, invest a quarter and take the plunge. I told him that I wasn't ready because I had not rehearsed what I was going to say. Also, I had to pick the perfect place to meet. Somewhere not too busy but not too quiet either. Someplace where I would not be seen, in case she was a two-bagger. These were all strategic decisions that had to sound spontaneous during the conversation.

Decisions of the heart require private reflection. Such issues should not be resolved in a Gerry conversation while sitting at the ICB. I knew all Gerry would be concerned about before calling was whether he had a sufficient supply of condoms and if his almost limitless platinum Visa card was maxed out. Two cappuccinos were enough for one Sunday morning. I said good-bye to Gerry and I went home to read my newspaper.

6

I always enjoy my walk home from the ICB. There is something about a walk down Wellington Crescent that feels good. Every spring I feel this sense of accomplishment that I persevered through another prairie winter and nature has rewarded me with a warm spring breeze blowing in my face. In spite of this refreshing outing I got nervous every time I passed a pay phone. At my age it was silly to be so nervous about calling a girl. She left the note. It wasn't like I was making a cold call trying to sell aluminum siding. I just didn't want to sound too ethnic or boring.

Home was a converted attic of a crumbling Tudor mansion in the prestigious 400 block of Wellington Crescent. The address gave people the impression that I was somehow tied to old money, like I was the third cousin on the estranged side of the Bronfman dynasty. Where I grew up, appearances were everything and that included your address. It was the way people measured each other in my neighborhood. I could have won the Nobel Prize for physics and all my neighbors would talk about was the cash value of the prize and that it was too bad I wasn't a real doctor. It was pathetic, that even as a student living in an attic, I was concerned with the image of my address.

I walked up the back stairs to my penthouse, just as the servants used to do when the grain barons lived in this mansion. I had to climb three flights of stairs to reach my apartment. As I walked in, I focused on the most potentially exhilarating sight for a single, thirty-four-year-old male on a Sunday. The flashing red light on the answering machine. Someone wanted to talk to me. I knew no one was returning my call because I hadn't called anyone. In fact, the machine indicated there were two messages, which is a good start for 11:30 A.M. on a Sunday. Who could be calling? My first guess was that it was my mother, whose message would be so long it took her two messages to tell me everything. With some apprehension I hit the play button. This moment of anticipation, just before finding out who is calling, is the same kind of rush you get from playing craps as you watch the dice roll, end over end, with a bet on the hard eight on the hop.

The first call was from Sarah Goldman. "Hi, Ben. What happened to you last night? I turned around and you were gone. Anyway, I hope you are all right. Give me a call so we can talk. Best of luck with the interviews. 489-6802."

The second message was from my cousin John. He said he was sorry that we did not get a chance to talk at my graduation party but I should call him so we could catch up. The truth was we didn't get a chance to talk because I avoided him. All he does is talk about himself and his wholesale shoe business. He was the first distributor of athletic shoes in Western Canada. He left three different numbers but I promptly erased the message so there would be no risk that, in a lonely moment, I would return his call. I can always blame it on a faulty answering machine.

I was curious about the motive behind Sarah's message. But I dismissed it. Instead, I stared at the folded piece of paper with my initials on it that I had strategically placed beside the phone. That's what mattered. I could not handle a relationship with two women at the same time. In fact, my record indicates that I can barely handle one relationship at a time. Not that either of them was so quick to go out with me. But I had to consider all possible contingencies. After weighing the options, I decided that Julia would get the first call. My track record with Jewish girls wasn't any better than the Chicago Cubs in World Series play.

I hadn't decided how to handle the call with Julia. What would I say? When should I call? Where would we meet? After much reflection and indecision, I decided to just call and get it over with. This is likely a case where the anticipation is far more complex than the act itself. So, I went to the bathroom, brushed my teeth and combed my hair in preparation for the call. I was a matador in the ceremonial dressing room knowing that in a few minutes I would experience either the adulation of the crowd or be gorged by the horns of the predator bull.

I sat down beside the phone and dialed Julia's number. It seemed as though it took forever to answer. Finally, on the third ring, an unfamiliar voice answered. "Nurses' residence, fourth floor." A dream come true, Julia Windsor was a nurse. There is something about the healing professions that makes the women in them uninhibited about sex. I asked to speak to Julia Windsor and was told to hang on by someone whose tone of voice suggested that I was her third call in the last thirty minutes. I listened as the dangling receiver hit the wall with a most disturbing bang. After what felt like an eternity, a voice came on the phone which sounded intriguing as any woman I'd ever heard. It had that deep yet feminine tone. I told her it was Ben Stein calling and asked if she remembered leaving a note on my chair at the graduation. She laughed and said of course she remembered. She had only left one note that day. Already, I was not doing so well. Unexpectedly, she jumped right in and asked if I wanted to meet her. That was a great relief. I said, of course I did. She told me that she was working until 9:00 P.M. at the hospital and could we meet at the bar of the Fort Garry Hotel after she got off work. I never had it this easy. A Sunday night rendezvous in the Drummer Boy Lounge was more than I could have ever hoped for. It was the perfect place. A bar in one of those hotels frequented by old money. It was such a liberating feeling to have the prospect of going out with a girl who wanted to go drinking at the Fort Garry. I knew right away I would not need a condom, if the occasion should arise.

I was in love. All my strategic thinking of when to call, what to say and where to meet had been a waste of time. Then, just before she hung up, she mentioned that I looked better in person than my picture in the newspaper. I was crushed. I just can't shake my Stein heritage. I laughed, trying to portray casual amusement about the announcement. But, in fact, it was humiliating and confirmed why I needed a fresh start.

7

I was at a loss as to what to do for the rest of the day. Every few minutes I looked at the clock and calculated how long before I should leave the apartment and the route I should take to the Fort Garry. I had to arrive at the perfect time. Considering I only lived fifteen minutes away from the hotel it was not much of a logistical challenge. I felt like an athlete in nervous anticipation of the big game even though I had never actually experienced such a feeling. My athletic ability ranges from mediocre to awful but, if I were a great tennis player about to compete in center court at Wimbledon or a golfer in the final grouping at the Masters, I sensed it would be the same type of feeling.

I spent the afternoon calling my friends to casually mention what was going on in my social life. Everyone I called was out. It was frustrating trying to find someone to impress on a Sunday afternoon. Out of desperation, I returned Sarah's call. What could it hurt? It's not like I was chasing her. She called me. It could give me a certain satisfaction if she knew that I had a social life which transcended the pages of the Jewish community phone book.

"Hi, Sarah, it's Ben," I said as she answered on the third ring.

"Where did you disappear to last night? I turned around and you were gone without even a good-bye. You're a little too mysterious for a law student."

"Well, I had other plans. I was meeting a friend at the Italian Coffee Bar." She didn't have to know that my friend was a male and we didn't actually meet until the next day. Already it was a relationship founded on deception.

"Really? That's one of my spots. I stop by there when I'm in the neighborhood. How come I never see you there? What shift are you on?"

"I generally go early in the morning and after dinner as part of my evening walk. I live close by in a house on the Crescent." I had to slip that in.

"Are you going for the interviews tomorrow?"

"Not sure . . . I haven't looked at the interview schedule and I'm not sure that I want a job. The prospect of working with lawyers every day does not make me want to jump out of bed early in the morning. I'll decide tomorrow. If I get up on time I'll go to the interviews. If not, I'll be an educated street person." Perhaps I was revealing too much. "Are you going for the interviews?"

"I'm going but I haven't really decided what I'm going to do. I might take some time off. Maybe sit on the beaches of Indonesia and decide what to do while watching a Bali sunset."

That sounded good to me. "How late did you stay last night?"

"Not very . . . it got boring trying to sound nostalgic about my years at law school. Truthfully, I'm relieved it's over and I can finally do something for myself. I'm finished pleasing my parents. Although it would be easier if I had my parents' blessing."

We continued to talk for some time. She didn't have a voice like Julia Windsor but there was something about her that put me at ease. She had a certain bluntness which I found very appealing. I even forgot for a few minutes about my date at the Drummer Boy Lounge. We arranged to meet the next day during the noon break of the interview schedule. That is, if I went for the interviews. I would not commit to it in advance. It never pays to appear too eager or someone might think that you actually needed a job. I said good-bye to Sarah and immediately speculated whether I could handle relationships with two women at the same time. Which one would be the other woman? These are challenging questions for our time. Anyway, I doubted if I would have to face such issues. My relation-ships had always been serial, at best, with long stretches in between. Two relationships at the same time would be a logistical nightmare, unprecedented and a dream come true.

I spent the rest of the day trying to keep busy. I went on a few errands, drove out to school to check the interview schedule and did some food shopping. I had to clean the apartment just in case I should have a visitor, if you know what I mean. Sloppy has a certain Bohemian appeal but it still must be clean sloppy with an ample supply of toilet paper. You've got to have clean sheets regardless of how many dishes need washing. So, I did the big clean-up. I checked for snack food and a bottle of wine. No Gimli Goose tonight, it would be beaujolais all the way.

I meticulously put everything in place, making sure the apartment still displayed a sense of interesting disorganization. I displayed certain books in strategic places so it would look as if I had eclectic taste and was not just another unidimensional law student. Neatness and order are anal subversive notions. Anyone who has time to be that neat has no life. These are people who go to gun shows and shoot people who park their cars over the yellow lines. Neatness won't get you laid unless you were dating someone your parents approved of.

I looked at my watch for the seventeenth time, it was finally dinnertime. Everything I had done that day was geared to my evening rendezvous with Julia and I would not risk having Mexican beans or Cajun food. Nothing with onions would do and anything like garlic bread would have to wait. But I knew that I had to eat or else, after two drinks, I would be just another Semite who couldn't hold his liquor. Anyone with a name like Windsor could drink me under the table. I decided that a pizza would do the trick. It is filling, not smelly and a traditional Sunday meal for a single person.

I ordered a pizza and sat back to watch some television. I did not get dressed for fear that I might spill on my wardrobe of khaki jeans and a designer denim shirt, classic student elegance. Sunday night television consisted of either Walt Disney, the late NFL game or the Sunday night ABC movie, a rerun of *Apocalypse Now*. I have never understood what the deep meaning of this movie was. But we live in a time where the less entertaining the movie the more likely it would be described as brilliant filmmaking. By this measure, *Apocalypse Now* is an all-time classic.

As 9:00 P.M. approached, it was time to focus on the coming event. What should I say? Should I try to be funny? There is nothing worse than a failed attempt at humor. I could always resort to the conventional to insure that I fill the silent void. All these issues and so little time. Being a sensitive 80s guy, I decided to find out who Julia Windsor was and then try to get laid. I could have used more time to prepare so I would have to wing it. I didn't know anything about nursing so I could always ask about that. Well, I figured, better to have talked and failed than never to have talked at all . . . or something like that.

I wanted to be slightly early. No matter what time she'd get there, I'd say that I just got there five minutes before. I decided to

30

sit at the bar if I got there before she did. It would give an impression of familiarity with the place. Also, the cashew cups are refilled more quickly if you sit at the bar. Most importantly, if you sit at the bar and get stood up it is not as obvious as sitting alone at a table set for two. I could always pass the time by talking to the bartender.

I arrived at the hotel at 8:50 P.M. I found the perfect seat at the bar which gave me an unobstructed view of the entrance but in a way that did not look obvious. While sitting at the bar, I went over again in my mind what I would say. I should have written down a list of topics on the inside of my shirt sleeve. Anyway, I could always rely on the standard fare and talk about my career, living accommodations, travel and perversion. Maybe I better hold off on that last one until we got to know each other well enough to spend an afternoon at the city zoo. There's something about those monkeys that breaks the ice in any new relationship.

As I sat there picking out the cashews, I heard a soft deep voice very close to me.

"Hi, Ben."

It startled me and as I turned around my elbow hit my Bloody Caesar and it spilled all over the bar. A river of Clamato Juice went floating down the length of the bar and I was lucky that the lip of the bar surface prevented the drink from spilling all over me. What a start! Julia laughed sympathetically and I laughed too. As I looked for napkins to soak up the liquid I said, "Did you ever notice that when you spill an eight-ounce drink it seems like five gallons and there are never enough napkins to clean up?" As she slipped into the seat beside me, Julia said this was too dramatic an introduction and that we should start again. I agreed.

Julia captivated me by her beauty and presence. She had silky white skin with emerald-green eyes and auburn, shoulder-length hair. She was a few inches shorter than me which is a good thing because there aren't many NBA players who won't play on Yom Kippur. Her perfume smelled tropical, hopefully, passion fruit. I couldn't believe that I was sitting beside such a stunning woman and it was not a coincidence.

Once we ordered her drink and replaced mine, I told Julia that the graduation ceremony was my first and that, if I had known that I could meet women like her, I would have gone to my previous three. My obvious attempt at flattery was a way for her to inquire into my academic past and figure out my age. She did not bite. She told me the note was a spontaneous gesture. She had seen the movie *The Godfather* two nights before and I reminded her of Al Pacino so she decided we just had to meet. *What a relief,* I thought, *at least I didn't remind her of Clemenza.*

We had a wonderful time. She told me about nursing and her work in pediatrics. She had a genuine tenderness mixed with a streak of tough-mindedness. It was an imposing combination. Julia was funny, beautiful, engaging and she drank vodka tonic. I had never been with a woman who ordered a vodka tonic. In fact, I didn't know what a vodka tonic was other than what the name suggested. She didn't seem to care about the names I dropped, whether my family had money or my stellar academic accomplishments. I had never felt more at ease but, at the same time, I had never felt more self-conscious. I was in unfamiliar territory and enjoyed every minute of it. All this and she was beautiful too. I didn't want to screw this up. As we talked, I found myself more and more entranced by her. Finally I stopped thinking about what to say and became uncharacteristically spontaneous.

Inevitably, our conversation turned to the future. As two recent graduates, the anticipation of what was to come was close to the surface. When you live in Winnipeg any contemplation of the future always involves thoughts about moving away. In Winnipeg every family has a child or sibling who has moved away. The outbound flights are usually filled to capacity.

Since the day I started law school, I knew that one day I would be leaving Winnipeg. I just hadn't worked out how to do it. I didn't have the strength of character to just pick up and leave. I needed some sort of purpose, like a job to go to. Also, I had no idea where I would move. All I knew was that I needed more space unencumbered by my past or stifled by my lack of anonymity. I told Julia that my motivation for leaving was lack of professional opportunity and a curiosity for change. This was a lie. I needed to unshackle myself from my ethnic background and I could not do it in Winnipeg. Julia did not have a need to leave. Unlike me, she was not desperate to move away from friends and relatives. She was the first girl I had ever met who had a sense of freedom and freshness that could function within what I considered to be a claustrophobic environment. *Maybe,* it occurred to me, *I had it all wrong.* Or was it just my luck to meet a girl who forced me to reevaluate every image I had of my surroundings just as I was plotting my escape?

Julia had a wide and varied circle of friends ranging from doctors, which you would expect since she was a nurse, to professional hockey players. She knew a lot about hockey and it quickly became evident to her that I knew nothing more than the names of a few players. We couldn't have been more different and that is exactly what I found so attractive about her. It was as if I had found a whole new city that had been hidden from me all these years and, through Julia, I'd been given a peek inside. It was like discovering Middle Earth and it emphasized to me how parochial my upbringing had been and how narrow my cultural outlook was.

Four vodka tonics later, the bartender told us it was closing time. Our time sitting at the bar had passed too quickly. I did not want the evening to end. I did not want to face that awkward moment at the end of a wonderful evening. I had done pretty well with her, been funny and interesting without seeming ego-driven. Julia told me that she had taken a taxi to the hotel and asked if I would give her a ride home. Of course, she knew I would but it was nice not to be taken for granted. We bid the bartender good night and he winked at me as if to tell me that I should hold on to this one. His acknowledgment made me feel special. I was leaving with a spectacular woman. We walked through the lobby arm in arm and made our way out to the car. The combination of vodka tonics and Julia's sparkling emerald green eyes in a 5'6" 110 lb. frame made me feel like I had never felt before. I was special, at least for a fleeting moment. But I still didn't know why she had picked me.

I took the longest route I knew to get to the nurses' residence and timed my driving to catch every possible red light. We listened to Marvin Gaye and sang his songs together. If I did resemble Al Pacino, I unfortunately sang like him too. We shared a relaxed closeness in a way that I had never known before. Julia seemed at ease with the evening and even attracted to me. I made a mental note to ask that bartender for the recipe for vodka tonic.

In spite of my best intentions, the car ultimately came to rest in front of her residence. She stuck her tongue in my ear, kissed me on the cheek and asked me to call her some time. Before I knew it, she was out of the car and had disappeared into the grey pre-cast concrete building. It happened so quickly that I wondered if it had all been a dream. Maybe it was finally my turn. Oh how I wanted my turn.

8

It was 2:00 A.M. by the time I got back to my apartment. The red message light was flashing on my answering machine but it was only a curious distraction from the euphoria of my night out. Already I was planning my next call to Julia and wondering how soon I could see her again. She did tell me to call her. How long should I wait before I called so I did not appear overbearing or desperate? This was no time to hold back and no time for subtlety in matters of the heart or other parts of the body. Anyway, subtlety is an overrated preoccupation which drives grown men to madness as they search for the perfect moment to act. There was nothing subtle about a Stein going out with a Windsor. It was real assimilation into the fabric of Canada. Anyone can get a law degree and learn how to golf but not everyone can share an evening with Julia Windsor.

Being single, I was always seduced by the flashing message light. That night there was a near record-breaking three messages . . . and it was only Saturday night.

Message 1: 9:48 P.M.

"Ben, it's Michael from the law students union. Just calling to remind you that interviews start at nine A.M. sharp but you should come early to pick up your orientation materials from the law firms."

I hate those student keeners. Don't they have anything better to do on a Sunday night?

Message 2: 10:03 P.M.

"Ben, this is your mother calling. I have ordered thank-you cards for you from *Comet Press*. I've made a list of everyone who gave you a graduation gift, including the guests from out of town, so you can send them a thank-you note, too. Come over on Wednesday when the cards will be delivered from the printer. I'll write the notes, address the envelopes and you can sign them 'Sincerely, Ben'. Let me know what time you will be coming. Maybe we'll have a little brisket for dinner."

Message 3: 1:45 A.M.

"Just calling to tell you that I had a great time. Call me soon. Why has it taken you so long to get home? You're not out with another girl, are you? Don't call back tonight. It's too late and I'm going to sleep. Pleasant dreams."

I sat there beside the phone in my overstuffed black leather armchair with my feet up on the ottoman. I didn't dare move for fear that it was all a dream and I would wake up. What a way to end a perfect night. Here I was torturing myself about the right time to call Julia so I wouldn't appear desperate and she simply picked up the phone and called me. I had dreamed about women who would call men. Female liberation was all very nice when it came to getting a job but women still expected men to call them for a date, open the door for them and walk on the outside of the sidewalk. Not Julia. I wanted to get in the car and take her out to one of those all night Salisbury houses for a stale bran muffin. But, I forced myself out of my armchair and went to bed full of anticipation at the thought of calling Julia the next day. I could barely stand the wait. It was my turn . . . I could just feel it.

I woke up early and fully relaxed, as if I had gotten laid all night. Everything looked good to me. Everything I heard on the radio or watched on television reminded me of Julia. I couldn't wait to see her again. With that in mind, I prepared myself for the job interviews. I decided that I might as well go and see what they were like. Even if I were offered a position, it didn't mean that I'd have to accept it. I wouldn't compromise who I was for the sake of a job. If some law firm wants me they would have to accept me just the way I am. I put on the same blue suit, my only suit, that I had worn to my Saturday graduation party but with my other tie and pale blue shirt and off I went to the interviews. Little did the recruiters suspect that I would be the one doing the interviewing and that the firms would have to prove themselves if they wanted to recruit me.

When I got to school I used my counterfeit faculty parking pass. There was something ironic about using a fake parking permit to go for articling interviews. It was not something that was widely known but it demonstrated the kind of initiative a clever recruiter would recognize. Recruiters were relegated to the guest parking lot which was a brisk fifteen-minute hike from the law school. You would think that with all the law firms scouring for students with initiative, my forged faculty parking pass would be an obvious signal. The dilemma was that, by revealing my handiwork, I would have to confess to counterfeiting. I was sure the recruiters were not ready for such candor on a first date. I mentally recorded this conundrum as my first legal-ethical problem.

The interview times were posted in the main foyer of the law school. Each interview would be twenty minutes long with ten-minute breaks in between. As I ran down the list, I considered just walking out and forgetting about any idea of a job in a law firm. It's not like I had to account to anyone and no one would know the difference or care. But, there is really no commitment if I go for an interview and it may be good experience. Most likely I won't get an offer so what could be the harm in just confirming that I was not cut out for one of these articling positions? Again, I looked over the list of firms, still not sure what I wanted. I didn't think I had the right temperament for litigation. There were so many rules of evidence and it was too obvious whether you win or lose. Ignorance of the rules could be very embarrassing in front of a judge. With solicitors work, it was all about making a deal. If the deal falls through you just blame it on the intransigence of the other side. It was a no-brainer. I had signed up for eight interviews with law firms ranging from old-line WASP firms to a solicitors' boutique.

The morning interviews were with a variety of local general practice firms. Typically, these law firms are populated by pedestrian lawyers except for the one or two partners who had reputations that transcended the firm. There was a sameness about the interviews, as if all the recruiters had gone to the same continuing legal education course about ineffective interview techniques. They all asked the same questions in one form or another.

"Why did you go to law school?"

"What was your favorite course in law school?"

"Do you know what kind of law you want to practice?"

"What outside organizations do you belong to?"

"How do you feel about putting in long hours for weeks on end?"

The interviews were so uninspiring and I had to invent ways to keep my interest up. I started thinking about the person in law school the interviewer most resembled. It was pretty easy. They all resembled second-quartile scholars who sat around in groups of four talking about the night before at the pub, constantly trading study notes. Those were the guys who would never miss a class reunion and would keep in touch with everyone in the hope that someone they knew might turn out to be somebody who they could later call upon for a favor or at least drop their name. Once I tired of that game, I challenged myself to give the most outrageous answer I could concoct. I told one interviewer that I was suffering from post-Olympic depression having come seventh in the two-man luge competition. The Canadian Olympic Committee had arranged for psychotherapy and I was coming along except that every time I see a sleigh I break out into uncontrollable sobbing.

Before I knew it, the morning sessions were over. As I left the last one I was somewhat depressed at the thought that I might end up working at one of these firms. I would never last. Plumbing supply was looking better all the time. I left the law school for the graduate student dining room where I had arranged to meet Sarah for lunch. I hoped that the afternoon interviews would be more inspiring because the necessity of a job was weighing heavily on me. I kept reminding myself that soon I would call Julia and go out for vodka tonics. Things suddenly looked up when I realized I was going to lunch with one woman and would probably be going out with another later. At least that was the plan.

Sarah was on time and she looked terrific. She wore navy blue, pinstripe pants and a white silk shirt. This girl knew how to dress for an interview. I figure she had family money because she was so confident and her Hermes belt spelt GELT. You could almost smell it. It was the scent of cash. In Winnipeg that could mean only one thing, the garment business. We laughed our way through lunch mostly talking about our experiences from the morning. She gave me no hint that she was interested in me other than having someone to talk to on interview day. She was not at all inquisitive about my social life nor did it appear that she even cared. Sarah told me that besides these interviews she had applied for graduate school and to clerk at the Court of Appeal in either Ontario or British Columbia. She didn't aim low. Her approach was relaxed and she was in no panic about getting on with her legal career. She was still considering going to Bali instead of getting a job. I tried to sound equally as casual but my suit gave me away. I had that $40,000.00 student loan to repay.

Our time together passed quickly and I have to admit that, in spite of my aversion to the stereotypes, I did like her. As we were getting up to leave she asked me if I would like to go out later to celebrate our survival of the initial interview process. I was taken by surprise by her interest in me. This was my chance to get even with all the Sarahs who had turned me down since I was fourteen years old. I told her that I was seeing a woman at the moment and was not available. Oh how I enjoyed that moment! All those years, being on the receiving end of the brush-off from women like Sarah, and now it was my turn. This was better than a blow job on a bus tour . . . almost. I really wanted to drop Julia's name to show that I did not need the Jewish phone book to get a date and I casually suggested that if she wanted, she and a friend would be more than welcome to come out with Julia and me. I couldn't think of a way of inserting Julia's last name but the seed was planted. It wasn't like her name was Rachael or Ruth. Sarah tried to keep smiling and said that it would be great and she would call me to confirm the day. We left it at that but I knew that she would never call. She was more accustomed to giving the brush-off than receiving it.

As I walked back to the law school, I could barely contain myself. Not only was there a promise of another date with Julia, but I was able to use it to give Ms. Hermes Belt the brush-off. This was turning out to be a great day. I went into the afternoon interviews with a sense of confidence and anticipation. My first interview was with the prominent local firm of Bloom & Company. This was the Jewish firm, a remnant of a bygone era when it was impossible for someone like me to get a job in a WASP-dominated profession. Over the years, these lines of discrimination have broken down, mostly because the rich wanted the best lawyers regardless of their religious beliefs. Although I hated the idea of pursuing a Jewish firm to get a job there was an undeniable reality which I could not dismiss.

As I entered the room, a lawyer named Lorne Wiseman introduced himself as the Bloom & Company representative. I have to admit that being interviewed by a Jewish lawyer put me at ease. I could lower the anti-Semite antenna and not worry about double meanings that could be taken as veiled discrimination. But I couldn't escape the paradox. Here I was trying to break away from my cultural identity and, at the same time, finding solace with my own kind.

Wiseman was one of those lawyers who worked at looking the part in his perfectly tailored blue blazer and a crease in his pants that could cut like a knife. He wore the appropriate Turnbull & Asser shirt with a striped tie identifying an Ivy League school which he likely never attended. His wardrobe had been carefully selected to separate him from the image of an immigrant's son living in an attic. It was hard to relate to a guy who wore a shirt that cost more than one month's rent for my attic. I didn't even like the shirt.

In the interview, Mr. Wiseman tried desperately to find some third cousin twice removed whom we had in common.

"Stein, are you related to Helen Stein? I knew her when I went to B'nai B'rith camp in nineteen sixty-five." If this was his notion of putting me at ease, it was not an endearing quality.

"No, I never heard of her," I said curtly.

"I took sociology with a Michael Stein whose family is in the ball-bearing business in Brandon. He was a very good student."

"No," I said confidently. "I don't think I've come across them at any family events."

"Perhaps you know the Steins who sold off-price merchandise to the discount stores in Minneapolis. Boy, those guys knew how to make money, until they got caught not paying the export duty."

"No, not related to them either but they sound like an interesting bunch." This was getting to be too much to tolerate. "My family is in the plumbing supply business and my parents came from White Russia. I am the first generation of Steins born in this country," I said.

"What a coincidence, my great-grandfather came from White Russia. Some czar chased him out of the country for fooling around with his distant cousin. Where in White Russia did your family come from?"

"My dad came from a little village called Lachva which does not exist anymore. It was wiped out in the war."

"My geography is not good for that part of the world but I bet that we had relatives all around there and, who knows, you might even be my cousin."

"Funny, you don't look like a Stein. But, all the Steins have a birthmark in the crack of our ass. If you want to pull down your pants, I can take a look and see if you are a real Stein. I mean, if we are long-lost relatives what could be the harm? I know a Stein asshole when I see one, and from the sounds of it, you could be one."

"Well," he said, definitely uncomfortable with the prospect of finding out if we were related. "White Russia was a big place and most of my family was infertile anyway. Chances are we are not related. But, I'll ask my parents about it and get back to you if there are any Steins on the Russian side of the family."

Needless to say that interview did not run over the allotted twenty minutes. I can't imagine why we did not hit it off. I guess he was not really a Stein. More likely he came from the Wiseman family of assholes or some other cavity. I just could not help myself. Here was this second generation whatever-he-thought-he-was, patronizing me in some desperate attempt to connect so we could relate on some undefined level. All I was looking for was an articling job and I wasn't even sure I even wanted that. I did not need a commitment to be a member of his family or invited to his house for Passover. I consoled myself that Lorne Wiseman had likely never gone out with a woman like Julia Windsor.

The next couple of interviews were no more inspiring than the Bloom interview. I refrained from suggesting to the interviewers that they pull down their pants to see if they were long-lost relatives but the process was starting to depress me. I knew that I had to persevere because there were no more degrees left for me to get and I was maxed out on my student loans. This growing-up business was not what it was cracked up to be. My basic problem with growing up and having a career was growing up and having a career. It had all gone downhill once they had made those student lounges non-smoking.

My final interview of the day was with a national law firm of Lord & Bishop. This firm was the quintessential WASP outfit. They represented banks, insurance companies and breweries. For them, hiring the Archbishop of Canterbury would have been an ethnic compromise. I was surprised to discover that their recruitment representative, David Black, seemed like a decent fellow with no obvious airs. We got on quite well and he was nothing like what I was expecting. He was not a fly fisherman and he didn't play polo. His family came from a farm in southern Ontario and he did not seem overly impressed with himself. He was one of three partners that Lord & Bishop had sent from Toronto to open the Winnipeg office.

The conversation moved along quite smoothly. It was apparent that I was the one being interviewed not him but he was very engaging. He told me that he was building a house in the Tuxedo area of Winnipeg. It's funny that no matter what your ethnic origin was, building a house in Tuxedo, north of Corydon of course, is what you did if you made it. He told me about all the problems he had with the plumbing and faulty faucets and shower heads. I mentioned to him that my father, Nathan Stein, was in the plumbing business and he might want to call him. This was pretty dangerous territory I was getting into and the anti-Semitic antenna were fully extended and ready to receive any and all communications.

"Your father is Nathan Stein, from Forward Plumbing?" The business was named after my mother's family.

"Yes, that's my dad." I thought that I had really put my foot in it now. My dad must have been the supplier who sold him all those dripping faucets and now Mr. Black was going to get back. "Do you know him?'

"I sure do know your dad. I went to him after I got into this big plumbing business mess and he was the only one who understood the problem and could help me. He didn't even charge me an arm and a leg. He is a fine man and I sure appreciated him saving me from the vulture contractors."

"Well, he is known for quality service and I will pass on your comments to him. I know he will appreciate it." His flattery left me with a sense of relief and pride. I lowered the antenna . . . just slightly.

From that point on, the interview was a piece of cake. I could say nothing wrong. I could have called his mother a third-rate whore from Dauphin, Manitoba and it would still have worked out fine. I left the interview with a renewed sense of optimism. Maybe I do have future in the law. And I got this break because of my family. I was so determined to break away from my background and it was that connection that had opened the door to a firm like Lord & Bishop. Go figure. This ethnic stuff is more complicated than I ever thought possible. Boy, could I use a vodka tonic.

9

The next three weeks were the best three weeks of my life. Everything was going my way. I did not see Julia every night but when I was not out with her we would talk on the phone for hours on end. While we were together, it seemed like no one else in the world mattered. I even started to plot how I would break the news to my parents that I was in love with a Windsor. This was not going to be easy. The image of a Christmas tree in my living room was not easy for me to reconcile, not to mention how my parents would react. I would have to buy them a portable defibrillator for Chanukah. If my mom sees a Christmas tree lit up in my apartment, those paddles will come in handy. It might seem a bit premature to have been worrying about such things considering that I had only met Julia four weeks earlier and it was six months until Christmas but these inevitable problems of conflicting cultures were always on my mind.

We went to movies, caught the local bands on the university summer concert circuit, drank at the student lounge and, in between all of these activities, smoked various concoctions of marijuana and hashish. Ultimately we did make love but I was in no hurry. I didn't want her to think that it was all I was interested in. When it finally happened on our second date it was sensational. She had this sense of freedom and adventure, which coupled with her beauty, was an addictive combination. I was captivated. When we were together, my attic apartment felt as romantic as Venice. In fact, I bought a toy gondola at K Mart for us to play with in the tub.

The one speed bump in our relationship was that Julia was a vegetarian. In a moment of passion and weakness, which for me always seems to go together, I told her that I would give it a try. It must be love to give up delicatessen. I starved but my lust for Julia was greater than my passion for my mother's brisket. Still, I must confess, I was not completely faithful. On two occasions I disguised myself in a baseball cap and sunglasses and snuck over to Oscar's

Delicatessen for a pastrami on Russian rye with a side of pickles. I could not help myself. I was ashamed by my lack of self-control but what could I do? It's not like there is an organization called Deli Anonymous where I could call someone in a weak moment. I come from a long line of deliholics and I was born with fetal deli syndrome. Still, I was careful not to leave any tracks of my addiction. I always paid in cash, ordered take-out and flossed my teeth afterwards to eradicate any trace of my weakness. Julia told me how proud she was of me that I had overcome this filthy delicatessen habit and would comfort me by pointing out the best places in the city for brown rice with almonds. There was never a line-up at those restaurants. Lentils for dinner was a testament to the depth of my infatuation with this woman.

During those glorious weeks, I was also going for second interviews at law firms. I was invited to three interviews. Bloom & Company did not extend an invitation. I presume Mr. Wiseman did not have the Stein birthmark. Also, my post-Olympic depression held me back from another second interview. I might have a human rights complaint. But, two of the larger local firms invited me for second interviews as did Lord & Bishop. Thank the Lord my dad knows his plumbing supplies. I arranged my schedule to go first to the local firms so I could tune up for the interview with the Lord. I kept questioning if I should bother going to these second interviews given my ambivalence about the law and working in a law firm. But my competitive instincts kept pushing me on. I wanted the assurance of knowing that I could secure a position as good or better than the other students in my class. I would rather have the satisfaction of turning down these firms than knowing they rejected me.

At my first interview, I met with the senior partner, Nash Richardson. He was the first person I had ever met who was named after an automobile. If I was going to name my kid after a car it sure wouldn't be Nash. I would name my son Bentley or my daughter Mercedes. He told me about the great opportunities at his firm. That was interview double speak meaning the pay is lousy. In fact, they were the lowest-paying firm in the city. I told Nash that, since we were on a first-name basis I sensed we could speak frankly. It wasn't that I cared so much about the money but my landlord did and so did the grocery store and the gas station. What choice did I have? Nash assumed that a Stein would care about money so he made a point of telling a thirty-four-year-old graduate that I should be patient and it would eventually pay handsome dividends. It was rather like the Button King's advice that our future lay ahead of us. But, at thirty-four, I didn't have the patience to wait for this future windfall. Also, I somehow could not picture Nash and me out there on the Winnipeg River fly fishing. I took my leave.

The second interview went better than the first, but it was no more inspiring. This was another local firm of thirty-five lawyers started by a group of six young lawyers who had left an established firm and took more than their share of the clients with them. They had a certain intellectual bent and were known as an up-and-coming group of professionals. I met four of the founding partners in a group interview session. It was an interesting experience, particularly when it degenerated into an argument between two of the partners that escalated into a yelling and swearing match about the meaning of their mission statement. It was finally resolved and they explained to me that calling each other stupid bastards was a healthy venting experience and assured me that I would not have to do a personal injury case. In the spirit of our candid discussion, I told them all they were full of shit. My candid comment was not taken as a healthy venting experience. I learned that, when your employer encourages you to be candid, be on guard. They never mean it. These guys tried so hard to portray a summer camp camaraderie but down deep they were all suffering from Nash Richardson disease. The thought of fly fishing with them was not any more appealing than with Nash.

Now I was ready for the Lord's interview. Their reception area had an air of permanence about it. There were no Leroy Nieman prints or pictures of prairie scenes on their walls. This was E.J. Hughes and Group of Seven territory. Everyone dressed for their respective roles and spoke with a quiet confidence. This was the place to launch my legal career if I were going to have one.

I was met by David Black and he escorted me through the interview process. He was, I think, repaying the courtesy my father had shown to him. The lawyers I met were casual and at ease. When you come from old money you are taught from an early age that you have an inalienable right to belong. These guys had that aura of quiet confidence. Although the Stein family was not known for quiet anything, I did feel surprisingly at ease. However, the antenna was fully extended as I waited for the remark. I could stand being the token Jewish lawyer as long as I didn't have to eat like a Gentile. I could always resort to the vegetarian excuse which would also keep me on side with Julia. This diet issue was getting complicated and I wasn't sure a legal career was worth the dietary sacrifice.

Eventually, the Lord called Ben Stein to enter the promised land of private practice. Here was my chance to reject the entire legal establishment by rejecting their offer of employment . . . but I didn't. I rationalized it by convincing myself that I could always quit later. Taking a job with Lord & Bishop officially ended my academic career. Although my overall plan was to move away from Winnipeg, that was now on hold, given my revived social life and a real job. In fact, I was excited about starting my professional career even though I would never have admitted it. This job was my first real step in breaking out of the immigrant equation. I was a thoroughbred in the starting gate anticipating the start of the race. I may not have been the favorite to win but the odds were not embarrassingly long.

A celebration was in order. During these weeks with Julia I had withdrawn from my friends and had not returned their calls. I wanted to preserve every moment with her and concluded the only way to do this was by not falling back into my usual routine. Still, I wanted to let the world know about my good fortune. I wanted Julia to meet my friends but was scared that she would see a side of me that contradicted the image which she had built up in her mind. I did not want her vision of me to be compromised by my other reality.

This job offer and my acceptance was a good excuse to convene one of my too-infrequent nights out with my friends. For years, dinner with them had always followed a poker game but, as we got older and some of my friends married, the poker game was dropped. We still managed to find time to get out but it was less frequently. This dinner would be particularly fruitful because, not only would we celebrate the end of my academic career and my joining the working world, but I would come out of the closet about Julia. I took the initiative of calling everyone and arranging the time and place for dinner. I knew Gerry would come on a moment's notice. The only condition he ever imposed was that no one pass around pictures of their children at the dinner and no one could tell stories about their brilliant children who were actually dumb as posts.

Paul had a lot of spare time on his hands and would use any excuse to get out of the house. His marriage was on shaky ground because of this trust account misunderstanding and the less he was home the better. I had met Paul at Sir Edmund Hillary Secondary School when he approached me to join the youth wing of the Conservative Party. I thought he was joking but, when I realized he was serious, I took it upon myself to free him from this evil trance. By encouraging him to smoke marijuana, regularly masturbate and give up disco dancing, I helped him come around. In a final symbolic exorcism, Paul set fire to his Conservative Party card and used the flame to light a carrot chilum of hashish. We've been friends ever since. Paul became an accountant but he has never been satisfied with his lot in life. He had this vision of himself as an industrial titan but instead has been relegated to the role of designated driver and bartender for his often drunk siblings and their spouses. He made awful drinks. Clamato growers were disavowing any association with his recipe for a bloody caesar.

Murray Wall had the most demanding schedule of all of us. Murray and I met while standing in line at a convenience store at 3:00 A.M. one winter morning. I was buying a package of Zig Zag rolling papers, a jumbo-size box of Old Dutch ripple chips and a case of twelve popsicles. Murray was standing behind me in the line waiting to pay for the same products that I had and he was just as stoned as I was. We looked at each other and broke out into uncontrollable laughter which prompted everyone else in the line to laugh too. As it turned out, everyone in the line was stoned and buying something to satisfy their early morning cravings. It was the golden age of ripple chips and Zig Zag papers. Murray Wall became a doctor, married and had five kids. Based on personal necessity, he started a clinic to revolutionize male vasectomies. We affectionately called him Dr. Free Willie Wall. He worked long and unorthodox hours and it was not easy for him to get away on short notice. But, the stigma of being the one who did not show up was always enough to insure his attendance.

The fifth member of our group was David Kaplan. We were in a carpool together in high school except that he was the only one with a car and drove every day. The rest of us chipped in for gas. David never seemed to have a bad day. He was a patent lawyer but we were never quite sure what he did. No matter what time you called him, he always had time for you. He was the glue that kept the five of us together because everyone kept in touch with David

47

and no one ever had a bad word to say about him. His only short-coming was that he always spoke using analogies which often did not make any sense unless you were drunk or stoned. Then his comparisons had the clarity of crystal. Unfortunately, we could never remember later what he had been talking about.

We arranged to meet at the dining room of the Old Bailey restaurant at 7:00 P.M. I reserved the corner round table which comfortably sat five. It was one of those spots where you would always be seen but not disturbed. As usual, dinner started out with a series of non-stop stories ranging from our time at Sir Edmund Hillary Secondary to the unfortunate effects of the sneezing moyel. In between these wide-ranging stories, I injected my first piece of big news.

"I want to make an announcement. I got a real job." This brought the conversation to an abrupt stop.

"What exactly do you mean by a real job? Is it like a real job or a job running a projector in a movie theatre?" Murray went for the pun.

"I got a R-E-A-L job." I spelt it out so there would be no misunderstanding as to what I had said.

"Do you mean like a real summer job or a real regular job that will go past registration date at school?" Paul inquired.

"No more summer jobs. This is a real full-time permanent job that does not involve wearing a hair net or having a name tag. I got a job at the law firm of Lord & Bishop as an articling student." It took my friends a few seconds to absorb what I had told them but when they did, they toasted my good fortune with Tequila shooters and beer chasers. This officially marked the end of me being the object of ridicule for having overstayed my welcome in school by about ten years.

Now that I had raised the subject of a job my friends turned the focus of conversation to work-related matters. Paul told us about his business trip to Budapest where he had hoped to wholesale lottery tickets. He knew nothing about lottery tickets and less about Hungary and this was another one of his schemes that would further deplete his share of the sibling trust account. Murray told us about a vasectomy patient who had a wife so ugly that he advised the patient that all he really needed was a proper pair of eyeglasses to prevent any risk of procreation.

I waited for the next lull in the conversation to casually drop Julia's name. I had to be careful not to sound too committed for fear that I would later regret my declaration of eternal love. They were so entranced by the story of how we met that you could hear a pin drop. Murray remarked that, from a medical standpoint, he had noticed a certain calmness about me which could only have come from sex on demand. I judiciously said nothing. Evasiveness is much more mysterious. They wanted to meet her and I wanted my friends to meet her too. But, I wanted to arrange this coming out on my own terms. I would find the right circumstance to introduce Julia to them but it will be in a setting which I could control. I knew that once I had told them about Julia, my private life would be exposed. The thing I hated most about Winnipeg was the lack of anonymity. I always felt like I was being watched and judged. Now that I had this relationship, which I had so longed for, I wanted everyone to know about it. How do you reconcile the desire for privacy and the need to prove that you can break away? I left the restaurant and all I could think about was calling Julia for reassurance that we were still together. But I was never entirely confident that she would be there when I called. Since I needed to sleep off the vodka tonics from dinner, I decided not to find out if she was out with some other man.

10

Julia and I were having a terrific time. I knew nothing of her friends and she knew nothing of mine. We were living on the planet Pluto and we did not seek out life on other planets, although I knew that eventually I would have to return to Earth and deal with all those petty Earthling issues. My friends would have to meet Julia, but I did not want it to be obvious. Our coming out required a certain subtlety so, if the gathering was a bust, I would not be tagged as the host of the event. My strategy was like buying a new car and parking it where everyone would notice it rather than calling your friends to come over and kick the tires. I did not want to risk showing off what might turn out to be an Edsel. I decided that the best way to introduce Julia to my world was simply to go where my friends hung out and let nature take its course. By going to the right place at the right time on the right day, we would run into the predictable crowd. I would have my coming out with Julia and no one would be the wiser.

Thursday night was the best night of the week to engineer a coincidental meeting. Since the Italian Coffee Bar had obtained a liquor license, the place seemed to attract not only the likes of the four Tonys, but socialites on a night out. I did not dare tell anyone of my plan nor did I make any arrangements with my friends on this appointed night. But this was Winnipeg and the same people go to the same places on the same nights. These were creatures of habit who never stray from their routine for fear of the unknown. I made a few calls to insure there was no intervening event such as a Three Dog Night concert at the Centennial Concert Hall. Having assured myself that Eli was not coming, I focused my attention on planning my coincidental night out.

Julia came over to my apartment after dinner on that fateful Thursday night. We drank some wine and smoked hash out of a pipe made from industrial plumbing parts I had scavenged from my dad's warehouse. As we sat on the couch talking about nothing in particular, Julia suddenly focused on two framed pictures on the middle shelf of my floor-to-ceiling bookcase. She got up and took the two pictures off the shelf and sat back down beside me. The first picture was of my parents on vacation in Minneapolis in 1958. They were standing proudly beside my dad's new Chrysler New Yorker. It was their first new car and they were very proud of everything that meant. My dad had spent $3,200 for that car and it was his way of announcing to the world at large that he had arrived. I explained to Julia the importance of that car and she only seemed politely interested but not particularly engrossed by the story.

"Who is the other picture?" she asked.

"That's me at my Bar Mitzvah. I was thirteen years old."

"You're Jewish?" she asked, sounding genuinely surprised.

"Couldn't you tell by my name?"

"I never thought about it. I don't think I ever went out with anyone Jewish before. Although I don't make a practice of checking."

"How do you like going out with one so far?" My antenna was starting to rise.

"It doesn't make any difference to me. How long have you been Jewish?"

In all my years I had never been asked such a question. It stumped me. I wasn't sure how to answer. I'm not observant, even though I go with my dad to synagogue on High Holidays. I don't participate in the Jewish community. Maybe I had stopped being Jewish without even realizing it. But, I'm not sure when.

"I'm not sure how long I've been Jewish. I started out that way but now I don't know what I am. I am the product of 100 generations who never forgot. But at the moment I'm not sure what I am."

"I didn't mean this to be such a hard question. What aren't you supposed to forget?"

"We carry with us a hundred generations of sacrifice and persecution to maintain our identity." I started to explain.

"So why are you going out with me?"

"You are what I want to be. You are not burdened by history or irrelevant tradition. When I'm with you I feel a sense of anonymity and freedom which I never felt before. It feels good." I paused, almost afraid to ask what I wanted to know. "And what do you see in me?"

"You reminded me of Al Pacino."

"That's it?"

51

"Not entirely. All the places we go and all the things we do seem new to me when I am with you. Even familiar places seem different when we are together."

There was a silence between us as we both considered the meaning of what we had said to each other. I wasn't sure if we were more distant now or if it had drawn us closer together. Neither of us ever mentioned that conversation again.

Without prompting, Julia decided that we should go for a walk in the neighborhood. We set out down the Crescent, turning on Lilac Street toward the Italian Coffee Bar. I suggested that we stop for a drink. Hashish has a way of making you thirsty and we both wanted a cold vodka tonic. In fact, I could have used a double in anticipation of my coming out. Everything was falling into place.

It was a typical Thursday night at the ICB. I said hello to the four Tonys and took a seat at the large round table by the corner front window where there would be ample seating for anyone to join us. Also, a round table has a certain intimacy. Everyone can talk to each other while maintaining eye contact. We hadn't been sitting for fifteen minutes when Gerry walked in with Barry Altman. Without any hesitation, Gerry sat down beside Julia and introduced himself and Barry.

Barry Altman was an engaging sort of fellow who never talked about anything which could lead to controversy or opinion. He did quite well buying and selling restaurant equipment which gave him the inside track on every new Chinese restaurant in the city. He collected expensive toys such as sports cars, a speed boat, a cabin on the Winnipeg River and a four-seater plane to get there. He used these toys like pieces on a chess board to capture a queen for the weekend. He never seemed to have any relationship which lasted longer than a tank of gas for his plane—two round trips to the cabin.

Gerry already knew about Julia but he kept it to himself. Barry was only interested in Julia as someone new to tell all his old stories. The conversation was light-hearted and the laughter was spurred on by numerous rounds of drinks. My coincidental coming out strategy was going well.

As the evening progressed, we were joined by two more of my friends, Loa and Arlene. Like us, they had gone for a walk after smoking some hash and decided to stop by for a drink. I had known Arlene for twenty years and we hung out together at school. It was nothing more than that. She was a bit shorter than I was, 5'6", with shoulder-length, curly flaming red hair and was seductively thin. Arlene was a gifted student but she became an artist of pedestrian ability whose family was well-known in the community. She concentrated on securing art commissions from well-heeled friends of her parents. She would routinely go to their open beam-and-exposed-brick homes and tell them how well their Royal Doulton figurines and Peter Max prints fit together. She would sell them large abstract paintings and talk about how wonderful it had been going to school with their nephew. This ethnic marketing strategy worked marginally well and it made her a meager living but nothing more. For many years I had been taken with her but, being from a lower caste, I knew that it could not be. As she grew older and was still single, my rating improved and she seemed more interested in me. I might have climbed a couple of rungs on the Jewish totem pole by going out with her but I had never really gotten over the earlier rejection.

Loa was much more of a mystery. We had never spent much time together and she was a friend of friends of mine. Everything she said bordered on sarcasm but she started every conversation with how good it was to see you. She worked in a hospital helping parents cope with the reality of having sick kids. However, she seemed to have become less caustic after her father went broke and her mother had to do the unthinkable; work for a living. Loa and Julia got on well since they both worked in a hospital. In fact, they knew some of the same doctors. They even exchanged phone numbers and arranged to call each other. I was uneasy with them getting together because who knew what Loa would tell Julia about my past. I had not anticipated Julia having anything in common with my friends and it made me nervous. It was too close for comfort.

As the six of us sat there and enjoyed each other's company, I was satisfied with the execution of my plan. No one suspected that I had orchestrated this chance gathering at the neighborhood watering hole and I knew only too well that by morning my new relationship would be the latest subject of widespread gossip. I could tell that Arlene sensed that there was more to me and Julia than I was admitting but she did not press the point and went out of her way to make Julia feel at ease. It was a gracious gesture which I knew would be followed by a phone call to me no later than 10:00 A.M. the next day. Arlene prides herself on getting the inside scoop.

After two hours of drinking and telling stories, it was time for us to go. I wanted to be the first to leave so the others would have time to speculate as to what was going on between me and Julia and how I could be going out with such a fabulous woman. It was the perfect ending to this perfect coincidental gathering.

As we walked back to my place, Julia was unusually inquisitive. She wanted to know how I had met these people and how long they had been friends of mine. I tried to downplay these relationships for fear of my being labeled by association. It was a puzzle to her and she was trying to figure out how the pieces fit together. I explained that I was more an observer than a friend of these people. They were part of a community that I watched from afar. I did not want to admit that for me these relationships were more complicated.

Once we got to the apartment, I went to open the door for Julia to come in. Julia hesitated and told me that she was tired and preferred to go home. I accepted her explanation at face value, given the drinking and smoking. It was the first time she hadn't wanted to stay over. I responded as best I could without sounding concerned or disappointed that our evening had come to an end. For me, there was never enough time of being together. But it always seemed to be on her schedule. We walked back down the driveway to my car and I drove her back to the nurses' residence. I didn't take the long way. She kissed me goodnight, no tongue in the ear, and got out of the car.

I felt that something had changed between us, but I told myself it was the drugs, alcohol and fatigue. I had no reason to be concerned. What could have happened? We had a casual night out with no apparent tension and we met people who were good company. *My anxiety was in my imagination,* I told myself. I dismissed my fear of losing her as nothing more than nerves and drove home to get some sleep. When I got in I checked the answering machine but the red light was not flashing.

54

11

The next morning I woke up at my usual time, 6:00 A.M. My first thought was the coming weekend. This was my last weekend before I started articling at Lord & Bishop. After that I would be just another suit working in a downtown office. As usual, I turned on the ABC morning news where some economist was trying to explain how you can have a tax cut, spend more and end up with a balanced budget. You'd think that with the advent of the $4.99 calculator these economists could master some simple arithmetic.

The first call of the day came at 8:30 A.M. It was from Gerry.

"Hi, did you get laid last night?"

"No . . . we were too tired from all the drinking and smoking. How about you?"

"Of course not. With that crowd you'd need an engagement ring and, by the way, don't BS me. You weren't that tired. She said that she was tired and you agreed."

"Well, that might be closer to the truth, but I was tired. Anyway, what are you doing?"

"I just closed a deal with a customer with only three teeth. He's buying thirty-thousand pounds of old computers to be shipped to Belize, wherever that is."

"I think it's in the Caribbean. Isn't selling computers by weight an odd way of pricing them?"

"Used computers are junk and I get more per pound from a customer in Belize with three teeth than the local junk dealers will pay me."

"You're showing your age. Junk dealers are recyclers, the new generation of environmentalists. How much a pound do you get?"

"I average about fourteen dollars and fifty cents per pound U.S. while the local environmentalists give me ten dollars and fifty cents CDN. I'm doing my part to raise the Third World out of the depths of their own ignorance at a profit of seven dollars and twenty-five cents per pound Canadian Delivery Network. I'm a regular Peace Corps. And, by the way, if she says she's tired then the end is near."

"Look, sometimes you can be tired." He had hit a nerve.

"You're never too tired to get laid. Have you ever been that tired?"

"No, I've never been that tired. Anyway, it's not like we're getting married. We've only been going out for thirty-four days. We're nothing more than passing ships in the night."

"So how long does it take for two ships to pass? It doesn't even take thirty-four days to pass through the Panama Canal."

The casual pretense I had to assume about my relationship with Julia was hard on me and Gerry knew it. But, I would not admit to anyone, especially myself, that something might have changed. "What did you and Barry do after we left?"

"What do you think we did? We talked about you and how you convinced a girl as beautiful as Julia to go out with you."

"She thinks I look like Al Pacino in *The Godfather*."

"I've got news for you. You look more like Clemenza. Anyway, I got to go. By the way, Barry says that you are hopelessly in love."

"Tell Barry he's got it all wrong. This is just a fling . . . no commitments. Talk to you later."

After I hung up all I could think about was how to protect myself from the big fall and the inevitable depression which would follow. I could not face the possibility that my flight for freedom with Julia could end in a spectacular crash landing. The only way to protect myself from being dumped was to downplay the relationship to the point of indifference. Anyway, there was no reason to worry. Nothing had happened between me and Julia to make our relationship take a turn for the worse. I took a shower and started to plan for the coming weekend. Of course I wanted to spend it with Julia but we had not made any plans.

Just as I went to get dressed, the phone rang. I'm not used to getting calls in the morning. I hoped it was Julia telling me she was on her way over to catch up after going home early last night. "Hello, House of Stein," I said, trying to sound uplifting.

"Are you in love?"

"Arlene, you had seventeen minutes to spare," I said, glancing at the clock on the answering machine that flashed 9:43 A.M.

"What are you talking about? You're in love, I can tell."

"I'm not in love. We've been spending some time together, that's all. Anyway, why do you care?"

"I know you're in love. Women can tell these things. Loa and I both said it was written all over your face. I'm jealous."

"You are an incurable romantic. We've just gone out a few times. It's nothing more than that."

"Have you told your parents? What are you going to do about a Christmas tree? Will you let her have one in the apartment? Your parents will go crazy and pour ashes on their heads."

"As far as my parents are concerned, the reform synagogue catalogue has portable defibrillators for such contingencies."

Arlene laughed. "Really, how did you meet her?"

"She left a note on my chair at graduation. She thought I looked like Al Pacino. I know, don't say it, you think I look more like Clemenza."

"Who's Clemenza?" Arlene was a pal. "I can see a resemblance to Pacino. This is so romantic. How long have you been seeing her?"

"Not very long. Every day for the last thirty-four days. Just kidding, but we do spend a lot of time together."

"Have you taken her to the zoo yet? That's the big ice breaker for you . . . those monkeys in the spring."

"I didn't have to resort to the zoo."

"Don't change your style. The zoo strategy is non-denominational and it works. I wish I was as uninhibited as those monkeys in the cage."

I'd known Arlene long enough to know that she would think going out with a Gentile was a big problem. She was too caught up trying to make a living from her parents' friends. Arlene didn't understand that Julia was exactly what I needed to release me from the suffocating stereotype that I had been living. Julia was my chance to lead an anonymous life without cultural expectations or borders. She couldn't understand how Julia opened up my life. Arlene could have used a one-way ticket out of here.

"Arlene, you know I haven't had much of a social life these past few years. Julia is a breath of fresh air for me."

"I think you're cute. I mean you look more like Al Goldstein than Al Pacino but haven't we had something brewing between us that we've never admitted to?"

It never rains but it pours. I only look good to them when someone else gets interested in me. "Don't be crazy. You were never interested in me. You were nothing more than curious. You always aimed higher than me."

I didn't tell Arlene that I knew about her medical problem which was what really turned me off any chance of a relationship with her. Every time she got excited, and I mean really excited, she threw up. She was famous for it. I had heard about her condition while playing poker with my usual crowd. One member of the Wednesday-night poker group was going out with her and gave us all the details. But I did not have the heart to tell her that her queasy stomach was common knowledge. You can't even throw up in this city anonymously. Can you imagine? If you're in bed with her and it's lousy then everything is fine. But, if you're having a great night, look out! What a way to climax. I was not prepared to use rubber sheets or, even worse, not need them.

Arlene wished me good luck, told me not to deny that I was in love and said she wanted to get together again soon. I told her we would stay in touch . . . sort of. I had to get dressed and get out of the apartment for fear of another morning phone call. I needed a double espresso to calm my nerves. I was out of the apartment within ten minutes. I stopped at Mr. Cohen's store to get the morning paper, and as I walked in, Mr. Cohen seemed unusually animated when he saw me. As usual, he was standing behind the counter wearing a white shirt and black tie tucked into his pants.

"So Stein, you're sleeping with a Gentile."

"Mr. Cohen, where would you hear such a thing? *The Globe* please and make it today's paper."

"You can't fool me. Jane is no Jewish name. Look, buy some condoms. You'll need them with those kind of girls." He winked at me, "if you're lucky." He pulled a carton out of a drawer. "These are private label with the Progressive Conservative Party logo printed on them. I got them cheap after their last convention. Their slogan was 'It's safe to vote Conservative.' They had lots left over." I tried not to show any emotion. "Look, if you went to a convention with the women's auxiliary of the Conservative Party, you'd expect to have cases of condoms left over too. I got them from one of those surplus dealers."

"I'm not in the market for Conservative Party condoms but I'll keep it in mind. But, I am in the market for today's *Globe*. By the way, her name is Julia, not Jane. How did you hear about my social life anyway?"

"My daughter, Beth, carpools with Loa over to Children's Hospital. Today was Loa's turn to drive and Beth was running late so I was talking to Loa while she was waiting. She told me all about Jane and how you will break it to your parents before they see the Christmas tree. If I were you, I wouldn't say a thing until the last possible minute. It will kill your mother and she should live as long as possible without her boy causing her so much pain. Couldn't you find a nice Jewish girl so you wouldn't need those condoms?"

"Mr. Cohen, thanks for the paper and I'm sure you'll be kept up to date."

"Come anytime, Stein, and next time bring Jane so I can meet her. I'm sure she is a nice girl but she'll never stick around. Down deep they still think we killed Christ."

What a morning. It was only 10:30 and already I'd been accused of being hopelessly in love, was told that Jane/Julia was in the process of dumping me and a Christmas tree in my apartment would kill my mother. All of this before my first espresso or the morning paper.

The Italian Coffee Bar was an island of tranquility from this tornado of innuendo and free advice. I acknowledged the four Tonys and sat down to read my newspaper. I sensed that this was going to be the only quiet time I would get the whole day and I had better savor every minute of it. I read an article about the shortage of corporate lawyers in Vancouver. The article was about the extent national law firms would go to recruit corporate lawyers. Condos at Whistler, leased sports cars and cash incentives seemed to be the standard enticements. It was too early to ask my firm for a transfer considering that I had not even started and I didn't know exactly what a corporate lawyer did. Anyway, Julia was in my life now and I was not ready to move. I made a mental note to call Julia for some assurance. Three espressos and one morning paper later, I was ready to face the day.

When I got back to the apartment there was no flashing light. I called the nurses' residence and was told that Julia had gone out and that she was not expected back until after her shift at the hospital. I decided to surprise her and bring her an order of brown rice with almonds and tofu. I know the way to a girl's heart.

I walked into the vegetarian supermarket to pick up my order and felt like I was in a pornography store. I was afraid of leaving any evidence that I had been a customer. I paid cash, asked for a plain brown bag and would not take advantage of the 10 percent off day by simply filling out a form and signing it. With a meal in hand and love in my heart, I drove over to her hospital in the hope of overwhelming Julia with this gesture of my eternal affection.

I walked down endless hospital corridors looking for the Pediatric Ward. Finally, when I found the pediatric nurses station, I was told that Julia was in the staff dining room. I found Julia sitting with a doctor in the dining room. I wasn't sure if I should turn around and leave or continue on. I couldn't let the brown rice go to waste. I caught her by surprise and for the first time since I'd met her, she seemed flustered. I told her that I was in the neighborhood, so I had brought her a little snack. This was not an entire lie since everything in Winnipeg is within half an hour from everything else, so you are always in the neighborhood. She introduced me to Dr. What's-His-Name who I noticed was somewhat uncomfortable by my sudden appearance. He quickly left on the excuse of having to go save someone's life. I understood.

"This is quite a surprise to see you here," she said. "What's the occasion?"

"Well, with all those people showing up last night, we really didn't get a chance to talk. So I thought I would come by and we'd have a snack together."

"It was fun last night but I was tired and I really needed some sleep," she said, apologizing.

"Me too. I need my strength for work on Monday." I kept on going. "I was hoping tomorrow you would help me find some clothes for work and then we could go for dinner. Once I start work I'll have less free time for our evening walks."

"I won't have time to go shopping with you. But, I'll see you for dinner. We could try this new Indian vegetarian restaurant. I heard the pakoras are to die for." I noticed that her emerald-green eyes did not have the same shine as when we first met.

We talked for a few more minutes about nothing in particular and then she told me she had to get back to the ward. My unexpected visit was not well received. I had intruded into a part of her life which she was keeping separate and apart from our relationship. I thought that sharing brown rice might bring us closer but it turned out my presence had the opposite effect. She was uncomfortable with me at her place of work. I was uncomfortable too because, suddenly, I seemed to be chasing after her, which was true. We made some tentative arrangements about her coming over around seven on Saturday night and we would go out for dinner from there. I walked with her back to pediatrics, kissed her on the cheek and left. She did not kiss me back but I told myself it was not the appropriate setting for a tongue in the ear. I could not admit to myself that our romance had taken a major turn for the worse. She was losing interest . . . and fast. But, there was no rational explanation for this change. I went into denial and drove off to buy my business wardrobe.

12

With my legal career about to begin in two days, I felt like a soldier on the eve of being shipped out. It was a volunteer army but it felt like being drafted and life as I knew it was about to change. I wanted Saturday night to be special and I hoped it would rekindle our relationship. I decided to take Julia where it all began, the Drummer Boy Lounge.

You can never go back. This time the Drummer Boy Lounge was just another bar. Our conversation was strained and Julia seemed preoccupied. She sat there out of a sense of charity. She did not have that same inner glow as the first time we met. I tried to disregard the obvious by drinking too much but the combination of vodka tonics and moments of deafening silence was very uncomfortable. We were just another stale couple sitting at another stale bar. Something was very wrong. I knew Julia would not be staying the night when we left. I drove her directly to her residence without asking. She didn't argue. I was waiting for her to say the awful words but that didn't happen either. I convinced myself that not every night is perfect and left it at that. I went directly home after dropping her off. There were no messages on my answering machine and I fell asleep watching a rerun of *Saturday Night Live* with Steve Martin doing the King Tut skit. The casket prop of Martin's routine seemed ominously appropriate.

The next morning, I decided to resume my Sunday routine. I would watch TV news then take a walk down the Crescent to pick up a newspaper and have three cappuccinos at the Italian Coffee Bar. For me, there is something comforting about a routine. But, as I settled in to watch the news programs, the phone rang. It was Julia. My heart soared until I realized she called to say that she might have left her wallet in my car and could I check. We talked for a few minutes but it felt as if our time together was all in the past. She sounded like she was apologizing but did not quite come out and say the words. I was sure that her call was a prelude to one of those "It's me, not you" conversations. I could never understand why my failed relationships were never my fault but I was the one who always got dumped. I could use some no-fault insurance. I knew it was over but would not admit it and Julia never quite said the words. I rationalized it all away that this was just a temporary setback and we were still kindred spirits destined to be together. I was still her Al Pacino even though I was feeling more and more like Clemenza.

My mother called to wish me luck on my first day at work. She wanted to know my work phone number and address. I did not know either but I told her that I would call her from my new office with the information. At her urging and promise to make me salami and eggs, I agreed to go to my parents' home for Sunday brunch. I wasn't going to see Julia so I might as well drop the pretense of braised tofu and brown rice. I hadn't seen my parents for a few weeks and I had never told them about Julia. I wanted to avoid having to deal with the whole *shiksah* issue. At least now I would not need to order the portable defibrillator from the reform synagogue catalogue.

Although brunch with my parents always has its share of tension, the sense of family is comforting. While my mother made brunch, I sat in the den with my dad discussing the news of the day as it appeared on television. First, Reagan warned us about the evils of government and then announced the largest deficit in the history of the world. Next, Prime Minister Mulroney was telling us it was important to fix our constitution to include Quebec, but no one outside of Ottawa could care less. The constitutional debate was the fourth item on the news after the story about grain farmers complaining about the weather. Finally, there was the human interest story about an elephant that could paint and whose pictures were being sold to some Upper East Side New York gallery. My father shook his head in disbelief. Ten years ago I would have argued with him, defending my pretentious definition of art, but with age I have come to realize that he is usually right. Anyway, what's the point of arguing? It wouldn't resolve anything.

My mom prepared a Sunday feast: toasted bagels, lox and cream cheese, salami and eggs, chopped herring and freshly squeezed orange juice to wash it down. It was a meal fit for King Solomon except he'd have the good sense not to split this brunch with anyone. Between courses, we talked about my forthcoming legal career. Although I could never admit it, I was looking forward to doing something outside of academia. I assured my mother that I had the proper clothes. She was very concerned and managed to talk my father into giving me his five best ties so I could look fresh every day. I accepted their generous gift knowing that, if I didn't, it would be a family fight which I would lose in the end anyway.

After lunch, while my mother cleared the dishes, my dad and I went in the den. This was my dad's favorite room. One wall was dominated by a floor-to-ceiling book case and the opposite wall had floor-to-ceiling windows which overlooked the garden in the backyard. He had his own special Eames chair adjacent to the gas fireplace where he sat and watched television while the guests sat on a distressed brown leather, over-stuffed sofa. There was an air of warm informality to the room that lent itself to frank and friendly conversation. I asked my dad what he thought of David Black.

"Mr. Black was a nice young man. He had been taken by some crooked contractor who put in cheap fittings for all his faucets. His faucets dripped more than his kids' noses. The noise of all that dripping was so loud that he couldn't sleep and he came to me looking for help."

"How did he find you?" I was curious.

"I supplied the plumbing for his neighbor, Rothstein, so they recommend me."

"How did he take the news that he had been taken by his contractor?"

"I never really came out and said that his contractor was a crook. That contractor may be my next customer. But I explained how the leaks came about in technical terms and he drew his own conclusions. He understood that it was expensive to fix and he paid the entire bill right away, about ten thousand dollars. Afterward he called to thank me. He was very gracious."

"He seems to have an engaging way about him."

"Yes, except for that one strange characteristic. When he came to see me on a Saturday afternoon, he was wearing a suit and tie. I can't remember the last time someone walked into my warehouse on a Saturday dressed like that."

"Maybe he was coming from work," I said in his defense.

"Maybe, but it didn't seem like it. It looked to me like he got dressed up to come to see me. I'll tell you one thing, he wasn't going to a *minyan*. Anyway, it's a free country. He can dress any way he wants. I'm just not used to customers who put on a suit to talk about leaky faucets."

"I guess I will need those extra ties of yours if I go to work on Saturdays." I was getting restless. "Enough about work. Do you want to go for a walk with me down the Crescent?"

"Sorry, I have my Immigrant Benefit Society meeting today. We are arranging naturalization of some Jewish immigrants from South Dakota into Manitoba."

"Are you sure it's South Dakota?"

"South Dakota? I get these names confused by it's south something. Actually, I think it's South Yemen but we would help Jews from South Dakota too, if they asked. Anyway, I have to go to this meeting and make sure those Dakotans or Yemenites are treated right when they come. We don't want them to get brainwashed by those Reform Jews and their crazy rules about women leading the Saturday services. We've got to make sure they have a good first impression or they will end up dating who-knows-what and going to Tony Roma for Friday night ribs."

"Well, you go to Tony Roma."

"Yes, but when I go, I know better. These new immigrants shouldn't think it's okay."

This would not be a good time to mention Julia, unless he had already heard about her and it was his way of telling me to stop. Just then my mother stepped into the doorway of the den, wiping her hands with a dish towel. I was tempted to break it to my parents just for the shock value but I held back until I knew where I stood with Julia. You'd think that, at my age, my parents would accept anyone who was important to me. But, when it comes to intermarriage, there is no limitation period on a parent's right to be critical. I kissed my mom good-bye, shook hands with my dad and went on my way.

I decided that a newspaper and cappuccino were in order. I stopped by Mr. Cohen's store to buy a paper and hear the gossip of the day. Like always, he was there leaning against the counter. Mr. Cohen had no new gossip except to ask me about my new girlfriend, Jane, and give me more advice about unprotected sex. He had bought a lot of those Progressive Conservative condoms. I got my paper, checked that it was that day's edition and continued to the ICB for cappuccinos.

I entered the coffee bar through the side door, said hello to the three Tonys, Milan Tony had gone home for lunch, and took my usual place at the round table in the corner by the window. I was not halfway through the Sunday Homes Section when I heard a familiar voice.

"May I join you?" I looked up and saw Sarah Goldman flashing her beautiful smile. I could not get over how terrific she always looked. No one looked better in a pair of jeans and a white T-shirt than Sarah. The contrast of the white against her tanned skin was captivating. It was great to see her. I stood up, kissed her on both cheeks, very European, and told her how wonderful she looked. She sat down beside me and I ordered cappuccinos for two.

"Sarah, what brings you here?" I asked, hoping she would say that she was looking for me.

"I was on my way to my dad's lawyer to have him sign my passport application. I am early so I came for a cappuccino and the newspaper to waste some time."

"Why do you need a passport?"

"I've decided to travel around Southeast Asia until next fall. I'm in no rush to start a career. When I get back I'm going to clerk at the B.C. Court of Appeal so I'll be moving to Vancouver. What about you? I heard you're going to Lord & Bishop."

"It's all true but I can barely believe it myself. Starting tomorrow, I'll be an articled student at Lord & Bishop helping the downtrodden banks and insurance companies get a fair shake. I'm a regular do-gooder. I'm not sure how long I'll last, so save me a spot on the beaches at Bali."

"I'm sure there's plenty of sand to go around. I thought you were going to move away."

"That was the plan. But, my personal life got complicated."

"With a girlfriend? Are you still seeing the same one from last May?" She looked straight through me with her sky-blue eyes.

"She never was my girlfriend. We just hung out together. We have the same interests so we often went to the same places. It was nothing more than that."

"Sorry to hear that it didn't work out."

"It's not what you think. We just spent some time together." Unconsciously, I crossed my arms in defense.

"Come on, there isn't a guy in this world who thinks of a girl just as a friend. You tried, it didn't work and now you have been relegated to 'friend' status. It happens to all of us. Maybe you should come to Bali and meet an Indonesian girl. I'm told they are beautiful."

There was no point continuing the conversation because I was lying and Sarah knew it. We each read our newspaper and spent the better part of the next hour discussing the various stories in the paper and enjoying our time together. As she was about to leave, I asked if I could see her before she went to Asia. She told me that she was pretty busy for the next two weeks but after that she had some free time before she left. It was the polite brush-off coupled with the faint hope clause. She had got me back. I wished her well and asked her to call me when she returned to Canada. I told her I could always be reached at the office. Imagine, I was telling someone to call me at the office and I had not even started working.

I was experiencing that lonely Sunday feeling as I drove back to my apartment. I noticed that everyone walking down the Crescent was either in couples or with their dog. Some of the dogs were even in couples. I was alone. I thought about whom I could visit on a Sunday afternoon for a little social distraction. No one came to mind. Perhaps the red message light would be flashing.

I walked into my apartment and went directly to the answering machine . . . no flashing light. This would be an opportune time to take inventory of my wardrobe. Appearances are everything and I had to look the part. The problem was that I wasn't sure what my part was. Should I be the academic turned professional? I did have all these degrees but I wasn't sure if I should play that up or not. I could dress like the ambitious professional who knew that in time he would be made a partner. But, I wasn't even sure I wanted to work in a law office, never mind become a partner. Or, I could play the eccentric who worked unconventional hours. That was getting closer except I had no idea what kind of work I'd be doing. The problem was my entire wardrobe was comprised of one blue suit, a blue blazer and two pair of gray pants. This did not open up many options. I looked like just another downtown guy. I opted for the blazer, gray pants and my dad's red-and-blue-striped tie for the first day. Then I settled back to watch the Sunday afternoon movie. It was a World War II movie which is always a favorite. You've got to like a movie where the Germans get it in the end. As I was eating my bucket of freshly popped popcorn, the phone rang. Just my luck. I had resigned myself to a quiet Sunday afternoon and now someone was calling. Still, it might be a better offer than the movie. I already knew that the Germans lost in the end so I was open to something different.

"Hello."

"Hi, Ben, this is Barry. How are you doing?"

"Barry Altman, this is unexpected. I thought you go to your cabin on the weekends."

"We have relatives visiting from out of town and I had a family party this weekend, so I stayed in the city."

"So what's new?"

There was a nervous pause in the conversation.

"I wanted to warn you that you should get to a doctor. I got a case of herpes and you should get yourself checked out."

"Why would I be exposed?"

"Julia, if you get what I mean. Get yourself checked out."

I was speechless. I felt like I had been hit in the stomach by a wrecking ball. I had so many emotions going through me at the same time that I wasn't sure how to react. I broke out in a nervous sweat. After an awkward moment of silence where I managed to compose myself, I tried to give Barry the impression that Julia was nothing more than a casual affair and that both Barry and I had been caught with our pants down, so to speak. I wasn't convincing but it got both of us off the hook. I told Barry that I would check into it, made a little joke, and ended the call as soon as I could.

I was crushed. Then I was furious and my heart was pumping so hard that I could hear it. How could I be so naive to think that I could change from the old pattern of my social life? I let down my guard and I got kicked in the balls. God was punishing me for sleeping with a Gentile. Barry knew that I was going out with her. He could get laid anytime he wanted. Couldn't he have found somebody else? Maybe I shouldn't have told everyone that we weren't serious about each other. But, did they have to believe me?

I was crushed that Julia would get laid by someone I knew. For sure this story would get out. She could have left me with some morsel of self-respect. But, no such luck. I could just picture them together in bed having a good laugh at my expense. I wondered who else knew or worse, who else was sleeping with her. I wondered how many of us would be standing in line at the herpes clinic. Imagine, there I was enduring brown rice with tofu and she was in bed in exchange for a cheap thrill in a four-seater Cessna. It couldn't have ended any worse. And I had hoped that it was my turn.

13

I didn't sleep that Sunday night. Aside from being crushed about Julia, I was nervous about the prospect of work. I played out every possible first-day scenario in my mind so I wouldn't be caught off guard. What would I do if I forgot a name? What would I order if the partners took me for lunch? Would I call the partners by their first names? When would I know it was time to go home? Should I take off my jacket when I was in the office? How should I refer to the secretaries? I didn't know the answer to any of these questions, and I was sure that I would commit at least three career-limiting errors of etiquette by 10:30 A.M.

On top of all that, there was Julia. I couldn't decide if I should feel anger or self-pity. Anger/self-pity, anger/self-pity, anger/self-pity. The yin and yang of my social life. Anger was like an orgasm. It was all-encompassing but hard to keep up. Self-pity had a milder punch but with staying power. You can wallow in self-pity for a long time. It oozes all over you like a Calastoga mud bath and sticks to the skin. The one thing I was sure of was that my emotional turmoil was not going to be resolved in one sleepless night.

I was out of bed by 5:30 A.M., washed and ready to go to work by six. But it was too early, so I turned on the TV for the morning news. It was so early that the Monday morning news was still the Sunday late-night news. There hadn't been enough time for anything new to happen, not even in the Middle East. I decided to go downtown and have breakfast in one of those downtown breakfast places. Perhaps I could do some networking. Of course, this was not going to be easy. I didn't know my office phone number. I didn't have a business card. I didn't know if I would have a secretary. And I was on the lowest rung of the legal profession . . . an articling student. Perhaps I could network with other articling students or an apprentice fax machine technician who might one day be president of IBM.

I ate breakfast at one of those nouveau diners and read the morning paper. I was finished eating and ready to go to work by

7:30 A.M. But, I was still an hour early. I wandered around downtown and tried to look like I was going somewhere. I kept thinking about Barry in bed with Julia, laughing at me eating brown rice and tofu. It was too early to be angry so I opted for self-pity.

I found myself in front of the Lord & Bishop building by 7:45 A.M. To hell with protocol, I'd get an early start. I'll meet the other people of the firm who come in early. At least I'll have something in common with somebody in the place. I took the elevator up to the 14th floor reception. The lobby entrance was locked. I couldn't believe it. Where were those solicitors I always heard about staying up all night working on international financial transactions or the litigators preparing for the cross-examination of the so-called unbiased expert witnesses. Where were all these lawyers hiding and why was the front door locked? I stood there, frozen, with nowhere to go and nothing to do.

After standing at the entrance for a few minutes, a very attractive woman, approximately my age, got off the elevator carrying a stack of newspapers in her arms. As I later found out, she was the slotted early morning receptionist. In a downtown law firm, it is not politic to refer to someone on a "shift" but rather a "slot." She unlocked the door and I followed her inside.

"Can I help you?" she said.

"Yes, my name is Ben Stein. I work here, starting today. I was told to ask for Mr. Basil."

"It's student orientation day? I should have known it was going to be one of those Mondays."

"Is student orientation a bad day?" I tried to sound engaging.

"All day the new students will be running around looking for Mr. Basil and they expect me to keep track of him as if it were my responsibility."

"Is Mr. Basil in?"

"Mr. Basil does not get in until eight-thirty. Let me check if your name is on the list. We'll try and get you started." She ran her finger down a list of names as she shook her head. "Strange, there is no notice of any students starting today. Are you sure that you were to start today?"

"I'm pretty sure. Could you check again? S-T-E-I-N."

"Sorry, no Stein on this list." She looked somewhat sympathetic but I knew she thought that I didn't have a job there and nobody had told me. "I'm sorry, we have a strict security policy here and only staff are allowed in prior to our normal opening time."

"What time is normal opening time?" I asked. This was not the kind of start I had expected.

"The office opens at eight-thirty but we make exceptions if we're notified in advance."

"Could I be an exception and wait for Mr. Basil in the reception area?" I smiled.

She looked at me for a long moment. "Has anyone ever told you that you looked like Al Pacino? You know from *The Godfather*."

"As a matter of fact, I have been told that." *Great,* I thought, *I had to be reminded of Julia.*

"Come in and wait," she smiled at me. "At least you don't look like that other guy in the movie."

"You mean Clemenza?"

"No, Moe Green." Green . . . Stein, I got the connection. I hadn't even begun and already I was being stereotyped as the gangster Jew. This day had not started well.

Promptly at 8:30, Mr. Basil came out to greet me. He was surprisingly short for a man named Basil but he was dressed for the part. He wore a tweed sports coat, grey slacks and a white shirt with a blue-and-red paisley tie.

"Good morning, Mr. Stein. My name is Basil. I'm the office manager. I trust you haven't been waiting too long?"

"Hello, Mr. Basil. It's nice to meet you. I came in early on the off chance I could get started. But, you are exactly on time."

"I'll be giving you your orientation. As it turns out, you are the only student starting today so the orientation will not take as long as when we have a group."

"I'm looking forward to getting started."

"Just so you understand my role, I am the resource for the lawyers in the firm. If you have any questions or problems, you can come to me to solve the issue or look for advice. In the Lord's system, these matters are kept in the strictest of confidence unless you indicate otherwise. Is that clear?"

"Yes it is."

"Then let's get started."

Mr. Basil took me into his office and presented me with a folder of documents to sign. He suggested that I sign all the documents and read them later. He stood over me until I voluntarily decided to dispense with reading the documents and signed on the designated lines. The documents provided for health benefits, set up payroll deductions, gave me security clearance for the building and registered me with the Manitoba Law Society. Oh yes, and the last document waived my right to severance pay in the event that I was terminated for any reason. Small detail. After signing my name at least five times, I officially became a member of Lord & Bishop. I was on paid time.

Mr. Basil took me around the office and introduced me to some of the lawyers. When it was over I couldn't remember any of their names but I don't think they bothered to remember mine either. Their areas of practice were completely foreign to me. I didn't have a clue what aborginal law was but I later learnt it meant screwing Indians out of their right to fish for Goldeye. I didn't know what an environmental lawyer did but later found out it had something to do with helping mining companies dump mercury into rivers. The highlight of the orientation was when Mr. Basil showed me my office. It was small, with one window looking out at an adjacent office building window, but it was all mine. I loved the sense of privacy no matter how small it was. After showing me to my office, Mr. Basil left. That was the end of my morning orientation.

I sat at my desk and wondered what I was supposed to do. My first instinct was to call someone. Lawyers make phone calls so I might as well get started. Julia was constantly in my thoughts and I couldn't forget about this herpes problem. I called Murray Wall's office and, after managing to talk my way past two receptionists, I finally got through to him.

"Murray, it's Ben. Guess where I am?"

"Ben, it's great to hear from you. Where are you?"

"I'm calling you from my very own office. It's my first day at work."

"What's it like finally joining the ranks of the working poor? Do you have a mortgage yet?"

"No, but I'm paying too much in taxes and the cost of parking downtown is robbery. I should fit right in." I paused before I had to reveal the real reason for my call. "Listen, I want to ask you a question. I'm calling for a friend."

"Happy to help. What can I do for your . . . friend." Murray said. He'd obviously heard that one before.

"My friend might have been exposed to herpes through sexual contact. He wants to know if this is possible and, if so, what should he do."

"What a coincidence, there seems to be a minor epidemic of friends calling me about herpes problems. Yes, you can get herpes from sexual contact."

"What should my friend do?"

"He should go to the Sexual Disease Clinic at the University Public Health Project and get checked out."

"How exactly do they check you out?"

"Your friend isn't going to like this. A nurse comes and sticks a swab up the hole in your penis. They grow a culture and let you know in a couple of days if you've got the clap."

After a few more minutes of small talk, I thanked Murray for the information and hung up. The thought of the examination left me in a cold sweat. Some nurse is going to grab my mulroney and stick a Q-tip up its hole. What happens if I get an erection when she grabs me? I will die from embarrassment. I was going to have to concentrate on something so I would stay flaccid. How could this have happened to me? I fell in love with a Windsor who played around with an Altman and now I have the clap. This was no way to celebrate the multicultural diversity of Canada.

I had nothing to do. I was introduced to my secretary Gloria who explained to me that she worked for five students so I should not expect anything more than occasional typing. She made a point of telling me that I'd have to manage my own calendar. *This should not be a burden*, I thought, *since I didn't have any clients, appointments or anything else to schedule.* When I finished taking my instructions from One-Fifth Gloria, I sat in my office waiting for something to happen. It was the perfect opportunity to order office supplies from the stationery room. I got two pens, a three-hole punch, lined legal-size pads, time sheets, paper clips and a stapler. Here I was ready, willing and less than able but with all the essential equipment to take on complex legal problems. I supposed someone from the firm would find me now that I was fully equipped.

It was close to lunch time when David Black came by my office to see how I was settling in. It was reassuring to see a familiar face. David explained there was a tradition at the firm that, on a student's first day, they are taken out for lunch to the Assiniboia Club by some of the partners. He led the way and off I went with five partners, including David, to the hive of the WASP establishment. I had never been there before but I was sure that I would be the only Stein in the dining room.

Everything about the Assiniboia Club was old. The furniture was old. The waiters were old. The members were old and so were their jokes. I tried my best to hate the place but, the truth is, I wanted to fit in. I wanted to reject this scene rather than be rejected. I pretended that I was accustomed to such places and almost succeeded until it came time to order. The drink order for our table consisted of two martinis, two scotch and sodas, one gin and tonic and one cranberry juice. The food order consisted of two steak sandwiches, one baron of beef, two rib eye steaks and one turkey clubhouse on multigrain. I made a note that my diet would have to change if I was going to eat and drink with this crowd. The only vegetarian item on this menu was the onion rings.

The conversation over lunch was not that different from talking to the four Tonys at the Italian Coffee Bar. We talked about sports, cars, weather and work. The only difference between these suits and the four Tonys was their income. At the coffee bar, they talked about Oldsmobiles while at the Assiniboia Club it was Mercedes. At the coffee bar, they talked about soccer while at the Assiniboia Club it was golf. Thank God neither group mentioned fly fishing. The partners were a decent group and they tried to make me feel welcome. I left lunch determined to be accepted by the partners and looking forward to my first assignment. They had ignited my competitive instincts and I wanted to get started.

That afternoon, Mr. Basil, still short but with a haircut, reappeared at my door to continue my orientation. The first order of business was to teach me how to record billable time. Although I was being paid $22,000 a year, they were billing me out at $95 an hour and expecting me to bill 1,700 hours a year. Now I understood why they were so nice to me. I was a cow about to be milked dry without the residual benefit of the farmer's daughter pulling my udder. Mr. Basil told me never to round down when recording billable hours. I should be generous to myself, he said, when recording my time or I would be selling myself short and selling the firm short. Selling yourself short was the code phrase for not billing enough hours. He never mentioned anything about value or about the client but he didn't need to worry. I was determined never to sell myself short.

The second thing Mr. Basil taught me was how I would get my assignments. The first six months I would be drafting documents and writing opinions for solicitors who draft documents and write opinions to clients. The next six months I would be working in litigation doing much the same thing. The lawyers of the firm were my clients. Each lawyer decided for himself whether they wanted to send me work. So, if I don't get the hours recorded, then it would mean the lawyers in the firm didn't want to use me and that would be the signal that I should resign. The key to the system was to have the confidence of the partners, bill the shit out of the files and never sell myself short. It was a system which bred competition among the students and associates and did not encourage a collegial atmosphere. We were all competing to connect with the busiest partners to insure a steady stream of work and billable hours which would always be at the expense of someone else in the firm. To survive, you had to latch on to the right partner, figure out what he needed and then make yourself indispensable. I knew that my animal science degree would come in handy someday. This was survival of the fittest and, although I had mixed feelings about working in any law firm, I was determined to succeed and be wanted. I spent the rest of the afternoon meeting more members of the firm, not remembering their names and getting accustomed to my new surroundings.

Near the end of the day, one of the junior associates came to introduce himself. He invited me to come out after work for a few drinks with some of the other students and associates. I assumed this was part of my orientation so I graciously accepted. There were seven of us who went to a downtown bar called The Vault which was in one of those converted bank buildings. You didn't actually sit in a vault, it had been converted into a combination wine cellar and walk-in cigar humidor. These gatherings, I discovered, were a well of office gossip about the partners and their more sociable secretaries. All that was required was to go and draw from the well. I sat beside an attractive second-year lawyer, Margaret Hibard, who was a solicitor drafting agreements. She explained that she was fourth in a group of four lawyers. She had never met a client but she had spoken on the phone to clients' secretaries. I ordered a stiff vodka tonic to overcome my approaching depression and take my mind off that unspeakable medical examination that was looming.

I learned a great deal from the associates. My one-fifth secretary was having an extracurricular social life with one of the senior partners. I was advised not to antagonize her. That meant I should not give her any work and make sure to offer her coffee when I get one for myself. Also, I learned which partners were in favor and which were on the outs. The distinction between the ins and the outs was those who got work versus those who were given work. Any lawyer can do the work but it takes a special skill to get the work. I was relieved that my contact, David Black, was near the top of the "in favor" list and considered a leading candidate for managing partner.

I limited myself to two vodka tonics and gracefully left when the conversation turned to dinner and the next bar. I was pleased that I got on well with these associates but, in this jungle, first impressions can be deceiving. I went home and fell asleep in front of the television. The message light was not flashing.

14

Julia was constantly in my thoughts. How could she hurt me like that? Did she know that I heard from Barry? I wanted to call her but I was not sure what to say. "Oh hi, Julia, did you know that you gave me the clap? Barry let me in on your little secret." No, too bitter. "Julia, I got a call from Barry. He told me he's been fucking you and I was wondering if he had to eat braised tofu and brown rice to get laid?" No, too sarcastic. "Julia, this is Ben 'Al Pacino' Stein, I was wondering when you were going to tell me that you dumped me and humiliated me in front of all my friends." No, too much self-pity. "Julia, don't concern yourself. I understand. I know it's not me, you're just not ready to be with one person. You didn't mean to make me the laughing stock of all my friends and poster boy for the I TOLD YOU SO calendar of Jews who try to assimilate. By the way, thanks for the clap." No, too everything.

The fact is I was still crazy about her and I could not bury my feelings of betrayal. Could I get past the image of Julia in bed with my friends while I was subjected to a tofu burger and waiting for her to call? I would have done my best to accept any explanation she would offer so we could move on. Maybe she was drunk or stoned and did not realize what he was doing. Maybe she bent over to pick up her keys and Barry was following too closely. There was no satisfactory explanation but I was willing to be convinced.

The next day, I went for my medical examination. Murray had described the procedure accurately. I wore new boxer shorts and my body behaved itself. The nurse told me to call back in three days and quote a twelve-digit number to get the result. I found the long serial number curious and wondered whether twelve digits was indicative of how many tests they'd performed. There must have been an epidemic in academia.

Over the next few days, various partners sent me a series of minor assignments which were nothing more than grunt work. I was sent to the library to update some creditor statutes; I checked limitation periods for filing corporate reports; I inquired if a corporate officer can use blue ink to execute a land transfer document. In my best legal reasoning, I explained that the Land Titles Office requires black ink and peacock blue would not do. It had not taken three years of law school to prepare me for this. I could have used five years. Diligently, I wrote down all my time and made sure that I did not sell myself short.

I never spoke to the lawyers who sent me these assignments. They would send me written instructions which were left by their secretaries in my IN box. In turn, I would write a memo in reply and leave it with one-fifth Gloria who, in turn, would send it back. I never received any feedback or comment about the quality of my work but the memos kept coming. No feedback was good feedback.

Within a few days I fell into a work routine. The mind is a flexible muscle and it can adjust to many circumstances. The memos piled up in my IN tray and I just kept working my way through them and sending them back up the pipeline. I was determined to get the memos back in record time as part of my strategy to be noticed. I had no idea how my work fit into the grand scheme of a file or if my opinions even mattered. Maybe it was a test on the limits of my boredom. Now I understood when Margaret Hibard told me that she had spoken to the secretary but not the client. This one degree of separation from the client was a professional accomplishment which I had not yet achieved.

By Thursday, I was feeling pessimistic about my legal career. I was doing these uninspiring memos and generously recording my time so as not to cheat myself. I could not believe that someone would pay $95 an hour for what I did. I was having second thoughts about a career that was only four days old. But, if I was going to leave, it was going to be my decision rather than theirs. That's what kept me going and justified my long hours at work.

My medical results were due back on Thursday. Work had not been a sufficient distraction while I was waiting for the results of the medical test. I delayed calling until the afternoon so it would not ruin the whole day. I called the special number for retrieving test results and was immediately put on hold and told I was fifth in line for a lab technician to answer. After I had listened to eleven minutes of Tony Orlando and Dawn classics, a voice came on the line and asked me for my twelve-digit reference number.

"Mr. Stein, could you give me your date of birth? We do this as a security precaution."

"Sure, March 29, 1952. The same day Harry Truman announced that he would not seek re-election."

"We don't have a Dr. Truman here. Are you sure you've got the right number?"

"That okay, I'll call his Missouri number."

"Thank you, Mr. Stein. Your test results are negative."

"Negative . . . is that good?"

"Mr. Stein, that's good. It means that we did not grow a culture."

"Is that good?"

"Yes, Mr. Stein, that is good. You don't have the clap."

"Thank you very much. Have a nice day."

"Same to you, Mr. Stein. Don't venture into any strange places, if you know what I mean."

"No chance. I'm staying close to home. Good-bye."

What a relief. Now that I was clean I could deal with my unfinished business with Julia. The problem was that Julia already thought of us as finished business. But for me, it was not finished and I needed to finish it. As I was driving home from work, I kept thinking about what I would say to her. I did not want to sound like some wounded puppy looking for someone to scratch my stomach. I wanted her to know that I knew what was going on and I had stopped eating that awful brown rice. Long live hard salami on Russian rye.

When I got home, the message light was flashing. I wasn't in any mood for messages. Eventually, though, my curiosity got the better of me and I had to know who would leave me a message at 3:45 P.M. I pressed the play button. It was Julia.

"Hi stranger. Give me a call and let's hear about your first week at work." How could she leave such a casual message and sound as if nothing had happened? Maybe she didn't know about Barry. I wanted to call her back and get it over with. After staring at the phone for what seemed like hours, I called her back. What struck me was how similar my emotions were after hearing her message that day and what they had been the first time she left a message on my machine. I was still drawn to her sultry voice. But it would be

80

hard to risk another round of intimacy for fear of further humiliation. My heart couldn't take another blow this soon. She was too
tough for me . . . and way out of my league.

"Hi Julia. I got your message. How've you been?"

"I've been working nights so things are a bit upside down. But
I'm going back on days so it should get better. What's it like being
a downtown lawyer?"

"Well, I am starting right at the bottom . . . a legal crustacean.
But not as valuable as a lobster, more like a shrimp."

"Be careful you don't end up in hot water."

"Actually, I think you're the one who boiled me in water, except
that it didn't kill my sense of feeling."

"What are you talking about?" There was a certain caution in
her voice.

"Julia, I got a call from Barry. He told me to get a herpes test.
It turns out I don't have herpes but it broke my heart."

"I think Barry overreacted. He was not in any real risk."

"The issue is not my medical risk. The issue is how little you
felt for me. If you didn't want to see me, why didn't you say something rather than lead me on?"

"It was just sex. It's not that big a deal and it was just for a few
nights. Barry means nothing to me."

"It's not just sex. I guess I read too much into our time together.
I thought it was more, at least it was for me."

"You take these things too seriously. We were having a great
time together."

"When I was with you it was special for me and I never thought
about being with anyone else. You, obviously, did not see me that
way."

"Well I didn't intend to devote my life to you." There was no
emotion in her reply.

I'd had enough. "I should go . . . see you."

"I understand. Stay well." She hung up.

I was mad when I got off the phone. I was hoping that she
would have been embarrassed, apologize or come over for the great
reconciliation. But she didn't. Julia ended the conversation with such
finality that I knew it was over. Strangely, though, it didn't feel like
an irrevocable closure. I couldn't stand sitting in my apartment a
minute longer. I grabbed my jacket and headed out for a rebellious

smoked meat on rye with hot mustard and a pickle on the side. If I was going to have a case of heartburn, at least I was going to enjoy it. I wish someone would invent Maalox for bad relationships.

15

Although it was only my second week as an articling student, the work was getting me down. Check the IN tray, go to the library, write the memo and send it back through the pipeline. I soon developed a routine of long days. On a typical day, I started by reviewing my IN tray to see who was sending me work. I hoped that the quality of the assignments would improve as an indication that my work was being well received and as a direct result of the speed of my turnaround time. My IN tray was on a table with the IN trays of the other four students. Out of curiosity, I looked in their trays to see how my assignments compared to theirs. At seven in the morning, there was no one around to see me. As best I could tell, it was pure chance that determined which file landed in which tray. Until you had a track record, the secretaries had as much to do with who got the assignments as the partners. I realized it was too early for the partners to make a judgment about anyone's work in a way that would distinguish one student from another. Still, it was discouraging listening to the other students and junior associates drop names and talk about the complexity and challenge of their respective assignments. In fact, there really was no qualitative difference between any of our assignments. All their name dropping and law talk was their way of avoiding the mundane reality of the work. A law graduate is not special and an articling student's work is tedious. But, no matter how mundane I found the work, I was determined to excel. Better to quit than be fired.

One morning while leafing through the IN trays, I noticed an assignment to draft a consulting contract between an insurance company and a group of consulting actuaries. This file should have gone to me. As a graduate actuary, I understood what actuaries did better than most. By nothing more than bad luck, the assignment had been placed in the tray beside me. It was not in the best interests of the firm. For the good of the firm, I told myself, I should take this file.

As a team player, I wanted to do the best for the firm. No one could question those motives. Here was my chance to break out from the crowd and distance myself from the rest of the students. Anyway, no one would know the difference. I took one of my files having something to do with registering a grain elevator and traded it for the consulting contract file, switching names on the routing sheets of the respective files. It was as if the assignment change never happened. Surely I couldn't be taking the work away from someone else if they never had it. My career was about to be launched.

My first order of business was to get some intelligence on Bill MacIntosh, the partner who had sent the actuary assignment. Mr. MacIntosh could open up opportunities for me beyond this assignment. I found out from the other students that he was general counsel to World Insurance Corp., one of those Western Canadian insurance companies that had become a national company by charging exorbitant premiums and only paying out on policies as a last resort. The company was majority owned by a consortium of three trust companies who carved up its cash flow like a pig at a reform Bar Mitzvah.

I was warned that Bill had a health problem. In certain circles he was known as Bill "OPEC" MacIntosh. This man could pass gas to rival Saudi Arabia. It was difficult to be in the same room with him as his problem tested the limits of two senses, sound and smell. The big challenge was not to break down into uncontrollable fits of laughter in his presence. You had to put up the appearance of neither having heard nor smelled anything. I got most of this inside information from One-Fifth Gloria who, I was told by another secretary, had been the latest receptacle of Mr. OPEC's pipeline. Gloria was candid and advised me to avoid Mr. OPEC after 2:00 P.M. which was one hour after he usually finished eating lunch. One-Fifth Gloria restricted their interactions to the mornings. The more I found out about Bill MacIntosh, the more complicated the assignment seemed. I decided to communicate with Mr. OPEC by memo rather than risk losing my composure.

The second step in my research was to call a former professor of mine from actuary science to get his guidance on how actuary consultants deal with their clients. The subject of consultants always interested university professors because all academics believe they are underpaid and underappreciated. It gives them joy to recite the incompetence of these experts who were once their students. To academics, these so-called consultants are charlatans who do nothing more than photocopy, borrow your watch and charge you for telling the time.

I had been Professor Winslow's teaching assistant for two years, in 1974 and 1975. He taught me actuary science and I taught him how to swear in Yiddish. In the midst of our mutual education he bummed cigarettes from me which made him the *shlemeil* and me the *shlemazel*. I arranged to come to his office at four that afternoon so he could give me his insight into the "bunch of thieves with the fancy hourly rates." I knocked on his door at precisely 4:00 but had forgotten that university time is not the same as downtown time. Professor Winslow arrived at 4:30 which is close enough to the appointed time if you're a tenured professor. We spent the first forty-five minutes reminiscing about my graduate school days, which seemed appropriate since I was billing this time to the World Insurance Company. I was getting quite adept at recording my time. Otherwise, it wouldn't be fair to me or the firm. When we finally got around to the topic at hand, the professor was very helpful. He told me anecdotes about the consulting scam. These guys took the practice of billing to Herculean heights. I took copious notes, listened carefully and interrupted only to compliment the professor on his insight while asking him more questions in the hope he would reveal as much of his experience as time would allow. One surefire strategy to get these university people to talk is to tell them how smart and practical they are.

After leaving Professor Winslow's office, three hours later, I took a long walk to the car and reacquainted myself with familiar surroundings. After all those years thinking that I never wanted to leave this place, it had lost its attraction for me. I felt like a stranger. I was skeptical about the utility of it all and the endless debate and wasted money that went on at the university. I was embarrassed that I had participated in heated discussions about subjects that had no relevance to anyone other than those of us who populated the university lounges. When time has no value, you can afford to wallow in endless introspection. But, at $95 an hour, time takes on a different perspective. You record it.

The next day I asked that all my calls be held, even though I wasn't getting any, and I told One-Fifth Gloria that I was not to be

85

disturbed. I organized the information Professor Winslow had given me, my own research and the contract language precedents and proceeded to draft the actuary consulting contract. It was going to be the best agreement that Mr. OPEC had ever reviewed. I thought of everything. I tied up those consultants as tight as a drum, including their so-called expenses. I defined the allowable scope of their disclaimer; I set out the mathematical tolerance levels which we required from their statistical work and I detailed the structure for their reports. By the time I finished the first draft, these consultants would never again take advantage of the World Insurance Company. Representing the underdog can be rewarding at $95 an hour.

After three drafts of the consulting agreement, I was ready to send my work back up the pipeline. I was a portrait artist about to reveal his creation of the willing subject. The problem was how to get maximum recognition. I confided in One-Fifth Gloria to get the benefit of her experience with Mr. OPEC. In the end, I decided to send my work back the conventional way. I wanted to leave the impression that this was just an average effort.

Friday, three days after sending my masterpiece up the pipeline, I got a call from Mr. OPEC. He asked me to come over to discuss the draft consulting agreement. I made sure to go in the morning. The fish had taken the bait and all I had to do was reel in the catch. MacIntosh's office was a dedication in his honor. He had the solicitor's ego wall, with an entire wall of grip-and-grin photos with various political celebrities and business titans. He also had medals, certificates and trophies from various charitable and athletic institutions. It was an impressive display of self-importance.

"Come in, Ben," he said as I opened his office door. "I don't think we've been introduced," he extended his hand. "The firm has gotten so big that I can't keep track of everyone."

"I know who you are," I said as we shook hands. "I'm told that you are the king of the insurance solicitors."

"I can see we'll get along. You've got a good attitude." He motioned for me to sit down on the chair across from his desk. "If only we could establish a royalty system in this place."

"Actually, I think we do have such a royalty system. The firm name is no coincidence." He laughed and I was relieved to see that he had a sense of humor. I had taken a big risk but I knew if I could break the ice right away it would be to my advantage. It was nothing more than playing the fish by giving him a lot of line.

"Did you draft this agreement by yourself?" he said, leafing through the pages.

"I have no one else to blame. I got some advice from an old actuary professor of mine but he never saw the draft and I didn't tell him why I was asking all the questions. He was willing to help me because I had been his teaching assistant."

He leaned forward on his desk and looked straight into my eyes. "In all my years of getting memos from students, this is as good a job as I have seen."

"Thank you, Mr. MacIntosh. It was an interesting project. I tried to think of all the ways these consultants can pass on the risk and not take responsibility for their work. Also, I tried to find some way to limit their fees," I said, staring right back at him but smiling.

"Please call me Bill. I confess that I didn't understand all of the statistical language but this is a good piece of work."

"If you have any other projects I would appreciate it if you would consider me. This project was more interesting then finding out that real estate deals must be signed with black ink."

"Keep producing this quality of work and we'll be spending a lot of time together. In fact, here is a file. Three insurance companies are forming a partnership to process premiums. We'll need a contract for their partnership. Read it over and then come and see me."

"Thanks, Bill, and I'll get started on this right away." I stood up to leave.

As I left his office, I heard what sounded like the muffled version of the Concorde breaking the sound barrier. At least he had the decency to wait until I left. It didn't matter. I had handled the actuary project like a lawyer. I was on a first-name basis with Mr. OPEC, I'd learnt the basic rules of the game and now was manipulating those rules to my advantage. Finally, I had broken away from the pack. I had abandoned my academic life and this was the real launch of my professional career.

16

I became known as the student of choice for a group of the most senior partners. Bill MacIntosh had shared his opinion of my work with a number of the partners and, in turn, those partners sent me work. I was assigned the complex legal questions involving the largest transactions in the office. But, as my career as an articling student was progressing, it was becoming increasingly stressful. I worked fourteen-hour days to produce legal opinions in record time and was acquiring a reputation as the hardest-working and most committed of the articling students. In truth, I was just trying to keep up with the workload and avoid getting fired.

During my six-month rotation with the solicitors, I spent time with the most senior lawyers in the office. I met with them rather than communicating only by memo and, routinely, I went to their offices to discuss my research. I was the only student who interacted with the partners this way. I went for lunch to the Assiniboia Club so regularly I had name recognition with the club concierge. I was determined to fit in and even disregarded the fact that this club had a history of excluding minorities. I started ordering steak sandwiches, medium rare, fried potatoes and diet Coke.

I didn't socialize with the other students because of the workload and I had little in common with them. I was ten years older than the rest of them and I worked hard to distinguish myself from them. I was not about to do anything that would put me back into the generic student group. I had no social life. I started my work days at 6:30 A.M. and stayed until 9:00 P.M. I worked every weekend to the point that even when I was not working I was too tired to go out. I was not hanging out at the Italian Coffee Bar or seeing much of my friends. When I did talk to them, I found that I had little to talk about outside of work and my phone rang less and less. Everyone assumed I was working, with no time for anything else. Work came first and there was no close second. The good thing was that work helped me take my mind off Julia and the humiliation of our separation. We were finished but she was not forgotten.

On one particular Sunday morning, I was lying in bed trying to gather the energy for another day at the office. I didn't have it in me. This first Sunday in October was a beautiful fall morning. It's the nicest time of the year on the prairies. I had missed the entire summer working in the office and I decided not to miss one of the few last great days of autumn. I loved the sound of the leaves crunching under my feet as I walked down the Crescent. I decided to walk to the ICB, read the Sunday paper and visit my parents. It had been months since I had taken a Sunday off from work and I was not about to waste it. I quickly got dressed and went for my walk.

My first stop was Mr. Cohen's store to buy the Sunday paper. There was Mr. Cohen behind the counter gossiping to the customers, as usual, and offering advice on the topic of the day.

"Mr. Cohen, how are you? Do you have the Sunday paper?"

"Stein, where've you been hiding? I thought you moved to Toronto or Los Angeles where the doctors make a lot of money."

"I'm not a doctor, Mr. Cohen, I'm a lawyer and I've been here all along. I've just been busy working."

"A lawyer?" Mr. Cohen seemed genuinely surprised. "I thought you were smarter and with such a smart father. You could have been a cardiologist. So what kind of lawyer are you?"

"I'm an articling student, but I might become a commercial lawyer if everything goes well. Mr. Cohen can I have that cigar with my paper?" I said, trying to change the subject and pointing to the white labeled Cohiba in the humidor behind the counter. "How much do I owe you?"

"Special for you, eight dollars including a box of wooden matches. You know everybody charge for matches, but not me." Now it was Mr. Cohen's turn to change the subject. "By the way, Stein, whatever happened to that girl you were going out with? Did you marry her?"

"No, we did not get married and I don't see her anymore."

"Oh! Did she dump you? I won't tell." He leaned against the counter.

"Thanks for the paper and cigar." I put the bag in my coat pocket and continued on my walk to the Italian Coffee Bar.

Sundays were always busy walking days and it seemed everyone was out. I nodded to familiar faces as I walked along. As usual, most people were walking in couples or with their children or dogs. It reminded me of the solitude of being an only child and made a mental note to consider getting a dog for companionship. Maybe I could just rent a dog for Sunday mornings.

I walked into the coffee bar and made my way to the corner table by the window. I said hello to the four Tonys who looked at me as though something was not right. They asked me if I had been on vacation because they hadn't seen me around. I explained that I'd been busy working. This satisfied their curiosity and they returned to watching the soccer game from the black market satellite feed. I ordered the first of my three cappuccinos and settled in to read the paper.

"Hey stranger, is this billable time?" The voice was familiar and as I looked up I saw Gerry Smith and David Kaplan standing in front of me. It was great to see them. You can never replace the familiarity of old friends no matter how long it's been. They immediately sat down and we started catching up on the months that I'd been out of touch. They had stories about everyone. I had little to offer because all I'd been doing was working, but David was curious about life in the fancy WASP firm.

"So what kind of work have you been doing in that fancy law firm of yours? Are you riding the elephant or sweeping-up behind it?"

"I do my share of sweeping but I wouldn't want to give up show business," I responded, trying to make light of my career. "I'm in the corporate rotation doing legal research for insurance companies and banks."

"How much time are you spending at it?" David pushed on.

"I'm billing about seventy-five hours a week."

"Seventy-five hours a week!" There was an obvious tone of surprise in David's voice. "I hope the Lord appreciates your effort. Be careful, partners don't give a shit if they grind you down like crushed matzoh."

"Actually, the partners are considerate."

Gerry jumped into the conversation. "What exactly is the valuable service you are performing for insurance companies, keeping the world safe from policy holders with claims?"

"These insurance companies are misunderstood. They take great financial risk to provide money in time of need," I said, sounding defensive.

"In time of whose need?" Gerry continued, "No one should defend these bloodsuckers who take our premiums then fight their customer when its time to pay off, after using our money for thirty years."

When I revealed that I had never spoken to an insurance client and that all I did was write memos for lawyers in the firm, David could not believe it. "You mean to tell us that you work these kinds of hours without the client ever knowing? Even if you worked twenty-four hours a day you would not be caught up, so why bother? The work will be there the next day no matter how many hours you put in." David gave me the benefit of his experience and said that if you don't deal directly with the clients, you'll never have a practice. I knew David was right as soon as he said it. All these billable hours were not worth the benefit of name recognition at the Assiniboia Club. It was becoming a depressing day for my too infrequent days off.

We moved on to lighter topics and they filled me in on Paul's latest get-poor-quick scheme. After discovering that he couldn't sell lottery tickets in Budapest, Paul had decided to open a Cuban take-out deli in a strip mall in the South End of the city. Now everyone knows how they line up to order a Castro Clubhouse or a Bay of Pigs bacon burger on the Canadian prairies. I could just picture it. Paul's Cuban Counter with a bunch of kids taking orders for Fidel Fries with a side of Guevera Guacamole.

Eventually, like always, the conversation came around to women. Gerry was getting laid regularly but he had to go out of town to find Miss Perfect. By Gerry's definition, Miss Perfect was anyone who would sleep with him. David still had the same girlfriend but they had an understanding, whatever that meant. As for me it had been a dry spell since Julia. I considered telling them the real Julia story when Arlene walked in, spotted us, and came directly over to the table. As usual, she was in jeans and T-shirt. In some ways, Arlene was one of the boys. She could talk about her lousy social life and the losers she dated. She could smoke dope like a real trooper and knew some great gossip. She kissed us all, sat down and insisted on hearing the latest Paul story.

After a couple of hilarious hours, Gerry and David left for their family Sunday brunches. They invited me to come along but, somehow, I didn't want to intrude. Anyway, I hadn't read my newspaper yet and I still needed one more cappuccino to meet the morning quota. This left me and Arlene. She asked me about work, I dropped a few corporate names and she was suitably impressed with my career. Ultimately, the topic of Julia came up and she had to know everything that had happened. I couldn't bring myself to tell her the real story but I had this feeling that she knew more than she was letting on. There aren't many secrets in this city. After I told her the amended version, she accused me of still being hopelessly in love with Julia. She was right about the hopeless part.

Once I finished the Sunday newspaper and met my coffee quota, there was nothing left to do but leave. Arlene walked with me back down the Crescent. This felt better than renting a Sunday dog for company. We've always enjoyed each other's company and it was great walking and talking with her on that crisp fall day. It was the first time in weeks that I had laughed. Before I knew it, we were in front of my apartment. I invited her up to smoke some hash and eat some cold pizza. We hadn't seen each other in such a long time and what could be better than having some hash and a cold pizza chaser with an old friend?

After one round of hash and some fond memories from fifteen years ago, we landed on the bed. The condition Arlene imposed was that this would be a one-time diversion. It was never to be mentioned again, not even between us. Of course, having not been with a girl for months, I would have agreed to any terms for endearment. I think Arlene decided this would be a take-pity turn in the sack. Regardless, we had a passionate afternoon in the attic. Arlene ran for the toilet and vomited three times. The sound of wretching in the toilet after sex is not the greatest turn on but I knew what it meant and I could stomach the compliment. Just five months ago I was in the same bed with Julia and now, I am relying on my social circle from high school for a passionate diversion. This was not progress but at least I didn't have to buy dinner.

Eventually the moment came when we both wanted to end our afternoon frolic and go our separate ways. It was awkward to ask her to leave so I simply waited her out. She felt just as awkward. Finally, I told her that I had to get to the office and she told me that she had family plans for dinner. She wanted to get home and take a shower. Who could blame her after two hours of sex and twenty minutes of vomiting? We kissed good-bye, very adult, and she left.

I went to visit my parents. It had been six weeks since I had been at the house and two weeks since I had called. In fact, my mother called me every Monday night reminding me how awful it was that grown children neglect their aging parents. So, that Sunday, I did not call ahead because my mother always loved a surprise visit. As I walked into their house, I noticed that the plastic was off the living room furniture. This could mean only one thing . . . guests. I should have turned around and walked out, but my conscience was being tested. I decided to stay. Who could my parents be having for dinner on a Sunday night who would merit taking the plastic off the furniture? And why wasn't I invited? Could this mean I'd been disinherited?

I found my parents sitting in the den with my cousin John, the shoe mogul, and his wife Miriam. John had this odd sense of social decorum. Instead of bringing flowers or wine for dinner, he brought my parents the latest technological innovation in athletic shoes. In fact, my parents had a closet devoted exclusively to athletic shoes which John had given them over the years. Their closet was a historical exhibit of running shoe technology over the past fourteen years. One thousand years from now, an archaeology team will dig up this house and find this closet of running shoes and do an academic treatise on twentieth-century man and his shoe fetish. It will be a discovery equivalent to unearthing King Tut's tomb. No one will ever know that this was just about my cousin John being too cheap to spend fifty dollars on a bottle of wine when he came for dinner. As I walked into the den, we saw each other at the same instant.

"Ben, what a nice surprise," my mother exclaimed. "You'll stay for dinner and I'll set another place at the table." Before I could answer she was on her way to the kitchen. Within fifteen minutes she appeared and informed us all that dinner was ready.

Unfortunately, the dinner conversation was focused on me. John reminded me that we had not gotten together since my graduation party and he wanted to catch up on what I had been doing. Catching up for John meant him telling me about what he had been doing for the last six months. My father, adding to my discomfort, kept feeding me questions so I could impress John and Miriam with my stellar career as an articling student. I descended to the occasion by dropping names of bank and insurance company clients without letting on that I had never met or spoken to any of them. I even mentioned having lunch at the Assiniboia Club with the partners to impress my family with my early success. Here was proof that I could succeed without relying on them or their friends. However, I don't think it impressed anyone other than my mother. My dad looked concerned. I could sense why. He did not want me to rely on any employer and, particularly, a Gentile one. John and Miriam were to preoccupied with themselves that I don't think they even heard what I was saying.

As we were finishing dessert, my mother's famous lemon pie, my dad motioned to me to come into the den. We both stood up and excused ourselves for a few minutes. I sat down on the couch in the den and my dad uncharacteristically sat down beside me.

"Ben, I'd like you to do me a favor." He didn't hesitate for a moment.

"Sure, Dad, what can I do?"

"You know the Benevolent Society to help Jewish Immigrants who come to Canada?"

"Of course, you've been active with that organization a long time."

"I gave this fellow, Abe Zimmer, his first job when he came from Poland. He worked for me for two years and then he opened a Jupiter Tire franchise with his brother."

"You mean 'The greatest tires on earth come from Jupiter' . . . with the catchy tune from South Pacific?" I asked.

"Yes. Well, he called me up and told me that he was having some problems with the franchise and he needed a lawyer to give him advice. He asked me to recommend someone but he was concerned about how much it would cost. I told him that I would try to help."

"Our firm doesn't do that type of work. In fact I don't know anyone who does franchise work. Also, with our client list it might be a conflict." In reality, I did not want to get involved with a Polish immigrant who fixed flat tires and had a small claims dispute for $1,400 but I had to find a way to get out of it without hurting my father's feelings. Simply saying no was not an option.

"Could you talk to Abe and give him some advice about what he should do? He isn't sure where to turn."

"I'm a law student and I'm not sure that I would know how to help him."

My dad put his arm around my shoulder as if he was depending on me. "Listen to his story and, if you don't know what to do, you've got two floors full of lawyers. Someone must know. He may turn out to be your first client."

"I guess I can call him and point him in the right direction." I got the message and it was loud and clear.

"Actually, he'll be calling your office. I knew you'd help." He got up. The conversation was over.

It was late and time to leave. I had to be at work early and I needed to get some sleep. At John's insistence, I told him my shoe size and he promised to send me the newest trend in athletic shoes. Something to do with air in the soles. It was his way of avoiding buying me lunch. I kissed my parents goodnight, took the brisket that my mother had wrapped in tin foil and left. I love my parents. I know that I should see them more often but I could sure have used a vodka tonic.

17

November marked the halfway point of my articles. I switched from the solicitors rotation to litigation. I was not looking forward to my litigation rotation with all its rules and constant worries about limitation periods. But, to my surprise and relief, the work was much like my solicitors rotation except that it was litigation questions I was researching. Files would appear in my IN basket and I would prepare a memo and send it back up the pipeline. As an articling student at Lord's, you never saw the inside of a courtroom unless you were bringing a file to a lawyer who forgot it at the office. And I still never met a client, not even the secretary of a client. I had a better chance of encountering the Loch Ness monster than a client.

I had developed a work routine during my solicitor rotation that I continued into my litigation rotation. I was in by 6:30 A.M. and never went home before 7:00 P.M. That winter was bitterly cold and the combination of work and weather was grinding me down. The most comforting part of my day was looking at a weather map and finding a city in Canada that was colder than Winnipeg. It was usually Regina or Ottawa. Days added up to weeks and then into months. Some of the work in litigation was interesting but I had no interest in people who had to resort to the courts to solve their problems. I never divulged to the litigation partners my real opinion about their work and I would routinely fake a work orgasm about my litigation assignments. In truth, I was looking forward to finishing my litigation rotation.

On the second Tuesday in February, I came in early as usual, ready to face the assignment of the day. It was colder than a ditch digger's ass and it had been that way for almost four months. I never understood how it could be so sunny but yet so cold. The phone rang and I glanced at the clock on my desk, 7:13 A.M.

"Good morning, Ben Stein speaking."

"Hello, Mr. Stein?"

"Yes, this is Ben Stein."

"My name is Abe Zimmer. I met your father at the Benevolent Society and he told me that I could call you about a legal problem I have."

"My dad mentioned you, but that was months ago. Are you the gentleman with the tire store?"

"The greatest tires on earth come from Jupiter . . . that's me. I didn't call before because I've been very busy and I wasn't sure if I actually had a legal problem. Have I left it too long to see you?"

"No, it's not too late. I can see you. But, you should understand that I am an articling student and the best I can do is listen to your story and help you find the right lawyer."

"Don't be so modest, Mr. Stein. If you're half as smart as your dad I'm sure you can help me. Nathan told me that if anyone can figure out what to do it would be his son."

"He might be overstating my ability but I'll try to help. When would you like to come in?" I opened my empty appointment calendar. "We could probably find some time later next week."

"I was hoping to see you now."

"You mean today? Mr. Zimmer that is very short notice. I am quite busy today."

"I didn't mean later today. I mean right now."

"Where are you calling from?"

"I'm in the lobby of your building at the pay phone. Did you know they raised the price of a call to twenty-five cents? I could have saved the price of a call and just come up but, without an appointment that's impolite. I would rather pay the bloodsucker phone company than barge in unannounced. Mr. Stein, could I come up and see you now?"

I had to think fast. If I saw him right away I'd be rid of him sooner. I didn't have an appointment anyway. In fact I rarely, if ever, had appointments but that was something a lawyer or even an articling student would never admit. I wasn't sure what to do but I told him to come up. I'd listen to his story then send him to a local firm in a neighborhood strip mall which would take his $500 retainer and deal with his problem. My clients were banks and insurance companies, I reminded myself. I did not want to get involved with a tire franchise with who-knows-what kind of problem. This was exactly the type of career that I wanted to avoid. If I was going to practice law, which was far from certain, it was going to be a meaningful career.

Within five minutes, I walked out into the reception area to meet Mr. Zimmer. I braced myself for the worst. Mr. Zimmer walked in wearing pressed green work pants and a matching shirt with a fleece-lined nylon jacket embroidered with the Jupiter logo on the back. He was between fifty-five and sixty years old, neatly groomed, with salt-and-pepper thinning hair. I introduced myself and quickly showed him into one of the client interview rooms in the hope that we wouldn't be noticed.

"You look a lot like your father, Mr. Stein," he said in an engaging manner.

"I have pictures of my dad when he was my age and there is a distinct similarity. He had less hair than I do but he assures me that I'll catch up. Tell me, how did you meet my father?"

"It was very bad for us in Poland. When we immigrated, the Canadian government sent us to Winnipeg as part of the agreement to let us into the country. When we got here, we called the Orthodox synagogue to see if they could help us and they put us in touch with the Jewish Benevolent Society. I needed a job and, through the grace of God, I was introduced to your father. He gave me a job in his warehouse. He was very kind to me and made sure I got most of the overtime to help me get on my feet."

As I listened, I got the sense that this was a man of some substance and not just another immigrant looking for free advice. He embodied every immigrant's dream of a new life in Canada. I became even more curious.

"After two years of working for your dad, I realized that, to get ahead in this country and provide for my wife and daughter, I needed my own business. I saw how wealthy Canada was and everyone had two cars. Every one of those cars has four tires and those tires wear out, plus you need a second set for the winter. So me and my brother opened a tire store."

"How did you get a Jupiter franchise?"

"I took all the money my brother and I had saved, plus what we could borrow from the Benevolent Society, for the down payment on the franchise. I raised forty thousand dollars. The bank would not lend money to an immigrant with ambition but no collateral. They'll only give you money if you don't need it. If I had the kind of assets they wanted as security I wouldn't need to borrow their money."

"How has the store done?"

"When I opened the tire store three years ago, it was a tough struggle. I had a bad location. No one could find us. No one drives under the Salter Street Bridge. Imagine a store under a bridge. I couldn't afford a proper location because the rent was too high. My whole life savings had been spent on this franchise so I wouldn't give up. I had to find a way to make it work. As it turned out, that terrible location was the best thing that ever happened to me."

"I don't understand."

"I had the idea that I couldn't afford a good location then I should go to the customer instead of the customer not coming to me."

"How do you take a tire store to the customer when you need shop equipment to install the tires?"

"Mr. Stein, your father was right. You are a smart boy. That was the problem. I worked out a way to build a portable wheel balancing machine and I installed it in the back of my van. No one had ever done it before. My competitors all assumed that the customer had to come to their store. Anyway, I made the portable tire installation equipment, bolted it to my van and I became the only mobile tire dealer in the city. Instead of customers not looking for my store under a bridge, I come to their office or home and install the new tires while they go about their business. You never have to wait in a dirty tire shop or interrupt your normal day."

"How did you learn to make portable tire equipment?" I was impressed with Mr. Zimmer's ingenuity.

"In Warsaw, I was a professor of mechanical engineering and these things come easy to me. But, no matter what they say about the new Poles, they haven't changed since the war. I would never be more than an assistant professor there and, even then, I was not welcome. We had to leave."

"And the business, are you making a go of it?" I was very curious and respected his tenacity to succeed.

"God willing, we keep getting better. We have five trucks on the road full-time and each truck is selling between sixty and eighty tires a day, six days a week. We don't work on Saturdays. But, we change tires on Sundays while my customers are in church praying for forgiveness. You wouldn't believe how many tires we install in church parking lots."

"It sounds like you have everything under control. Why would you need a lawyer?"

Mr. Zimmer picked up the accordion folder he had brought which was stuffed full of papers. He explained that, as a Jupiter franchisee, he paid a franchise fee based on a percentage of gross sales, plus a prorated portion of marketing expenses along with all the other franchisee owners. He got a bill every month for the franchise fee and his portion of the expenses. There was an automatic deduction taken from his bank account in the amount of that bill. Mr. Zimmer thought he was paying too much and couldn't understand the accounting for those expenses. He gave me a whole binder of loose-leaf pages which included the franchise agreement, copies of his monthly statements, reports to the franchisees about the Jupiter marketing activities and his cancelled checks.

I was slightly overwhelmed. "Mr. Zimmer, I'm an articling student and you should be seeing an accountant."

"No, I need someone who thinks like a lawyer. I want you to look at this problem. I can trust Nathan Stein's son. Your father gave me my start in this country and if he says see my son then you are the one I want to see."

"Mr Zimmer, you are one franchise. How do you expect to last in a fight with a company as powerful as Jupiter?"

"I can fight if I have to. But you have to tell me if I have a case. Please look at my records. I'll leave it all with you and you tell me what you think."

"By the way, how many franchises are there?"

"I'm not sure of the exact number because it keeps changing. But it's about four hundred."

I couldn't say no. I remembered my parents telling me about the family who helped them when they came to Canada and how much it meant to them. It was now my turn to return the favor. The immigrant story seemed to have come full circle. I didn't want this type of client, but I didn't have it in me to say no.

This case is probably nothing more than a franchisee who had a bad deal and now he was trying to find a way out of his commitment. They'll sign anything to get into business and, as soon as the franchise starts making money, they don't want to pay the fees. But

Mr. Zimmer had a certain dignity about him and I promised my dad that I would look after him which meant at least looking at the documents. I told Mr. Zimmer to leave everything with me for a couple of weeks and I would let him know what I thought. At the end of our conversation, he pulled a jar of pickles out of a paper bag and gave it to me. He told me his wife made the best pickles west of Thunder Bay with a secret recipe she smuggled out of Poland. It was my retainer. At least I won't be a starving articling student, just a thirsty one.

18

It's hard to maintain your enthusiasm about anything in the middle of winter on the prairies. It is bitterly cold with no relief in sight. February is the worst month of all and every day seems colder than the day before. The only real uncertainty is whether the temperature will dip to a record low or just stay at a balmy −20c. The wind and cold are so biting that you walk backwards down the street to avoid facial frostbite. But on the brighter side, the plunging cold caused my billable hours to skyrocket. I was billing 40 percent more hours than any other student and more than most of the associates and partners in the firm. My enthusiasm for work was the result of a combination of the weather, a non-existent social life and I couldn't afford a winter vacation in a tropical paradise. I was still ambivalent about my career but leaving the firm would be my decision, not the Lord's.

In spite of my propensity for work, I did not look at the Jupiter file. For ten days following my meeting with Mr. Zimmer, I stared at the Jupiter file on the floor in the corner of my office and I did nothing about it. I wished the documents would walk out on their own but they never moved. I didn't want to get involved with Mr. Zimmer but I had eaten the pickle retainer so I had no choice but to do the work. I knew that I must review the file before my dad asked me why I had not helped Mr. Zimmer.

One morning in February, I got a message to see Rupert MacIntosh. Rupert was Bill's older brother but, thank God, Rupert did not have the same genetic code as his brother. Rupert came to work early and I often saw him in the lobby waiting for the daily newspaper to arrive. The group of early morning lawyers at Lord's was a cult. We didn't have a secret handshake but we were members of the fraternity of the early. We were somewhat smug in our view that only we understood the true meaning of work.

Rupert Macintosh was on my floor so I walked to the southwest side of the building where he had his corner office.

"Mr. MacIntosh, you wanted to see me."

"Yes, come in," he said. "I've never properly introduced myself. I'm Rupert MacIntosh and you must be Ben Stein, the student my brother is so keen on."

"I did a lot of work for your brother during my rotation and I enjoyed the opportunity."

"I expect it wasn't entirely enjoyable, Mr. Stein." He smiled. "I know his nickname. I know he's sleeping with your secretary and I know he goes for lunch with students to that club for the walking dead. And you're telling me that you enjoyed that?"

"But he did give me interesting files and if it weren't for him, I would still be registering grain elevators at the Land Title Office."

"How about litigation, would you like to try some court work?"

"I don't have any interest in personal injury claims, family disputes or people who can't find a way to solve their own problems. I just can't see myself as another ambulance chaser down at the courthouse, waiting for my turn to be heard by the judge." I couldn't believe my candor.

"I wouldn't want to be one of those ambulance chasers either. But that's not how the smart litigators do it. The trick is to be in the ambulance before it leaves the parking lot. Leave the chasing to the rest of them. If you want a litigation practice, make sure you know rich guys who fuck up and can afford to defend it. Then the world of a litigator will unfold as it should."

"I'll keep it in mind. But, how am I going to meet these people when all I do is write memos? I appreciate the opportunity of working for this firm but I've never met a client, never mind getting to know one." I didn't want to mention Mr. Zimmer and my pickle retainer. I couldn't take the risk that Lord's might try to poach my first client.

"Ben, we all have this frustration when we start out. But, the trick is to watch for an opportunity and seize it when it comes around. The difference between a successful litigator and one who does slip-and-fall cases is nothing more than taking advantages of an opportunity when it comes. Somehow, it always comes."

"And how are you so sure that this opportunity will come?" I challenged him.

"Every lawyer gets his shot. The problem is that most don't see the opportunity when it comes around or they are too timid to take a chance. So, it just passes them by. It's sad, but it makes it a lot easier for the rest of us who can spot an opportunity and are willing to take the necessary risk. The trick is to spot it. It's the same as being in court. At some point in a trial, the other side will make a mistake. No one runs a perfect case. If you recognize the error and shove the mistake up their ass, you will win more cases than you deserve. If you miss it or let it pass, then you'll get what you deserve and you'll have to rely on the dumb client's pathetic lies. That's the difference between winning and losing."

"I must admit that you make litigation sound intriguing. It would certainly keep me alert."

"No one knows when opportunity will knock. But I guarantee it will happen and the rest will be up to you. Now, I called you about this file. I want you to look at this issue. Can you use a 'without prejudice' settlement as evidence of subsequent conduct? Read it over and give me a call if you don't understand what's going on." He pushed the file across his desk.

"Sure, happy to help. I'll look at this file within the next few days if that's okay."

"That's fine. By the way, in case you're wondering, my brother's nasty digestive problem does not run in the family. He should stay away from that Assiniboia Club food. It's methane waiting to happen." He winked at me as I got up to leave.

I kept thinking about Rupert MacIntosh's advice as I walked to my office. I could not decide if it was the voice of experience offered to a student or a pointed warning because of something he heard about me. Maybe his advice applied to more than the practice of law. The difference between success and failure was recognizing and seizing the opportunities that comes along. This was different than my strategy. I was counting on success being a combination of hard work and brains, the classic son-of-an-immigrant story. I didn't think that any more was necessary. If Rupert was right, then the difference between success and failure was a very thin line. It was nothing more than being in the right place at the right time and realizing it. All those hours and days of writing memos would only lead to more hours and days of writing memos. If Rupert was right, my entire working strategy was flawed.

That night I took the Jupiter file home. I didn't want to do the work at the office because the work was not billable and I didn't want to explain the circumstances. It was hard to concentrate on one tire store's problems after talking to Rupert. I had been counting on hard work and intellectual excellence to advance my career and here I was being told the real key to success was recognizing and seizing the moment. There was no point spending any time on Mr. Zimmer's problem for a jar of pickles retainer. Jupiter was not an opportunity knocking at my door. But, it was a request from my father so I couldn't turn Mr. Zimmer away, at least not for now.

I took the documents out of the accordion file and laid them in neat stacks on my kitchen table. It soon became apparent that this franchise problem was not a small claims case of $1,400. Although Mr. Zimmer had a small business with fifteen employees, his franchisee obligations were complex and comprehensive. Even if I worked three or four hours every night, it was going to take at least five nights to understand the business relationship and work through the issues. I had to call him.

"Hello, Mr. Zimmer, this is Ben Stein."

"Mr. Ben, how are you? What can you tell me?"

"Mr. Zimmer, I started looking at your documents and this is a complicated problem. It's going to take some time to sort through it all."

"Take all the time you need."

"Mr. Zimmer, this is not as simple as reading a few documents and giving you some advice."

"I'm sure someone as smart as you can handle it. But your effort should be rewarded, so I'll send you over another jar of pickles and one for your dad."

"That's very generous. But this is a problem that requires an experienced lawyer. It's beyond me."

"Don't be modest, Mr. Stein. Your father told me that you can handle any legal problem. He's a fine man, your father. You take all the time you need. I'll get you those pickles. We don't have many left from this year's batch, but for you we'll find."

"Thank you, Mr. Zimmer, I'll keep in touch. Good night."

Two jars of pickles were on my desk by 9:30 the next morning. I was committed. I didn't have a trust account to deposit this retainer in but I made room in my fridge, segregating them from the food meant for general consumption. Over the next two weeks, I spent every evening reading and working through the stacks of Mr. Zimmer's documents. The more I read, the more interesting the problem became and the more confused I became. I saw it as a puzzle of how all the franchise agreements, invoices and correspondence fit together. And like any jigsaw aficionado, first I looked for all the straight-edged border pieces and then worked my way to the middle.

The franchise documents were the standard set of Jupiter documents where you fill in the blanks to identify the franchisee, his address, the down payment and expiry dates. It was obvious that the franchisor drafted the contracts and could do anything he liked. The franchisee sublet the premises from the franchisor, bought all his goods for resale from the franchisor, paid a franchise fee of 4 percent of sales and paid a proportionate share of all marketing costs. In addition, the franchisee had to use a designated bank and the franchisor could withdraw funds automatically from the franchisee's account to satisfy their bi-weekly invoices. Also, the franchisor could come in at any time to audit the franchisee's books to check if he was paying the proper fees.

The most intriguing group of documents were the sales and marketing bills from Jupiter. Based on Mr. Zimmer's bills, I calculated that the franchisee group in total was paying $3,000,000 a month for the marketing expenses of Jupiter. This seemed excessive considering the franchisees were also paying a franchise fee of 4 percent of sales, a mark-up on the goods purchased from the franchisor and rent for the signs and all the fixtures and equipment.

By the end of my review, I concluded that the marketing invoices were out of line for the services contract. It warranted a full investigation. This would take more work than a deli retainer and would be far more interesting than writing a banking memo. At least I had met the client. But, at the same time, I did not want to be just another ethnic lawyer servicing a narrow ethnic community and having to attend ethnic fundraising dinners to insure that I had clients. I had taken the job at Lord's to break away from a stereotyped practice. I was determined to broaden my horizons and leave my family's past behind. I was not going to depend on the Jewish Benevolent Society and my father's connections to sculpt my career. I decided to tell the Lord partners what I had been doing and solicit their advice. If this Jupiter file went any further, a partner would have to take stewardship of the work and I would take a graceful exit.

106

I met with David Black and Rupert MacIntosh, I explained to them how I got the file and the work I had done on my own time. They reminded me that once you work at Lord there was no such thing as work on my own time. Time had only two categories, billable and non-billable. My own time was not a recognized category. All legal work was in the billable category. I didn't want or need a lecture on the theory of billable hours and articling servitude, but I sat there and nodded in agreement.

Both David and Rupert advised me that the file was more work than it was worth. As long as the franchisor had the power to terminate the franchise agreement, then all the franchisees would fall into line and any claim would ultimately be dropped. A claim against the franchisor would put the franchisee claimant at real risk of losing his business. Years of litigation would follow with no assured result. They recommended that I tell Mr. Zimmer that he had no case but to remind him that it was only the view of an articling student. David might have slain Goliath somewhere in the Middle East but it's much tougher in litigation on the Canadian prairies. It would take a lot more than a sling shot to bring down the Jupiter Corp. When I left them, I suspected that I should have stuck to my original plan and sent Zimmer on to some suburban strip mall law firm. I knew David and Rupert were right but I was not quite ready to send Mr. Zimmer to the strip mall.

19

During the next few weeks, I worked on the Jupiter opinion. Even though I intended to transfer the file to another law firm I didn't want my successor to think that Mr. Zimmer got a shoddy opinion from a student of the Lord. I produced a thirty-page document which dissected the franchise relationship and concluded that the invoices for marketing services, considering the other fees, were likely inflated by as much as 40 percent. Because my work was non-billable, if you disregarded the three jars of pickles, I typed the opinion and put it on plain paper so as not to implicate the firm. By the end of March, the final draft of my opinion was done and I called Mr. Zimmer to pick it up.

"Hello, Mr. Zimmer, this is Ben Stein."

"Yes, Mr. Ben, how are you? And how are your parents?"

"We're all fine, thank you, and how is the tire business?"

"Business is good. In fact, this week I put another installation truck on the road. We're selling our share of tires but the franchise fees are killing us."

"That's the reason for my call. The franchise opinion is ready for your review."

"Do I have a case?"

"Mr. Zimmer, I'm just an articling student and I don't have enough experience to offer an opinion."

"Don't be so modest, although it seems to be a family trait. We both know you're smarter than most of those lawyers at your fancy law firm. I could see it as soon as I walked into your office. What do you think? Do I have a case?"

"It took me thirty pages to explain so it is not that simple an answer. You may have a case. But, you would be David fighting Goliath or maybe worse."

"Mr. Stein, I found a way to get out of Poland alive and away from those so-called academics who were agents of the secret police.

I'm sure I can find a way to handle a tire company and their crooked invoices. Leave the opinion at your reception desk and I'll pick it up. I'll read it and get back to you. By the way, how much do I owe you?"

"Well, counting the three jars of pickles as a retainer, I figure we're about even as long as you send me one jar of pickles every year from now on at Rosh Hashanah. It's a steep price, I know, but I put in a lot of time on your opinion."

"I'm confident you're worth it, it must be a good opinion to warrant such a fee."

"Best of luck. I'll pass on your regards to my parents."

I was relieved. My obligation to Mr. Zimmer was coming to an end. I'd probably talk to him after he read the opinion and then it would be over. Although it was an interesting problem I was better off leaving this to others. I didn't want an ethnic-based practice and the sooner I was rid of Zimmer's case the better. I would refer him to another law firm and I would not have to convince him that he could not fight a giant such as Jupiter. I did what I was asked to do and my father would be happy, Mr. Zimmer would be happy, the lawyer I'd send it to would be happy and I'd never worry about it again. We would all live happily ever after.

The next few months went by quickly. Winter was turning into spring and usually I'd be getting restless. But it was easy to stay focused on my work because of my non-existent social life. I stayed in touch with my friends but none of us made much of an effort to get together. They talked about their family businesses while I was doing work for the biggest companies in the country. It wasn't that I was turning into an articled student snob but I was dealing on an entirely different scale than my friends who clung to the safety of the local business. I was tired of the petty gossip about the same people doing much the same things. It was of little consequence to me and boring.

In June, 1985 I was called to the Bar. It was a relief shedding my status as articling student to emerge as a lawyer. At age thirty-five, I was ready to stop being described as a student and tediously explaining why I was ten years older than the next oldest student at Lord's. I still had no idea what was to become of me and I had serious concerns about a career in the law. On the occasion of my being called to the Bar, the managing partner of Lord's came to my office to congratulate me and told me I was being offered an associate position in the corporate commercial group. This group, the largest group in the firm, was headed by David Black and Bill "OPEC" MacIntosh. The offer was described to me as a long-term opportunity. That concerned me because every time someone referred to something as a long-term opportunity it always meant the pay was lousy.

"Ben, you've done great work and the partners would like you to stay on," the managing partner reassured me.

"I appreciate the offer. What would I be doing if I stayed? If I'm going to specialize in corporate work I'd like to understand my prospects with the firm." I was remembering Rupert's advise about recognizing an opportunity and capturing the moment. I wondered if this was one of those moments to capture or avoid. It didn't feel like the moment had come.

"As a first-year lawyer you will be paid fifty-five thousand a year with a bonus depending on how the firm does and how much you contribute. You will work mainly on mergers and acquisitions and be part of the team that goes in and does the deal. There is no set agenda and you will get as much responsibility as we feel you can handle. It all depends on you."

"Will I be dealing with the clients?"

"That depends on you and the nature of the work. Some lawyers are very good business getters while others don't do well with clients. We'll take it one step at a time. But, we'll get you a corporate membership to the Assiniboia Club. This will give you a chance to meet some of our clients."

He kept saying that everything depended on me but I didn't feel in control. At least it was my decision if I stayed or not. Just as I was about to ask about transfers and temporary assignments to other Lord offices, the phone rang. Instinctively, I picked it up.

"Hello, Ben Stein," I said.

"Mr. Ben, how are you? This is Mr. Zimmer, you remember, 'the greatest tires on earth come from Jupiter.' "

"Of course I remember you, Mr. Zimmer. Did you ever sort out your franchise problems?' "

"That's why I'm calling, Ben. Our national franchise conference is being held in Vancouver. I was wondering if you could get on a plane and come here. I showed your opinion to the franchisee executive board and they want to meet you and ask you some questions about your opinion."

"That's not much notice. I just got called to the Bar today and I was going to celebrate with my friends tonight."

"Ben, I think you'll have more cause to celebrate if you come here than if you go to Rae & Jerry's to drink rye and Coke. There is a business class ticket waiting for you at the airport and you can make the six o'clock flight and be here by seven with the time change."

"Mr. Zimmer, I can't take pickles as a fee anymore. Don't misunderstand, your pickles were delicious but I'm going to need a harder currency."

"I would expect nothing less."

"Give me your number and I'll see if I can change my plans and I'll call you back."

I apologized for the interruption and explained that it was a potential client who wanted me to fly to Vancouver tonight for a meeting. I sensed a certain skepticism from the partner that, on my first day as a lawyer, I had been asked by a client to fly 1500 miles for a meeting. He suggested that a senior lawyer go with me but I wanted no part of that. I explained that Mr. Zimmer was a friend of the family and he would not understand why I would bring a stranger to the meeting. I kept thinking about Rupert's advice about seizing an opportunity. This felt like it and I was not about to let some legal bureaucrat from Lord's take what may be my opportunity away. Besides, the meeting would likely not evolve into anything more, so I figured I may as well go myself.

I called my parents with the news that I had been called to the Bar and offered a position with the firm. I told them I had accepted an associate position with the firm but I hadn't decided if it would be in the commercial law area. At least that was my choice. Then I went to Speedy Printers to order business cars. The only thing missing was that I had no one to share my good fortune with. There was no girl to kiss me and tell me how proud she was of me and to wait in my apartment until I got back from my first business trip. A vodka tonic and Julia would have been a great way to celebrate but it was not to be. Randy Neuman, it's lonely not just at the top.

20

Sitting in business class on my maiden business trip was orgasmic. There is an aura of arrogance sitting in the front of the plane. Business class has its own unwritten rules of etiquette even though the people sitting there would deny it. First, you can never admit that sitting in the front of the plane is a special event. In fact, you must appear somewhat impatient with the whole experience as if you partake in this luxury on a routine basis. You must act casual about the good fortune of having a larger seat, more leg room and edible food.

Second, you must never make eye contact with the passengers walking by you into the steerage section of the plane. Economy passengers are intensely jealous and you can't even acknowledge their humanity as they walk by. They will look at you with envy and curiosity but you can never return the look, not even a glance. The best strategy is to look occupied by taking out a document of any sort and write something. It leaves the impression that you are so busy working and so accustomed to business class travel that you wouldn't even notice the amenities of the flight, let alone enjoy them.

Third, never strike up a conversation with the person beside you. Be polite but never familiar. This gives the impression you are too deep in thought with weighty problems to waste time on idle conversations with total strangers who are likely flying on frequent flyer points. You have no time for casual social engagement. Moreover, the less you say the more you look like you belong in this privileged part of the plane where you pay four times the price of an economy ticket for eighteen inches of leg room and a meal worth $5.00 more than the slop in economy.

Finally, never ask for second helpings, even though they're free. You can always spot the upgrade passengers or the ones flying on points because they are asking for quadruple cashews and endless rounds of double rye and seven, the indigenous drink of Manitobans. In fact, passing on the meal is the ultimate indication of belonging in the front cabin. In spite of religiously following the four rules of business class etiquette, I couldn't stop smiling. Finally, I got a tangible benefit from all my years of post-secondary education; eighteen additional inches of leg room and worth every inch.

The fact was, though, I did have work to do on the plane. I had not read the Jupiter opinion in weeks and I was going to a meeting where I would be questioned about what I had written. The fear of the upcoming meeting was sufficient to keep me focused on the task at hand. But the flight was not long enough. Just when I had gotten accustomed to the luxury of business class travel, we landed.

As I got off the plane and headed for the row of waiting taxis, I knew that it didn't matter if I was going to be retained by the franchisees or not. I had been well-compensated by three jars of pickles and a business class ticket to Vancouver. Anything after that would be a bonus. I sat back in the taxi and smiled. I decided not to refer the file to a strip mall law firm, quite yet. Those lawyers wouldn't appreciate the luxury of the front cabin. It was my turn. I was a member of the Lord's team.

I went directly to the Bayshore Hotel where the Jupiter franchisee group was meeting. The doorman at the Bayshore, in his Beefeater uniform, took my bag from the taxi to the bellman who in turn took my bag to the check-in counter. There was a reservation in my name with a note that the room was being charged to the Jupiter franchisee bill. Another bellman took me and my bag up to a corner suite in the tower overlooking Coal Harbor. By the time I got to the room, I had tipped the doorman and two bellmen for carrying one bag a total of approximately 100 feet. At this price, I couldn't afford to go much further. The client paid for everything except the mini bar and pay-per-view movies. But I wouldn't dare pick a porno film for fear that the title would be typed on the bill. I did not realize that the name of the movie or the time you charged it to your room is never shown on the bill. Next time I'll know better.

With the two-hour time change, it was just around sunset when I got to the hotel. The sky was the color of one of those cheap paintings you can buy at an abandoned gas station. I was captivated by the sharp edges of the mountain set off against the orange sunset. Even better, there were no screens on the windows because mosquitoes don't like the West Coast. I fell in love with the city and knew this was a place I could live. It had everything: the anonymity of the big city, no snow, no mosquitoes and no past. Who could ask for anything more?

Once I turned away from the view, I noticed that the message light was flashing. Mr. Zimmer had left a message that I should be at the Orca Room on the convention level at 8:00 A.M. the next morning for a meeting of the franchisee executive board. He told me that casual dress was the norm but I hadn't carried a suit on the plane to let it hang in the hotel room closet. I was going to look the part of the lawyer on a business trip even though I had only been practicing a total of twelve hours.

To calm my nerves, I went for a walk on Denman Street. I wanted to get something to eat and take in the sights of the west end of Vancouver. I bought some take-out souvlaki and washed it down with champagne gelato. Eating outside on a park bench by the water, with the ocean breeze on my face, made everything taste better. It was a glorious West Coast evening and a perfect introduction to the demands of business travel. All this and frequent flyer points too.

I didn't sleep that night in anticipation of my first client meeting. This could be the opportunity that Rupert MacIntosh was talking about and I was not about to squander it. I kept rehearsing what I was going to say. Should I be funny or take on the role of the humorless no-nonsense professional? Should I swear if I want to emphasize a point or should I take the role of the proper English solicitor? Should I raise my voice or should I appear cold and aloof? They had not taught me any of this in law school or in my articling year. I came to the conclusion that I'd do exactly what the clients did. If they swore, I'd swear. If they were clinical, I'd be clinical. If they took a bathroom break, then I would too. I was out of bed by five, Pacific Standard Time, and totally confused about how to act. As a last resort I decided to act like myself. It was the best I could do and I'd had a lot of practice in the role. I only hoped that the role fit the play.

I walked into the Orca room at 7:58 A.M. with briefcase in hand. Of the twenty-four members of the executive board, about half were there on time. I introduced myself and gave them each my freshly printed business card. By 8:15 A.M. all the executive members were present and accounted for. The meeting began with Mr. Zimmer introducing me as the brilliant young lawyer he found sinking in a snow bank in Winnipeg. He explained that I was here to review the opinion and advise the committee if the Jupiter Tire Company had lived up to the terms of the franchise agreement.

Now it was my turn. I had decided to treat them like the innocent victims.

"All of you know that Jupiter hasn't been treating you fairly. But that's not what you came to hear. This is not about fairness but rather this is about using the franchise documents to get some of your money back. We're going to discuss whether there is a legal avenue to refund your money and reduce the sales and marketing fees going forward." I took them through the franchise documents and constructed the argument section by section. The compulsion of greed made them a receptive audience. There was a writing easel in the room so I took off my suit coat and I talked to them as a teacher would to his students. It was a role I was comfortable in from my days as a teaching assistant at the University. As I stood up in front of a room full of people with an easel and felt pen, I felt in charge.

"Solidarity among the franchise group is essential. If Jupiter can't pick off one franchisee at a time to scare the rest of you, and if we can get at the real documents, then you can win this case. It might take a long time to accomplish but the potential damages are substantial and it would secure the financial future of your businesses. Jupiter is bleeding all of you dry and if you do nothing then one day you will be replaced by other franchisees who will be bled dry just as you were. You are fighting this case for your families' futures."

Tire people speak their own unique dialect of English . . . Tireese. They wanted to know the chances of a blowout. When will the rubber hit the road. Would the case leave any lasting skid marks and was there a spare strategy if we should need it. We talked about how to keep the franchise group inflated and where they could get chains for the icy patches. I gave them answers using tire analogies. You'd think I was an heir to the Firestone fortune.

After three hours of standing at the easel and answering questions, the executive told me that it wanted to consider what I had said and they would get back to me at 4:00 P.M. They were going to a luncheon on a boat that tours around English Bay and they would discuss their options in the privacy of the boat. I thanked them for the generous accommodation and plane ticket and wished them luck regardless of their decision. Mr. Zimmer followed me out of the room and told me that my dad would have been proud and that I did a good job. I thanked him for his support and that I looked forward to the 4:00 P.M. decision.

I spent the afternoon walking around the seawall at Stanley Park and enjoying the view. By four I had put my suit back on and was back in the Orca Room listening to the chairman of the executive committee. He asked me if I was willing to take on the case and devote my energy to this matter. I told him it would be a privilege to give this my personal attention. The executive committee was concerned that the case would be handed off to some junior. But no one could be more junior than me. I had been called to the Bar less than thirty-six hours. He handed me an envelope and the meeting was over in fifteen minutes. My dad told me that once you get the order, get the hell out of the customer's office as fast as possible. I shook a few hands and was gone.

Back in my room, I sat out on the balcony and stared at the envelope. I trembled as I opened it. In the envelope was a letter retaining my services and a retainer check made out to me for $500 per franchisee, a total of $196,500. I counted the numbers on the check three times. I was numb. I was a member of the legal profession and I'd gotten a check to prove it. The fact that someone was willing to pay for my knowledge went a long way in overcoming my ambivalence to the practice of law. I was in no hurry to quit. I was in the game and, I admit it, I liked it. Now all I had to do was figure out what to do next. A minor detail in the world of the law.

21

I was a Roman legionnaire returning home with treasure from the conquest of far-off lands. Given our modern system of currency, I was not burdened by a chest of gold, tiger skins or bolts of exotic silks. The envelope in my breast pocket was more than sufficient. Due to the flight schedules, I was not able to get a flight back to Winnipeg until the next morning so I had a minor celebration that night sitting by myself on English Bay watching the sunset with a split of sparkling wine.

I was back at the office by 10:00 A.M. the next morning. I went straight to see Bill MacIntosh and David Black to report on my first client meeting. My timing was perfect because that left the better part of the day for the gossip drums to beat out the news of the conquering hero.

"So, how was your trip?" David asked.

"It was terrific. I've never been to Vancouver and I loved the city. I stayed at the Bayshore, walked around the seawall in Stanley Park and ate champagne gelato on English Bay."

"How did the client treat you? Was it steerage all the way?" Bill inquired as if I had gone to a third-class trade show.

"Actually, the client could not have been more gracious. I flew business class and stayed in a corner suite overlooking the harbor and the mountains. The suite even had a big-screen TV with video games." That would shut him up for a while.

"How was the meeting?" David took back the conversation knowing that I found Bill's attitude somewhat demeaning.

"Well, I was nervous at first but as we got into it I became more comfortable. By the end, I sounded like I knew what I was talking about. I think I made a good impression or at least didn't embarrass myself." I wanted to set the hook in deep to get the maximum reaction when I pulled out the envelope.

"How did you leave it? Were they going to let you know if you got retained?" David asked.

"Actually they told me on the spot. They wanted to retain the firm as long as I would give them my personal attention. They wanted me to describe how we would manage the file."

"Did you make it clear that these cases are expensive and can go on for years?" Bill's question no longer had a demeaning tone.

"I don't really have an understanding how the billing would work. Since I've never seen one of our bills, I had to wing it. I knew enough to ask for a retainer. I'm not sure I asked for enough." Now the hook was set and it was just a matter of finding the right moment to yank the rod and pull these two giant fish into the boat.

"You know it would cost up to twenty thousand dollars to map out the strategy and prepare the demand letter and statement of claim." Bill was concerned about the firm's exposure. It was time to yank the rod. These fish were ready and mine.

"I didn't realize it would cost twenty thousand dollars but I managed to get a retainer." The fish were flopping in the boat. I reached into my pocket and put the envelope containing the retained check on David's desk.

"Who gets this check?" I asked. It was like shooting fish in a barrel. Bill reached for the envelope, opened it and took out the check. There was silence and a look of disbelief written all over his face. He passed the check to David without saying a word. David glanced twice at the check. They looked at each other, looked at me and didn't say a word. I had been a lawyer only three days and I had brought in a new file after my very first client meeting with a retainer check of $196,500. The fish were jumping.

"This should certainly get us going. In all my years of practice I've never managed to get an initial retainer of even half this amount." David, sitting erect in his chair, said with a big grin on his face.

"Well, the first trick is to ask for it." I was flying high and felt I could take certain liberties with the facts. "And if you don't know how much to ask for then aim high. They might give you less but they'll never give you more."

"Ben, how can we help you?" Bill couldn't do enough to assist.

"The first thing is to deposit the check. I've been nervous carrying it around and I'd like to be relieved of the burden. Then, I'd like to put together a small group of lawyers to work on a proposal of how we're going to run the file. This will take some time so I need to know that the firm supports the priority that I must give the file."

"That shouldn't be a problem. I can think of one hundred and ninety-six thousand, five hundred reasons why this should be given your priority," David said.

"Also, I'll need some administrative support, like my own secretary, and a large enough office to accommodate the paper. There will be a lot of documents."

"I expect we can handle these problems. I'll talk to Basil and make sure this gets done quickly without any unnecessary debate. You know, some people are quite sensitive about things like office size but we'll take care of it." David wrote a few notes on the yellow pad of paper on his desk as he spoke. He assured me it would all get done to my satisfaction and stood up to shake my hand.

"Thanks so much for the support. I can't wait to get started. By the way, how do I open a file? I've never opened one. I want to be the billing lawyer with the two of you reviewing all the bills before they go out." This was my way of letting them know who was in charge of the file.

"It appears that you've already thought your way through these issues. You won't have any problems learning how to open a file or sending out a bill. It's not likely you'll underbill," Bill commented with a certain admiration for my strategic thinking.

"I'll leave this check in your good hands. I'm sure you'll find a way to get it into our trust account." I left the check lying on David's desk. "I haven't been in the office for a few days so I'd like to go check the mail and finish my current projects to clear the way for the Jupiter work. See you later."

"Meet us for a drink at the end of the day. We'll have a little celebration." Bill never passed up an opportunity to drink on the office expense account.

I asked my secretary to open a file for Jupiter Franchisees and name me as the billing lawyer. She gave me a strange look, as if I was doing something wrong, but I assured her that this was absolutely proper and I had gotten the go-ahead from David Black and Bill MacIntosh. I asked her for my mail which consisted mostly of congratulation cards for being called to the Bar and some insurance forms that new associates had to fill out.

By the time I got a chance to get some work done, the phone started ringing. Partners and senior associates from the office were calling to congratulate me on accepting the associate position and to tell me they had heard about this Jupiter file. They all assured me that if I needed any help or advice I could count on them. It was a bit awkward having partners ask if they could assist me since I worked for them. I thanked them for their good wishes and willingness to help and told them that I could use all the help I could get. I left it at that.

Among the cards, all from relatives and the tailor who makes legal robes, I noticed an envelope from someone named Mr. & Mrs. Windsor. It was a wedding invitation.

Cecil and Mary Windsor
request the honor of your presence
at the marriage of their daughter
Julia Catherine Windsor
to
Robert Elliot Acheson
son of
Dr. and Mrs. Acheson
Saturday the fifteenth day of August
six o'clock in the afternoon
United Western Church
34 Airdrie Street, Chicago Illinois

Julia had done it again. At the height of my ecstasy, she was still able to reach out and deflate me. She must have known that I would never go, so why would she send me an invitation? She was rubbing our relationship in my face. The truth was that I had never entirely given up on the possibility that, with the passage of time, Julia would come back to me and all would be forgiven. In fact, in some dark corner of my mind I was hoping for it. Her invitation came right out of Paul Simon's Kodachrome. Had she invited all the men she had known when she was single and put them all together for one night? I put the invitation in my desk drawer and moved on to other issues. I had no intention of being part of her Kodachrome wedding. That would acknowledge the reality of losing her. I spent the rest of the morning concentrating on my work and answering calls from lawyers in the firm congratulating me about the new client.

By noon, the administrative wheels of Lord & Bishop were in full motion. Mr. Basil came to tutor me on the basics of sending a bill. He took me through the code system but I didn't have a clue what he was talking about. He pointed out that my hourly rate had been increased to $150 per hour. Underbilling at this rate could become very expensive. Also, I no longer had One-Fifth Gloria as my secretary. What a shame, our one-fifth relationship had become so meaningful. Gloria had been replaced by Three-Quarter Dana. Another lawyer, a senior associate, would use Dana as back-up for up to ten hours a week in case his secretary got too busy. But, it was made clear to Dana that my work was the priority.

The biggest change was a new office. At Lord's there is an office space caste system. As a student, I had a one-window office facing an office building. There was no doubt about my status. Four window offices were for senior partners; three window offices for junior partners; two window offices for senior associates and one window offices for junior associates and students. Secretaries did not get a window unless they were sleeping with a four-window partner. Besides the number of windows, there was the view factor. The important view was overlooking the river. Your status slowly diminished as you went clockwise from the river, ending up with the view of the building across the street. David Black was a four-window partner overlooking the river. The challenging question was whether a four-window office facing the building next door had a greater status than a three-window office with a view of the river.

All the associates watched in great anticipation where Mr. Basil was going to move me. I had heard from One-Fifth Gloria that there was a heated debate amongst the partners about the appropriate office for me. What should a $196,500 retainer get you? Finally, the moment came. I got a two-window office with a view of the river. It was an unprecedented jump in status for a first-week associate and the subject of comment in the hallways.

I did not take my good fortune for granted. The Lord giveth and the Lord can taketh away. The only lawyers who were genuinely pleased for my success were the senior partners who would profit from the Jupiter file. The junior partners thought I was coming up too fast and the associates were worried that I was passing them by.

Even though the other associates congratulated me, I knew it was not genuine. As I was walking by one office I heard three associates talking.

"Oh, you know how pushy they are," one said. "We can't let this become the new standard of performance." As they saw me, the topic turned to baseball. My anti-Semitic detector antennae were extended. I was succeeding according to the Lord's own rules but my success was being stereotyped as the work of just another pushy Jew. It made me wonder why I should even bother trying. I would not be judged on merit. I buried my feelings and decided to enjoy my moment in the sun and the extra window, but I never forgot the chill and anger that came over me.

By the end of the day, I had moved to my larger office with the river view. I was worth $55 more an hour and I had Three-Quarter Dana right outside my door. I didn't have any more legal ability than I had three days before when I was billing $95 per hour and looking at the building across the street from a one-window office with One-Fifth Gloria. But, in the real practice of law, the combination of a big retainer and two windows with a view is one route to the pinnacle of professional success. *A few more files like Jupiter,* I gloated, *and I'll be the professional liaison from the firm to the law school and teaching a course.*

After work, a group of ten lawyers took me for drinks to celebrate landing the Jupiter file. There were three senior partners, two junior partners and five associates, including me. The partners came to avoid going home and the associates came because the partners came. The evening consisted of alcohol consumption and stories told by the senior partners about judges who slept during a trial, lawyers who prepared the wrong file for the following day's court application, witnesses who changed their stories as they testified and one lawyer who wrote a legal argument in the same poetic syntax as Yellow Brick Road. It was a mildly entertaining evening, but chiefly because of four vodka tonics. I had prepared myself to leave before someone got embarrassingly drunk, specifically me. You never want to face people the next day if you've made a spectacle of yourself. But, just as I was about to go, the waiter wheeled out a cake with sparklers on top. The cake was in the shape of a tire and on it was written "MAY THE LORD BE BLESSED BY THIS TIRE." Everyone sang, "For He's A Jolly Good Lawyer," and I was given a large knife to cut everyone a piece of the tire cake. The symbolism of cutting up the tire to satisfy the various appetites of lawyers was not lost on me. I left as soon as I could.

It was ten o'clock when I got home. The message light was not blinking so I knew Julia hadn't called. I thought about her and the wedding invitation. In a way, her wedding was a relief because it provided some sense of closure. Still, I missed her and wanted her back. Julia's infidelity was not a mortal wound but even a healthy heart takes time to heal. At least now I could accept the healing rather than entertain some romantic notion that we would be together again. I had my turn and it was over.

22

The next morning, the first order of business was to call my dad. My career got a boost because my father insisted that I help his immigrant friend.

"Hi, Dad, I know I can always find you at work early."

"I do a lot of business before my competitors get out of bed. Are you the first lawyer in the office?"

"I'm not the first but I'm one of the first."

"So why would my fancy downtown lawyer son be calling a plumbing supplier at seven A.M. Are the toilets overflowing?"

"We have enough of that flowing here without the toilets breaking. At one hundred and fifty dollars an hour, it's continuous flow."

"Still, it's better to buy a toilet then have to sell one. That's why you went to school so you wouldn't have to go into the plumbing supply business. What do I owe the pleasure of this call and, by the way, is this billable?"

"This not billable time, I called to thank you for helping me."

"What did I do besides maintain my infinite patience and open my wallet throughout your academic career?"

"Do you remember when you asked me to help Abe Zimmer with his tire franchise problem?"

"I hope you could help Abe. He is a good person with a good mind."

"Actually, Abe Zimmer has a very good mind and, as it turned out, it's been a terrific opportunity for me. He sent me the biggest file in the office. Because of Mr. Zimmer, I have a two-window office with a view of the river and three-quarters of my own secretary. His case has really given my career a big boost."

"He only has one store. How could his case be so important?" My father sounded skeptical.

"Mr. Zimmer got all the franchisees together, all three hundred and ninety of them, and they hired me as their lawyer. That's how I got a two windows with a view of the river."

"Ben, don't be impressed by an office with an extra hundred square feet and a view of a polluted river."

"It's not the size of the office. But it means the firm wants me and now it's my choice if I want to stay or not. Let them depend on me rather than me depend on them."

"You're right not to rely on these Lord lawyers too much. Never lose your relationship with the customer. As soon as you lose touch with the customer, you can be replaced. You stay close to Zimmer and make sure that he's treated right. Don't let anyone come between the two of you. Remember, he hired you, not the firm."

"We'll make sure that Abe is treated right. He gets first class treatment."

"Why are you talking like it's 'we'?"

"It's just a figure of speech," I said defensively.

"That's fine as a figure of speech but Abe Zimmer put his trust in *you* and this is your responsibility no matter how many lawyers work on the case. You must never forget that he hired you and not your fancy firm. Don't think in terms of 'we'. It will only lead to grief." He spoke in that fatherly advice tone that I remembered so well growing up.

"Don't worry, Dad, I know what Mr. Zimmer has done for me and I will make sure he's treated right."

"Good, come by the house. You haven't seen your mother in weeks."

"Give her my love and I'll see you soon." When I hung up I thought about taking care of our own. My parents' generation believed success came from excelling within their community where they principally dealt with each other. What they didn't understand was that inward focus has limited our vision and segregated us from a broader experience. My parents' generation always faced inward. The difference between us was that they assumed Lord & Bishop would be an inevitable disappointment. I saw the firm as a means to broaden my horizon beyond the cultural cocoon.

For the next two weeks, I worked on the Jupiter proposal. I had calls from lawyers in the firm who wanted to help but I made up excuses to put them off. I knew that if I called on everyone who wanted to work on the case, I would lose control of the file. I sought the advice of specific individuals on specific issues in the proposal but I did not confide in anyone. I could not risk bringing any senior lawyer into my confidence. Although I did not accept my dad's basic distrust of anyone who was not Jewish, I was not about to test his view.

One part of the proposal that was problematic for me was the fee estimate. I had no experience or the remotest idea what a case like this could cost and I had to show the proposal to someone to get their advice on fees. I decided to ask Rupert, in spite of my misgivings about him. He would never underestimate a fee. Rupert read the proposal and gave me some suggestions on how to improve the document and he offered a fee estimate. He reminded me that just because we had a retainer, the client could still change solicitors before the claim was filed. In effect, he said I should still be promoting the client and that the proposal was one more step in closing the sale. His advice had the ring of experience although I was still cautious about his motives.

Once Rupert got rolling with advice there was no stopping him. I took notes which filled four sides of my legal pad. In three different ways he told me that I should leave an impression with the client that their case is the most important matter I am dealing with and that I would work on it day and night. Also, I should portray an aura of competence that made them feel no one in the world knew or understood the case better than me. They hired the best. I had to use the proposal to convey a vision of the case and strategy which would be so compelling that any reasonable person would obviously have to agree with our position. He told me that the proposal should tell a story and not to get bogged down in detailed facts or boring statistics. The best advocates are the best storytellers. The pedestrian lawyers rely on precedents and reading from endless and tiresome briefs of law. The client wants to hear their story told back to them and that always convinces them. Then you can send a big bill and move on to the next case. This was the perfect opportunity to raise the fee question.

"How much should I put down as a fee estimate?"

"I don't know. Tell them ten times the retainer. That should be good enough. If it turns out to be low, we can always blame the other side for trying to milk the file and say we had to respond to protect our client's position." When he saw my surprised reaction to his cavalier attitude Rupert smiled and continued, "You're in the ambulance, Ben. Fasten your seat belt and enjoy the ride. The best

126

part is we get paid even if we lose the patient." At least being in the ambulance means I didn't have to chase it.

I called Mr. Zimmer and told him that our proposal would be delayed by two weeks to give us time to fully consider all the issues and decide on the best strategy. He told me that the next franchisee meeting was in four weeks in Toronto and we should aim to review the proposal then. He would take care of any problems because of the delay. The timing was perfect and I knew it would all be ready in time for the Toronto meeting.

I did a complete rewrite of the proposal, keeping in mind Rupert's advice. Tell the client's story in a compelling way and estimate the fees at ten times the retainer. That was clear enough. The legal part of the proposal was in the appendix since franchise litigation was in its infancy and there were few statutory regulations. It made the case difficult because we had to rely on a combination of basic legal principles, common sense and the skills of advocacy. But I convinced myself to worry about that later. I could always find some eager associates to do some basic legal research and let them think they were part of the team. If they did a good job, I'd reward them by introducing them to some of the clients.

I gave the second draft to Rupert for his comments. He told me to include color-coded tabs in the document book. It always impressed the clients. He said they think you know what you're talking about if you have tabbed pages under a clear plastic cover with CONFIDENTIAL typed in red ink. In his own unique perspective, Rupert likened the proposal to a program at a football game. He described it as the client's litigation souvenir for the game about to begin and that was a better memento than a pen and pencil set or personalized scratch pads. The amazing part, he reminded me, was that the proposal was prepared at the client's expense.

Four weeks to the day, I was sitting in the business class section of the plane on my way to Toronto. I was a seasoned traveler by now, this being my second trip in the front of the plane. I didn't hoard the cashews. I made the appropriate casual remarks and looked mildly bored. The proposal was complete so I could relax and watch the movie. Between the flight time and the time change, I arrived at 7:30 P.M. and went straight to the hotel.

I was booked into the King Edward Hotel, the most expensive hotel I had ever stayed in and the first one that had ever charged for a bucket of ice. I have observed that the more expensive a hotel is the more likely you get charged for services that are free everywhere else. At Motel 6 there is enough free ice to build an igloo but at the King Edward, at $7.00 a bucket, it would cost $15,000 to build that igloo. I was starting to understand the meaning of exclusive; exclusively filled with schmucks on expense accounts who will pay extra for frozen water.

My meeting with the franchisees was scheduled for 9:00 A.M. I was up and dressed by six and spent the next three hours going over what I was going to say, reading the morning paper and watching the weather channel. It's the only channel on television where there are no repeats. I was in the appointed meeting room at 8:55 A.M. and watched as the directors drifted in, feeling the effects from their social event the night before. The room was set up to accommodate the twelve franchise directors plus a couple of extra chairs. Four tables were joined at the corners into a square so there was no apparent head table. The significance of that was not lost on me. Because I had already met this group in Vancouver, there was a greater sense of informality at this meeting. The difference now was that they were paying for my time and wanted to make sure they were getting value.

"How much of our $196,500 have we spent on this proposal?" The Chair of the franchisee committee inquired. He was the only one in the room who brought a file.

"I haven't done the calculations but I estimate around twenty thousand plus disbursements. You must keep in mind that the more thorough the preparation up front, the more you will save later because there is less uncertainty and thus, fewer changes." I hadn't been prepared to answer questions on what we had spent to date but I noticed on the routine billing summary that we had spent about $20,000 of time. Sometimes you just get lucky.

"What is the key to winning our case and how long will it take?" The Chairman continued.

"The key to winning will be in Jupiter's documents. Everything we need is documented somewhere in Jupiter and we will have to squeeze it out of them. If we can find those documents, then we'll be two-thirds there to making our case. In that vein we should do as much as we can as fast as we can. Delay works to Jupiter's advantage. They'll try everything to wear us down and maybe even buy back some franchises. If we can hit them hard and fast right from the start we will increase our chances of success." That question I was ready for, no luck this time. But I soon realized this was not some law school assignment. These were real clients talking about real money.

"What if they just shred all the documents?" Mr. Zimmer asked, throwing me a softball.

"They have to account for their bills. Somewhere there is a record of all the expenses they have been charging the franchisees. As long as we have the will to keep digging then no amount of shredding is going to cover their tracks."

"What are the fee arrangements with your firm?" The Chairman had a one-track mind this morning. I wondered what set that off.

"It is set out in the Proposal. I propose that you make a special assessment of the franchisees of $100 per month per franchise. You should start now, and if you collect more than what is needed, then you can always return the surplus. We will bill you monthly and give you a quarterly report on our progress. We have to be careful what we write in the reports so not to divulge anything to the other side."

"What is the history of other cases like ours?" Mr. Zimmer lobbed another softball.

"Franchise claims are new to the courts. Historically, franchisors did what they wanted. Each franchisee had to start a separate lawsuit because each had their own franchise contract. Only within the last two years have the courts considered that franchisees might qualify as a class and start a single lawsuit. Our research indicates that at the present time, we would only be the third such case in Canada and certainly the largest to date." The directors liked the notoriety. "Jupiter will fight us on the franchises joined together in a single action. That is one of the major hurdles we will have to get over. You will see this discussed on pages twelve through fifteen of our proposal."

By the end of our meeting, there was a sense in the group that I understood the case and had thoroughly answered all their questions. Rupert had been right. The client has to think that you care more and know more about their case then anything else. They said they wanted to discuss the proposal in their private afternoon session and asked me to return the following morning.

I had some time on my hands and was curious to visit Lord's Toronto office. It was an opportunity to introduce myself to some of the Toronto lawyers which, I thought, might prove useful for my career. I called David Black and asked him to arrange an introduction with the managing partner, Bob Sutherland. Lord's office was right in the heart of the Toronto financial district in one of the bank towers. It was an impressive building with Lord occupying five floors starting on the 45th floor. The lawyer directory at Lord's was equally impressive with a list of 325 lawyers, twenty-three of them had names ending in LAND. There was Blackland, Creland, Friland, etc. There were no Steins, but, I did see three Bergs . . . Goldberg, Silverberg and Schwartzberg. They were all in the tax group which must have been reassuring for those who thrive on stereotypes. The firm's reception area was impressive. Their annual bill for cut flowers must have been more than my annual salary. The paintings were modern Canadian realists hanging on the pillars between the floor-to-ceiling windows looking out over the city. Everyone talked in hushed tones and everything was very proper. I asked for Mr. Sutherland and the receptionist immediately asked if I was Mr. Stein. I like name recognition. I was shown into one of the boardrooms where I was soon joined by Robert Sutherland and James Winter, Chair of the Associate Committee. These two fit the image of big-time solicitors. They were both tall, over six feet with perfectly parted salt-and-pepper hair and both wore tailored grey suits with white shirts and striped ties.

"Hi, I'm Bob Sutherland," he said, extending his hand, "and this is Jim Winters. We've been expecting you. Black called to say that you would be coming around. He told me that I should be on my best behavior."

"Thank you for seeing me on such short notice. I hope my visit is not too inconvenient."

"Not at all. No one thinks a managing partner does anything anyway." We all sat down in unison. "What brings you to Toronto?"

Here was my chance to impress these guys. A first-year associate traveling at the client's expense and controlling a major piece of litigation. "I have a client meeting at the King Edward. As it turns out, I had the afternoon free so I thought I would come by and introduce myself." I was sure their curiosity would be aroused and they would ask me more, but they didn't.

"It's not often we see lawyers from the other offices here in Toronto. Usually, we see them at their offices. We seem to do more of the traveling," Jim Winters commented.

"These clients I am seeing hold meetings all over the country and I just follow them around from meeting to meeting." I thought that would get them curious, but they didn't take the bait.

"Well, would you like us to show you around?" Bob inquired, "I have an appointment in just a few minutes but Jim will give you the tour if you don't mind."

"No, of course I don't mind. In fact, I appreciate that you would take time from your day to see me at all."

"Okay, let's be on our way and maybe we'll have time to grab a cup of coffee downstairs with some of the associates when we're finished," Jim Winters suggested, getting up.

The offices were as impressive as the reception area. The art collection was a great display of twentieth-century contemporary Canadian art ranging from the Group of Seven to Colville and Riopelle. The furniture was all leather and all the containers, from glasses to paperclip holders, were crystal. We passed a wall displaying the photographs of all the dead partners over the last 100 years. This wall represented the pinnacle of legal success. I couldn't help but wonder if I would be on that wall someday. It was almost worth dying for. The library housed 100 years of law books and three snobby librarians who showed off the collection. These women were as brittle as the bindings on their 100-year-old books.

As we walked the corridors Jim talked about the history of the firm and described some of the current projects. It was obvious he took some pride in being the self-appointed firm's historian. I met solicitors working on a $500 million bond issue for the Government of India; associates who were going to Brussels on an international taxation arbitration; lawyers who were working on the financing for the privatization of the Denmark oil fields and other lawyers preparing for court applications over the sale of a municipal airport to a group of investors. No wonder neither Sutherland nor Winters were curious about my file. It was going to take much bigger bait to hook these fish. Business class from Winnipeg to Toronto wasn't much compared to a trip to Brussels or Denmark. I was way out of my league. Abe Zimmer and the Jupiter group were small potatoes for this crowd. I was in one of the national enclaves of establishment power and a Stein with $196,500 retainer was not a showstopper. It's one thing to be recognized by the concierge at the Assiniboia Club but quite another to sit in the 45th floor boardroom and discuss a $500 million bond issue with the Minister of Finance for India.

I was overwhelmed by it all. I knew right there and then that it would be next to impossible to get noticed in this club. Even meeting the 'Berg' lawyers didn't give me much comfort. The scope of their work was out of my reach. It is difficult to look mediocrity in the face and see your own reflection, even with two windows and a river view.

On the final stop of my office tour Jim introduced me to sixty-eight-year-old John Bishop, the grandson of the original Bishop, the one on the letterhead. Surprisingly, he was my height and very fit. Mr. Bishop had a five-window corner office with a view of Lake Ontario and the Toronto skyline. His office was impeccably neat with not a piece of paper out of place. There was a putter leaning against the corner of his desk indicating that we had interrupted his practice time. Mr. Bishop claimed to be very interested in the opinion of Lord lawyers from the other offices and Jim left us alone to talk.

"So, what do you think of Lord & Bishop?" John asked as he rocked in his office chair, his hand combing through his thinning hair.

"It has been interesting. I am getting good work and I enjoy the people I work with."

"Actually, I meant what do you think about us here in Toronto?" I found this to be a very odd question. *This guy thinks so much of himself, he is sure that everyone else in the whole country must be preoccupied with thinking about them,* I thought.

"Well, I never hear anyone talking about the partners in Toronto. It's not a topic of conversation among the lawyers I talk to."

"Come now Mr. Stein . . . may I call you Ben?"

"Of course." There was something odd about this man.

"We realize there is a certain animosity about how we control the firm and how we decide partner compensation. You must hear about this sort of thing."

Unless I said something, he would not let go. The shorter this conversation would be the better I would like it but I had to dream up something. "I've heard a bit about the conduct of the Toronto partners when they're working at the other offices. They don't let any of the lawyers from the other offices work on the files. All we're allowed to do is file material and provide a photocopying service for these guys. We really would like to contribute." I figured he'd believe that since he lived at the center of the earth. This seemed like the kind of stuff he would want to hear. He looked at me thoughtfully and said something about having to do a better job getting work into the outlying offices.

Without warning Bishop got up from behind his desk and came over to the couch where I was sitting. He sat down beside me, put his hand on my knee and said he could arrange for me to work on more interesting files. Who would ever have believed that a Bishop from Toronto would try to play hide the bishop with a Stein from White Russia. Mr. Bishop then proceeded to tell me that if I came back at 6:00 P.M., he would introduce me to some of the "special" partners and we could all go for dinner at his private club. I shot up so quickly that I twisted my knee and told Mr. Bishop that I had to get to my next appointment. I thanked him for his time and he reminded me that discretion among the lawyers is expected as I limped out of his office as fast as my bent knee would allow.

So this was what they called the center of commerce. I had met lawyers who made $500 million deals, sat with a Bishop who tried to grab my crotch and then retreated to a hotel that charged for frozen water. Who would ever have believed it? This had been a truly multicultural experience. Frankly, I would have preferred a little less culture. As I limped back to my room, what I had experienced of Toronto in one afternoon would last for a while. I was famished so I ordered room service. I didn't want to go out for fear of being mistaken for a delegate at a proctological convention. I stayed in and watched *The Godfather* . . . "It's just business, Sonny, not personal."

The next morning I was back with the Jupiter group in one of the King Edwards' extravagant meeting rooms. As I greeted everyone and sat down I noticed a pitcher of freshly squeezed orange juice in a bucket of ice on the credenza in the corner of the room. At $7.00 for a bucket of ice, I could only imagine what this place would be charging for a pitcher of juice. We got down to business right away. The executive committee complimented me on how quickly I had mastered the material. They were anxious to get started, on the condition that I lead the project and not pass it off to juniors. They still had not caught on that, in spite of my age, I was the junior. There was no one after me to pass on the case. They told me they had formed a committee of three franchisees to deal specifically with the litigation: Mr. Zimmer, a franchisee from Guelph, Ontario and one from Montreal. But, even though the three franchisees had equal authority, Mr. Zimmer was the contact client and I should report to him on an ongoing basis.

Once I was sure the case was mine, I got out of there as quickly as possible. I went straight to the airport and caught the afternoon flight back to Winnipeg. I was ecstatic at what I had accomplished for the firm but, at the same time, nervous about how I would turn talking about the case into running the case. I did not preoccupy myself about the Toronto office or that I was working in a branch office. As for Mr. Bishop, I didn't tell anyone about his Toronto hospitality, at least for the time being.

23

I was so consumed by the Jupiter case I didn't take on any other assignments. In fact, I was sending memos to other lawyers in the firm to do research for me. It was a sensitive issue that the most junior associate lawyer in the firm was sending work instructions to more senior associates. I was still reluctant to take anyone, other than Rupert, into my confidence on the overall strategy of the case. I was trying to calculate how much Jupiter had been improperly billing the franchise group since that was the heart of the claim. Every week I received more documents from the franchisee group. Soon I had a room full of file boxes piled six feet high. I was drowning in paper and we were just getting started. The truth is the case was beyond me. I didn't have any experience and I didn't have a mentor to confide in. When I wasn't sure what to do next I asked Rupert, Bill or David who pointed me in the right direction but never followed up.

No one knew my schedule and my travel for work took on a mysterious aura. It seemed like every second week I was flying to a franchisee meeting. The franchisee Executive Board met in the best of places and stayed in the best of hotels. The travel expenses were mounting but nobody seemed to care. It all came out of the monthly franchisee allotment. It's as if the clients expected exorbitant expense bills. I became so accustomed to business class travel that I would take a later flight rather than tolerate the rear cabin. The flight attendants started to recognize me and brought me two packages of cashews. My career was moving ahead at supersonic speed and I would have been ecstatic, if only I knew what I was doing. But no one at the firm questioned what I was doing or the quality of my work as long as the monthly retainer checks kept coming. I was a first-year lawyer but not accountable to anyone. No one challenged or questioned me. I avoided associate meetings and I always timed my trips so I would be out of town when they held firm functions. I was billing seventy hours a week which in law firm language meant DO NOT DISTURB, BILLING MACHINE IN OPERATION. And nobody disturbed me.

I was learning fast how the business of the law really worked. Keep busy, don't tell anyone what you do and make sure the bills get out. That's all there was to it. You don't have to know very much but you better know somebody who knows something. That was my problem, I was having trouble finding a person who knew what to do. In that hot prairie summer, I worked late every night for the benefit of the office air conditioning. My social life stopped completely which was not much of a sacrifice since it didn't have much momentum. The red light on my answering machine never flashed. Everyone assumed that I was too busy with my career and I never did anything to indicate otherwise. Professional success and the road to partnership was paved with billable hours and that became my goal. I was going to be the youngest partner with the most billable hours in Lord history. My place on the wall of fame was assured.

By mid-August I had gathered all the franchisees' documents. I was exhausted trying to make sense of the boxes of documents. We had not filed our claim against Jupiter yet and I had countless questions about our own documents, never mind what we'd eventually get from Jupiter. Most nights I went home around eight and picked up a pizza for yet another evening of watching TV until I fell asleep. One particular night, I was nodding off in front of the television when the phone rang. I was too tired to pick up the phone and instead I listened for the message.

"At the sound of the tone please leave your message."

"Hi Ben, wish you were home. I sure would like to talk. Anyway, if you . . ." It was Julia. I grabbed the receiver just as she was about to finish her message. I was wide awake in spite of being half asleep a few seconds before.

"Julia, I just walked in and heard your message."

"Why didn't you RSVP my invitation? The wedding was yesterday."

"Congratulations, so you went through with it."

"Of course I went through with it." Her voice sounded as captivating as ever and I wanted to reach through the receiver and hold her. "It was a perfectly beautiful wedding and the party went on forever. All my friends came except you."

"I'm sure you'll be very happy." The rational side of me kicked in and instead of euphoria I told myself to be cautious about her motives. "Where are you calling from, Chicago?"

"I'm calling from a Honeymoon Suite at Caesar's Palace in Las Vega. My husband, it's so weird calling him that, is downstairs playing roulette."

"You just got married, you're on your honeymoon, you're sitting in your fancy suite alone while your husband is gambling and you're calling me? This doesn't sound to me like a great start." She didn't answer and I couldn't stand the silence. "What does your husband do?"

"He's a doctor."

"How did you meet?" I thought if I kept asking her questions about herself I would avoid having to talk about any of our old memories.

"He was in Winnipeg giving some sort of lecture at the hospital. We met in the staff dining room and before I knew it, here I am Mrs. Robert Achison sitting in the Honeymoon Suite at Caesars."

"It's that easy?" I said, trying not to sound jealous.

"It just sounds easy. Actually, it's your fault. How could you let me do this? Why didn't you come and rescue me from this wedding? Then we could have lived happily ever after. How could you let me go through with this? Didn't you care enough to fight for us?"

I could not believe what I was hearing. She fools around with my friend, laughs it off by saying that it was just sex and I get the Q-tip test in return. She dumps me and now she blames me because she's sitting alone in the Honeymoon Suite at Caesar's. I could barely contain my anger and yet there was a part of me that was thrilled to hear from her no matter what the circumstances were. "Julia, you dumped me. How could I possibly know that you wanted me to come after you? This is ridiculous."

Julia changed the subject and started reminiscing about the great nights we had in my apartment and the way she introduced me to vodka tonics. It felt so good talking to her but I knew better than to let my guard down. What kind of game was she playing anyway? She just got married. How many old boyfriends had she called from the Honeymoon Suite before she got to me? I wondered if she went in alphabetical order. She had really hurt me and I would not let one call in a weak moment reopen the wound. I asked her for her number

137

and address in Chicago in the unlikely event that my work might take me there. I was invoking the faint hope clause of failed relationships. Perhaps something would occur that would bring us back together. I didn't have to worry about saying any more because just then she heard her husband at the door and told me she had to get off the phone. I wished her luck and said good night. When I hung up, my first thought was to question if the call had actually occurred or if it had been a dream. Once I saw her address on a scratchpad I knew it was not a dream. I leaned back on the sofa and pictured her and her husband on their wedding night. Why, after one day of marriage, was she calling me? I thought of Barry Altman and wondered if he got a call tonight.

I did feel some satisfaction that she had called me. She had broken my heart during our few weeks together when I desperately chased after her and put aside all self-respect. Now here she was calling me the day after her wedding. It was confusing but it felt good. Maybe it was still my turn, only this time it would be a married woman and much more complicated. I thought of my mother and knew that if I told her about this I would have to get her a heart-lung machine for Chanukah. The defibrillator would not suffice. On second thought, perhaps it wouldn't be so bad. An affair with a married Gentile woman was safer than a relationship with a single one. Less chance of intermarriage. The portable defibrillator might still do.

The next four weeks went by quickly. I didn't hear from Julia again and I didn't call her. I concentrated on work. I consulted with Rupert on various aspects of the claim to insure that I did not make any glaring errors. I had our corporate search department working overtime verifying the correct corporate names, addresses and directors of the franchisee companies. It was a laborious task just to get the proper information on all the franchisee companies. Next, we had to decide where we would commence the lawsuit. Since the franchises were all across North America, we had a choice. We decided to keep it close to home and chose Manitoba as the forum of convenience. We calculated the claim at $40,000 per franchise per year starting from the most recent franchise agreement. Jupiter did a re-draft of the agreements every ten years and 1980 was the latest agreement. With punitive damages, interest and costs, the claim amounted to about $125 million. That should get someone's attention, even in Toronto.

I regularly reported to Abe Zimmer who became quite a student of the law. We decided to file the claim on September 16, 1985, the day after Rosh Hashanah, the Jewish new year. We both felt it would be a good way to start the year. I assumed that Jupiter must have known by then what we were up to but they wouldn't likely know our timing. I had this image of blowing the shofar at synagogue, wishing everyone a happy new year and filing a $125 million law suit the next day. It fit together like chopped liver on rye bread.

24

Every Jewish New Year I went to synagogue with my parents. My mother insisted that we go to the Orthodox synagogue because that was the best place to find a nice Jewish girl. In the Orthodox synagogue men sit separately from women. If all the women are seated in one area it's easier to spot the hot prospects. When my mother was president of the synagogue sisterhood, she tried to pass a rule that the single girls sit separate from the married ones but it never passed because of definition disagreements. Where would you sit if you're separated but not divorced? Where would you sit if you had a boyfriend and he bought you a watch and met your parents? Where would you sit if you were a lesbian? Who was going to mediate individual cases and what if there was no agreement? It became a hopeless mess and the idea was dropped after twelve executive board meetings and four proposed amendments all of which were defeated.

It always makes for interesting sociological observations where you sit in the Orthodox synagogue. No rush seats when it comes to God, everything is reserved and show your ticket at the door. The closer to the front the better. As for me, I did not aspire to the front because everyone notices when you come late and whether you have rib sauce on your tie which you will deny to your grave and claim it is the blood of Christian children. Anyway, I liked being close to the exit doors which were about midway down the sanctuary. It allowed for a quick exit without being noticeably pushy. As my dad was a medium-size donor at the synagogue, $10,000 a year, midway seating fit in quite nicely with our generosity.

We always looked forward to the Rosh Hashanah services, because everyone attends. It is an opportunity to renew old friendships and catch up on the gossip, which mostly focuses on who died or got divorced. If you don't go to synagogue on Rosh Hashanah, then you are assumed to be in one of the two above categories. The highlight of the Rosh Hashanah services is the sermon and the blowing of the shofar. The theme of the sermon is always the same. We are at risk of cultural extinction and we must stand together to keep our heritage alive. All of this translates into donating money. On that particular day, the rabbi warned of an attack on Judaism from within, the dreaded intermarriage. Do business with them, fine. Work with them, fine. Eat with them, fine. Sleep with them, not fine but we understand. But, never, ever marry them. If you do, you will be forsaking 3,000 years of Jewish life. As I sat surrounded by my people, I tried to imagine how a little passion could break the bonds of 100 generations. I wouldn't want to shoulder that kind of responsibility. So, in the end I donated $2,500 to help pay someone's salary at the Jewish Family Services to counsel me against partaking of the forbidden fruit. The truth is, I didn't need a social worker to explain the threat of intermarriage. I just needed to get laid.

My closest friends went to our synagogue. Murray Wall sat directly behind me, where he was often seen handing out free Willie retractable pens. Paul sat up at the front because his family donated the interlocking brick driveway to the synagogue entrance. Gerry Smith sat near the back because he didn't give anything to the synagogue except advice for which he did not insist on a tax receipt. As he explained it, if you start giving it would never end and then they'll think you're rich and that's the kiss of death. Our family donated the water fountains and faucets. Those faucets were the gift that kept on giving. The interlocking brick needed replacing every two years from the winter frost but the faucets last forever. During a break in the services, I arranged to meet my friends the following evening after the family dinners. We had not seen each other for months and I was looking forward to it.

The New Year service ended at one o'clock and my mother, like always, had our relatives and close friends over for lunch. She has done this for the past thirty years and, by that time, everyone took it for granted. That year we had twenty-seven people for lunch, an average crowd made up of the usual suspects with a few additions. As much as I liked to complain about these gatherings, there was a certain feeling of warmth and security sitting in my parents' home with all the relatives and friends all talking at the same time, nobody listening to anybody else.

My parents didn't have a dining room table big enough to seat twenty-seven so the food was always served buffet style with the guests sitting anywhere they could find a seat. The house was full of flowers, sent ahead by the guests, and you'd have thought a mafia boss had died. The only one who didn't send flowers was my cousin John. He brought my parents the latest in athletic footwear. Another two pair for the closet. The table was a site to see, a virtual cornucopia of cholesterol. There was chopped everything including eggplant, herring, liver, eggs and mushrooms. There were four different varieties of smoked salmon and the greatest delicacy of all, Goldeye. For the meat lovers, my mother had made her famous sweet and sour brisket and purchased a variety of cold cuts such as salami, pastrami and any other "ami" you could make from some portion of a cow. Not one morsel of tofu or a hint of brown rice. For the real gourmets there was *karnatzel* from Schwartz's. For those exercising restraint because it was only lunch there was stuffed, orange-glazed turkey. And to wash it all down, Diet Pepsi. There was Diet Coke for the reform Jews. This was a crowd of calorie counters.

Within 60 minutes of the guests arriving, the buffet table was the site of complete devastation with twenty-seven people using any horizontal surface that could be used for seating or eating. Three people sat on the staircase leading upstairs, six sat around the kitchen table and the rest found seats on the couches in the living room and the den. My dad's friend, Henry, the efficiency expert, sat on the toilet in the guest bathroom. In one end and out the other.

There were the usual incidents of spilling. Like every year, I had a wager with my dad on who would be first to spill the red wine. I always bet on my cousin "The Eraser." This guy spilled so much he should have been buying gortex ties to avoid the dry cleaning bills. To make matters worse, he would usually spill red wine on his crotch and then spend the balance of lunch with a paper napkin covering the wet spot, hoping that no one would notice. Kosher wine is very sticky due to the high sugar content so the napkin would often stick to his pants and he would walk around the house with an "It's a Party" napkin stuck to his crotch while engaging in small talk. No wonder he never married.

By three o'clock everyone had finished eating and had started to leave. Most of the same people would gather the next night for dinner which consisted of the same meal but with candles on the table. The venue for the dinner changed from year to year but there was always a sense of continuity because most of the menu never varied. My mother shared her recipes but always made the brisket no matter who hosted the dinner. There is nothing quite as compelling as the combination of religious and culinary traditions.

I had been sitting on the piano bench throughout lunch for fear that if I got up someone would take my seat and I would have to stand for the remainder of lunch trying to balance a plate and a glass while engaging in small talk. The downside was that, because of the strategic spot of the piano bench in the living room, everyone passed by my seat on their way out and stopped to engage me in small talk. The conversation consisted of mainly two topics: what a wonderful host my mother was, as usual and the New Year's resolution to see more of each other during the year and not wait until next Rosh Hashanah. The truth was, though, that everyone who said they regretted not getting together more often was quite happy not getting together sooner, including me.

As the last of the guests drifted out, my mother, wearing her standard hostess uniform of grey skirt, darker grey silk blouse accented by a gold rope chain came and sat down beside me on the piano bench with a plate of food. She was always the last to eat because she was so busy keeping all her guests happy. Now, both tired and relieved that everyone had come and enjoyed her lunch, she could relax.

"Mom, you see most of these people once a year, why do you go to such trouble when they don't make any effort to keep in touch except coming here for High Holiday lunch?" She swallowed a piece of smoked salmon and prepared to answer.

"Your father and I always wanted a home where our friends and family would gather for holiday occasions. I wouldn't have it any other way and I wouldn't exclude anyone, no matter how I felt about them."

"But most of them don't even try to keep in touch. Why bother if they don't?" I reached over and took the pickle from her plate and she affectionately slapped my hand.

"Some of our friends and relatives have never experienced what it's like not having anyone to call and invite over. They don't place the same importance on keeping in touch as your father and I do." She ate the second pickle from her plate before I could grab for it.

"I don't know what you mean." She placed her left hand on my knee, which is her way of signaling that she was about to tell me

143

something which I would not likely appreciate until some years later. "We came to this country to find a better life. It has been very good to us but, at the same time, we left part of our lives behind. You can never replace your lifelong friends and family or even just familiar faces. You cannot replace those places which hold your history. Sometimes I miss it so much but I know it was for the best that we left. Having everyone over for lunch year after year is my way of creating a new history for our family and making our home the place for new memories to be created for our family to take away with them. I know that I can't replace the past but I can create something new."

As I sat there and listened, I realized how much of an emotional impact this topic had on her. It was more than casual conversation. "Mom, I never realized that you had such strong feelings about leaving Europe. You were barely eighteen."

She put her plate down on the piano and sat back on the piano bench. "I left behind more than I care to talk about. Your father and I talked a great deal before we decided to leave and it was more difficult than you can imagine. It is the curse of all immigrants who want to hold on in some small way to their past but know it is best to move on. It's not easy to walk away from your past. In my own small way, on this speck of earth I call my home, lunch once a year is my way of keeping everyone in touch with each other so I can have memories to share with you and which one day, you will pass on to your children . . . if only you'd get serious and find a nice girl to marry."

We both laughed and, as I wiped the tear from her cheek and kissed her on the forehead, I told her I'd get right on it but not today because I had to get to the office. She nodded like it was something my father would say. I was going to the office to return a few phone calls. It's not right to work on the Jewish New Year but I saw no harm in it since I had gone to synagogue, stayed awake for most of the sermon and attended my family's lunch. I was trying so hard to break out of the claustrophobic mold of my parents' culture and my mother was trying so hard to preserve it. She saw it as something of incalculable value. The new year had started just like the last one had ended, in utter confusion and uncertain resolve.

"By the way, Mom, why do we have a piano when nobody knows how to play?" I said as I got up, hugged her and made for the door. She went into the kitchen and came out with a bag of leftovers for me, dragging my father behind her. We wished each other a good year and I left.

When I arrived at the office there was a lot of general confusion because of the presence of a television camera crew in the reception area. They seemed to be waiting around for someone but it was not clear to me who exactly that was. As I made my way to my office, Three-Quarters Dana gave me a pile of messages. What I was about to learn, was incredible and brought back to mind my father's advice.

That morning, Rupert MacIntosh had called two members of the franchisee committee and convinced them to let us file the claim that day. Mr. Zimmer and I had agreed to wait until after Rosh Hashanah but Rupert had taken it upon himself to convince the clients otherwise. He told the two members of the franchisee committee that we had to file or we would have to redate all the documents. Someone in word processing had put the wrong date on all the documents and Rupert decided that we should file rather than go to the trouble and correct the documents. In addition, he was giving interviews to the local television stations where he was described as the senior counsel for the plaintiffs, all 390 of them. I was furious but there was nothing I could do about it. The horse was already out of the barn. My venting would have to wait.

I called the two franchisee representatives and explained that I had always intended to file that day but Rupert had not been part of that discussion. Also, as Rupert was a senior partner, we had both decided it would look more impressive if he was the face for media interviews. I assured the franchisees that I was still in charge but just using Rupert's name would look more impressive. I convinced them but that it was all part of the plan and events were unfolding as they should. The truth was that events were overtaking me and I was losing control of the file. I was still the named lawyer on the court documents but no one looks at documents when you are getting air time on the six o'clock news. Mr. Zimmer knew what had really happened and he called to reminded me to be careful and stay in charge. I told him that I had foreseen this contingency, which I hadn't.

Two of the messages I received were from news wire services asking for interviews. I had never been interviewed before and I was afraid that I would look and sound like a young Henry Kissinger. I recognized that Rupert, as the senior counsel, should return these calls. I went to see him about it but he insisted that I should respond. I had no choice but to agree or I would further diminish my profile in the case. Still, I was suspicious as to why Rupert was so willing to step aside. I went back to my office to make the calls. The first was to Mr. Palmer.

"Hello, Mr. Palmer, my name is Ben Stein. I have a message here that you were calling."

"Stein, oh yes. Are you the franchise lawyer in the lawsuit filed today?" He sounded so casual.

"Yes, that's right. How did you get my name?"

"We have people who check the court registries for interesting lawsuits and your name is on the documents as the franchisees' lawyer."

"How can I help you, Mr. Palmer?" I was somewhat more relaxed knowing how he found me.

"I read the documents and I was wondering what you think your chances of success are in this action?"

"There is no amount of rubber that will protect Jupiter from penetration by our clients." I was so used to using tire speak with the franchisees that I didn't think about what any of this meant but it sounded clever. "The Jupiter Corporation has financially assaulted its franchise group and this assault will not be taken lightly."

"How long do you think the lawsuit will take to be resolved?" Palmer pressed on.

"The climax of this case will come when Jupiter screams for relief. I don't know how long that will take."

"Thank you, Mr. Stein."

The moment I hung up it hit me what I had said. How could I have been so stupid. It must have been that sermon. All that talk about sleeping with Gentile girls. I had come into the office for two hours and now my whole career is at risk. God was punishing me for working on Rosh Hashanah.

25

The next morning I went to work early hoping to intercept the newspapers before they reached the reception area. I was waiting in the building lobby by six A.M. for the carrier before he distributed his papers throughout the building. Just like clockwork, fifteen minutes late, he arrived. I took the Lord & Bishop copies from him and there, on page five of the Business section was the headline "FRANCHISEES ALLEGE ACCOUNTING FRAUD." So far, so good. I read through the article that speculated on a new wave of litigation by franchisees and at the end found my quote about rubber and penetration and climax. It was bad enough that I had said it but to actually see it in print was devastating. Maybe I could claim I was quoted out of context. But, what context could justify such a stupid mistake? I decided to leave the paper in the reception area and move on.

By 7:30 A.M., the better part of the free world had read the Jupiter article. Calls started coming in. Unexpectedly, the Jupiter franchisees were thrilled with the article. I guess when you're in the tire business these puns take on a different complexion. The comments from lawyers in the firm were not as supportive. I got a message from David Black suggesting that the franchise group retain a media spokesperson for the duration of the litigation. He mentioned something about this being raised in the morning executive meeting and I should refrain from further comment. His message ended by advising me that Rupert, at least for now, was designated as the Lord spokesman on the file. I was starting to understand why Rupert insisted that I do the interview. I'd been taught my first lesson in office politics.

By mid-morning, I had a stack of messages from people who had read the article. Even my mother called, although she never read the Business Section.

"Hi, Mom, I got your message. What's up?"

"What kind of law firm are you working for with all this bad language about rubber and penetration and climax? You aren't one of those lawyers who help pornographers make those videos you get in hotels, are you?"

"No, Mom, don't worry, I'm suing a tire company and it has nothing to do with pornography. How did you find out?"

"I went to the hairdresser this morning for a combing because I'm going out for lunch and Sterling, my hairdresser, showed me the article. He asked if I was related to that Ben Stein. Anyway, couldn't you have worn a nicer tie for the interview?"

"What do you mean? My picture wasn't in the paper."

"Exactly. If you dress better the newspaper would have taken your picture and put it with the article. They don't want a picture of some *shleper* lawyer in their fancy business section."

"Thanks for the advice, Mom. I'll try to do better next time."

"I just sent a thousand dollar check over to Dad's tailor. You go get a nice blue pinstripe suit and a paisley tie. That way, next time the newspapers will take your picture for their article."

There was no point arguing about the logic of her generosity. The path of least resistance was to graciously accept. "Thanks Mom, and tell Dad thanks too."

"Anyway, we are very proud. Come and visit soon."

"I love you, Mom, good-bye."

I told Three-Quarter Dana to hold my calls and decided to hide for the rest of the day in the document room used for the Jupiter litigation. I hadn't been there for a few weeks and I thought this would be a good time to re-acquaint myself with the boxes of documents that the franchisees had gathered up and sent over. As I walked into the room, I found two eager students sitting at desks surrounded by file boxes full of documents. I didn't know what this was all about and I frightened them as much as they frightened me. Although I had the impression they already knew who I was. In any event, I introduced myself and they, in turn, introduced themselves. They were both named Bob. To keep them straight, I decided to call the tall one Bob-A and the shorter one Bob-B, or "A" and "B" for short. They told me that they had been assigned to catalogue the documents on what had been described as a six-week project. They reported to Rupert MacIntosh and took all their instruction from him. Although I knew I could use the help, this was the first I had heard about this assistance. I kept thinking about the advice my father had given me. Don't lose control, he had said, but I *was* losing control. All on the pretext of efficient management of the case. I was prepared to accept this reasoning but, in my gut, I knew Lord & Bishop was taking the case away from me. I thanked Bob-A and Bob-B for their commitment to the project and told them that I would be checking in with them from time to time.

I went straight to see Rupert and David Black. I wanted to discuss our respective roles as the case developed. I tried to calm down and think strategically about what I wanted to say. When I got there, I was told that Rupert was out of town on business and would not be back until the next week. Now I knew why he had been in such a rush to file the lawsuit. If he had wanted to be seen in control, he could not be away when the litigation became public. He must have told word processing to put the wrong date on the documents knowing that neither Abe Zimmer nor I would be available to object. As I suspected, word processing confirmed that they had received a written requisition three days earlier from Rupert to change the dates on the documents in preparation for yesterday's filing.

I didn't manage to catch up with David Black until the end of the day. I explained to him that I appreciated all the help I was getting from the lawyers of the firm but I wanted to be clear on the division of labor now that we started the litigation. I told him about the two students Rupert had assigned to the document organization without telling me. I also told him that Rupert giving interviews to the media as the senior counsel might not sit well with the clients as they expected me to be in charge. David could see I was agitated and motioned me to sit down.

"Ben, we are very impressed with how you brought this case to the firm and your work on the file. You've done a terrific job with the clients and securing our fees. But, we are a team and, as a team, we organize the work in the best way for the firm, not for any single lawyer."

When I heard the reference to the "best interest of the firm" I knew it was really about self interest and I was the one being sacrificed. "My managing the file is in the best interest of the firm because that is what the client wants," I shot back.

"The clients never know what they want. We tell them what's good for them, they don't tell us. We just let them think that they are telling us what to do. They repeat back what we tell them and we give them credit for the idea." David was speaking from experience and he knew I could not rebut that argument.

"What does all that mean in terms of my role on the Jupiter file?"

"We discussed this in the firm management meeting. From the client's viewpoint, you will be one of the two lawyers running the file. Rupert will take the lead in the litigation and you will work with him. The two of you together will decide how the work will be assigned and who will deal with the issues as they arise. You will arrange for Rupert to attend one of their franchisee meetings so he can be introduced."

"Who will be running the file from the firm's viewpoint?"

"Rupert." David said without hesitation.

"Shouldn't I have been consulted? I'm the one who knows the client and the file better than anyone else."

"Ben, the senior lawyers here know what is best for the firm, what is best for the client and what is best for you. Sometimes we do things for reasons which are not obvious but you must assume that we know what we're doing. As part of managing the firm, we make decisions about how to distribute the work. You have a bright future here and you should support what is best for the firm. In the long run, it is what's best for you."

The dreaded words "future" and "long run." I'd heard those words before. Every time someone talked about my future I knew that I was about to get screwed. But what could I do? There was little point in going to another firm and I was not ready to go out on my own. I'd co-operate, keep busy and pick the right moment to exercise my influence. But I could use some advice before I really screwed it up.

That night, I went to dinner at a cousin's house with the same twenty-seven people that I had lunch with the day before. It was amazing that they still had things to talk about even though they had been together just thirty hours earlier. The menu was the same as lunch except that what had been smoked was now pickled and there was matzoh ball soup. I was meeting my friends at the Italian Coffee Bar afterwards and excused myself by eight. My friends and I always try to meet at the New Year as a way of starting things off on the right foot. This is not that much different then what my parents do.

I was the last to arrive and Paul, Murray, David and Gerry were already there, seated in the corner round table. As I walked in, I acknowledged the four Tonys who immediately called me over to their table.

"I saw in the paper," said Milan Tony, "that you are the lawyer for the leaky condom case. You know, we used those condoms. Do you think we can get any money out of it?"

"No, my case is not about condoms or anything leaky." Even here I was haunted by that interview.

"But, we read in the paper about you suing over rubbers and something went wrong in penetration and climax," Venice Tony joined in, not taking his eyes off the soccer game on the big screen TV. "So, what could have been wrong with those rubbers except if they leak? Don't tell me they were too tight and they exploded."

"No. Tony, the rubber refers to tires on cars, not rubbers like in condoms. The case is about people who sell tires. It has nothing to do with sex."

"Well, do you know if anyone is suing over leaky condoms? Because that's how I ended up with Tony jr.," Milan Tony asked, concentrating on the soccer game.

"No, I don't know anything about that but, if I hear who is suing over leaky condoms, I will let you know."

"Thanks anyway, but since my wife got her tubes tied I've been doing my riding like Tonto, bareback." This remark prompted fits of laughter among the four Tonys which diverted their attention from the big screen and started a discussion about all the women they had slept with but never married. I gestured good-bye and went to sit with my friends.

When I arrived, Paul was complaining about his Cuban delicatessen. He had been so confident that he would do more catering for Rosh Hashanah. How many Cuban Jews did he think lived in Winnipeg? As Paul spoke, I could picture the family trust account shrinking before our eyes and his siblings circling for the kill. One by one my friends and I talked about the past year and highlighted something ridiculous that had happened to each of us. It was our tradition. Murray told us about a married woman, who remained nameless, and how she brought three different guys in, inside of two months, to free their Willies. Not one was her husband and none knew about the others. Gerry told us about how he had convinced an official from Saudi Arabia that his surplus computer parts were worth more because the hard drives had records of various export transactions made by Israeli companies. He charged the Saudis double the going rate. David told us about a client who pulled up in his Harley-Davidson and brought with him $150,000 in 50's and 100's to close a real estate transaction. Then he had offered David a pound of marijuana at cost. When David explained to him that a deposit of that much cash had to be reported to the banking authorities, the guy packed up his money, took back the marijuana and left. The deal never closed.

When it was my turn, the questions came faster than I could get the answers out. They had all read the newspaper article and wondered why I would say such stupid things. I told them I had done it for the good of the firm and that it had gotten a great response from the clients. Then I confided to my friends how I was losing control of the file and asked them what they thought I should do. Advice was never lacking at our table.

Paul told me to demand a partnership but did not have an alternate plan if they said no. Murray did not offer any advice but he had the good sense to recognize that his professional experience did not lend itself to office politics. He did not take in partners and paid the doctors in his office on a per-head rate. David offered advice which, at first, seemed like the path of least resistance. He said that I had gotten all the credit I was going to get for bringing in the file so I might as well cut back my hours and treat it like any other assignment. If Rupert MacIntosh wanted to take the lead role so badly then I should let him because he would also have to take the responsibility if the case failed. I should bow out, he said, and cut the risk of a bad result. The problem with his advice was my commitment to Abe Zimmer. How could I let my dad down after he convinced Abe to use me? David conceded that he had not considered the father/son guilt factor. His backup position was to marry a Gentile girl and still take his advice about the file. That way my parents would be so preoccupied with the dreaded intermarriage that the Abe Zimmer issue would be forgotten. Marriage seemed like a heavy price to divert attention from a problem at the office but the logic was undeniable. I didn't dismiss his suggestion out of hand and it brought back memories of Julia and our latest phone call. Gerry listened to all of the gratuitous advice and put his own simple wisdom to it without being clouded by post-secondary reasoning.

"Look, you work for a business that is controlled by people who control the work. The whole trick is how to maintain influence over the file in the face of your bosses trying to pry it loose for themselves. You can't have an out-and-out fight over it because you don't have any alternatives. So, what you have to do is make sure that the retainer checks continue to come to you and that you continue to send the bills. That way, you will know who is doing what on the file and you will keep in touch with what is going on. Also, you should keep working on the file. If one of the senior lawyers screws up, that may open up an opportunity and you could take over."

As usual, Gerry's reasoning made perfect sense. "How do I make sure that I keep the billing?"

"You talk to Abe Zimmer and tell him that you need a favor. Tell him this plan will protect him from the partners inflating the bills because you will see every bill. Have him send a letter insisting that you review and sign every bill. He'll figure you are repaying him for sending you the work and he will want to do right by Nathan Stein's son." As usual Gerry's reasoning made perfect sense.

"Is there a Plan B?" I asked.

"At the same time that you are doing all this Jupiter work, you must prepare for your exit from the firm. Guys like you can't hang around these big firms. There will be one lawyer or another for the next twenty years pulling rank on you and telling you that you have a great future. You've got to get out on your own. So you might as well start preparing for it. Otherwise, you'll be kissing the Lord's bishop for the next twenty years."

"Look, there are some great lawyers at Lord's who have terrific careers," I said in their defense. "It can work out. There are three hundred and twenty-five lawyers in Toronto doing some of the largest files in the country, five hundred million dollar deals for the Government of India. There are a few 'bergs' in there too. But I admit they are all in the tax group."

"The fact is, those lawyers in the big firms are replaceable parts and, if left on their own, they wouldn't have enough street savvy to fill out the unemployment insurance forms," Gerry added while tapping his fingers on the table. "Guys like you suffocate in these WASP nests and, to breathe, you must get out on our own."

Gerry's comments were very disturbing. I had gone to Lord &
Bishop because I didn't want an ethnic practice and saw it as my
chance to break away. Now, my best friend was telling me that I
couldn't succeed in a place like Lord's. I had to go out on my own.
He had given me good advice about handling the Jupiter file but I
was not prepared to give up on the Lord. I'm no atheist.

Everyone sensed that the conversation was getting a little too
serious so we changed the topic, ordered more drinks and switched
to stories about women. Julia's name came up. I said that I had not
spoken to her but I heard third-hand that she had moved away. Some
things are so private you can't even tell your lifelong friends, even
after four vodka tonics. Wounds of the heart take time to heal. In
any event, we were having a great time together and the time was
going by quickly. Soon there was no one left in the place except the
guys in the back room at the all night poker game. Even the four
Tonys had gone home. We had one last drink, toasted each other a
Happy New Year and went our separate ways. On the way home, I
took a detour and drove by the nurses' residence. The light was off
in Julia's old room. I kept on driving and, when I got home, I looked
for the message light on the answering machine. It was not flashing.
I debated if I should call. Then I remembered the pain and embarrassment and decided not to. She got married and it was over.

26

All weekend I thought how Jupiter was slipping out of my grasp and my future at Lord. You can prepare for all consequences but it usually comes down to making the right decision within a ten-minute window of opportunity. I would have to deal with Rupert on Monday morning and I better know what I wanted and how to get it. I took a long walk down the Crescent, my favorite autumn activity. The cool autumn breeze combined with the warm sunshine was invigorating. I looked at the stately homes and wondered what it would be like to live in one of these stone mansions. What went on behind those manicured hedges? I had always assumed that the quality of life inside was much like the quality of the homes, refined and orderly. In fact, what went on behind those iron gates was likely more sordid than the stately appearance of the dwellings.

I noticed that one house had a Henry Moore sculpture in the front yard with a snow fence around it. It was only September and too early for a snow fence. But, it occurred to me, the fence might have been put up to keep the dogs from pissing on the sculpture. It was reassuring to realize that the dogs of the rich could exercise such judgment about art. Why pee on a fire hydrant when you can pee on a Moore? If I had the chance, I might be inclined to piss on a Moore too. Of course, for me, it would be a spur of the moment thing, like jumping into a pool with your clothes on. You don't plan to do it but sometimes you've just got to. It's there and you get the urge. Anyway, the snow fence sufficiently discouraged me from relieving myself on Mr. Moore's creation.

Before I realized it, my walk had taken me to the gates of City Park where there was a steady stream of cars going in and out. The gates of the park have an egalitarian effect of transforming all those who enter into a homogeneous status. You cannot distinguish rich from poor or the educated from the illiterate while you are in the park. Everyone is there for the same reason.

I made my way to the food pavilion to get a hot chocolate, extra whip. I stood in line and slowly made my way to the hot drink area. In the line in front of me were two elderly women with walkers making a life-defining decision on whether they should have a heated muffin or a chocolate croissant. I smiled but my patience was wearing dangerously thin. I considered coming back late at night and taking out all the handicap ramps to the pavilion, thus permanently ridding the cafeteria of the indecisive aged. This gesture would not have affected me because I was from the Peter Pan generation. We will never grow old. In the spirit of a true Canadian compromise, they finally ordered one of each and split them.

I ordered a tall, non-fat hot chocolate with double whip. I was perfectly aware of the contradiction of my order but I stared down the clerk and moved on to pay. As I was looking for a seat, I noticed one of the Lord's associates, Margaret Hibard, sitting in a corner. She was a third-year associate working in the securities group. She was a one-window associate but with a view of the river. She had a future with Lords but the partners did not consider her a star. Margaret was the kind of lawyer every national law firm needs to get the work done, a journeyman with little prospect for client contact. I had spoken to her several times and found her friendly and knowledgeable in the law.

"Hi, Margaret. May I join you?" I stood in front of her table so not to frighten her.

"Oh hi, Ben, of course you can. What brings you out here?"

"I was taking a walk down the Crescent and, before I knew it, I was at the park gates so I came in for a hot chocolate, double whip. And what brings you here?" I sat down.

"Sophia, my niece, is doing a science project. We're looking for leaves and acorns and I'm taking a short break from my supervisory responsibilities."

"How come an aunt has these responsibilities on such a beautiful autumn Saturday?"

"I'm just filling in. My parents normally take their granddaughter out on Saturdays but they are working at the Greek bazaar so I volunteered to take Sophia to the park."

"Hibard doesn't strike me as a Greek name."

"Actually, my family name is Hibakis but my parents changed it when they came to Canada. They thought it would be easier to pronounce Hibard than Hibakis."

"I would have never guessed. Is it easier being a Hibard?" I blew on the hot chocolate, hoping to cool it down.

"There's not much Hibakis left in me. I was born in Winnipeg and I have never been to Greece. My Greek heritage was never part of my upbringing." I watched as Margaret took the cap off her muffin and ate it first.

"What about weddings and family get togethers?"

"Oh sure. I enjoy those times, but they're no different for me than if I were at a Turkish wedding. It's fun, the food is great and the change refreshing. But, I don't really feel part of it."

"I hope you don't mind me asking questions. I find this subject very interesting."

"I don't mind you asking. It's not something I think much about." She paused, searching for the right words to explain. "I am a Hibard in every sense of the word. I don't really know anything else and I am quite comfortable with this lifestyle. I don't even like souvlaki and I don't frequent the Greek Orthodox Church. My parents' history is not my history."

"Do you think you could be a Hibard by day and a Hibakis by night?"

"I don't know. I've never tried to be a Hibakis, by day or by night." She knew exactly where this conversation was leading. "It sounds too confusing to me. I was born and raised in Canada not Greece. I don't carry the baggage of my Greek ancestors around with me. Hibard has worked for me," she said, baiting me now. "And what about you, are you a Hibard by day and a Stein by night?"

"Well, in my case it's a little more complicated. I was brought up with my family's heritage front and center and I wrestle with trying to expand my horizons beyond my upbringing. I don't want to forget my heritage but I don't want to be limited by it either."

"But isn't the natural tendency to give yourself a label?" Margaret asked. "Ultimately, you have to make a choice and you live with the result. Didn't you make that choice by coming to a firm like Lords?" I found Margaret's question more a revelation than an inquiry.

"I wanted Lords because it was one of the best firms doing some of the best work. But, I admit that it was my proclamation to the world that I was not going to be confined by my parents' heritage. I wasn't interested in Bloom & Company." I had never revealed this to anyone. "The Bloom recruiter had the wrong birthmark." She looked at me as though she did not understand. "Please don't make me explain. It was too much of a stereotype and I wanted to avoid being labeled."

We spent the next half hour talking about how to decide where to fit in. I barely knew this woman and I was telling her things that I hadn't told my closest friends. For some unexplainable reason, I did not feel at risk. It wasn't one of those chance meetings where you end up getting laid. Our conversation did not bring out those emotions. But, I had a strong feeling that a Greek Hibard could get along quite well with a Russian Stein. Maybe Gerry was right and maybe there was no room for a Stein at Lord & Bishop. Maybe I would have to abandon my past to have a future in a place like Lords. Maybe that's what the Button King meant when he talked about abandoning buttons for velcro. By the end of our conversation, I was more confused than ever. I wanted to be compatible in a place like Lord's without changing my name from Stein to Stone. Why was a name change from Hibakis to Hibard so important? It was just a label. You're still the same person with the same values. But changing your name is a public declaration to the world that you have changed. Hibakis gets a different reaction than Hibard. A name change is an identity change. My parents raised me to be a Stein, not a Stone.

As I said good-bye to Margaret I felt like we were two passing ships in the night. Without saying a word, though, we had both understood that our conversation would not be tomorrow's office gossip. It was our secret.

The walk home from the park in the late afternoon when the sun was not as warm seemed longer and colder. On the way home, I tried to sort out what I should do about Rupert, but it was enough introspection for one day. All I really wanted was to go out and have some fun. After all those seventy-hour weeks, I wasn't sure if I knew how to have fun anymore. I could not bear the thought of climbing three flights of stairs to face an empty apartment and no messages, so I walked past my apartment and toward the Italian Coffee Bar. It was still afternoon so I was not worried about looking like I was alone on a Saturday night with nothing to do. Perhaps I would see someone coming in for a late afternoon latte and we'd make an evening of it. Otherwise, it would be another night of pizza and a rented movie with a popcorn chaser.

On the way I stopped at Mr. Cohen's store to buy a Saturday newspaper. I hadn't been there for some time so I knew that I was in for some gossip.

"Stein, where have you been? Have you moved away?"

"Hello, Mr. Cohen. No, I still live here but it's been very busy and I haven't been around much. May I have today's *Globe*, one #2 Dominican cigar and some matches?"

"By the sounds of it you're still single. Too bad. My Beth found a boy in Toronto and she is getting married. His family makes wire hangers. You know you could do my Beth a favor and not get your shirts folded at the dry cleaner. You make sure to tell them to put everything on hangers and don't be one of those, God forbid, recyclers who brings the hangers back."

"Congratulations, I'm sure they'll be very happy and no more folded anything from the dry cleaner. I promise."

"So, Stein, why don't you have a girlfriend? You're a good-looking, smart boy. Don't you like girls? If you know what I mean." He winked.

"Mr. Cohen, I like girls. It's just that I'm not seeing anyone right now." I had to find a way to change the subject. "How much do I owe you?"

"You should go to the singles dance at the synagogue. You are a real catch and I'm sure you could meet a nice girl, maybe one with money or, better yet, real estate. I'm not saying you should look for a girl with money, but you shouldn't hold it against her. Eight twenty-five and I'll throw in the wooden matches. You know some people charge for matches, but not me."

"Yes, I know. Thank you for the matches. Now, it's today's paper? I don't want old news."

"Of course I gave you today's paper. I save the old papers for the widows who can't see anyway. Even if they can read, they forget what they read yesterday, so it's always new to them. Call them my special customers. But, I would never do this to the son of Nathan Stein. A Stein deserves the latest news."

"So, what is the news in the neighborhood?" I said, checking the date on the paper.

"It's been so long since I've seen you. There's a lot I could tell you."

"Try me with the latest."

"Let me see. Oh yes, do you remember my daughter's friend Arlene, the artist?"

"Sure, I have coffee with her at the Italian place sometimes. I haven't seen her in a while." I wasn't about to tell Mr. Cohen about that twitchy stomach of hers or how well I really knew her.

"Anyway, she had been going out with this fellow named Rubin something-or-another who was training to be a professional bicycle racer." Mr. Cohen looked at me over his bifocals. "I don't want you to repeat this."

"I won't tell a soul. I've never known anyone who wanted to ride a bicycle for a living. Where would you go for something like that?"

"I think he was training for that race in Europe. The Tour de Franks." I sensed Mr. Cohen was embellishing to keep my interest. "Anyway, he was bicycling somewhere near the park and he hit a pothole in the road and went over the handle bars. To make a long story short, and just between you and me, he was stabbed in the crotch by one the brake handles. It cut something or another and now he's running on a flat tire, if you know what I mean."

"Oooh, that must have hurt. What is he doing about the flat?"

"He's going to some special hospital in Florida. No one knows if it will work."

"How is Arlene handling it?"

"The word is she was going to dump him because she couldn't see how a poor artist could make it with a poor bicycle racer. Someone has to make a living and he wasn't much of a prospect. Now she feels stuck with a guy who can't make a living and has a permanent flat tire."

"How could such a terrible thing happen to her?" I wondered out loud.

"Now, there's a girl for you. She could use a nice Jewish lawyer with working parts. I think her family may have some real estate. Maybe I could get the word to her that you're available."

I had to get out of there. "Mr. Cohen, as always, it's been nice to talk to you and I hope to see you soon."

"Come by any time. Say hello to your parents. They are wonderful people. Stein, don't fall into any potholes," Mr. Cohen could barely contain the laughter.

160

"I'll make sure to pass on your regards and you can be sure I'll avoid those holes in the road."

I must be really out of touch. No one had called me with this piece of gossip. I guess the silver lining is that Arlene's stomach must have settled down. At the first pay phone, I stopped to call Arlene. She was my best prospect for a little Saturday night companionship. Last time, she had felt sorry for me so this time I would gallantly return the gesture. I wondered if she'd respect me afterwards.

"Hi Arlene, it's Ben, how are you doing?"

"You're calling because you heard about Rubin."

"I don't know what you're talking about. What's a Rubin besides a sandwich?"

"Oh, Rubin is this friend of mine who got into an accident while riding his bicycle."

"Did he get hurt?" I was curious how she was going to phrase it.

"He was injured pretty seriously and there may be some permanent damage."

"What kind of damage?" Let her try to get out of this one.

"Something internal, I don't understand these medical words."

"Sorry to hear it, whatever it is. Is there anything a lawyer with a background in animal husbandry can do to help?"

"No, he is getting good care. So to what do I owe the pleasure of this call?"

"Well, I haven't been in any bicycle accidents or any other kind of accidents for that matter. I was on my way for a late afternoon cappuccino and I was wondering if you would join me?"

"Usual spot in fifteen minutes?" she asked without hesitating.

"Terrific. See you. Bye."

I liked arlene, but almost in spite of herself. Her idea of success was living a life much like her parents. She had no interest in unchartered territory. I could never overcome this difference between us. But, for some unexplainable reason, I was always attracted to her unbridled enthusiasm and energy-packed 110 lb. frame. She was one of those women who looked like she went out of her way not to look like she went out of her way to look her best. In keeping with her artist image she always wore jeans and a T-shirt. But on closer inspection, you could see she had spent a lot of time to get her hair just right and she wore designer jeans and a Chanel tie-dyed T-shirt.

161

In spite of all her contradictions she was kind, something I found very appealing.

Arlene was always twenty minutes late for everything. Thirty-five minutes to the second after our call she walked into the coffee bar and took a seat beside me at my usual corner table. I like a woman who sits beside me rather than on the opposite side of the table. I could tell that she had changed into her going-out jeans and T-shirt but neither of us would ever admit we were out together. I decided that an alcohol and coffee combination would be the appropriate libation on a cold autumn afternoon and ordered two double Spanish coffees made with espresso. That way we could get high and stay awake at the same time.

After we spent a few minutes catching up, Arlene told me about the art commissions she had gotten from friends of her parents. *She'll never change*, I thought. She didn't mention anything about Rubin and I didn't want to push too hard, but I was dying of curiosity. After three drinks and 90 minutes of conversation we were loosening up and I finally asked the question.

"So, how long have you been seeing Mr. Sandwich?"

"His name is Rubin and we've been together for about four months. Actually, he is very nice," she said, crossing her arms defensively.

"What was this permanent injury of his?" I moved my chair closer to her.

"Rubin is a professional bicycle racer and he got hurt falling off his bicycle."

"How do you make a living riding a bicycle?"

"You get sponsors who pay you to race."

"Did Rubin have any sponsors?"

"It's hard to find a sponsor. Bicycle racing isn't that popular in Manitoba. But he had some local support."

Now I was curious who would sponsor Mr. Sandwich so he could race around on a bicycle with their name on his back. "Like who?"

"One of his sponsors was the Manitoba Car Wash Association and his other major sponsor was the Manitoba League of Competitive Snowblowing. They have contests to find who can clear a one hundred foot driveway the fastest."

This was an impressive array of support from prestigious organizations. When you get those competitive snowblowers behind you, the sky's the limit. "Next thing you know," I said, "he'll be sponsored by the leaf rakers." I tried to keep a straight face but it wasn't easy and both of us burst out laughing at the same time. Then Arlene told me that since his accident the sponsorships had dried up. Those car wash and snow blower guys were a heartless bunch, she said. Rubin was looking for a new sponsor but the search was not going well, given his permanent injury. She described it as a penile erectile deficiency latitude, PEDL, which in cycling jargon means Arlene was cycling alone.

The flood gates of her personal life opened once the hinges were greased by multiple Spanish coffees. She was having a Duracell social life since Mr. Sandwich's accident. If she were a man she'd have carpal tunnel and impaired vision. But she felt she could not dump him in his fragile state even though it was obvious that their relationship was not moving in the right direction. A starving artist and an injured bicycle racer did not add up to a match made in heaven. I told her that we could both use some fun and convinced her to go out for dinner. We decided on Greek food as a throwback to our student days. The food is plentiful, the wine is cheap and the restaurants are noisy. You can't go wrong because the boisterous atmosphere gives it an air of informality which neutralizes the stigma attached to going out on a date for dinner. It was a wonderful idea because we drank, ate and laughed for two and a half hours. As always when we were together something sparked between us, but it never seemed to last.

After dinner we went back to Arlene's apartment which was a large warehouse space that doubled as her studio. The outer walls were exposed brick with supporting wooden beams held together by rusted metal fasteners. Throughout the apartment were bright abstract paintings leaning against the brick walls. These were paintings given to her by her artist friends in trade for work she had done. Knowing Arlene's work, I'd say she traded up. Being on the top floor of the warehouse building, Arlene had skylights and she had placed her furniture directly underneath them to maximize the sunlight. We laid down on her bed to look up through the skylight at the evening stars. The bed was large enough that we could both lie down without touching each other. It was too cloudy that night to see the stars but the reflection of the apartment lights on the bird excrement that had stuck to the skylights did resemble the faint white twinkling of the stars.

"Arlene, what do you want to be when you grow up?" I asked. I put my arms behind my head and looked up at the skylight.

"I am grown up." She was lying on her side facing me.

"I mean really grown up, like your parents."

"I want to be happy."

"You mean like Happy the Clown happy?"

"No, just plain happy. But I always did like that red ball on the end of his nose. What about you?"

"I want to live an interesting life." I turned toward her.

"Don't you already with that terrific job of yours?"

"No, my life is too much like my parents. It's secure, predictable, not interesting and it's suffocating me."

"Does that mean you want to be an astronaut or something?"

"I'd consider all options. I want a life that I define for myself rather than becoming stereotyped and precast by my cultural up-bringing."

"It's a luxury to have your problem. I'm just trying to make a living. Your problem is too complicated for me."

Inadvertently, we fell asleep in each other's arms. I will always remember that night as one of my first experiences of adulthood. It was the first time I had gone to bed with a woman and only slept while all my body parts were functioning normally. It was an odd experience but it felt good. We awoke about three in the morning both feeling somewhat self-conscious and slightly hung over. But, there was a certain closeness between us that was undeniable even though neither of us would admit it. I kissed Arlene good night and we made some vague commitment to get together soon. I got home around four, prepared to face the emptiness of the apartment. To my delight the message light was flashing. It was more than likely my mother. So, to avoid the disappointment, I decided not to check my messages until the morning. I was so tired that I fell into bed fully clothed still not knowing how I would deal with that son of a bitch Rupert MacIntosh. But at least I felt relaxed.

27

Message 1 . . . 5:45 P.M.

"Hi, Ben, this is Sarah Goldman. I just got back from Asia and I saw your name in the paper so I thought I'd call to say hello. I'm leaving tomorrow for my job clerking at the B. C. Court of Appeal. Call me if you get to Vancouver. You can reach me through the Court. Sorry I missed you. Bye."

A Saturday night with Arlene instead of a Saturday night with Sarah. This was the second time I missed her for the sake of another woman. We just couldn't seem to get together. I guess it was fate. I wondered what she meant by "you can get me." Maybe it was an invitation for intimacy or just poor vocabulary. A girl as smart and beautiful as Sarah Goldman must choose her words carefully. In fact, I heard that before you could buy a Hermes belt you had to pass an etiquette and language test. It never seemed to be my turn, not with a Windsor or a Goldman. When would it be my turn?

The message from Sarah was a brief distraction from the problem at hand. My career launching file was slowly but surely being taken away from me and I had no strategy to reclaim the case. If I couldn't get it back I would just be another associate working on a Rupert MacIntosh file. I had broken out from the pack and I was not about to falter in the back stretch. I was learning that it took a lot more than competent legal work to excel at Lord's. In fact, the quality of work was secondary. With less than a day to decide on a strategy, I decided to ask my father for advice. I knew he would have my interests foremost in his mind. I called my mom and invited myself for Sunday brunch. Every time I did this my mother got excited, hoping that I was bringing over the girl I was going to marry. She was always disappointed when I came alone. In spite of her disappointment, my mother still made me the best salami and eggs west of the Stage Deli. Pure cholesterol and proud of it.

No matter how much I cherished my privacy and living alone, I found it comforting to be sitting at my parents' kitchen table and talking to them. There was a sense of security and warmth that I had never been able to duplicate in my apartment. I sat at their table eating classic Sunday fare and I felt protected from all the problems of my world. It was very relaxing in spite of my looming confrontation with Rupert. I made a mental note to visit my parents more often.

After brunch, I sat in the den with my dad and we watched Sunday NFL football. Neither of us cared much about football but the Sunday game was always a good backdrop for conversations. I explained to my dad the problem I was having, how I was losing control of the Jupiter work to the senior partner of the firm. I told him that the Jupiter file was an opportunity that might never come my way again and if I lost control of the file I would be losing the chance to launch my career.

"Ben, a career lasts a long time and you can't rely on one case to decide your entire working future. Are you sure that you're not overstating the importance of this case?"

"Dad, I walked into the office with a retainer that senior partners had never seen before. Most lawyers never see a case of this magnitude in their whole careers."

"When I was starting out in the plumbing business . . . Did you see the Raiders score again? You can say *Kaddish* for the Rams. Anyway, when I was starting out, there was this big apartment complex being built in St. James. At that time, I was selling one faucet at a time. The builder took a shine to me and he gave me certain advantages for bidding on the work. It included all the interior plumbing fixtures for over four hundred apartments. I never dreamed I'd ever be bidding for such a project. The biggest suppliers in the province wanted that job and I knew that I didn't have much of a chance even with the builder trying to help me."

"So, what happened?" I got up to change channels because this game was as good as over.

"I got the word out that I had the inside track and then I went to one of the major suppliers and made a deal to put in a joint bid. I told the builder that, with a project that size, he should have me and a major supplier as back up support with their engineers. The builder thought I was giving up part of my profit to insure a quality job. I got the job and he has been loyal to me ever since. That was over twenty-five years ago."

166

"Are you saying that I should divide up the work?"

"Look, I never worked in a law office but I have been in the plumbing supply business a long time. Leaving something on the table for others has paid off handsomely over the last twenty-five years. Maybe you're grabbing too much."

My dad did not say anything else but he knew that I would think about what he said. We spent the next two hours watching various sporting events and eating my mother's endless stream of pastry. Finally, we got to the point where the only thing left to watch was curling. We drew the line there. Neither of us could stand curling, even though the two-time reigning world champion came from Carmen, Manitoba. It was time to go home. I kissed my mother good-bye as she handed me a brown bag filled with my favorite cookies and other assorted Sunday snacks. I kissed my dad on the cheek and was on my way. As I was leaving, I could hear my father's muffled cry, "Sweep, you *schlemiel*, sweep. You're so lazy, you should get an Electrolux." And all this time he had denied watching curling.

I didn't have any plans for the rest of the day but I couldn't relax. As long as the Jupiter problem was not resolved I couldn't not think of anything else. I decided to spend the balance of the afternoon in the office. Perhaps in the atmosphere of billable hours, it will all come to me. For some reason, I liked going to the office on Sundays. For one thing it was easy to get a good parking spot. There were no interruptions. Finally, there was no dress code on Sundays, although some lawyers never wear jeans, no matter the circumstances. It was an embarrassment for these lawyers to be out of uniform. It was a small fraternity of us who came in on Sundays and we had an unspoken camaraderie, a secret fraternity but without the handshake.

After I had settled down and just gotten comfortable, I looked up from my reading and noticed Mr. Basil in the doorway, looking like he wanted to tell me something. Even on Sundays, Mr. Basil wore tweed. He always dresses the part of the conservative business manager.

"Mr. Stein, may I have a word with you?" He had perfect posture but still barely made five feet seven inches.

"Mr. Basil, come in. What brings you to the office on Sunday?" I motioned him to come in and take a seat.

Mr. Basil began to speak before he even got comfortable. "Actually, I thought I might be able to help you. I wanted to talk to you about those two students who are going through all those boxes in the document room."

I nodded. "Every time I look in that room, there seem to be more boxes. It looks like a neverending job." There was an obvious tone of concern in my voice.

"Actually, that is the reason I wanted to have a word with you. These students have been largely unsupervised and they don't seem to be making any progress."

"Rupert is the named partner on the file. Shouldn't he be talking to them?"

Mr. Basil looked at me rather sheepishly. "As best as I can tell, there is no supervision for the two students. Their work is not being monitored and it is not entirely evident what they are doing once they shut the door to that room.

"We would have a major problem if we don't get those documents organized. It is a major piece of the case. Somewhere in those boxes is the proof of our claim. We need that stuff organized to quantify the amount of our damages." I was not sure what he was getting at.

"Mr. Stein, those documents are not being properly organized and I think someone must take stewardship of the file."

"Someone other than Rupert?" It was becoming evident what Mr. Basil was leading up to.

"Mr. Stein, Rupert is not known for his organizational skills. In fact, he is known to be somewhat cavalier in the management of his practice. You best get accustomed to that. He will never change."

"Do you have any suggestions as to how to get this document issue back on track?"

"I am not a lawyer, Mr. Stein. I am the office manager. But I do see the billings and this is a major file for our office. Since you brought it in, you must insure that it moves along properly. Rupert is the named counsel on the file but, if there should be an embarrassment, you will be held responsible."

"But if I'm not the lead counsel, how can I be held responsible for the result?" I leaned forward to insure I didn't miss a word.

"I've been here a long time, Mr. Stein. Trust me, when a file takes an unfortunate turn, the senior partner is never responsible.

The partners occupy a secure position. A file that a junior lawyer has brought it will not be a partner's downfall. There will be notes on the file covering the partner's backside and that means someone else will be responsible. Have you seen the file memos?"

"I never thought of looking. I don't send memos and I don't keep notes of office conversations."

"Curious, I must be getting along with my work. I'll see you tomorrow." Mr. Basil turned and walked away before I could thank him or even begin to consider the significance of what he had told me.

I knew the Jupiter case had attracted some attention around the office but I never thought that Mr. Basil would consider my vulnerability or bother to help me. Obviously, he had an opinion of the partners, just like any of the associates, and in his own proper way he was warning me. He knew more about the firm then any of us and, as office manager, he watched what everyone was doing. Rupert MacIntosh was not his favorite partner and I took Mr. Basil's comments seriously. That night I took the memo folder in the Jupiter file home.

When I had first moved in, it seemed uniquely elegant having this apartment on the top floor of a crumbling, Tudor mansion. The three flights of stairs felt like protection to keep away unwanted visitors. The staircase leading to my so-called penthouse had an aura of exclusivity. But, as time went on, the absence of an elevator became increasingly apparent. It was a lot easier carrying a pizza and a briefcase in an elevator than walking up three flights of stairs. My notion of exclusivity had turned into nothing more than the inconvenience of three flights up the back staircase of a big old house. I fumbled for my keys, managed to unlock the door and dropped my briefcase at the entrance. The message light was flashing. Even on the worst day, it's nice to know someone has been thinking enough about you enough to leave a message. I always feel uplifted by the anticipation of retrieving my messages. It triggers my gambler's instinct, betting on who had called. Maybe Julia was calling or maybe it was Sarah Goldman or maybe someone was calling to invite me out for dinner so I could put the pizza in the fridge and have it as a late night snack. I sat down heavily on the sofa and pushed the play button on the answering machine.

"Hello Ben, this is Rupert. I'm glad you're out on this beautiful fall day. Sorry to bother you at home but I didn't want to miss you.

I'd like to talk to you tomorrow afternoon. Leave a message with my secretary about a convenient time to meet. Perhaps around one-thirty. Bye now."

This was very odd. No one from the office had ever called my apartment. What could Rupert possibly want to talk to me about that would prompt a Sunday call to my apartment? Now I had no choice. I had to be ready for our Monday conversation and I had to settle on my strategy for this Jupiter work. Obviously it was on Rupert's mind too and he must have known what he wanted to do. I had to be clear about what I wanted and how to go about getting it. As a longstanding student, my first reaction was to write down and categorize all my options. I put out my pad and pencil and one hour later I had filled one side of a legal pad.

My friend Gerry had said I should prepare to leave the firm. Paul had said I should demand a partnership. Mr. Cohen said to marry a rich girl. My dad had said to give some of the credit to others. Mr. Basil said I should cover my backside and create a trail of memos to file. Mr. Zimmer said he would support me whatever I decide to do. Rupert told me when I first met him that when the opportunity comes you must go for it. The list seemed to go on forever and now I was more confused than when I had started. I had expected the solution to magically jump off the page. I was taught in university that what you write down is secondary. The benefit is in the process. That was all well and good except that by 1:30 tomorrow that process had better result in an answer or I'd be another lawyer of the Lord carrying some partner's briefcase and talking to the client's secretary. I had to take control of the file but still make Rupert believe that he was in charge. I threw out my notes and gave up on the analytical nonsense. Writing a list might have been productive in academia but now that I actually had to decide something a list was nothing more than a list. My solution required judgment and strategy. I needed a plan. I opted for the cold pizza and the late NFL game. The memo folder could wait till after the game. I was counting on the combination of heartburn and sports to inspire me.

I didn't sleep in anticipation of the Monday meeting. I tried to stay in bed but by 4:30 A.M. I surrendered to my anxiety and got up. I turned on the lights, put on my winter terry towel bathrobe, which I had mistakenly taken from the Bayshore Hotel, and went to the kitchen with the memo file in hand. I poured myself a concoction of various fruit juices and sat down at the kitchen table to read the file. After twenty-five minutes of reading Rupert's memos, it was clear that he was setting himself up to dodge the big fall and setting me up to take it. All the memos recounted our conversations in which he told me that I was the responsible lawyer in charge of the file. No wonder he did not object to my signing the bills to the client. The memos left the impression that he was only acting as a resource and the named partner for public consumption. Rupert did not believe in the case and he concluded the case would get bogged down in mountains of documents and endless motions. If the case succeeded, he takes the credit as the named senior partner and if it failed he relies on the memos and makes me responsible.

I was beginning to understand the meaning of office politics in the Lord's world. Senior partners had access to the best work the firm could offer and they were insulated from mistakes by holding the junior lawyers responsible. I didn't have an exit option from the firm and I didn't have a plan to push the responsibility back up to Rupert, but I still wanted to send him a message that the benefits of partnership were not as secure as he assumed. Rupert's position was fragile. He knew a lot of people and sent out big bills but, in fact, he knew very little about the law or the details of a file. He always made the same argument to the court regardless of the case and that was that his client had acted fairly. Oddly enough, this strategy seemed to work more often than not. His weakness was in the details combined with laziness and greed. He relied on others to prepare the case. His most proficient skill was taking a disproportionate income from the firm at the expense of his partners. It was clear to me that I had to do something so Rupert would withdraw from the file for fear of failure.

Status comes in many forms at a law firm. There are the obvious symbols, such as the size and location of your office. But, there are less obvious affectations, such as the location of your parking spot, especially in a city with a cold winter and huge snow falls. With my six-bit screwdriver in hand, I went to work very early that Monday morning and made some changes to the parking pecking order. All the reserved parking spots sported the name of the partner who laid claim to the spot and the parking lot was part indoor and part out-door. With another prairie winter approaching, no one wanted out-side parking where you had to plug in your car, walk on the treacherous ice and scrape the frost off the windshield before leaving after a long day at work. The Farmers Almanac predicted an unseasonably cold and wet winter, which prompted the landlord to raise the rates for indoor parking. That morning, I made some status adjustments by rearranging some of the assigned spots. I moved Rupert and a select few of his legal fraternity to outdoor spots. I made sure that Mr. Basil got an indoor spot as a way of repaying him for our Sunday conversation. As office manager, I wanted to insure that he would not seriously challenge the necessity of those temporary parking reassignments. I did not change my outdoor spot so as not to draw any suspicion to myself.

When I got to the office that morning, I found an old memo from the building management. I photocopied out the content of the memo so that all that was left was a blank piece of stationary with the building letterhead. I took a certain literary license and wrote a notice to all the tenants.

TO: ALL TENANTS
FROM: PORTAGE MANAGEMENT
AS PART OF THE ONGOING UPGRADING OF THE PARKING LOT AND BUILDING, THERE WILL BE CERTAIN TEMPORARY CHANGES TO THE ASSIGNMENT OF PARKING SPOTS. IN ADDITION, THE PARKING LOT ELEVATOR WILL BE SHUT DOWN FOR MAINTENANCE FROM TIME TO TIME BUT THIS WILL NOT OCCUR IN BUSINESS HOURS. WE EXPECT THAT THE WORK IN THE PARKING LOT WILL BE COMPLETED WITHIN SIX WEEKS. WE APOLOGIZE FOR ANY INCONVENIENCE. THANK YOU FOR YOUR COOPERATION.

I made copies of the memo and distributed them through the inter-office mail system to all the lawyers. I left a message for Rupert confirming our 1:30 P.M. appointment to discuss whatever was on his mind. Then I resumed my morning routine of reading the newspaper and drinking my first of five cappuccinos.

28

I had a plan. At precisely 1:30 P.M. I knocked on the open door of Rupert's office and he motioned for me to come in. I didn't know why Rupert wanted to see me, but nonetheless, I had a plan. I sat across from him while he argued on the phone with some developer. Rupert was trying to negotiate a discounted price for a condominium and in return he would promote the project to his friends. He was trying to impress upon the developer that his presence would lend prestige to the empty building. I only heard Rupert's end of the conversation, but it was obvious to me that the developer was not convinced. It's one thing to try to convince a judge based on some nineteenth-century legal principle but quite another to pick the pocket of a real estate developer. I was starting to understand just how cheap Rupert MacIntosh really was.

When he got off the phone, he swiveled in his chair toward me and said, "Sorry to keep you waiting, Ben. I'm trying to buy a condo for my daughter and this developer thinks he built Buckingham Palace. Well anyway, how are you? We won't be disturbed. I've told my secretary to hold my calls except if Goddamn Basil calls. I want to talk to him about my fucking parking spot."

"What's wrong with the parking?" I attempted to sound uninformed.

"When I came to work this afternoon, there was a No Parking sign on my spot and someone had moved me to an outdoor stall. Can you imagine what it will be like to have to park outside all winter?"

"Actually, there was a memo circulating this morning from the building management about parking. They are doing some sort of repair to the parking lot. My spot was not moved but I only rate an outside spot anyway. If I remember the memo correctly it's only temporary."

"Temporary or not, I want to talk to Basil about it." He swung around to look at the view and spoke with his back to me. "I wanted to talk to you about the Jupiter file."

"Sure. What's on your mind?"

"I suppose you were pissed off about my changing the filing date without talking to you first. The documents had the wrong date on it and instead of redoing the documents we decided to file early." He turned back to see my reaction.

I knew that was a lie but I decided to let him keep talking, giving him lots of rope so I could get the full picture of what I was up against. "Oh . . . I'm not mad. A day's difference didn't matter to me."

"What did you think about the media identifying me as lead counsel?"

"I expected something like that. You are the lead counsel. All I'm concerned about is that I understand my role so we get everything done the way you want it."

"Ben, I'm glad that you see it that way. You'll get your chance, but you have to be patient. As far as your role is concerned, I want you to take full control of the work. We must do whatever it takes to manage the file."

"I assume that means organizing the documents, drafting the pleadings and preparing all the legal briefs. Since I know the clients, I should keep in contact with them so they're up to date and informed if we need anything."

"Absolutely. Ben you call the client as you think best and you continue to sign the bills." The phone rang and he reached for the receiver without hesitation. "Excuse me, that must be Basil."

"Basil what the hell is going on with my parking spot? Why hasn't the building manager called you back? I have no intention of parking outside all winter. Partners don't park outside. Yes, I understand that it's temporary but I still don't like it . . . No. I don't want you to find me parking somewhere else. I'll freeze my ass off walking from the car to the building. I want to stay in the building but I do not want to park with the hired help in the outside spots. I don't care what our lease says. Okay, okay, but if this lasts one day longer than necessary someone will answer for this and that someone is going to be unemployed. Good-bye." He hung up the phone and undid the top button of his shirt and loosened his tie as the vein in his neck had expanded from tension.

"Sorry for the interruption, Ben. Did they move your spot, or did you already tell me?"

"I've had the same spot since I was hired. It's outside. What did Mr. Basil tell you?"

"He told me it's temporary. The building manager didn't know about any renovation and they will find out what is going on and get back to us. The building has the right to make such changes under the terms of our lease, of course, and we just have to be patient and hope the repairs can be done quickly."

I nodded and stood up. "Is there anything else, Rupert? I've got to get back to work." Rupert nodded in recognition but he was obviously irritated by the parking. I got out of there as fast as I could. It was clear what Rupert was doing. I was being set up. If someone was going to take the fall for the case it was going to be me. So far no surprises. As for the parking, I knew Mr. Basil would not push the building manager since I'd made sure he got an indoor spot. He'd be in no rush to check on the progress of the parking lot repairs.

I went back to my office to execute the next steps in my plan. I called Mr. Zimmer and the president of the franchisee association. I assured them both that the firm had sorted out the division of labor and they would not have to deal with countless numbers of lawyers all having some obscure sub-specialty which touched on the case. I assured them that I was still the contact lawyer and I was in control of the case. As a follow-up to the calls, I prepared a letter outlining the timeline for the next six months and how we were going to move the case along. I copied Rupert on the letter knowing there was an 80 percent chance he would not even bother looking at it.

The next item on the agenda was to go and see Bob A and B. Their work area was still wall-to-wall boxes and they did not appear to have made much progress. I noticed a deck of cards on the document table which led me to suspect they weren't working as hard as they should have been. I asked them to show me what they had finished to date and they took out a stack of recipe cards which listed the documents they had catalogued in alphabetical order under such headings as: Memo, Financial Statement and Correspondence. The documents were not cross-referenced so there was no way of tracing the correspondence to the referenced source documents. This was a serious problem. It was clear to me they had been left with no adequate supervision. I decided it was time to sit down with the two Bobs and have a little discussion about the work.

"This looks like a tedious job. How much progress have you made?"

"Actually, we seem to be falling behind. Every time we finish one box of documents, two more arrive. We could use some help." Bob A was the spokesperson.

"Let's stop for today. Tomorrow, first thing in the morning, let's say seven, I want to see both of you in my office." Their faces told me they never came to work before nine. They did their best to hide the inconvenience and agreed to meet at seven.

Next, I got a three-way call going with my friends Gerry Smith and David Kaplan. After exchanging the usual pleasantries, mostly about Paul's new business venture, I got on the topic at hand. David is one of those lawyers who predicted that computers would one day revolutionize the practice of law. He'd had a computer on his desk since 1981, had filled in all the legal forms on it and always used the computer to type the first drafts of his letters. I was content to use Three-Quarters Dana and let others have techno-fulfillment. But, it occurred to me that with the volume of documents the Jupiter case generated, a computer would be useful. It would also be an excellent way to exclude Rupert. He didn't understand the computer well enough to search for a document. When I filled them in on the plan, David explained that a new computer company in Seattle had developed a system for cataloging large volumes of documents. He told me about the type of computer equipment we needed for the project. Gerry said he could find the necessary equipment.

My plan was in motion. Gerry was going to find the equipment and I was going to retain David to teach the two Bobs how to input the data into the computer. The input of the documents would all be done within the next six weeks as long as the people in Seattle would co-operate. David promised to give me some lessons on how to use the computer to do a document search when he came to my office the next morning to meet the Bobs.

I was ready for the next step. I met with Margaret Hibard and Bill the Wasp. I wanted their help to prepare the court application to get the Jupiter documents. Margaret and I had maintained our friendship since our meeting in the park but I didn't really know Bill. He was one of those quintessential national firm lawyers who looks the part but would never be crucial to the practice. He would never do anything that would embarrass the firm. I wanted Margaret and

Bill to work with me. I promised there would be lots of work and the opportunity to deal with the clients. It was the latter point, I'm sure, that closed the deal. They were both third-year associates but neither one had ever spoken to a client. I knew they would both see Jupiter as an opportunity to jump-start their careers which, up to this point, had been predictably uninspired.

With the assistance of David Black, I put together a second team of lawyers to prepare our response to what we felt would be Jupiter's strategy to have a separate trial for each franchisee. Although we had not heard from them, I knew that would be their plan. The case could be won or lost on this issue. If each franchisee had to litigate separately, no single franchisee would have the resources or the stamina to go it alone. Not even Mr. Zimmer could afford to sacrifice his future as the test case. David picked the brightest and most energetic of the associate group to work on this issue. Once the word got out that I had fallen in line with Rupert as lead counsel, everyone was quite willing to help. There was no need to pick sides in the conduct of the case. He is a senior partner and he had a lot of influence in the firm. My plan avoided a controversy with Rupert so nobody questioned my motives. I was not being watched or second-guessed.

I called Mr. Zimmer and the franchisee president and arranged to meet the franchise committee on the first Monday of each month to give them an update and advise them on what to expect for the coming month. In this way, the clients would be fully informed and insured that the case would move forward. The meetings were usually held in Vancouver and would precede their monthly franchise meeting. As the next meeting was in four weeks, the first Monday in November, it was important that we could show the clients some progress in the move toward litigation. I pushed the lawyers to produce something concrete for the November monthly meeting. Rupert was quite content not to interfere because he held the view that the litigation was doomed anyway and he was happy to let me sign the progress reports. I believed in the case and I was willing to stake my future on it. With no established career and some ambivalence about private practice, this was not a high risk wager for me.

When I left the office at 6:30 that day, I was quite pleased with myself. All things considered, it had been a productive day. I had avoided a confrontation with a senior partner, set up two teams of lawyers to help on the Jupiter file, managed to maintain my contact with the clients and kept the billing authority. And, I had repaid Mr. Basil for his helpful advice with an indoor parking spot. To top it off, all the time had been billable, with the money already on deposit as part of the retainer. In the word of the Lord, who could ask for anything more?

It was a cold night as I walked to my car when I noticed that all the cars had a heavy layer of frost on the windshield. Then I noticed Rupert standing beside his car, swearing, holding his wrist and jumping up and down.

"Rupert, what's wrong?" I asked, puzzled by what he was doing.

"Why would you think anything was wrong?" he asked, nursing his wrist. "Isn't it perfectly normal to see a fucking grown man jumping up and down, screaming in agony? Of course there's something wrong."

"What happened?"

"Every Monday I have my car washed while I'm at work. The dumb bastard who washes my car left it in the outside spot. All the doors and locks froze. It would be easier to pry a donation out of those grain traders down the street then pry the doors open on this German popsicle on wheels."

"But what happened to your wrist?"

"I took out my lighter to heat up the car key so I could thaw the lock and the heat from the key burnt my finger. I dropped the keys and, as I went to pick them up, I slipped on the ice and fell on my wrist. It might be broken."

"Is the bone sticking out?" I asked with eager anticipation.

"No, but it's turning blue and it hurts like hell."

I could barely contain myself. There was a God and today I am one of the chosen people. I offered to take Rupert to emergency but he insisted that he would rather go home than wait around all night in emergency. He did not want me to drive him home so I helped him into my car and gave him a ride to the taxi stand at the Westin Hotel. As we left the parking lot, I took one final glance at his frozen BMW. I estimated that it would not take longer than five months to thaw. As he got out of my car, with the help of the Westin doorman, he had a pained look chiseled on his face. I waved good night but he only nodded his head, given the pain in his wrist. I made a note to move him back to his inside spot before he asked any more questions.

29

Four weeks went by quickly and it was time to leave for Vancouver to report on our progress. The three groups working on the case had prepared a progress report which I incorporated into my summary to the clients. I made a superficial effort to have Rupert review the summary but he left it up to me for editing and presentation. The document looked impressive, bound in a green suede folder with the firm logo in gold leaf at the bottom right-hand corner. It included a computer printout of the documents that had been catalogued. The list had a technological look which gave it instant credibility and left the impression that it had taken a lot of work and we knew what we were doing.

I booked a Canadian Airlines flight and confirmed my reservation at the Westin Bayshore Hotel. I had been flying so much that the airline gave me a gold card which entitled me to get on the plane before anyone else and wait for the always-late departing flight in a separate lounge of the airport. I coveted that piece of yellow plastic. I was amassing so many frequent flyer points that one day I'd get a free airplane ticket. Flying, even business class, wasn't as pleasurable for me as it had been in the beginning. In fact, it had become an irritating chore. The real reward for frequent flyers should have been a Lazy Boy chair and a remote control so I could sit at home instead of on an airplane.

It was a welcome relief coming to Vancouver in November. It was getting very cold at home and it would keep getting colder every day now until about March 25 when there would finally be a hint of spring. In Vancouver there were still leaves on the trees along the walking paths in Stanley Park and I could recapture the autumn season all over again. As soon as I got to the hotel, I resumed my West Coast routine of taking a walk down Denman, buying a souvlaki at the Greek take-out and sitting on a park bench to watch the sunset behind the freighters floating on English Bay. I cherished my sense of privacy and not being burdened by heavy outdoor clothing. It was a liberating feeling.

The monthly meeting with the franchisees went off without incident and I was becoming more at ease making these presentations. Some of the dealers were concerned that the case was not moving forward fast enough but I assured them that, once things started happening, they'd wish we could slow it down. Actually, I wasn't speaking from experience but it sounded good and everyone smiled and nodded their heads. The meeting ended by one-thirty so I had the rest of the day in Vancouver to myself. I was going to Seattle the next day to meet with the two computer programmers who were working on cataloging the documents. I walked down Robson Street and stopped for lunch. Then I wandered through the Vancouver Art Gallery which at one time had been the courthouse. The gallery is known for its Emily Carr collection and Jack Shadbolt butterfly paintings. I don't care much for artists who paint insects, even if the insects have wings, but Emily Carr knew how to paint a tree which would later be chopped down by some loyal British Columbian and shipped to Asia to be made into cheap furniture. I spent an hour at the gallery walking from room to room and looking for the escalator to take me to the next floor. It was a relaxing way to spend some time and I didn't have to resort to shopping.

After the gallery, I made my way across the street to take a look at the new courthouse. It was quite impressive in the sunlight and had the appearance of a giant sheet of glass laid on an angle. When I walked in I saw a red plastic pail collecting water from the leaky glass roof. *Even brilliant architecture can leak,* I thought. As I looked up to find the source of the leak, I heard a voice behind me. I knew the voice without turning around. I had heard it on my answering machine.

"Hi, Ben, I see you've taken me up on my invitation." It was Sarah Goldman. I had to think fast because I had truly not been looking for her. In fact, it had never occurred to me to look her up. But it was a pleasant surprise to see her.

"Sarah! You look terrific. I'm here for a meeting and I had the afternoon free so I thought I'd come by since I missed you in Winnipeg." I could always tell her the truth on our twenty-fifth wedding anniversary. Spontaneously, I kissed her on the cheek and, equally spontaneously, she responded in kind. I hadn't seen her for close to eighteen months and I didn't know where to start. She relieved me of this awkward responsibility and asked me if I wanted a tour of the building. "Of course," I said, and off we went.

"So how is your job?" I asked as she showed me around.

"We each get assigned a judge. Mine is a longstanding member of the Court of Appeal. We meet each morning to go over the day's agenda and then I'm on my own. I often sit in on his cases so I'll have a better idea of the issues which he'll want me to research."

"I guess you find out quickly who are the good lawyers and who are the bums."

"The judges talk among themselves and reputations are quickly made, no matter how unfair the comment."

"How do Lord and Bishop lawyers stack up?"

"I'm not allowed to repeat anything I hear in the judge's chambers, so all I can tell you is my opinion." She smiled coyly.

"What happens if I ply you with alcohol and take you out for an expensive meal. Would that do it?" It's my way of asking her out on a date while keeping it informal.

"It would certainly be worth a try. I'm free right now if you want to get an early start."

"It's a date." I took her arm and we headed back to the lobby.

It was only 3:15 but Sarah told me that, within her group of judges, this would often be the approximate time for convening to the bar at the Meridian Hotel. I fully endorsed such judicious consideration. I waited for her in the lobby of the courthouse while she got her coat. I noticed that the red bucket was half full and rising.

The bar at the Meridian is perfect. Cherrywood paneling, no windows but not too dark, and comfortable, tufted leather chairs. What's more important, they had a first class assortment of nuts with plenty of dry roasted cashews. The airlines could take a lesson. We sat in the northeast corner of the room that provided a strategic view of the entire bar and both of its entrances.

In the two and a half hours we spent there, I had four vodka tonics for which Sarah instructed the barman to use some obscure vodka the name of which I could not pronounce or spell. She had an equal number of mojitos that I soon learned was a trendy Cuban drink made with fresh mint leaves, lime and some variety of Cuban rum. She talked mostly about her trip to Asia and the strange experiences she had while traveling. I was fascinated listening to her stories

181

about the mysticism of Indonesia, the islands of Malaysia and the characters in the golden triangle of northern Thailand. But what should have tipped me off was that she spent too much time talking about the shopping. I kept my mind on how terrific she looked. She was not a stunning beauty but she had a presence which was captivating. It was the first time since I stopped seeing Julia that I was interested in someone for something other than the usual reasons. Maybe I would get my turn after all. Maybe it would come when I least expected it.

We decided to walk down Robson Street and have dinner. There was no lack of restaurants to choose from but we were both looking for something semi-intimate where we could continue our conversation. We found a little French restaurant in an old converted house that fit the bill. Sarah had been there before and the maitre d', Eddie, recognized her and gave her a flirtatious but polite greeting. He showed us to a nice little table in the corner by the fireplace where we sat side by side, ate, drank wine and talked about how our outlook had changed since we left law school. I asked her if she missed home.

"No, not at all. I like my privacy here and I don't feel like anyone is watching me. Although, I do miss my parents."

"You always struck me as someone plugged into Winnipeg society with lots of friends and always somewhere to go."

"Looks can be deceiving." Sarah smiled. "But, you are partly right. I have a lot of family and friends there but it got boring and it was holding me back. I had to get away. My trip to Asia and my job in Vancouver was my way of getting out."

I wondered if she found the answer I was looking for. "Did it work?"

"Well I'm still close to my parents but I speak to my friends less and less. I've made a point of not calling anyone from home who has moved here. I was determined to make a fresh start and I did not want to depend on my old friends for a social life." We both sat back and reflected for a moment on what she had just said. "When I first moved here and my phone rang, it was either long distance or a wrong number. But it's improving, slowly. I don't mind being alone after feeling for so long that everyone knew everything there was to know about me. How about you? How has it been for you since you left law school?"

"It's a big surprise to me but my world revolves around work. I didn't even want an articling job and here I am an associate at Lord's working seventy hours a week. I was seduced by the competition in the firm and determined to succeed. I'm not sure I want the prize. I still keep in touch with my old friends and, because of our long history we have a bond that will last for life no matter how infrequently we see each other. Work is my focus and I see it as a way to become self-reliant. I don't want to be beholden to anyone. I don't feel vulnerable if I am in control. It's the legacy of an immigrant ancestry."

Somehow, Sarah's search for anonymity and my need to break away fit together like pieces of a jigsaw puzzle. We were kindred spirits in search of similar goals. Somehow, it all fell into place while we were sitting in a bistro on Robson Street. We talked for hours, ate and drank until it became painfully obvious that the restaurant staff wanted to go home and we were holding them back. We didn't ever have that awkward moment at the end of the evening. I was happy just to be walking down the street with her and I sensed that she felt the same way.

"I had a great time, Ben. It feels like I'm still on vacation."

"I have to get up early tomorrow to go Seattle. I'm going to see two computer experts about a document problem I'm having."

"Have you ever been there?"

"No. I know there is a space needle from an old world's fair but that's about it."

"Seattle is a wonderful city and you should take in the market and the galleries."

"Could I convince you to take the day off and give me a tour of the city?" I couldn't believe what I was actually saying. "My meeting will be over by noon and we can spend the afternoon looking at the sites."

"Sure," Sarah said. "I'd love to. It would be fun."

I was stunned that Sarah would take up my invitation. She responded faster than I could change my mind. "What about work, won't that be a problem?"

"Ben, I'm a dedicated member of the public service, you know, you tax dollars at work. When you work for the courts no one keeps track of you. If I don't show up, the judges assume I'm doing research at the law library. These judges are all retired lawyers. They don't want to account for my time because then someone might want to account for theirs." I thought, *This is the difference between billing by the hour and working in the service of the public.*

As we walked back down Robson, we made a plan. She would come by my hotel at seven and we would take my rent-a-car to Seattle. I would work in the morning and then we would go to the galleries for the afternoon, have dinner and come home in time for me to catch the evening flight back to Winnipeg. As we parted, I kissed her on the cheek, she responded in kind and we went our separate ways.

My day in Seattle was a real education. The two computer programmers' new cataloging software was fascinating. In fact, they were looking for investors at $10,000 each for a half percent share of the business. I was ready to invest based on their enthusiasm alone. I took the prospectus on the share offering and left $2,000 as a down payment.

While I was at my meeting, Sarah checked into the Four Seasons Olympic as her little surprise for the afternoon. That's where I got my real education, the cost of luxury. I had never spent $400 for a hotel room before, let alone $6 for coffee, $32 for a fruit plate and $140 for a bottle of champagne. Sarah did the ordering and I did the paying. It was a strangely liberating experience since this is what grown-ups did. At the Four Seasons, I discovered the true meaning of service. If you tip enough all the staff somehow know your name, gratuitous clairvoyance. And they sounded so sincere. Not even the $700 Visa bill for one afternoon at the hotel was the real lesson. The real lesson was that if you go out with a girl who wears a Hermes belt, it probably means she shops there too. I didn't appreciate that simple fact of retail consumption at the time but it would later prove to have a real impact on my life.

30

When I returned home from Vancouver there was a message from Sarah on my answering machine. It did not surprise me but I thought it was a kind gesture. It reminded me of my first date with Julia. I was relieved. I called Sarah back and we talked about our time together, work and the weather, which was getting increasingly colder in Winnipeg. We decided to see each other again soon and she left it to me to work out the arrangements. We both tried to sound casual but we both knew this was not a one-night stand. Sarah had suddenly become an unanticipated and complicating factor in my life.

Although I had only been away for two days, there were developments in the Jupiter case. Jupiter's lawyers had filed an application in court to have our claim struck. They claimed that the franchisees, having their own individual franchise contracts, could not join together in a single cause of action. Jupiter wanted their application heard within ten days, which was a very short time considering the volume of material and the importance of the issue. That application would determine whether our case went ahead or not. We had anticipated this strategy and were ready to argue the motion but we did not want Jupiter to know that. I set the trap and called the other side.

Step number one:

"Mr. Billings please, Ben Stein calling." As I waited for him to take the call, I listened to the orchestral version of "Money" by Pink Floyd. This music was likely chosen by some branding consultant hiring a psychologist sub-contractor.

"Billings here."

"Mr. Billings, this is Ben Stein calling from Lord & Bishop. I'm working with Rupert MacIntosh on the Jupiter matter. We received your application and I thought we could talk about it for a few minutes."

"Of course, Mr. Stein, what would you like to talk about?"

"I was wondering if you would be agreeable to adjourning this application to the new year. We don't have the resources to prepare for this application in such a short period of time."

"Mr. Stein, the timing of our application complies with the rules and we have no intention of adjourning this matter. Our client would like this resolved before the new year and we are not prepared to delay this one day longer than necessary." He was nibbling for a settlement by using the term "resolved."

"If we go before the judge and ask for an adjournment, we'll likely get it, so why don't you consent and save all of us the time and needless expense." I wasn't going to take the bait quite yet.

"I don't agree that you will get this adjournment. We have followed the rules and the fact that you don't have adequate resources within this time period is not the basis for an adjournment. I'm sure Rupert MacIntosh knows that and so do I, so there is no reason to make this accommodation."

"Instead of fighting about the timing of the application, maybe our time could be better spent settling the whole case. Not even Jupiter could describe this litigation as productive." Now I'll set the hook. I wanted Billings to believe that we were thinking about settlement because we had a lousy, expensive case and were not prepared. I hoped that would lull them into a sense of overconfidence.

"Of course we would consider any reasonable proposal. But time is running and we won't adjourn our application."

"I understand the urgency and I will convey this to Mr. MacIntosh. I'm sure you'll be hearing from him."

"I look forward to the call and hope that we can settle this matter. Good morning."

Step number two:

"Hello Mr. Zimmer, this is Ben Stein. There is an issue which has come up in the case that I want to talk to you about."

"Go ahead, Ben. I'm sorry I could not get to the meeting in Vancouver but I was busy installing tracking equipment in the trucks."

"What did you mean by tracking equipment?" He always fascinated me with his engineering skills.

"I can track the location of my trucks by installing tracking equipment in the bumpers. It was developed by the Israeli army to track the vehicles of suspected terrorists. But, in my case, when the driver tells us he is on the way to the next customer we will know if that really is the case." He paused. "What can I do for you?"

"Yesterday, we were served by Jupiter with an application to throw our case out because it included multiple plaintiffs. As you know, we have been anticipating such a strategy and we are ready."

"What happens next?"

"The case will be heard in ten days, a week from Friday. It will be held in Winnipeg and I hope you and the rest of the committee can attend."

"You leave that up to me. Is there anything we can do to help?"

"As a matter of fact, that is one of the reasons I am calling. I want you to give us the authority to try and negotiate a settlement. Don't worry, the only settlement offer we would accept is complete capitulation on their part, but I want you to let me try."

"Do you really think that Jupiter would ever consider such a thing?"

"They will never settle. But I have my reasons for trying and I need your support to go ahead."

"I'm not quite sure what you're up to but I would never doubt the son of Nathan Stein. You go ahead and I'll take care of the others."

"Thank you for your support, Mr. Zimmer, and we'll keep in touch. By the way, if you hear from Rupert MacIntosh about any settlement offer, just be non-committal and . . . let me know."

"I don't know what this is all about but I'll do as you say."

"Thank you Mr. Zimmer. See you in court."

Step number three:

I called around the office and tracked down Margaret and Bill. I gave them copies of Jupiter's application and they were suitably impressed that I had predicted Jupiter's tactic. Margaret and Bill had written a first draft of the argument in collaboration with the lawyers who helped with the research. They were excited about having a meaningful role and eager to help in any way. We agreed to have the written argument in final form within five days which would leave us five days for court preparation and for any unanticipated changes.

"Now there is one thing I want to talk to you about which is important to the strategy of the case. But this must be kept absolutely in confidence." Both Margaret and Bill nodded their heads in unison.

Their demeanor indicated that they fully appreciated the seriousness of what I was about to tell them.

"Under no condition do I want either of you to show your work to anyone, especially anyone in this office. If someone wants to see the argument, you refer them to me. There are no exceptions. Even if Mr. Lord should rise from the dead and ask for our legal brief, the answer is no." Although Margaret and Bill both looked puzzled and amused by my instruction, they accepted it without question. "One more thing. All the old drafts must be shredded and you are to account for the whereabouts of all copies of the most recent draft. There can be no more than two copies of the most current draft in existence. At the end of each day, I want you to place both copies in a locked drawer and only the three of us can know where that is." Margaret and Bill found the mystery of these instructions seductive. They suspected we were following the clients' wishes and I was not about to tell them otherwise.

Step number four:

"Rupert MacIntosh's office, how can I help you?"

"Yes, Ben Stein calling. Could you please tell me if Rupert is available a week from Friday?"

"Sure, Ben. All he has is one appointment in the morning and lunch with the firm's finance committee."

"We've just been served with an application on the Jupiter file returnable that Friday. Could you change his morning appointment so he can be in court?"

"No problem. Consider it done."

"Please write in its place, Jupiter Application. I'll talk to him about it when I see him later."

"It's already changed."

Step number five:

So far so good and now I just had to deal with Rupert. I was nervous about seeing him but felt sure that he had not suspected a thing. I was still considered the loyal soldier and he was in command. I knocked on his door and went in without waiting to be admitted.

"Rupert, could I speak with you or should I come back at a more convenient time?"

"There is no convenient time, so we might as well talk now. It's as good a time as any."

"How's that wrist of yours?" I took a seat in one of his client chairs facing him. "It doesn't look too bad."

"I got lucky. It isn't broken, just a bad sprain. And I got back my parking spot. Curious, but I'm glad to have it. Anyway what can I do for you?"

"While I was in Vancouver, we were served with an application from Jupiter to have our claim struck because it has multiple plaintiffs. It will be heard a week from Friday."

"Can we get ready that quickly?" He seemed somewhat bored and distracted.

"Sure we can, and I checked your calendar, you are available. The big news is that when I was in Vancouver doing the monthly briefing for the client, they raised the issue of settlement. They are nervous about the costs and how long everything is taking. They want us to pursue the possibility of settlement. You are far more skilled at this than me, so I told the client that I would leave that to you." Rupert straightened up in his chair and smiled.

"Do they know what they want to settle for?"

"Mr. Zimmer is the contact for any settlement discussions and he would like us to pursue the best deal you can make, but it must be cleared with him."

"What about the timing?"

"He would like to get this done before the court application because, if we lose, then we have no case at all. He would like you to concentrate on the settlement issue."

"This sounds like fun. I'll get right on it." Bingo!

"Williams Billings is the Jupiter lawyer for any settlement discussion."

"Anything else?"

As nonchalantly as I could, I handed a document to Rupert. "Yes, sign this document as the lawyer of record for Jupiter's application. I'll take care of filing it. This will be academic once you settle the case."

"Sure. Where do I sign?" I laid the paper down in front of him and he pulled out the Dupont fountain pen and scrawled his signature on the appointed line. "Keep in touch, Ben."

"See you later."

31

The next ten days were frantic. We worked on the case day and night. Margaret and Bill produced a terrific memorandum of law. Margaret found a decision from the State of Delaware that stood for the proposition that, if a party perpetrates a fraud arising out of multiple commercial contracts, then all the victims of the fraud could join in a single action because of the common intent. This was the missing piece. It was exactly our situation with Jupiter. I told Margaret to exclude this case from the brief of law and not refer to it in the written argument.

At the same time that we were preparing the legal argument, Rupert was meeting with the Jupiter lawyers to settle the case. He had an offer which amounted to both sides walking away from the litigation and paying their own costs, with a hollow assurance by the franchisor that there would be no recrimination to any franchisee who participated in the litigation. He included the provision that, in the future, there would be a franchisee representative on the audit committee to consider a new formula for the apportionment of expenses amongst the franchisees. Rupert spent most of the week negotiating this settlement knowing it was still subject to the client's approval. As far as I was concerned, it was no more than capitulation cloaked in legal jargon. I stopped by his office.

"Hi Rupert, how is the settlement discussion coming?"

"I've been calling Mr. Zimmer but he hasn't been returning my calls. We have a settlement offer which we should grab and run with but I need his final approval to make the deal."

"Could you tell me about the offer?" I asked in a respectful tone.

Rupert went into considerable detail explaining the terms of the offer with a blow-by-blow description of all the time he had spent getting Jupiter's counsel into this position. Rupert was trying to convince me as if I were the client. The only difference was that I could see through the fancy terminology. He had gotten nothing. After a half-hour discussion, I told him that I would pass this information on to Mr. Zimmer and have him return his call. Almost as an afterthought, I reminded Rupert about the motion coming up in two days in case there was no settlement.

"I haven't even started to prepare. There's no chance I can be ready on such short notice."

"Well let's hope it settles because you have to be ready. You signed the document as counsel of record for the motion. It's marked in your calendar and we didn't apply for an adjournment when the dates were given to us. We've got no choice but to go forward."

"Is there a brief of law prepared? Has anyone drafted a written argument?" I knew I had gotten Rupert's attention because he didn't bother picking up his ringing phone.

"We should have something by the end of the day, but it is incomplete. It should be enough though to give you the basics for our argument. Anyway, don't worry, the case will probably settle. Let's call Mr. Zimmer right now and you can explain the offer. I certainly couldn't do it better than you can." I asked Rupert's secretary to call the client.

"Jupiter, the greatest tires on earth comes from Jupiter."

"Mr. Zimmer please. Tell him MacIntosh and Stein are calling."

"Hold the line please, I'll see if his spaceship has landed."

"Hello, Mr. Stein. Hello Mr. MacIntosh. I hope you're calling with good news. I got off my spaceship just to talk to you."

Sometimes I think they take this Jupiter thing too far. But he's the client and, if they want to play *Star Wars*, who am I to tell them otherwise? He sells a lot of tires and pays all his legal bills. I guess if he wants to come to my office on the space shuttle that's okay with me.

"Mr. Zimmer, this is Rupert MacIntosh." Rupert had taken the lead in the call. "We have been working very hard on an offer from Jupiter to settle your case and I think we have something worth talking about." Rupert went on for ten minutes without interruption explaining the settlement offer and its merits. He talked about how difficult the Jupiter lawyers were and how he had kept pushing to get the best possible outcome. He highlighted the risks of going ahead with the litigation and emphasized that he had managed to obtain a concession of having a franchisee representative on the audit committee to insure that expenses were properly allocated. This was used-car salesmanship at its best. It was fascinating to listen to Rupert's pitch knowing that he was not even prepared for court if the case went ahead.

Mr. Zimmer could have won an Academy Award for his role as the indecisive client. They engaged in a back and forth debate for about forty-five minutes, all billable time. Mr. Zimmer was noncommittal and did not give Rupert cause for optimism or pessimism as to whether he would accept the offer. Rupert became increasingly agitated. The clock was winding down. It was less than forty-eight hours to the court date. Finally, he used the ultimate weapon. He pulled the big arrow out of his quiver and aimed it right at the client's wallet. It had never failed to work in all of Rupert's years as a lawyer.

"Mr. Zimmer, we must decide by the end of the day. If we don't make this settlement the other side will withdraw its offer and we will lose the opportunity to settle on such favorable terms. The time for talking is over. It's time to decide. Do we settle or go forward with the uncertainty of the litigation? There are significant legal fees ahead for you if we go forward."

There it was, the legal fee arrow. That strategy might have worked with some bureaucrat from an insurance company or a banker petrified of losing a case and the impact on his career. It was not going to scare Abe Zimmer. In fact, I thought I heard a chuckle over the phone when Rupert spoke about the fees.

"Mr. MacIntosh, thank you for your efforts. I would like to think about it for the rest of the day. This is a very important decision to our franchise group and I must make a few calls before anything is decided. I presume you are prepared for our court date in any event, so waiting the day should not effect you."

"Yes, of course, we are prepared although we have a few more details to sort out. I look forward to hearing from you later today. It's time to settle and, if you want me to participate in any of your calls, I would be happy to help in any way I can."

"Thanks, but I understand the offer well enough to explain it. I will call you or Ben by the end of the day. I am confident that we will come to the right decision. Good-bye."

Mr. Zimmer had followed the script to the tee. He was noncommittal and kept Rupert believing that he was about to dodge yet another bullet in his overrated career. Rupert was confident.

"Ben, they'll take the deal. I haven't met a client yet who can withstand the final hours of pressure where there are big fees looming on the horizon. It works every time."

"I'm not so sure, Rupert. Perhaps you should look at the brief just to be on the safe side. You've only got today and tomorrow to prepare if they don't settle."

"We'll hear by five and, if they don't settle, I can take the work home tonight. My instincts tell me it will settle. You remember this conversation. This is a lesson in your professional development."

"Look, I don't have your experience with clients but it did not sound to me that Mr. Zimmer was eager for our deal. They don't really get anything out of that settlement."

"Would you care to make a wager that they take the deal? It's not right to take money from an associate of the firm but if you're so sure . . . I'll accept your wager."

"How much would you care to bet?"

"I don't want to make this too onerous on a young associate. But, it should be enough to keep both of us interested, you decide."

"Let's say, if I win, we switch parking spots for four months and, if you win, I'll buy dinner for eight at a restaurant of your choice."

"It's a bet." We shook hands and nodded as a form of confirmation.

By the time I walked back to my office there was a message from Abe Zimmer. I returned the call immediately. I congratulated Mr. Zimmer on his Oscar-winning performance. He wanted to know what was next and we arranged that he would not call Rupert by five and that I would coincidentally be in Rupert's office at that time and call him. We would make Rupert sweat it out to the last moment. I reassured him that we would be ready to go to court and we were confident we'd defeat Jupiter's motion.

I was busy for the rest of the day going over our argument and studying the Delaware case to the point that I had memorized the court's reasoning. Rupert was calling me every hour asking if I'd heard from Abe and then he started calling me on the half-hour asking why Abe had not called. He was so self-absorbed that it never dawned on him a client would act contrary to his advice. He was so smart and he had so much invaluable experience that anyone with half a brain would do what he told them to. But, Rupert had no idea. He kept telling me that Abe was going to take the deal and there was no need to prepare the court motion. It would be a waste of his valuable time. I kept telling him that he should not delay the preparation until the last day. But, by 3:00 P.M., I sensed his level of confidence was flagging even though he would never admit that to me. With our wager on the line and the weather getting colder every day, he could not admit that he had read the situation wrong and would have to endure an outside parking spot for the duration of a Winnipeg winter.

"Ben, its four o'clock, why hasn't that son-of-a-bitch client of yours called us with instructions to settle?"

"I don't know why he hasn't called and, by the way, Rupert, the court considers the Jupiter franchisees as your son-of-a-bitch client."

"Maybe you should call him and make sure he wasn't trying to reach me."

"Look, I'm sure you're right. The case will settle and if we don't hear from him I'll come by just around five and we can call him together."

"Good idea. If we call him together he won't think that I am too anxious. By the way, when you come, bring the briefing notes with you so I can take a look at them just in case we can't reach him. I'll need to do some work tonight."

At precisely 5:00 P.M., I knocked on Rupert's door and found him sitting behind his desk looking at the phone as if he were willing it to ring. He tried to make light of it and insisted that I call Mr. Zimmer right away because he wanted to make reservations for that dinner I was going to pay for. I fumbled around with the file pretending to look for Mr. Zimmer's phone number even though I had his number memorized. I knew that any kind of delay would drive Rupert further into a cold sweat. Indoor parking for the duration of a prairie winter; it gave me a toasty feeling all over.

We called Mr. Zimmer who explained that, after considering all the options with the group, they had decided not to take the settlement, principally because they had so much confidence in Rupert's preparation and ability as a lawyer. Rupert was completely shaken. Mr. Zimmer told us that he looked forward to seeing Rupert perform in court and wished us luck, in Polish. He also mentioned that the press had called and they would be attending the hearing.

By the time Rupert hung up he might as well have been in mourning at his own funeral. He knew nothing about Jupiter's application and he was the lawyer of record. I assured him that I would help in any way I could and left him with documents six inches thick, the correspondence file and a legal brief of twenty-two cases. I told him that once he went over all the material, I would come back to discuss it. Then I got out of his office before he could say another word. This had been a very good day at the office. I drove out of the lot that evening admiring my new parking spot. Rupert's car was still snugly nestled indoors when I left.

I got home and called Sarah. We talked for over an hour. I told her some of what had happened that day but left out the incriminating details. I proposed that, if I won the court motion, we'd find a suitably luxurious hotel somewhere and go off for a celebratory weekend. She was never the voice of fiscal restraint and immediately decided on San Francisco for our weekend getaway. The combination of my commitment to this case and my anticipation of a weekend with Sarah was the overwhelming inspiration for my upcoming day in court. If things went as planned over the next thirty-six hours, I would have retribution against a partner who thought he could outsmart a Stein, I would have advanced my career in the law and gotten laid all from one single motion. I have come to love the law.

I was late for work the next morning because I stayed home to watch the morning news. Also, I had stopped for a cappuccino. When I finally arrived, my new indoor parking spot was empty waiting for me. No more plugging the car in to keep the engine block from freezing and no more waiting for the defrost to clear the windshield. I noticed Rupert's car had two inches of snow on it which could only mean one thing, he had an early start.

There were five messages from Rupert on my answering machine, all from that morning, each one sounding increasingly agitated. When I went to see him I found him sitting at his conference table which was covered with papers and the briefing binder. I stayed with him most of the morning going over the brief and explaining our legal position, except, I forgot to mention that one case.

Rupert did not have a good day. He wanted me to take on part of the oral argument. He told me that since it was really my file I should not be left out in the cold. I reminded him that I was not left out in the cold because I had a new indoor parking spot. He did not find my little reminder amusing. But, Rupert insisted. We agreed that I would present part of the argument when the right moment arose, something we didn't need to decide that moment. Rupert was sure that he had found the way out by having me respond to those judge's questions which were sure to embarrass and it would be witnessed by the client and the entire national business press.

I left the office around six. Rupert was still in his office and, by then, his car was completely covered with snow. I had to turn down the heat in mine because it was a touch too warm. When I got home, there was a message from Sarah. She had made hotel reservations in San Francisco and all that was left for me to do was to win the case. If I flew out tomorrow night, we could both be at the hotel by ten. Assuming I won the motion.

32

I couldn't get to sleep that night. After all, this was my first major court appearance. My career could be determined by the outcome of this application, not to mention the prospect of renewed celibacy. This was the meaning of real pressure. I got up too early, paced around my penthouse suite and looked for any divergence to pass the time. I didn't want to go into work too early. I had completed the word jumble in an old newspaper and was working on the chess quiz when the telephone rang. Who could be calling me at 5:25?

"Hello."

"Ben, it's Gerry, what are you doing answering the phone after only two rings at this hour?"

"What am I doing? Why are you calling me at five twenty-five in the morning?"

"I'm in Hawaii and it's only two twenty-five. I just got back to the hotel and decided to call you before you run off to work."

"I'm not running anywhere at this hour. What couldn't wait?"

"I closed a deal with some Sri Lankan government officials to supply them with two hundred and fifty thousand pounds of used computer parts, delivery starting May first. I'm going to make twelve dollars U.S. a pound profit. It's the deal I've been dreaming about ever since I went into the computer junk business."

"That's terrific. Where is Sri Lanka and where are you going to find two hundred and fifty thousand pounds of computer parts? It sounds like a lot of used computers."

"That's where you come in. I want to set up franchise depots in the four largest cities in Canada. I want you to draft the franchise agreement. You know all about franchising, so you can structure the network."

"I'd love to help you, Gerry. Call me when you get back to town and we'll get together."

"Look, I don't want to deal with your fancy law firm. You and I will do it on the side and I will pay you cash."

"We can talk about that when you get back but I don't think I can do it outside of the firm. I'll think about it."

"Okay. Go back to sleep. But you have to admit that a new client is worth waking up for."

"I wasn't sleeping. I have an important case today and I was up anyway."

"I guess that means you didn't get laid last night. For me the night is still young."

"No, I didn't, but if I win today, I'll get lucky tonight."

"It sounds perfect. The client pays you to screw the other side and, if you win, then you get screwed. Best of luck in both screwings."

If there had been any chance of getting back to sleep before the phone rang, that chance was now gone. Why should I give Gerry's work to the Lord? He was my friend and I'd do the work. I could hire my own word processing. Anyway, I had plenty of time to work it out. Right now I had to stay focused on the court application. I took a shower, put on the blue suit with one of my dad's ties and I went to work. As I was parking in my heated indoor spot, I noticed that Rupert's car was already there.

I found Rupert in the main boardroom with binders of material covering the entire surface of the table. He looked somewhat awkward flipping pages with his left hand as his right wrist was still in a sling from his fall on the ice. He was not in an engaging mood and was abrupt with me. He pointed out that he had been there since four and it was all because of my stubborn Polack client who could not see a deal staring him in the face. It was curious that, as the case had gotten more difficult, it was my client but when he had filed the case and gotten press coverage he was lead counsel. I reminded him that he was counsel of record. I insisted that the case could still settle on the courthouse steps. The architecture of the courthouse entrance often makes the risks inherent in litigation more real. But, I knew that in this case the chances of settlement were nothing more than Rupert's desperate hope. We arranged to go over to the courthouse together and I said I would help him pack up the binders.

Although it was a chambers motion, we were on the trial list to insure that a judge would be available. There was an unusually large number of people standing outside our assigned court room waiting for the clerk to open the doors. Mr. Zimmer and four members of the franchisee group were standing in a corner. They made a point of making eye contact with Rupert and gave him a nod of assurance. Rupert looked almost pleadingly at them, hoping they would reconsider and take the settlement, but he got no such indication in response. Two business reporters from the national press approached Rupert and asked if they could have an interview when the application was finished. He could never turn down the chance of seeing his name in print and he agreed. Then a woman from the Federal Competition Tribunal introduced herself to us and commented on how interesting these franchise issues had become. The small talk was making me anxious so I walked away from the crowd. A few minutes later the doors were unlocked and we all went in single file.

At precisely 10:00 A.M., the court clerk took her seat and the judge entered through the side-paneled door. Everyone stood, the judge nodded in recognition and we sat down in unison as if we were members of an orchestra taking our cue from the conductor. There were brief introductions of counsel and some preliminary matters which I did not pay any attention to. We were ready to proceed.

Mr. Billings went first since it was Jupiter's application. He took up the entire morning meticulously constructing his argument by first laying a solid foundation of law and then applying it to the facts at hand. He gave us a history lesson on privity of contract and how different contracting parties were not normally allowed to join together into a single action as a matter of fairness. He argued that it was unjust for Jupiter to be required to defend itself against multiple and different franchise agreements as, in effect, they would be defending hundreds of separate cases at the same time. From an observer's standpoint, Mr. Billings did a masterful job and looked like a winner. The judge asked a few questions but was not unduly skeptical or intrusive. We could not help but feel a certain sense of concern for the outcome. Billings sounded persuasive and what he said fit together like pieces of a puzzle. No one said a word to us as we left the courtroom for the noon break. I kept reminding myself that it wasn't over.

Court resumed at two. Rupert handed up the judge our written brief with the supporting cases. The essence of his submission was that it was too expensive and time-consuming to expect one franchisee to handle litigation of this magnitude. In effect, Jupiter would be litigation proof because no single franchisee could afford to take on such a case.

"Mr. MacIntosh," the judge interrupted, "are you advocating a legal principle based on how much money a litigant is willing to invest in a lawsuit? Is that a legal principle we should enshrine into contract law?"

"My Lord, if you don't have access to the courts then you have insulated companies like Jupiter because of the size of their bank accounts."

"Mr. MacIntosh, what would be your position if the situation was reversed? What if the franchisees were enormously wealthy and not the franchisor? Would you be taking the contrary position? What if a franchisee won the lottery and could afford to pay for the litigation? Are we to base privity of contract on buying lottery tickets? I suggest that you respond to this court's concern."

This exchange between Rupert and the judge left a deafening silence in the courtroom. The reports were frantically taking notes and there was an undercurrent of whispering. The case for the franchisees was not going well and all eyes were fixed on the back of Rupert's neck. He could feel their penetrating gaze and beads of perspiration formed in the back of his neck. The judge announced the twenty-minute afternoon break to give us a chance to regroup and consider our position.

Rupert was uncharacteristically shaken by the judge's pointed questions and he nursed his wrist, which seemed to be throbbing. He was grateful when I suggested that I respond to the judge's remarks. He had exhausted the contents of the written submission and had nothing more to contribute. In fact, I suspected he wanted me to address the court so he could keep his name out of the paper as being identified as the unresponsive counsel. I had a few words of assurance for Mr. Zimmer as I walked back into the courtroom and kept thinking that, if I could succeed in the next forty-five minutes, my professional life could change forever and I would be on a plane to San Francisco for a weekend with Sarah.

When court resumed, I introduced myself to the judge and handed him the Delaware case. Both Rupert and Mr. Billings were caught by surprise because it was not in the brief. Both did their best to conceal their emotions. I methodically took the judge through the reasoning of the decision and demonstrated that Billing's impenetrable wall of logic had a faulty foundation. I was so focused that I didn't even have to refer to Margaret and Bill's briefing notes.

I was on a roll. "My Lord, this is not simply a privity of contract issue, as Mr. Billings would have you believe. Jupiter systematically and routinely engaged in the same fraudulent scheme of billing hundreds of its franchisees for unsupportable expenses. In effect, Jupiter treated all the franchisees as one. The common fraud by Jupiter justifies a common response, namely one cause of action."

"Are you telling me that if Jupiter can treat all the franchisees in a common fashion then the franchisees can respond in kind?" I had gotten the judge's attention.

"Yes, my Lord, that is exactly our point." My simple proposition resonated in the courtroom. Common sense has a compelling way of being persuasive. I could sense a palpable change in sentiment from the judge. Rupert's submission was long forgotten even though he had only finished it some forty-five minutes earlier. The judge challenged Mr. Billings to respond to our argument but Billing's wall of logical reasoning was crumbling like the walls of Jericho.

By four o'clock all the submissions were completed and the judge told us that we would resume in fifteen minutes at which time the court would render an oral decision. As we waited and speculated on what a quick decision could mean, there were as many opinions as people willing to speculate. I was very nervous and avoided everyone. I spent my time pacing the hallway by myself but could not help noticing Rupert's dejected appearance. He had been shaken by a first-year associate who had made him look ineffectual in the presence of a packed courtroom and the national press.

The fifteen-minute adjournment stretched into forty-five minutes. Perhaps the judge had a word with his counterparts and they had brought him back to Billing's way of thinking. Courts show a certain deference to seniority in the profession and how could a respected lawyer like Billings with over thirty years of experience lose to a first-year associate? Billings gets the sympathy vote of the court, no doubt about it.

At 4:45, the clerk notified us that court was to resume. We returned to our seats in nervous anticipation of the ruling. I was told by one of the reporters that a straw poll had been taken among the observers and Jupiter was the odds on favorite, although I had the sentimental vote. The courtroom was dead silent. The judge entered the court, sat down and immediately started to read his decision. He methodically reviewed all the case law and quoted from the relevant passages but gave no hint as to the result. He wanted it on record that he had considered all aspects of the law in coming to his decision. No judge wants to be overturned on appeal for not considering the relevant law. Then he came to the point.

"Mr. Billings' able argument is persuasive and thorough. It is based on accepted legal principles going back well over a hundred years. But these principles do not stand in isolation of common sense and fairness. Jupiter, if proven liable, constructed a scheme of defrauding all franchisees in a like manner. The franchisees should be entitled to an appropriate response. In this case that means joining together to assert the common claim. The motion by Jupiter is denied and the franchisees can go forward with their lawsuit, costs to the respondent. Court is adjourned."

For a brief moment, the courtroom was dead silent. Not a sound or a movement. It was as if everyone were holding their breath and absorbing the judge's words to make sure they had understood correctly. Spontaneously, there was an eruption of commotion. As it turned out, Mr. Zimmer had called my mother the night before and she was there to catch another one of my Kodak moments. At least she hadn't invited the out-of-town relatives. The blinding light of the disposable flash left spots in my eyes which made it almost impossible to identify who was congratulating me. Mr. Zimmer was first to extend his hand in congratulations. The press crowded around me, asking about the next step in the litigation and how this ruling would affect our strategy. Amidst all the commotion, no one paid any attention to Rupert as he quietly packed up his briefcase and left by the side entrance. Everyone could see that I had taken control of the case at his expense.

I was still reeling in shock but, as I was leaving the courthouse, I found a pay phone in the lobby and stopped to call Sarah. With victory in hand, I told Sarah the good news and confirmed our rendezvous that night in San Francisco. This would be the weekend that would finally erase any lingering feelings for Julia.

33

It was a perfect weekend in San Francisco. The warmth of the California sunshine was a welcome relief from the prairie winter. Shopping on Union Square, lunch at Fisherman's Wharf and multiple Irish coffees at the Buena Vista all contributed to a perfect weekend. The hotel was terrific and the bill was enormous, even without the exchange rate. I learned quite a bit about Sarah from our few days together. She was not shy about anything, including spending. But it was worth every penny.

During our most intimate moments we talked about the future. It was obvious to both of us this was more than a weekend fling. We talked about how I could arrange my work to be in Vancouver more often and about her coming to Winnipeg on the pretense of visiting her family. But these were only temporary measures. The reality was that long-distance relationships didn't last. One of us would have to move. Long-distance lovers only benefit the phone company and the airlines.

By the time I got home Sunday night, I was emotionally and physically drained from the constant high of euphoria. I felt both exhilarated and exhausted at the same time. I set a new indoor record because there were seven messages on my answering machine. I was too tired to listen to them all and decided they could wait until morning. When I finally got to them they were not as interesting as I had speculated the night before. The first three messages were from my mother asking me to come to a celebration dinner. She read me the whole article in the Saturday *Globe* paper about my stunning victory which required three messages to get through. The newspaper referred to me as an emerging franchise specialist. Then there was a message from David Black congratulating me on my victory and asking me to drop by his office on Monday morning. The fifth message was from Gerry about his Sri Lankan deal. The last two messages were from the cable company about renewing my service.

When I got to the office Monday morning, I noticed that the lawyers treated me differently. The partners, who normally didn't give me the time of day, made a point of acknowledging my presence. I was more than just an associate who had billed all those hours. I was a two-window associate. My first priority, however, was to speak with Rupert. He had left me a message on my office line to see him when I got in. I knew he was going to blame me for his poor showing and, one way or another, I had to deal with the issue. I was confident, having won the court motion, and felt he had gotten what he deserved. As I knocked on his door and entered his office. I sensed right away that this conversation would be blunt.

"Hello, Rupert."

"Why the hell didn't you tell me about that Delaware case? It would have changed my whole argument." He stood up from behind his desk.

"By the time you decided to prepare for the case there wasn't time to brief you on everything. So, I left it out of your briefing notes and I prepared it on the off chance it might be relevant." I looked him straight in the eye so he would know I was not about to back down.

"Bullshit. You kept the best argument for yourself and in the process you made me look like a fool. Is that what you call on the off chance?" He spoke in a tone of controlled rage.

"Rupert, I read your file memos setting me up as the scapegoat if we got a bad result. All you wanted was the publicity and you planned to hold me responsible if we had a loser. You were outplayed at your own game. The big surprise for you is that you're not as smart as you think and a first-year associate could see through your plan." I didn't take my eyes off him.

"Except there is one thing you forgot. I am the senior partner and you work for me. So don't think you can play me like that stupid Polack client of yours and get away with it."

"I've already gotten away with it. I bill more hours than you do, I brought the file into the office, I won the motion and I got your indoor parking spot. I don't depend on you for work, so what can you do to me?" I got up to leave. "Come and see me if you need some work. That is, if your brother won't help you. I don't think you'll be getting more calls from Mr. Zimmer about settling."

I knew a serving of sibling rivalry would drive him to the brink and I left his office before he had a chance to throw me out. Our conversation had set my fate in stone. My days in the Winnipeg office were numbered. Even with my own clients, and even if I could bill a million hours at full rate, Rupert would get rid of me. Time was on his side. I needed to talk to David Black before Rupert put out his own unique version of events.

My conversation with David was far more amicable. We discussed how I would manage the Jupiter case going forward. We talked about forming a franchise practise group. I told him that I wanted to continue working with Margaret and Bill if they were so inclined. We got along quite well and there was enough work to keep all three of us busy. David was willing to help in any way he could. He realized that Rupert had fallen short of the mark and did not even bring up his name or his future participation. His silence about Rupert spoke volumes. It was time to get down to the real reason for my visit.

"By the way, David, there is another matter I want to talk to you about. But you must keep this in the strictest confidence. No one is to know what I am about to tell you."

"Of course. How can I help?"

"I may want a transfer to Vancouver. I've been seeing this woman there and it is getting more serious than I expected. If this continues, one of us will have to move and the logical choice is me. I'd like to stay at Lord's but it would mean a transfer. I'm not ready to move but it may become an issue." I spoke quietly to make sure no one could overhear me.

"Congratulations. Besides all those billable hours you've managed to find time for a social life. And I was worried that you didn't have a life outside the office." He reached out and shook my hand. "I don't think we've ever had an associate transfer but that doesn't mean it couldn't happen. It would take some planning because there would have to be an opening in the Vancouver office and there may be other candidates."

"If I can keep myself and two associates busy with this franchising work then I would not be a burden and we would not need an opening. In fact, I could help the Vancouver office generate work spun off from my franchising clients. Of course, if I don't get any more franchising cases then I would need to fill an opening. Anyway, this is premature but I will keep you up to date."

"I won't mention it to anyone unless you tell me otherwise."

The next item on my morning agenda was to call Gerry about his Sri Lankan business. I had to find out where Sri Lanka was. We arranged to meet that night at the ICB where we could talk without being disturbed. We agreed that, until I decide if I was going to do the work through the firm, he better not come to my office.

Sarah called me at noon. I told her about my conversation with David Black and how I had raised the issue of a transfer to Vancouver. The reality of our relationship was sinking in for both of us and we were both more cautious than when we had discussed this lying in bed at the hotel in San Francisco. If I was going to move, it meant that we were serious. I wasn't going to move to Vancouver and not live with her. Even though I was approaching forty, these decisions seemed too grown up for me. I was learning that I could not avoid growing up, sooner or later. Although, later was coming sooner than I had expected.

34

By the first week of December, winter had a firm grip on the prairies. I was lobbying for increased sulfur emissions to accelerate global warming. I could risk a smaller polar ice cap in return for a stand of palm trees at Potage and Main. It was just my luck that a platoon of environmentalists has polluted the Manitoba civil service in defense of clean air. How clean does the air really have to be? In retaliation, I booked a winter holiday with Sarah to my people's traditional homeland, Miami. The venue was Sarah's suggestion and she booked the hotel. Warm Florida sunshine, Joe's Stone Crabs and a week with Sarah was the perfect three-part formula to cure me of the winter doldrums.

December 1 traditionally marks the start of the Christmas social season. Christmas has evolved into a multi-cultural social event highlighted by inventory reduction sales. We are reminded of the religious aspect of the holiday only by bad radio. It's hard to consider this a holy time of year while listening to Bob Dylan's rendition of Silent Night. Anyway, it's the time of year when we promise to see long-lost friends before the Christmas break. Some of those promises are kept and the rest go into the trash heap of good intentions. I have observed that those who make the effort to get together before the holidays are going on a tropical vacation over the break. Seasonal get-togethers afford these travelers the opportunity to tell those less fortunate about their coming vacation. By doing so, they plant the seeds of envy which are later harvested when they are seen wearing white to show off their golden tan.

It had been months since I had dinner with my friends. I called David Kaplan who in turn called Gerry, Paul and Murray to make the arrangements. David is such an engaging sort that when he calls no one ever turns him down, regardless of any prior commitment. Even Paul's wife, who must give the nod before Paul is let out, would never refuse a request from David.

As is our tradition, we booked the round table at the Old Bailey restaurant. I am never more at ease then when I'm sitting at that table with my four friends. We never seem to do this enough and there is always so much catching up that the evening ends too early no matter what time we leave the restaurant. As an only child, my friends take the place of siblings. Our only enforceable dinner rule is that the topic of children is discussed only in exceptional circumstances. They are all brilliant, beautiful and mature beyond their years. Thus, there is nothing more to say on that topic.

Murray Wall told us that he had expanded his Free Willie clinics to a pod of five. He now had offices in Winnipeg, Regina, Saskatoon, Brandon and Thunder Bay. Judging from his success, there is no imminent threat of a population explosion on the prairies. Murray was considered a terrorist by the condom industry.

David Kaplan continued to be the most even-tempered and consistent one of all of us. He told us about running out of gas one night and being picked up on Corydon Avenue by his Grade 4 Hebrew School teacher who insisted that they speak only Hebrew while in his car. The only Hebrew phrase David could remember after seven years of Hebrew school was I have to go to the bathroom. This prompted his former teacher to speed to the nearest gas station thinking David had to relieve himself. On the way, they were stopped for speeding by an unsympathetic traffic cop. The Hebrew teacher tried to explain that the only reason he was speeding was because David had to relieve himself. David repeated his plight in Hebrew which thoroughly confused the police officer to the point of where he let them off with a warning.

Paul's latest venture was opening a singing academy for recent immigrants so they could learn indigenous Canadian songs. He had read that singing helps people lose their accents and it had the added benefit of helping them adapt to their new country. He told us the songbook included Red River Valley, the Wreck of the Edmund Fitzgerald and American Woman. So far he had five Pakistani cab drivers, two Vietnamese cooks and a Chilean mechanic signed up but he was hopeful business would pick up. He was selling prepaid lessons as stocking stuffers. He wanted to talk to me about selling franchises. No doubt about it, a marketing genius.

Gerry told us about his new deal and drinking coconut whiskey with Sri Lankans in order to get their order for used computer parts.

These Sri Lankans evidently couldn't hold their coconuts. Gerry glued lead weights to the bottoms of all his used equipment before it was weighed and, in spite of the fact that micro chips continue to get smaller, Gerry's computers continued to get heavier. He justified this increase in weight by the increasing density of silicon. He explained that if you give the freighter's shipping manager two bottles of Chivas Regal and a carton of Benson & Hedges you could have almost any weight you wanted. The trick was to be the last guy to show your appreciation before he certified the weight records because the Sri Lankans bribe the same shipper to underweigh the goods. Gerry was always last in line and came bearing gifts.

Anytime we got together, sooner or later the subject always turned to women. When David asked us if we were getting laid, Paul reminded him that he got married instead. We reminded Paul that he never got laid when he was single so, in his case, marriage hadn't changed anything. Out of a sense of loyal friendship we pointed this out. Inevitably, my friends wanted to know about my latest social adventures. Ever since Julia, my friends had a newfound respect for the allure of my academic accomplishments. Paul was first to broach the subject.

"Ben, have you been screwing anybody besides your clients?" Paul has a subtle way of cross-examination.

"Actually, I've been seeing this girl who lives in Vancouver. We've spent quite a bit of time together and we've done some traveling."

"Have you taken her to the monkey cages?" In some respects, Paul knew me too well.

"I didn't have to. When you go out with a girl long distance, you assume you're going to get lucky. But the hotel bills are a killer."

"How did you find someone who would put up with you?"

"We met at law school but I didn't spend any time with her. The first time we went out was in Vancouver."

"So what's she like? Is she missing any limbs?" Gerry inquired.

"No I didn't call 1-800 amputee for a date. In fact, all her limbs are quite attractive."

"What are you going to do about the Christmas thing. Have you told your parents?" This was always a big issue to Paul.

"Actually, she's Jewish. At least if I tell my parents, I won't have to buy my mother a portable defibrillator for Chanukah."

"What's her name?" David wanted details.

"You wouldn't know her. She's younger than we are. I would guess about thirty."

"Come on, what's her name? This is no time to hold back. It's the season for giving, so give us her name."

"Her name is Sarah Goldman." This seemed to get Murray's attention. He looked at me as if I had hooked the big one.

"I knew a Sarah Goldman who graduated from law school a couple of years ago. She has an older brother about forty who lives in Toronto. We were both chasing the same girl in university. He won. I married her."

"I don't know if she has a brother. She never talks about her family and I've never asked."

"You didn't know this is the Goldman that gives away money all over the place and in return they put his name on buildings? You never heard of the Goldman Wing of the Jewish Seniors Home, the Goldman Library in the Faculty of Judaic Studies and the Goldman Center for Acid Reflux?"

"I had no idea. She never mentioned her family. But, she acts as though she's rich. She's too comfortable in expensive places. I assumed that her family had money but not like Goldman money."

"Her dad is the largest manufacturer of buttons and velcro in North America. He's known as the Button King."

Her dad was the Button king. This was the man whose advice at my graduation was that my future lay ahead of me. I had never gone out with fastener royalty before. I wondered why she was going out with me, a commoner. I would never have dreamed that the daughter of the Button King would be going out with a first-generation commoner from White Russia whose father was in the plumbing supply business. My mother would be speechless, almost. I decided it was better not to tell her for fear it would prompt another newspaper announcement.

This news about Sarah dominated the conversation. I tried to change the topic but, when you're sleeping with a girl whose father has $100 million, it's hard to get people thinking about anything else. By the end of the evening, I was convinced that Sarah and I had no future. I was servicing a lonely rich girl until she met the heir of the zipper fortune or some other fastener. Now I understood why she never mentioned her family. I could never keep her in the lifestyle she was accustomed to. I'm not prejudiced against rich, beautiful women. But, a first-generation Stein living happily ever after with the heiress to the button fortune was just not going to happen. I might as well enjoy it while it lasts. Her dad was wrong. My future didn't lay ahead of me. It's on the way to being behind me. This time I'll be better prepared.

35

The last three weeks before Christmas break were hectic at a law firm with solicitors working day and night to close their deals before the holidays. There was a general push to start the new year with a clean slate. The litigators renewed their efforts to settle cases in spite of their unequivocal declarations six months previous that they would never settle. In fact, most litigators need to settle everything for fear of losing.

Jupiter had adopted a new strategy after it lost the court motion. Because Jupiter was now required to produce all relevant documents, one option was to disclose the bare minimum and fight it out with multiple motions. Alternatively, they could inundate us with documents so it would be difficult to find the documents that mattered. Jupiter opted for the latter strategy. They sent us ninety file boxes of documents with a forty-page list identifying these documents in the most imprecise and generic way. Somewhere in those boxes were the documents which would make our case. I just didn't know how to go about finding them.

I met with Bill and Margaret to discuss the document problem. We had become the franchise practice group even though we only had one case. We did have some experience cataloging thousands of documents when we were trying to quantify our claim but, this was more challenging because Jupiter was trying to bury the relevant documents among thousands of documents that had no relevance to proving liability. We called Seattle for some advice and assistance. It was obvious to me that we needed help or we would drown in irrelevant paper. We needed a plan to tackle the identification and cross-referencing of the documents and we wanted that plan in place before everyone went their separate way for the holidays.

I worked every day on the document project. I was determined not to be out-maneuvered by Billings' strategy. In addition, Rupert was just waiting in the wings, hoping I'd fail. That would be his proof that we were engaged in an ill-conceived case that should have settled on the terms he negotiated. Our success resisting the Jupiter motion raised our stature in the firm, but we had a long way to go before we could claim victory in the litigation. We were in the game but the result was far from certain.

I took three trips to Seattle in the three weeks leading up to Christmas to meet with the software people. Their company was the leading authority on the cataloging and retrieval of large volumes of data and our case was a high-profile test on the capability of their computer software. In fact, among lawyers, we were considered at the vanguard for this type of computer application. We were using the computer for litigation in ways that were unprecedented to the profession. We could bring the equivalent of ninety boxes of documents into the courtroom on two floppy disks. Also, we could find and retrieve documents based on a word association program. We could search for documents using key words or logical word associations and we were betting this would reveal the needle in the document haystack. There was no fallback position.

With the guidance from our Seattle friends, we settled on a plan. We copied every document into the computer and then categorized the documents in different ways to see if there was a common denominator to link it all together based on the overhead charges to the franchisees. The two Bobs were fully occupied cataloging documents so we hired an outside firm to get the job done. By the time the Christmas break came, the plan was being implemented with completion slated for the second week in January.

I spoke to Sarah almost every day during those three weeks leading up to our vacation but I did not stop in Vancouver on my way to the Seattle meetings. I could have done it but I told her that I was working under a very tight schedule. The real reason was to keep my distance in anticipation that she was going to dump me once she found someone more suitable. In other words, when she found someone as rich as she was. The irony was that the less available I became the more she pursued me and she called me more often than I called her. My instinct was to respond in kind, but I stopped myself. I was not prepared to go through the humiliation of being dumped again and having one of those "It's not you, It's me" conversations.

213

In spite of my caution, I did drop tidbits of information about my family, hoping she would respond in kind. I was cautiously looking for ways to bring us closer and I was curious as to how she would describe her father.

"I spent yesterday evening watching Monday Night Football with my dad," I told her. "We've been doing it for years." I thought this might prompt a comment about her relationship with her father. Sarah did not take the bait. "I often go over to my parents' for Sunday brunch because my dad's office is closed Sundays." I thought maybe she might respond with something about her father's work. Again, she did not take the bait. "The dry cleaner keeps breaking the buttons on my shirts and I can't be bothered looking for matching ones so I throw the shirts in my bottom drawer," I told her. Now if that didn't work, I didn't know what would. Again, no bites. Not even a nibble.

Not a nibble. This convinced me that she was not interested in me enough to know more about my family or tell me anything about her family. I kept hoping that I was wrong and that she was just being cautious. However, there was no basis for optimism. She was thoughtful, interested in my career and enthusiastic when we were together. We even talked about my moving to Vancouver. But, on anything that had to do with her family or my family, she was evasive, unresponsive and disinterested. This was strange to me. In my family, everyone made a point of knowing everything there was to know about everyone. There were no secrets although everything was told in the strictest of confidence. Whatever dark secrets lurked in the Goldman family were not getting out to the son of Stein from the plumbing supply business. I was frustrated I had made no progress in my social standing since I was sixteen trying to get a date for the end of year dance at Sir Edmund Hillary Secondary. In my neighborhood, everyone knew their station in life and it was based on their parents' bank balance.

Sarah and I flew to Miami on Christmas Eve. We met in the Dallas airport where we got a connecting flight to Miami. Christmas Eve is the best day to travel because all the Gentiles are already at their destinations and the planes are empty. Except if you were going to Miami from Dallas. As a matter of fact when the flight attendant on the Dallas/Miami leg of our trip asked Mr. Cohen to identify himself for his kosher meal, seven men raised their hands.

Sarah knew her way around the Miami airport and I was happy to follow her lead. She had the demeanor of a seasoned traveler and I took advantage of her experience. On Sarah's advice, we rented a car to go to the Fontainebleau Hotel. She told me that the airport rate for a rent-a-car was cheaper than renting the same car at the hotel. I had no idea but was willing to accept her direction. She drove to the hotel without any hesitation about where she was. We talked during the drive and she paid very little attention to the street names. Obviously, she had done this many times before. I had taken a map from the rent-a-car kiosk but she did not refer to it once. She got us to the hotel entrance without one wrong turn. The doorman of the hotel took our bags and we went to the front desk to check in.

"We have a reservation. The name is Stein, initial B, from Winnipeg, Canada or it might be under Goldman, initial S," I said.

"Yes, of course Mr. Stein. And Ms. Goldman it's so nice to see you again. I hope you had a pleasant trip. Would you like your regular room?"

"Yes, that would be fine. I presume we will get the usual rate?"

"Of course, and what time would you like us to book your morning spa treatment?"

"Ten should be fine," she said in a matter-of-fact way.

I couldn't believe what I had just witnessed. The hotel clerk treated me as if I were the invisible man once he recognized Sarah. He didn't even ask for my credit card imprint. I had ventured into a world that I was unfamiliar with and unprepared for. Perhaps I was just one of a series of guests who have accompanied Sarah Goldman to Miami? Since she was going to dump me anyway, I decided to find out more. When a relationship has no future there is no risk of failure.

As we stood at the counter waiting for our room key, I couldn't resist asking. "Sarah, how do they know you so well?"

"My family has been coming here for years. My parents keep a suite in this hotel."

"How do you get a permanent suite in a hotel?"

"My dad comes to Miami on business so much that he has some type of arrangement where they guarantee him the same suite every time he comes. It's very convenient. I always take the suite beside him so we can talk while we each sit on our own balcony."

"How often do you come here?"

"When I lived at home I would come once a month for at least four nights but, now that I'm in Vancouver, I don't get here as much. You'll see, it's a great hotel. The service is terrific and we'll have a great time. I'll be your tour guide for Miami. I must warn you, though. We'll have one interruption to our vacation tomorrow evening."

"And what will that be?" I had no idea what she was talking about, but I was worried.

"My parents are here and we're having dinner with them tomorrow night."

"Are you telling me that while we're together, your parents will be next door? They will see us in our bathrobes tomorrow morning sitting on the balcony looking out at the view?"

"That's not exactly right. There are solid partitions between the balconies so they can't see us, but we can talk. Don't look so shocked. I've already prepared them."

"You prepared them! What about preparing me?" Sarah laughed, took my hand in hers and assured me that it would all be fine. I found it all very confusing. Perhaps I was wrong about Sarah. After all, she did want me to meet her parents. Meeting the parents is crossing the great divide in a relationship.

Out of nowhere we were approached by the hotel manager who proceeded to gush all over Sarah. She knew him on a first-name basis. He told us that we should call him on his personal line, day or night, if there was anything we wanted. I was going to ask him for a Lake Winnipeg Goldeye as a midnight snack just to watch him go pale. I decided to let him off easy, at least for now. He escorted us to our suite where a bellman was already unpacking our bags and hanging our clothes. This was a world I had never experienced.

36

I didn't sleep at all that night . . . for a couple of reasons, and I was up early hoping to avoid a morning introduction to the Button King. I could not imagine sitting on the balcony drinking freshly squeezed Florida orange juice and having a casual conversation with Sarah's father after having slept with his daughter the night before. I told Sarah, who was still half asleep, that I was going down to exercise on the beach. My ETA back at the hotel would coincide with her spa appointment and thus, I would avoid the morning gathering of the Goldmans on adjacent balconies. In fact, exercise was the last activity I was likely to do on vacation or any other time for that matter. I decided long ago that exercise was the greatest waste of time for me. Actually, it was the second greatest waste of time. The greatest waste of time was talking about it afterward. What is there to talk about when you pedal a bicycle or run on a treadmill that doesn't go anywhere? Nothing could be more boring then having a conversation about the feeling of exhaustion.

There I was, at 7:30 in the morning on the ocean boardwalk in my fitness gear ready to face a two-hour workout. But I had forgotten to bring one thing, matches to light my Cohiba #2, product of the Dominican Republic. I could not believe that not one of those early morning joggers or muscle stretchers had matches on them. Finally, a gracious elderly Miami citizen who was sitting on a bench watching the joggers go by as she sucked on her morning Winston obliged me with a light. She offered me the book of matches, in fact, if I would answer two skill-testing questions. She wanted to know whether I was single and where I was staying. I answered her questions, returned her wink as I lit my cigar, and walked on, decked out in my red nylon shorts, a Lord t-shirt and sparkling white athletic shoes.

The boardwalk seemed to go on forever and I decided I'd walk in one direction for an hour, take a rest and then walk back for the second hour. That would give me just enough time to say good morning to Sarah before she went off to the spa. Normally, if I indulged in this kind of activity, I would walk in one direction for two hours and then take a cab back. But my exercise shorts didn't have pockets so I had not taken any money with me. I was actually happy to have this time to myself. It gave me the opportunity to think about my relationship with Sarah and what I would say when I met the royal family of buttons. I won't wear a jacket with a zipper.

I didn't have much time for introspection during my walk because I kept being interrupted. Every time I passed someone on the boardwalk, they would say good morning or something about it being another beautiful day. Perhaps it was my T-shirt that attracted these salutations. A shirt with bold lettering that said "LORD" could attract some attention among the elderly in Miami. After forty-five minutes of repeated good mornings to complete strangers, I began responding by nodding my head and smiling. This understated response did not interrupt my thoughts about Sarah and how I would deal with her parents. Perhaps I had been wrong about Sarah. Maybe I was more to her than a passing fling. She had to be serious or why would we be vacationing next door to her parents? I wanted to be more than casual fun.

I considered the impact of going out with a girl whose father was a zillionaire. How would that look? I know I shouldn't discriminate against the rich, it's not her fault. I decided that anyone who cared about such things would think the worst, regardless of the truth. Still, I wondered if anyone would believe that I didn't know Sarah was the heiress to the throne of the King of Buttons when I met her. For the better part of my university days, I had tried to separate myself from the Jewish community. Now, here I was in the epicenter, Miami. Right in the eye of the storm. In truth, I was enjoying every minute as I walked along the boardwalk smoking my Cohiba #2. If you must suffer from inner conflict then it might as well be in a suite at the Fontainbleau.

Sarah and I met for lunch by the pool and then spent the afternoon touring around South Beach and looking in stores that sold $8 T-shirts for $120 because they had the name of an Italian embossed on the front. Sarah bought a white-on-white one with her gold American Express. By 4:30, we were back at the hotel which gave us just enough time for you know what, a shower and a drive to the restaurant where we were meeting her parents. I could get accustomed to this if I had to.

218

For the Goldman family, dinner is always at six. No matter what the circumstances or the time zone, the Button King insists on going for dinner at six. And, like any royal family, the king picks the venue and cuisine. On this night, Mr. Goldman had picked *The Le Table*. In Miami this was considered authentically French, one of those restaurants where you get one meal for the price of two. The kind of place where you walk in hungry, pay $100 per person and leave a little less hungry. On the way home, you stop at Wolfe's Delicatessen for brisket sandwich and a real piece of chocolate cake.

We arrived at the restaurant at 6:06 P.M. and everyone was already there. The Goldmans always came on time.

"Dad, I would like you to meet Ben Stein," Sarah said as we approached the table.

Mr. Goldman did not get up but he stuck out his arm for me to shake. "Nice to meet you Ben. Please call me Abe. This is my wife, Adele."

Adele smiled. "It's wonderful to meet you, Ben. Sarah has told us all about you."

I wondered what Sarah meant by friend and what she had told them about me. I suddenly looked forward to tomorrow morning's walk when I could mull over all the possible explanations.

"This is Mr. and Mrs. Schwartz," Mr. Goldman said as we sat down. I thought it was odd that they had invited another couple to join us until I learned a little more about them. Manuel Schwartz was the largest shirt manufacturer in Brazil and Mr. Goldman supplied his factories with all the buttons. Every shirt that Manuel manufactured had eleven Goldman buttons on it. When Mr. Goldman took a break from talking about himself, Manuel explained that his late father had started the business soon after moving to South America just before the war. His father had sold all his assets in Germany, bought precious gems and swallowed them to smuggle his wealth out of the country. Manuel's wife, I noticed, was not as shy as her father-in-law about showing off the family jewels. She was dripping in diamonds and emeralds which were suitably accented by her ample cleavage.

The Goldmans were a sight to behold sitting at the corner table of the restaurant. Abe wore pastel head to toe, all five feet seven inches of him. He had on a pastel blue jacket with white pants and a contrasting pastel green shirt. It was quite a contrast against his dark tan and salt-and-pepper hair. Adele was the pastel female equivalent but she was decked out in a pastel pink shirt and white pants. They could have been the cover of a Miami senior's tourist magazine.

Just as I was about to say something clever, the maitre d' came over and greeted the Goldmans by name. "It's so nice to see you, Mr. Goldman," he gushed all over him. "We brought in the veal you like, Mr. Goldman, and your favorite bottle of wine is being decanted, Mr. Goldman. Roger, your regular waiter, will be with you in a moment, Mr. Goldman."

It was clear that Abe Goldman was putting on a show and loving every minute of it. He was P.T. Barnum directing the greatest show on earth and making it clear to all concerned that he was in charge. The conversation throughout dinner centered around Abe's business accomplishments and philanthropy. He and his wife had the act down pat. Adele would introduce the topic of conversation and then Abe would take over. He was the consummate salesman and yet he was a likable guy. He was well read despite his grade ten education and had a clarity of purpose tempered by nerves of steel. It was all quite entertaining, if you could tolerate the fact that he only talked about himself, peppering his conversation with a healthy dose of name dropping.

The dinner lasted the better part of two-and-a-half hours. I was a willing spectator, but by the end of the evening I had had enough. Every so often Sarah would squeeze my thigh under the table just to remind me of what was to come later. She seemed quite relaxed in these surroundings and it was obvious that she had considerable experience attending such dinners. She challenged her father on non-controversial issues, recounted harmonious stories about her various trips to Florida and was a charming addition to the conversation. I listened politely but had very little to contribute. It amazed me that people with money have so much confidence and socialize with such ease.

Abe decided when it was time to leave. As in most regal gatherings, no one got up to leave before the king but, when he rose, the evening was over. Without any warning, Abe stood up, thanked all of us for joining him and started for the door. Accordingly, we got up and followed close behind. I noticed that he did not even get a bill or give anyone a credit card. There had been nothing spontaneous about the evening, or about Abe Goldman for that matter. He planned every detail and considered every possible contingency. I hoped this trait was not hereditary.

Sarah and I said good night to everyone and as we were about to leave, Abe motioned for me to step aside and have a word with him. He leaned in close and spoke softly so no one else would hear.

"Ben, when you go for your walk tomorrow morning at seven-thirty and smoke your Cohiba #2, I'd like to join you."

"Of course. I would welcome your company," I said, flabbergasted.

"Good. I'll meet you in the lobby of the hotel. And Ben," he said with a riveting stare, "bring some matches or buy a lighter."

37

I wasn't getting much sleep on this vacation. Two nights before I hadn't slept thinking about Sarah's parents listening to us through our common wall and last night I hadn't slept for fear Abe Goldman was watching me. This was fast becoming the most exhausting vacation I'd ever taken. I didn't tell Sarah that her father had me followed. All she knew was that I was going for a walk with him in the morning and she considered that an engaging gesture on his part. In fact, I expected my morning constitutional with her father would be anything but an engaging gesture.

I was in the lobby at 7:10 and headed straight for the newspaper stand where I bought two boxes of wooden matches for the two Cohiba #2s which I purchased on the way home from dinner the night before. By 7:20, I had positioned myself in a strategic spot that provided an unimpeded view of everyone using the elevators. As I watched the guests getting on and off the elevator, a voice behind me broke my concentration.

"Good morning, Ben. You're right on time. I like that." There was Abe Goldman dressed in his perfectly pressed white athletic suit.

"Good morning, Mr. Goldman, I didn't see you come off the elevator. Have you been waiting long?" He extended his hand and we shook. He does the two handed grab to give the impression of sincerity.

"No, I just got here. I came down the private elevator in the back. Are you ready to go?"

As we walked out the back of the hotel to the boardwalk, I kept looking around to see if anyone was watching us. There were no obvious candidates except the middle-aged man wearing a Hawaiian shirt selling free-range eggs.

"You can stop looking around. There's no one following us."

"I have to admit, Mr. Goldman, the thought did cross my mind. Where were they hiding yesterday and how long was I being followed?"

"Please Ben, call me Abe. A good magician never reveals his secrets but I'll tell you this one time because I like you. It wasn't a they but a she and next time be careful who offers you a match."

"I would have never guessed."

"And she's much younger than she looked. You'd never recognize her without the make-up."

We started walking and, as I expected, Abe Goldman led the way. He set off in the same direction I had taken the day before and I didn't protest. I was sure Abe had decided which direction he would walk well before 7:30 that morning. This was not a spontaneous man, even for a morning walk in the Florida sunshine. But, I had done some planning myself. This time I brought cab fare.

"So tell me, Mr. Goldman, why did you have me followed? What could be so threatening that you would go to the trouble of having me followed?"

"Ben, call me Abe. Although Sarah is thirty years old, she is still my little girl and one day she will be very rich. Sarah thinks that she knows the ways of the world. But even though she has traveled a great deal she only knows a very small and exclusive slice of life. She doesn't fully understand what the wrong kind of man would do to get at her inheritance."

"Mr. Goldman, I don't think you give your daughter enough credit. She can size up people pretty well and I have no interest in her inheritance. I didn't even know she was rich. Anyway, is that what you thought, that I'm desperate for your button fortune?"

"I didn't know what to think. That's why I had you checked out. Try to see it from my perspective. I've worked a lifetime to insure the security of my children and their children. I won't take any chances on a guy who stayed in school too long." He glanced at me sideways as we walked. "By the way, why did you study animal husbandry?"

"You really did check everything. How did you find out about the animal husbandry?" He had caught me by surprise but I didn't change my pace.

"When you get your name on a university building it's not hard to accidentally find an academic record. So what is this animal husbandry?"

"I was looking for something different to study and I was interested in this girl studying agriculture so I figured, what the hell."

223

"You mean to tell me that you took a three-year degree because you wanted to get laid? Actually, I can understand that."

"Mr. Goldman, you didn't invite me for a walk to discuss my academic background. I don't care about your daughter's money and I don't care about your buttons. In fact, I can't, at the moment, think of anything more boring than buttons. All I want is a winter vacation with Sarah and I hope the weather doesn't turn. You can keep your money and use it to put your name on another building for all I care."

"Call me Abe," he said. "Look, don't get upset. How can you be angry so early in the morning on such a beautiful day." He raised both arms as if he were an evangelical messenger of wealth. "If I didn't think you were genuine I would never have invited you for this morning stroll. Ben, I like you, and Sarah would be lucky to have you. I know you come from a good family. I checked. Now, how about that cigar? Did you bring the matches this time?"

"Yes, I brought the matches and they're wooden," I said pulling out a box of matches and two Cohibas #2. "But can I trust you? Or is this just your way of putting me at ease so you can continue to have me followed?"

"To show my sincerity, I'm going to tell you a little secret that I wouldn't even want my family to know. I offer this as a gesture of good faith."

"Mr. Goldman, I thought a good magician never revealed his secrets." We both stopped walking and stood in the middle of the boardwalk lighting our cigars.

"Yes. But I have this feeling that we'll be seeing more of each other so we need to start over. You know Manuel Schwartz from last night? That was his out-of-town wife, if you know what I mean."

"But what about the jewels?"

"Those jewels on Mrs. Out-of-Town Schwartz were as real as her cleavage. Adele and Sarah don't have a clue. My wife would be disgusted if she knew that we were socializing with her type. But he's a customer. I sell him buttons and he pays my bills. I'm not in business to judge the moral character of my customers. All I do is supply buttons for his shirts. Anyway, I found her to be quite charming in spite of her excessive use of zippers as a fashion statement." He made a fatherly gesture of putting his arm around my shoulder. "By the way, Ben, call me Abe."

"This is not the kind of conversation I thought we would be having. I didn't think I'd enjoy our morning walk this much. The sunshine is beautiful." I was starting to feel at ease with him.

"Just one last thing, Ben. I trust we can keep this conversation between you and me. I wouldn't want my Sarah to think that I questioned her judgment about men. I don't think it would benefit either of us."

"Mr. Goldman, I understand."

"Now, Sarah tells me you're a franchise lawyer. I have this idea for franchising retail carts in shopping malls where I would sell buttons and fasteners. We could put a cart in every mall on this continent. If we're going to do business together, first, you'd better call me Abe."

There were six days remaining of our vacation. We took day trips, or to be more precise, shopping trips around South Florida. We went to Boca Raton and Palm Beach. I hate shopping. Worth Avenue was not worth it. To me, the only good mall is a closed mall and, in South Florida, malls never close. Sarah cut a path of destruction through these malls like a tornado through a trailer park. She had the definitive shopping bag collection to prove it. I resisted complaining about shopping, talking about our future or volunteering my impression of her family. I didn't want to risk ruining our vacation.

We had dinner with her parents twice more and, on both occasions, Mr. Goldman brought along customers. Staying in character, Mr. Goldman chose the restaurants and always made six o'clock reservations. The restaurant managers always gave him personal service and, even at Joe's Stone Crab, where they don't take reservations and there is a constant 45-minute wait, there was a table set aside for Abe Goldman. He told the same stories at all the dinners but we all pretended they were new because of the presence of the customers. I could have won an academy award for spontaneously laughing at his retread jokes. When Abe Goldman told a joke everyone laughed because he always picked up the tab. Whoever said money talks forgot to mention that it can also prompt a laugh.

On New Year's Eve, 1986, our vacation came to an end and it was time to go home. Just before checking out of the hotel we went to say good-bye to Sarah's parents and thank them for their hospitality. As we were about to leave, Mr. Goldman gave me a gift-wrapped

225

box. Sarah and Adele did not look surprised. They were obviously in on the conspiracy.

"Go ahead, Ben, open it, it won't bite you."

I tore open the wrapping and pulled out . . . a Rolex. One of those gold and stainless steel Oyster models with the blue face and bezel. I couldn't believe how excessive this was and I wasn't sure how to respond. Maybe it had been coated with some sort of drug to prevent erections. I wouldn't put it past him. Or maybe it had a built-in homing device so Mr. Goldman could keep track of me everywhere I went. That too was a possibility. Finally I wondered if maybe it was just a gift from a rich guy who overdoes everything. I chose door number three.

"How do you like it, Ben?"

"This is far too extravagant, Mr. Goldman. It is difficult for me to accept such an expensive gift." I couldn't keep my eyes off the watch.

"My parents wanted to get you something to remember this trip to Florida," Sarah said, putting her hand on top of mine. "Now you'll have no excuse for ever being late for dinner. There's no more five minutes of grace once you have a Rolex."

"Mr. and Mrs. Goldman, I will treasure this generous gift. Thank you."

"Call me Abe, Ben."

"Call me Adele."

Little did Sarah know that, between being followed by a private detective and meeting Manuel Schwartz's out-of-town cleavage, there was not much chance I would ever forget this vacation. The watch was Mr. Goldman's way of insuring our little understanding that I would never mention anything to Sarah. This Rolex Oyster, I knew, joined me to Abe Goldman at the wrist. Actually, I pictured Abe Goldman with a drawer full of Rolex watches which he gave away every time he had some indiscretion that he didn't want mentioned. I envisioned a group photo of everyone who had been given a Rolex by Abe Goldman. You know, the picture where everyone smiled at the camera with outstretched arms showing off their time pieces set to various time zones as an indication of Mr. Goldman's worldly indiscretions. That photograph would be a timeless treasure.

When I went to check out of the hotel, I was told by one of the gushing desk clerks that Mr. Goldman had taken care of the bill.

Now I understood why they hadn't taken my credit card imprint. I was angry. The watch was one thing but I didn't want him paying for my vacation. I was not going to be one of those people who come to depend on the largess from people like Abe Goldman to maintain a lifestyle which the Goldmans got them accustomed to. He was like a drug dealer who gave away the first ten hits in order to get you hooked. I told Sarah that I didn't want her father to pay our hotel bill. She thought I was overreacting and told me it was just his way of doing things. Her parents stayed at that hotel all the time and it would go on the bill which was paid at the office. I didn't want our week to end in a fight about money so I did not press the point. I went back upstairs and, again, thanked them for their generosity and said all those things you have to say.

That evening Sarah and I flew to Dallas/Forth Worth where she was connecting for a flight to Vancouver via Seattle and I was getting a flight to Winnipeg via Minneapolis. We had three hours together in the Dallas airport where we celebrated the New Year. We ate nachos and washed them down with two bottles of California sparkling wine. We could have taken a room for a few hours but nothing was available at the airport. We talked about my moving to Vancouver and how the trip had brought us closer. It all sounded so serious except for the fact that we were both drunk from the sparkling wine. The conversation finally collapsed into laughter and necking. It was New Year's Eve.

In spite of the time change, I still didn't get home until 6:00 A.M. By the time we landed in Winnipeg, it was −20 C. without the wind chill. I was as relieved to get into a warm taxi as the taxi driver was relieved to get the fare. Even with a five-dollar tip I could not seduce the driver to get out of the taxi to lift my luggage out of the trunk. He pressed the trunk release button from inside the glove box and wished me a Happy New Year. I paid him back in kind when I didn't close the trunk and he had to get out the taxi to close it.

I dragged my luggage up the three flights of stairs to my apartment, looking forward to a hot shower, an espresso and watching the Rose Bowl parade. The message light was flashing but I expected nothing less since I had been gone eight days. In fact, it would have been depressing if no one had called. There were nine messages. Not bad. That averaged out to better than one a day.

Message One: "This is Dana. You've had some calls and I told them that you'd be back right after the New Year. What should I do with the urgent messages? Let me know where to direct the calls."

Message Two: "Hey, Ben, it's Gerry. I'm here at the bar in the Acapulco Princess with three girls from Cleveland who insist that I take them all out tonight because they want to experience a foreigner. Could you drop what you're doing, amigo, and fly down here and help out a friend."

Message Three: "Hi, Ben, its Arlene. Rubin and I have broken up. It wasn't meant to be. I was wondering if you would come with me to an artist studio New Year's party. It would be great to see you. Give me a call."

Message Four: "Ben, it's Dad. I know you're getting home New Year's Day and I was wondering if you want to come over and watch the Rose Bowl game with me. Call me when you get in."

Message Five: "Ben, it's your mother. We haven't heard from you since you went to Florida and I read in the paper that a tourist in Palm Beach died from an overdose of bad caviar and heat exhaustion from wearing too much cashmere. Please call me so I'll know you're all right. By the way, are you coming over to watch football with Dad? I'm making your favorite brisket."

Message Six: "Ben, it's your mother. I can't remember if I told you, but when you come to watch the football game I'm going to make your favorite brisket. We'll expect you around three. Don't eat that rich Florida food. A tourist in Palm Beach died from eating fish eggs."

Message Seven: "Ben, this is Margaret at the office. We've been going through the documents from Jupiter and I think I may have found something but I cannot explain it. Call me when you get back. By the way, Happy New Year."

Message Eight: "Hi, stranger. I thought I would call to say hello from Chicago and wish you a Happy New Year. Actually, I'm in Hawaii but I'm going home tomorrow. I've been thinking of you. Call me in Chicago next week during the day and we'll catch up. Aloha."

At that point I stopped the message machine. I didn't know what to make of Julia's message and I replayed it six times. What was I supposed to do? Call her back. And what was I supposed to say if I did call? She left a ten-second message and all the old feelings had rushed back. But this time it was different. I was smarter, or at least, older. She was married and there was Sarah. Julia had probably left the same message for five other guys just to find out who still lusted after her. Likely they all called her back. She was a high-risk proposition. I didn't play the last message. I looked at my Rolex and it was 7:04. I called Sarah to make sure she got home all right and to reassure myself that she really existed. No one answered.

38

Although I hadn't slept for days, I kept to my New Year's Day tradition. I watched the Rose Bowl parade whose theme was Man and Religion. A fundamentalist Christian group had entered a float depicting Adam and Eve in the Garden of Eden. They used 2,000 fig leaves to cover Adam's private parts. This float was larger than life. The Alliance of California Reform Synagogues had a float of Moses rollerblading across the split Red Sea. They used white tulip petals for the whitecaps of the parted Red Sea. I've always been fascinated with the statistics about these floats. This float was 110 ft. long, the height of a four-story building, took ten months to build using ten zillion carnation petals individually pasted on by 225 illegal Mexican immigrants within the last forty-eight hours. And who counted all those petals?

I went to watch the Rose Bowl game with my dad. He had bought a big-screen TV on the Boxing Day sale from Maniac Manny's Electronic Warehouse. Maniac Manny is one of those discount retailers who screams into the camera and offers you his sister and no down payment to buy a big-screen television within ninety minutes of seeing the commercial. This rear-projection monster had a sixty-inch screen and seemed to take up half the den. We both loved it. We watched the game, ate my mom's brisket sandwiches with a side of cole slaw and washed it down with Tahiti Treat. Nathan Stein had the last known stash of Tahiti Treat in the Western Hemisphere and only served it on special occasions. It was during the fourth quarter of a relatively boring game when I checked the time. That was a mistake.

"Ben, where did you get such a fancy watch? Niaomi, come and look at Ben's new watch."

"Actually I got it in Florida," I said, pulling my sleeve over the watch.

"Those street vendors in Miami sell watches you can't tell from the real ones." My father motioned for me to show him the watch.

At that moment, my mother walked into the den, took my wrist and commented. "What a big and shiny watch. It looks like one of those watches that the astronauts wear in space, an Oymayguh."

"No it's a Rolex."

"Not a real Rolex," my father said. "Did you see that catch? Nobody can beat the Bruins in the Rose Bowl. They're the home team."

"Actually, it is a real Rolex." As soon I said it I knew that was my second mistake.

My father was distracted watching the game but not too distracted to drop the topic.

"Did you get it at duty free? The duty free in the Miami airport has everything."

"I didn't get it at duty free." That was my third mistake. I should have let them think it came from duty free.

"Nathan, what's the difference where he got it?" My mother's comment helped me avoid the details. "It looks beautiful on his wrist and he should enjoy it."

"Only my fancy contractors wear such watches and that's because they don't pay their suppliers. How else could they afford them? It must have cost three thousand U.S. How does an associate in a fancy law firm afford such an expensive timepiece?" My dad never lets me forget his opinion of my law firm.

I was at the fork in the road. I could have come clean and told my parents it was a gift from Abe Goldman, which would have opened up an entirely new topic of conversation, or, I could have said nothing more and let them think I bought it. I opted for the sin of omission. "Oh don't worry, I didn't go into debt. I can afford it," I said. If I had told my parents how I got the watch, that would lead to a conversation about Sarah and the next thing I would know there would be an engagement announcement in the mourning section of the newspaper. I could see it now:

Nathan and Niaomi Stein are relieved to finally announce the engagement of their son, Ben, the successful franchise lawyer, to Sarah Goldman of THE GOLDMANS and soon to become the button-in-law of Abe and Adele Goldman. Look for further details as the blessed event approaches.

This timepiece was going to be more complicated than its jeweled movement. I didn't want to explain why Abe Goldman had given me the watch or my relationship with Sarah. I didn't fully understand either, myself. I could stop wearing it but I liked it too much. I wanted a lifestyle that was different from my parents' and here I was living the part of their social aspirations. I was not willing to embrace their world so I had to be careful how far I ventured into it. And, of course, there was still that message from Julia.

It was time to say good-bye. It was prudent to leave before my parents asked any more questions about my timepiece. My mom gave me some brisket, a small container of her famous vinegar cole slaw and a piece of marble cake. I kissed them both and went on my way.

I stopped at Mr. Cohen's store to pick up a newspaper. The only newspaper available on New Year's Day was *The New York Times* and Mr. Cohen was the only store open which carried the paper. Of course Mr. Cohen was there in his white shirt and black tie tucked in his pants and leaning against the counter as he does every day.

"Mr. Cohen, Happy New Year. How've you been?"

"I'm fine, Stein. It looks like a Florida tan you have there."

"How can you tell what kind of tan someone has? Tans all look the same."

"Lawyers and accountants go to Hawaii or Florida. You look to me like the type who would visit family so it's Florida."

"Mr. Cohen, you're right again. I'd like today's *New York Times*."

"This is your lucky day. I have one left. One of my regular newspaper customers is away and I forgot to cancel his paper so I have one left. You're getting the Abe Goldman's newspaper."

"Abe Goldman comes here for *The New York Times?*"

"Actually, he sends his driver every day at noon to pick up a newspaper and a Cohiba #2 cigar. The bill is thirteen dollars and fifty cents and he gives me fifteen and tells me to keep the change. He gets a fresh cigar and today's paper. I keep a box of Cohibas in my fridge so his wife won't find out."

"How long has this been going on?"

"Twenty-five years like clockwork and, to prove it, look at this." Mr. Cohen leaned over the counter, all 5'6" of him, and pulled up his left shirtsleeve to show me his watch. It was a Rolex Oyster with a blue face and bezel. Identical to mine. Instinctively, I pulled down my coat sleeve so he would not see my Rolex. There I was in a serious relationship with the Button King's daughter, being followed by private detectives and I got the same hush gift from Abe Goldman as his newspaper vendor. I wondered what secret Mr. Cohen was keeping for him besides the daily Cohiba. Maybe he was supplying him with pornography of women wearing nothing but zippers. I paid for my newspaper, checked that it was today's edition and left.

When I got home, I listened to the ninth message from the night before. It was from Arlene who was checking if I had gotten her earlier message about the New Year party and leaving me the address if I could make it. I replayed Julia's message a few more times and debated if or when I should call her back. There wasn't any point calling her other than my unquenchable curiosity. Instead, I called Sarah and woke her up. We didn't talk about anything in particular and both of us seemed to avoid any subject that was remotely related to any hint of commitment. We were both tired from our vacation. I wanted to get off the phone and told Sarah that I was late for the office. She seemed relieved to accept the reason without question even though it was New Year's Day and the office was closed. The office excuse was the best and easiest way to end any conversation.

Next, I called Arlene and explained that I had been in Florida and that was why I had not returned her two calls. She was about to tell me about her artist loft New Year's party when I suggested that we meet for a cappuccino and trade stories in person. It was already close to six o'clock but there's never a wrong time to go for coffee. We decided to meet in half an hour at the Italian Coffee Bar. I knew she'd be on time, exactly twenty minutes late. By the time she got there, I had already had my first espresso.

"So how was the artist party?" I asked after wishing her Happy New Year.

"It was an artistic blow out. Everyone got stoned, watched Dick Clarke in Times Square and engaged in some body painting. I had a bitch of a time getting the paint out of the various crevices and undulations in my canvas. The old canvas isn't as tight as it used to be. But, I think I managed to wash all the paint away."

"I think you have a very nice canvas but I'm not sure that would have been my kind of event."

"You always say the nicest things to me. Let's just say there were novel substitutes for paint brushes. You would have done just fine."

"I think that's a compliment but don't explain. Did you bring pictures?"

"No pictures that I'd admit to, just washable paint. Now tell me about your vacation."

"It was pretty standard for a vacation. I went to Miami and was followed by private detectives, had dinner with a whore from South America who had a reconstructed cleavage and got a Rolex from the Button King, Abe Goldman, for sleeping with his daughter. Just your average week in Miami."

"Ben, you're in love." Arlene is the ultimate romantic and she always assumes it's love. Arlene aspired to such social heights and I didn't have the energy or patience to explain otherwise.

"Arlene, I will never get you to understand no matter how hard I try. This is not love. It is nothing more than a mess." We left after two hours and three cappuccinos but Arlene didn't come back to my place although the thought did cross my mind. It didn't seem like the right thing to propose given our conversation. I went home and stared at the phone. I wondered if Julia would call. I checked the time on my Rolex and was relieved that in less than ten hours I would be back at work. If I was going to call anyone in the next ten hours, it would be Sarah. But, there were no restrictions on incoming calls.

39

Jan. 2, 1987. I went to work early, anxious to meet with Margaret and Bill and hear about their progress in the Jupiter case. I was sitting at my desk by eight and before long they were both sitting across from me in my office. Margaret dove right into the document issue.

"Jupiter has sent us ninety file boxes of documents and there are more coming. We have all of them on floppy disc, entered and catalogued with the help of our friends in Seattle. By the way, how can I get an office with two windows like yours?"

"The same way you get to Carnegie Hall, practice, practice, practice," Bill interrupted.

"Did you find anything?" I was intent on keeping us on topic.

"The documents raised more questions then they answered. But, somewhere in that pile of boxes is the smoking gun. We just haven't found it." Margaret was staring at my wrist as she spoke. "Where'd you get the fancy watch?"

"I got it in Miami." I was slightly embarrassed by the attention but relieved somebody had noticed.

"Boy, that must have been expensive. We better find those incriminating documents if you're going to pay for that hunk of Swiss engineering. Did you get it at duty free?" Margaret seemed unusually interested.

"No. It's a long story but let's just say it was a token of someone's appreciation."

"That's some appreciation. What did you have to do to be that appreciated?" Now Bill was curious and I was concerned this would get out of hand and I might have to reveal the story of the watch.

"Nothing improper. But, it would take liters of drinks to coax it out of me."

"So let's go to a bar," Bill said, hoping to get the real story about the watch.

"It's a little early but we can revisit the subject closer to happy hour." Again, I steered the subject back to the Jupiter document issue. At my urging, Bill returned to the subject and told me that when the bills were arranged in order of dollar amounts, some of the largest invoices had the same serial number. J-TCIC, recorded on about 100 of the largest expense invoices. None of us knew the significance of that number but we just assumed there was a simple explanation. Since there were thousands of documents, it likely wasn't significant. But as a matter of curiosity, I wrote to Jupiter's lawyer and asked what that reference code referred to. We would stay alert for any more documents with the J-TCIC reference until we had a satisfactory explanation. Finally, we divided up the work and set a time to meet at the end of the week to review our progress. I reminded them that I would be going to Vancouver in the first week of February to give the monthly progress report.

For the rest of that week, I reviewed the documents that others had reviewed before me, hoping something would just pop out like a jack-in-a-box. It didn't. The work was tedious even with the computer program that catalogued the documents. Every day I was at work by seven and never left before nine at night. I was obsessed with finding the needle in the haystack. Somewhere in all those boxes was the evidence that would make our case. The incriminating documents were well hidden by the camouflage of volume, but I knew they were there . . . somewhere.

By the time I got home most nights, I was exhausted but I would call Sarah. She told me how I had become more punctual now that I had the Rolex. Every time I looked at it I thought of Sarah and my pact of silence with her father. I told Sarah that I would never take it off. We talked about my moving to Vancouver but I could not consider moving until the Jupiter case was finished.

When I wrote Mr. Billings, Jupiter's lawyer, for an explanation about reference code J-TCIC, it took him a few days to reply. This code was an internal audit reference for accounts payable. I didn't understand what that meant but I assumed it was a standard accounting term and accepted Billings' explanation at face value. In the three weeks before I had to report to the client, Margaret, Bill and I couldn't find one incriminating piece of paper that proved Jupiter was padding the expense reports to the franchisees. We had made no progress other than organizing the documents into the database. I was not looking forward to informing our clients that, after spending

$165,000 of the retainer on document discovery and computer technology we found no hard evidence that the Jupiter expenses were inflated. We kept working and clung to our theory that the evidence was there, somewhere.

Meanwhile, Gerry returned from his extended Mexican vacation. He called me and we arranged to meet at the Italian Coffee Bar. I was looking forward to his stories about Mexican romance and arrived at the coffee bar early to secure the corner round table. I said hello to the four Tonys on my way to the corner table. Gerry was late but I didn't mind because it gave me a chance to read the newspaper. Suddenly, I looked up and he was there.

"Hi, Ben, great to see you." As we shook hands he glanced down at my arm. "Where'd you get the fake Rolex?"

"Fake? It's not fake. It was given to me by the Button King, Abe Goldman."

"I don't care who gave it to you, that's a fake Rolex. It's a good fake but there is no doubt it's a fake." I could not believe what I was hearing. "Are you still sleeping with his daughter?"

"I am, still. It can't be a fake and how could you tell so quickly?"

"You see, a Rolex second hand moves in a sweeping continuous motion. In a fake Rolex the second hand jerks every time it moves."

"How would you know? You don't even own a watch." I must admit I was annoyed.

"They're on every street corner in Acapulco. Take it off and I'll show you."

I took off the timepiece for the first time since going through the metal detector at the Miami airport. I noticed a green ring around my wrist where the watchband had been resting. It wasn't stainless steel and gold. Gerry showed me how the second hand jerked. He was right. My so-called Swiss timepiece was a Taiwan fake and Abe Goldman's so-called demonstration of generosity was nothing more than a cheap imitation you could buy on any Third World street corner. This watch wasn't a Rolex rolex, this was a Goldman Rolex, a Golex, a word I coined meaning a cheap imitation.

Over the next hour, I told Gerry the whole Abe Goldman story. I told him how he had me followed, how I met his South American customer and the so called out-of-town wife and listened to the Button King tell me how he was protecting his daughter from golddiggers. As I walked, I began to question everything about my Miami holiday. What could I believe, if anything, and was Sarah in on this practical joke at my expense? That sense of betrayal brought to mind images of Julia.

"Gerry, what do you think? I should confront that button bastard and tell him I know his watch is a fake and he never fooled me." Gerry sat there thoughtfully but did not say a word for fear of breaking out in uncontrollable laughter.

"Maybe he thought it was real and the store took him like he took me," I said looking for the easy way out.

"Not likely," Gerry answered. "Guys like Goldman aren't fooled easily and face it, this is a cheap imitation."

"If I tell Sarah she'll never believe me." I envisioned our relationship heading for a crash landing.

"But," Gerry leaned over to tell me, "if you say nothing, Abe will be convinced that you're after her inheritance or you're a greenhorn who can't tell a real Rolex from a fake." While listening to Gerry, I decided to confront Mr. Goldman but say nothing to Sarah, I could not believe she was in on it.

"The problem, Gerry, is what I am going to tell Sarah when she sees that I'm not wearing the watch."

"You're right, that's a problem."

On the way home, I stopped by Mr. Cohen's store to take a closer look at his Rolex. Imagine Goldman, that cheapskake, giving fake Rolex watches as a show of his appreciation.

"Good evening, Mr. Cohen. Do you have *The New York Times?*"

"Too late. We sold out by three o'clock."

"How about Abe Goldman's *New York Times?* Did he get his today?" I wasn't sure how to break the news to Mr. Cohen that his most prized possession was a fake.

"He's back from Miami and as usual he had it picked up like clockwork. The driver was here at noon for his newspaper and cigar. Abe Goldman is as dependable as my Rolex."

"Speaking of your Rolex, could you tell me what time it is?"

With a flurry of showmanship reminiscent of a ballroom dancer, Mr. Cohen extended his arm to show off his timepiece. He was so proud when he leaned over the counter to show me his gift from the great Abe Goldman. The second hand swept across the blue face without a hint of a hesitation. I couldn't believe it. Cohen had the real thing. Here I was playing hide the salami with Sarah Goldman, keeping her father's unsavory secrets and Cohen gets the real Rolex while I get the green ring. I wouldn't have had this problem with Julia's family. That reminded me that I never called her back.

I had another sleepless night, courtesy of Abe Goldman, as I played out the scenarios of what I would say to the Button King and all the possible outcomes. By six in the morning I was so exhausted and confused that I wasn't sure what I would do. But I was determined to call him and confront him about my Golex. I prayed he would say something that would make the whole problem go away. When I arrived at my office I called him at the office.

"Good morning, Goldking Investments," a polite but firm voice answered the phone.

"Abe Goldman, please. Tell him Ben Stein is calling."

"Yes, Mr. Stein, I'll see if Mr. Goldman is available." I waited on the line for what seemed like forever for him to take my call. In fact, it was only three minutes later when the receptionist came back to tell me that he was in transit and would call me back. I gave her my office number and hung up. He called me back within half an hour.

"Hello, Ben, how've you been?" He sounded happy to hear from me. "Do you still have that Florida tan or has it washed off yet?"

"Mr. Goldman, most of my tan has gone down the drain but I did manage to keep a green ring mark around my wrist."

"Please, Ben, call me Abe. How did you do that?"

"That watch you gave me had a copper wristband and it left a green oxidation mark. A real Rolex does not have a copper band."

"Sometimes appearances are, and need to be, deceptive. Why don't you come over to the house tonight. I'm sure we can straighten this out."

"When?"

"Let's say about seven-thirty."

"See you then, Mr. Goldman."

I worked as hard as I could all day hoping it would take my mind off my appointment with Mr. Goldman. Every time I took a break, all I could think about was what I would say to him. I had no idea what I would say but I was determined to keep my composure. I decided to be late and blame it on the watch. Depending how I handled this there was a lot of risk because I could not imagine Abe Goldman telling Sarah the real story.

Abe Goldman had an impressive home. It was a giant, stone, Tudor mansion dating back to the 1920s. You could not appreciate the enormity of it from the street because the house was set so far back on the property and there were twelve-foot-high hedge around it. I rang the bell at the gate, gave my name and soon a set of large iron gates opened with the smoothness of the second hand on a real Rolex. I walked up to the oak double door with an iron grate over the peep window and, just as I was about to knock, the left door opened and a woman who was obviously the housekeeper invited me in. She directed me toward a room beyond the foyer under a massive winding staircase. I asked her if she knew the time. It was a test. She pulled up her sleeve to reveal a Rolex with a blue face and bezel. No jerk, just a sweeping second hand. This did not boost my self-esteem.

Mr. Goldman's den was exactly as you would picture it with the usual array of grip-and-grin photos of famous people giving him awards of one type or another. The paintings on the walls were French Impressionists and the room smelled of fine leather. The couches were covered in chocolate-brown suede with a contrasting black arm chair and ottoman in the corner. There was a wall of books on the shelf, a design imperative, and a bronze Remington of a horse on its hind legs with rider. I walked over and tapped it. It did not sound real.

"Good evening, Ben, I've been expecting you," an engaging voice said from behind me.

"I'm late," I said, pointing to my wrist. "My watch is running a little slow."

"Yes, I can well understand how these things happen." He was smiling.

"This is a beautiful home you have. I like the fake Remington," I said, as I touched the base of the sculpture.

"How would you know a fake Remington from the real thing? There are respected art historians who have examined this sculpture. They swear it's authentic."

"Let' just say I'm a better judge of character than those historians are a judge of sculpture. You wouldn't pay for the real thing. I bet my Rolex is as genuine as your Remington and you know how valuable that is."

"I can see you didn't come over for small talk. Yes, your watch is a fake but you'll get the real thing if you and my daughter get engaged."

"You mean I have to earn your generosity?" I stood there facing him. "I didn't think generosity worked that way."

"Who said anything about generosity? I reward those who are loyal to me. It's about commitment. If you remain loyal to my daughter then you'll get the real thing." He motioned for me to sit down but I didn't move.

"You mean I just warrant the cheap imitation until you judge my character."

"In a word, yes. You should take this as a life lesson. People are always willing to give the rich the benefit of the doubt. If my wife wears a sparkling necklace, everyone assumes it's real. Why would I spend a hundred thousand for a necklace when I can get the same reaction for three thousand. My wife is happy. I'm happy. And everyone else is suitably impressed." I was so amazed at what I heard that I instinctively sat down on the couch. Mr. Goldman took a seat behind his desk.

"Don't you lose track of the difference between what's real and what's fake?"

"When you grow up, which you should have by now," he pointed at me, "you'll learn there is no difference between a real anything and a fake if you get the same reaction. It's all about impression. Nothing has intrinsic value."

"Do your wife and kids know you do this?"

"Adele and Sarah have no idea that most of the stuff in this house is fake. My son figured it out long ago and let's say we remain civil to each other while my wife and daughter are in the room."

"Then how does the newspaper vendor and the maid rate a real Rolex?"

"Every so often you buy the real thing and give it to someone. That insures the impression that everything else must be real. If Abe Goldman gave Cohen the newspaper vendor a real Rolex then the necklace around his wife's neck must be real."

I wanted to hate Abe Goldman, his cynicism was intolerable. But I admired his savvy. In some ironic way he was the real thing. I had to admit I saw his point. What's the difference if it's a real or fake Remington? Either you like it or you don't. Anyone who's that impressed by originals deserves to be taken in by a Goldman fake.

"Aren't you worried that I might tell your wife or daughter the real story? You wouldn't want Sarah to treat you like your son does."

"If you love my little girl you wouldn't do anything to hurt her, especially over a trinket. If you tell anyone then you should understand that no one has led a perfect life and yours might have its own interesting imperfections." Abe Goldman stared right through me and smiled.

"So what should I do about this watch?"

"Here's what I would do. I would go out and buy a real Rolex and chalk it up to a life lesson. It will only cost you five thousand and you'll never forget our conversation. I can give you the name of a jeweler who discounts these watches and, if you give him cash with no receipt, he'll forget about the sales tax."

"You want me to keep this quiet and then go out and spend five thousand dollars for a real one?" I shook my head is disbelief.

"That's what I would do if I were you," Abe Goldman said matter-of-factly.

"You know, Mr. Goldman, I'm starting to understand why they call you the King. The strange thing is I can't even hate you for what you are."

"Of course you can't hate me. One day I might be your father-in-law and you are going to be my lawyer for my franchising business. Can I show you around the house?"

"No thanks, Mr. Goldman, I think I'll be going." I stood up to leave and we shook hands.

"I presume our conversation is between us." He put his arm around my shoulder. "By the way, call me Abe." As I left I hung the Golex on the Remington. It was a match made in heaven.

The message light was flashing when I got home. It was Sarah.

"Hi, Ben. I called to say hello and I can't wait to see you. I just spoke to my dad. He sends his regards and says that you should give him a call when you have the time. I think that's his way of asking if you're enjoying your Rolex. Speak to you soon."

40

January was bitterly cold with the temperature never rising above −20C. The combination of the cold and the wind made every extremity of the body susceptible to frostbite. I was grateful there was no minimum order size for take-out Chinese. And I was especially grateful for my indoor parking spot. I almost felt sorry for Rupert having to park in my outdoor spot and getting into a frozen car every night. In a weak moment, I even considered giving back his indoor spot as a gesture of reconciliation. I came to my senses before it was too late.

The cold weather kept me from distractions that would interfere with work. I worked on the Jupiter document search day and night, feeling the pressure of the approaching monthly client meeting. We tested every far-fetched theory trying to uncover the bogus expenses. We kept coming up empty. We did not find one piece of paper that would prove Jupiter was padding the expenses. I was in touch with Mr. Zimmer who told me that the senior Jupiter executives were confident about their case. He speculated that his franchise could be in jeopardy if we weren't successful. He kept reassuring me that he had confidence in me and I would find the needle in the haystack. This was his gentle way of keeping the pressure on. I only had seven days left until I reported to the franchisee committee.

I took Mr. Goldman's advice and looked up his jeweler. The Rolex cost me $3,800 and I paid in cash. The watch came by mail in a plain brown shipping envelope from a store in Sarnia, Ontario. I didn't ask. It was a lot of money for a first-year lawyer and it just about drained my savings account. In fact, since I had started going out with Sarah my expenses took a dramatic increase. I was finding out that socializing with the rich, though fun, is very expensive.

As I'd done every morning since I started at Lord's, I was at work by seven and took the reception desk newspaper to my office for twenty minutes of uninterrupted reading. I love the newspaper for the sheer variety of subject matter. The lead story in the business section was about Air Canada buying ten jumbo jets from Boeing. I was casually looking at the photograph of the tail piece of the jumbo jet when it caught my eye. I couldn't believe what I saw. It was so simple. I tore the page out and returned the rest of the newspaper to the reception desk. I could hardly contain myself and waited anxiously by the reception entrance for Margaret and Bill to get in. I had the answer.

"What took you so long to get in?" I asked as I saw them get out of the elevator.

As usual, Margaret answered for both of them. "We always get in just before eight. We're right on time."

"Today, on time is late. Take off your coats and meet me in my office." Within five minutes Margaret and Bill were in my office with puzzled looks on their faces.

"So what's going on? What couldn't wait?" Margaret asked.

"Look at this story in today's business section of the newspaper." I pointed to the article lying on my desk. "Tell me what you see." They both stood over my desk reading the story about Air Canada ordering these jumbo jets.

"What?" they said in unison.

"The picture," I said pointing. "The picture of the tail wing of the plane."

"Yes, I see the picture," said Bill "So what? It's a picture of an airplane tail wing."

"Look what's painted on the tail, A-CBJJ."

"I can read. What's the point?"

"The point is J-TCIC. Jupiter Tire Corporation. That's no audit trace code, whatever that means. It is the identification code for their corporate jet. Those invoices are the expenses they have been charging to the plane account. That's how Jupiter has been padding its bills and hiding it. They've been charging personal expenses to the corporate jet account and passing it on to the franchisees. This is the needle in the haystack we've been looking for."

For a full minute there was complete silence in my office. All three of us stared at the picture of that jumbo jet tail wing as we worked out in our minds how the pieces of the puzzle fit together. We had found the answer and our deafening silence was the roaring sound of us savoring the moment. Then we all began talking at once.

We got so loud that lawyers in nearby offices looked in to find out what the noise was about at eight o'clock on a Monday morning, with the outside temperature of −34C. We were too excited to explain. Then we settled down to work out the strategy.

Bill knew someone who knew someone who worked at the airplane registry section of the Federal Ministry of Transportation in Ottawa. He managed to get the guy on the phone and to have a search done of the Jupiter plane while he was on hold. This was much quicker than the official four-week delay and the nine-page form they required at the Ministry. We were right. The Jupiter Tire Corporation had two private jets with identification numbers J-TCIC and J-TCID. We wrote Mr. Billings, to make his day as well as ours.

Dear Mr. Billings:
re: J-TCIC

It has come to our attention that the internal audit code J-TCIC, as you described it, refers to at least one, if not both the corporate jets registered to your client. We are enclosing the list of invoices which have referenced this number. Pursuant to our demand for documents, we require the original invoices in support of all the documents with the J-TCIC reference code. In addition, if there are any additional documents with the reference code J-TCID, we want all of those supporting documents. We look forward to hearing from you in the very near future.

Yours truly,
Ben Stein

I didn't get any work done the rest of that day. Between the euphoria of uncovering the document deception, relief from the mounting pressure of the upcoming client meeting and the sheer exhaustion of working day and night, I had no energy left for work. However, my sense of guilt would not permit me to do the rational thing and go home to sleep. So I sat in my office with the door shut and leafed through my telephone directory, looking for an excuse to call someone. Before I knew it, and without realizing what I had done, I dialed Julia's number. When I heard her voice, I had to think quick. Should I hang up or speak?

"Hi Julia . . . Happy New Year. I didn't expect to find you at home."

"New Year? It's almost February. What took you so long?" She was as surprised to hear my voice as I was to hear hers.

"It must be either Ukrainian New Year, Indonesian New Year or Argentinean New Year. Anyway, somewhere someone is about to celebrate the New Year so Happy New Year."

At first our conversation was awkward but, as we kept talking, it became apparent that there was still something between us. For me, the old feelings came rushing back, affection and betrayal. But I told myself I was not going to allow those feelings of infatuation trample my sense of caution.

"How come you're home?"

"I don't work anymore and it's too cold to walk down Michigan Avenue. So here I am reading catalogues and watching TV."

"It sounds like you're bored."

"It's not that bad. We have a condo in Florida and, if it gets too boring or cold I got to Florida for a few days while my husband is working. I'm there in three hours."

Neither of us suggested that we should meet but we did talk around the subject. We talked for forty-five minutes and we promised to keep in touch. For the rest of the day, I kept replaying the call in my mind and trying to understand the real meaning of her remarks. Did she imply that we meet in Florida? I was elated that Julia was still interested in me but, at the same time worried that it could lead to something very complicated and messy. I called Sarah, hoping her voice would snap me back to reality. What I got was Sarah's recorded message. I left a message about seeing her on Sunday in Vancouver and told her that I missed her very much.

That night, I went out with Bill and Margaret for a minor celebration and we billed the dinner to the client, of course. We talked about the case and speculated about the phone calls between Billings and Jupiter once they realized they had been caught. We agreed not to consider any settlement offer until we got those supporting documents. Also, we decided to hire an accountant to put the documents together in some logical format so we could demonstrate how much Jupiter had spent on those so-called airplane expenses. We weren't sure how this would unfold but we knew that we were on the right path to uncovering the fraud.

That evening, for the first time, the three of us talked about our future at Lord's. This was a sensitive subject because, if it got out that we were talking about leaving, that would end our careers at the firm. The single uncompromising principle at all of these large law firms is blind and unwavering loyalty. You can fight among yourselves, pass hurtful gossip or manipulate the other lawyers in the firm to your advantage. But, you can never hint that you might leave. Disloyalty gets you fired on the spot. These large firms are constantly on guard that lawyers will leave and take the clients with them. The senior lawyers believe the firm owns the clients and any hint of a lawyer leaving, partner or associate, with a client in tow is the worst form of disloyalty and grounds for immediate termination.

The three of us were, for all intents and purposes, functioning as a self-contained unit. Lord's was not providing us with anything more than office space and secretarial assistance. Lord's wasn't even a potential source of work for our franchising practice. We had the Jupiter case and we were doing Gerry's work, setting up his dealer depots. We were optimistic that more work would come and speculated what it would be like to have our own firm. We decided not to talk about it until the Jupiter matter was well in hand. Also, I was entertaining the possibility of approaching Mr. Goldman about his idea of franchising carts in shopping malls. I chose not to mention it to Bill or Margaret since that venture was complicated by my relationship with Sarah.

For the balance of the week I waited for Mr. Billings to respond. I wanted to hear from him before I went to Vancouver on Sunday. I didn't want to appear anxious, although I was, so I was reluctant to pick up the phone and call him. Finally, on Thursday, he called. He wanted to get together and have an informal conversation about exploring some resolution to the litigation. In keeping with our plan, I told Billings that we would be pleased to meet with him as long as he sent along the documents we were requesting. He told me that he was hoping to avoid all that work but I assured him that the work was unavoidable. It was obvious from the call that Jupiter's strategy of hiding the truth among thousands of documents was in the midst of collapse. Jupiter's arrogance would soon be transformed into high class begging. They were about to pay handsomely for all my sleepless nights.

41

I was anxious to get to the monthly meeting in Vancouver. I was scheduled to travel Sunday morning, spend the day with Sarah, meet with the clients on Monday and then return to Winnipeg on Tuesday. However, that winter had been one of the coldest on record so I decided to stay an extra day and enjoy what seemed like the subtropical temperatures of Vancouver. Also, in my darkest and most private moments, I had come to admit that I enjoyed the indulgences of business travel. I like flying business class. I like the VIP lounges in the airports. I liked the spaciousness of hotel suites and I had developed a minor addiction to the airlines' roasted cashews.

On Saturday, Mr. Zimmer called to tell me there had been a change of venue for our meeting. They wanted to meet at Whistler, B.C. There had been record snowfalls in the mountains and the franchisee committee wanted to go skiing. For me, this was not good news. From my perspective, the only good snow was melted snow. Coming from the prairies, snow is nothing more than a household expense . . . snow removal. You shovel it out of the way to get your car out of the garage and hope you don't get stuck in it while you're driving. But Whistler was where the clients wanted to meet, so that's where we would meet.

I called Sarah to tell her about the change in plans. She was enthusiastic about a few days in Whistler. As an overworked soldier in the legion of justice, she never hesitated to take a furlow. No one at the courthouse seemed to object or know whether she was there or not. She had no fear of losing her job while I was petrified of being fired. Security of employment and my economic future had become a concern to me. I wanted to maintain my newfound affluence. But, for Sarah, work was nothing more than an amusing divergence.

While we were on the phone Sarah asked if I had the right clothes for an alpine adventure. I told her that I would be wearing my regular wool winter coat with the appropriate cold-weather accessories. I wasn't going on an alpine adventure and I didn't know anything about alpine fashion. She sensed my ignorance and encouraged me to outfit myself in the appropriate clothing. I told her not to be silly. I didn't ski and my only reason for going was to attend a client meeting. I had no alpine anything on my agenda. Sarah warned me that, if I didn't dress the part, it would be like going to a Bar Mitzvah without a shirt and tie. She would take it upon herself to outfit me. I agreed reluctantly. I wanted to avoid any obstacles between us. As I looked at my Rolex I just knew that alpine fashion was going to cost more than I had bargained for.

Sarah met me at the airport with three shopping bags stuffed with alpine fashion. For the bargain price of $1,900 plus tax, I owned a made-in-Switzerland orange ski jacket with contrasting white stripes and matching gloves, a toque from Holland, an Italian cashmere sweater depicting deer running across my chest and a tartan wool shirt. I looked like a regular United Nations, all appearance and no substance. Actually, I looked exactly like some schmuck from the prairies who just got off the plane on his way to Whistler. Sarah assured me that I would fit in, as long as I remembered to cut off the price tags. It was a defining moment for my distaste for ski resorts which would remain a lifelong loathing. I'd rather play the accordion at a costume party than socialize with the alpine set as they order their half caf-half-decaf-extra-hot soy lattes while they discuss the quality of snow. Fresh mountain air is overrated and I preferred the aroma of car exhaust.

My meeting with the clients was a success, but a bit tricky. We had not secured the documents which would prove Jupiter was padding the expenses on the airplane accounts so I advocated a position of restrained optimism. I failed. By the end of the client meeting, they were discussing how they would divide up the damage award and which hotel in Las Vegas they should book for the victory party. I must admit their enthusiasm was contagious except that I was the one who had to deliver the check. The meeting lasted all of Monday morning after which the clients went skiing and I had the next day-and-a-half off.

While I was at my meeting, Sarah went to the hotel spa and got the full Whistler treatment: massage, mud bath, facial with cucumber treatment and a steam. We met back at the room for lunch. She felt silky smooth and it had only cost $600. We ordered room service, drank champagne and lay in bed looking at the view of the alpine meadow against the mountain backdrop. Lying there, I reflected on how my life had changed. Three years earlier I had been sitting in the student lounge of the law school drinking coffee, bumming French cigarettes, debating philosophical nonsense and mocking a career in anything. Now, here I was with the Button King's daughter in a suite at Whistler, drinking champagne, wearing my Rolex Submariner watch, with an $1,100 orange ski jacket in the closet. This was not how I had thought things would turn out.

Sarah and I stayed at Whistler the balance of Monday and all day Tuesday. The place was really a camouflaged shopping mall with a mountain attached, populated by self-indulgent tourists. All the same, we had a great time walking and talking for hours. Both of us felt we were closer than we had ever anticipated but neither of us spoke directly about it. As for me, I kept trying to avoid the truth of what had become of me.

On Wednesday, we drove directly from Whistler to the Vancouver airport. We timed it perfectly and I arrived at the gate exactly thirty minutes before my scheduled departure time. That might seem like I was cutting it close but Air Canada is always at least twenty minutes late so I had plenty of time. Once I was at the airport, I called the office for my messages, returned a few calls and had time to pick up a pastrami sandwich to go.

Between the flying time and the two-hour time change, I didn't land in Winnipeg until 6:00 P.M. local time. I didn't go into the office but I did call Margaret. I was eager to hear if Jupiter had delivered the documents and, if so, what it all meant.

"How was the snow?" Margaret asked.

"White and yellow in spots. They drink a lot of beer at Whistler."

"Did you ski?"

"No, I wasn't even interested in trying. I spent a couple of days relaxing and trying not to think about work."

"Oh, so you met a girl there."

"No, I didn't meet a girl at Whistler. The alpine set is not my kind of crowd." This was a bit of a lie, but not technically. I hadn't met Sarah at Whistler. I had brought her with me and I wasn't prepared to explain my personal life to people from work. "Did we hear from Billings?"

250

"We sure did. He sent over about a third of the documents we asked for with an attached letter. He wants to set up a meeting."

"Did you look over the documents he sent?"

"We did, and if the rest of the documents are anything like what he sent over, they have a lot of explaining to do. They've been doing a lot of socializing on the account of our clients."

"Great, send a letter to Billings and tell him we want the balance of the documents before we meet. Then ask him if he's had a call from the Toronto Stock Exchange regulators. Ask him if he has any suggestions on how we should respond if we receive such an inquiry."

"But we haven't had an inquiry from the stock exchange."

"I didn't say we had an inquiry. I said ask him if *he* had an inquiry. Tell him we'll be prepared to meet once we have all the documents. Send the letter out under my name and we'll talk about it in the morning."

42

By February 1987 the polar jet stream swept south over Manitoba down to the Gulf of Texas. It was a month of record-setting cold temperatures in Winnipeg. Now I understood why Canadians have a global reputation for being frigid. Everything was frozen stiff and I counted the days until Sarah would come to visit.

The Jupiter documents surpassed my every expectation. For the next three weeks I was consumed by them. With the help of an accountant, we identified and categorized every questionable airplane expense charged to the franchisee group for the last three years. These expenses were listed as corporate travel but were far more. They included tickets to sporting events, personal travel to summer homes using both corporate jets, casino bills in Las Vegas, shopping trips to New York and unspecified entertainment disbursements labeled as miscellaneous expenses. It was difficult to put an exact total to it, but the so-called expenses were at least $2 million a month. In addition, Jupiter was charging the franchise group proportionate rent and utilities for their head office.

I called Mr. Billings to arrange the meeting. I asked him to bring along the two principals of the company, Harland Jupiter, the founder's son and Isaac Bloom, his longtime partner. The two had met at a right-wing non-think tank while attending university and had been friends and business partners ever since. During my telephone conversation with Billings I told him that, given the magnitude of the damages, it would be prudent to have Jupiter and Bloom attend. Without them, the meeting would be a waste of time. Billings understood. It felt to me as if he was about to concede that there were expenses that should never have been charged to the franchise group. We agreed to meet on March 7 in Winnipeg since Jupiter was coming from Toronto and Bloom was in Vancouver. Also, I reasoned that the cold would focus their attention on work. It was too cold to even go for a walk.

I had never attended a meeting like this, I was even more nervous because I would be the spokesperson for the franchisee group. I had seven days to prepare and needed some strategic advice on how to conduct the meeting. It was all about tactics and little about the law. I knew that Rupert MacIntosh had the best insight into such matters. Before I could reconsider and change my mind, I walked down the hall and knocked on his door. He was just as surprised to see me as I was to be standing in his doorway.

"So, how's my parking spot?" he asked with a certain edge to his voice. Rupert had never quite gotten over our wager, especially since it had turned out to be the coldest February on record.

"Your parking spot is just fine," I said, smiling to break the ice. "Both me and my car appreciate the relief from the cold. By the way, has your wrist fully healed?"

"The doctor tells me I won't be doing much golfing this year but you didn't come here to talk about my wrist. Tell me what's on your mind and get it over with."

He hadn't asked me to sit down but, to assert my status in the firm, I sat down anyway, opposite him, as if I were one of his peers. "I need your advice on the Jupiter case. I know you are the most able person in this office for the situation."

"I don't know what you're talking about and I doubt if I want to help you. But, let's hear what it is before I tell you to get the hell out of my office." This was not a good start but I decided to press on. I tried to tell a compelling story and I got his attention. Rupert had never known much about the law but he was strategic. I could sense that he was considering the options as I spoke non-stop for ten minutes. He didn't say a word the whole time and stared out the window to avoid looking too interested. When I finished talking, I waited for a signal to stay or leave. I sat there while he said nothing. It felt like an eternity. Finally, he handed me a pad of paper and a pen.

"Stein, take notes. The most important thing to Jupiter and Bloom is their reputations. They already made a fortune so the money won't get their attention. Jupiter and Bloom are some of the most dedicated social climbers in the free world. Your claim didn't scare them. What got their attention was the risk of a tarnished reputation amongst their fancy friends. No amount of money will put them in those fancy charity balls in Palm Beach and Palm Desert if they are labeled as common thieves. It's the risk of disclosure that got their attention. Otherwise they couldn't care less."

"Okay, I think I understand. But what about the fact that I am a junior lawyer and they won't take me seriously?" This was the entré to get Rupert reconnected to the case.

"Treat them respectfully, like at a job interview. Come thoroughly prepared and don't be afraid to tell them what you want. Have a letter ready which details the most important examples of their bogus expenses and make sure they understand that it will be part of the court record which anyone, especially the press, can access. Make sure they know you're not impressed with their social status. The sooner you get them over that issue the sooner they'll get serious about settling."

"Who should I take to the meeting?" I spoke while jotting down some of Rupert's thoughts.

"Take anyone you want but make sure they are people who add value. I suggest you take an expert in securities regulation and disclosure issues. The Jupiter team must be convinced that if they don't get serious at this meeting then we'll go public and to the security regulators. Also, don't meet in our office. That way, it's easier to find a reason to leave. If you're already in your office there's nowhere to leave to."

We talked for at least another thirty minutes. I listened carefully and took notes. His advice was valuable and could not be found in law books. I tried to absorb his logic. Although nothing directly was said, by the end of the meeting we had come to some sort of reconciliation of our past differences. Still, I was not about to confuse reconciliation with trust and I still had his parking spot. When there was nothing left to say, I stood up and thanked him. Neither of us extended our hand to shake.

"Stein, one last thing. Don't ever take your eyes off these arrogant assholes. Once you see them squint and nervously fidget in their chairs, then you know you've got them and it's just a matter of how big a check you want them to write. But I expect you won't aim low."

I prepared for the meeting day and night as if it were a final examination. I memorized facts. I thought about alternative arguments. I considered the words I would use which would have the greatest impact. I made notes to focus my thinking and then made notes of my notes. I distilled all the information onto one side of a single page and then reviewed that piece of paper and reviewed it again until I had it memorized. But more importantly, I kept thinking about what Rupert had told me and how I would sense their weakness. I even went to the trouble of buying a new tie. It always feels good when you put on a new tie. I had a friend who owned a clothing store and he always knew the right tie for any occasion.

We were all set. I arranged the meeting at Billings' office. I took a securities lawyer of the firm with me who briefed us on the violations of the securities regulations. Margaret and Bill stayed at the office in case I needed to retrieve any information from the documents. I wasn't sure if Jupiter and Bloom would be intimidating to the franchisees so I decided not to take them along. But, I arranged for the franchisee committee to be available by conference call if I needed them. I had the calculations of the damages in summary form. Everyone was in place to provide me with information on demand.

Billings' office was just what you would expect if you had a client named Harland Jupiter. We were escorted into a boardroom that had a table which comfortably sat thirty-two. There were paintings of what appeared to be a dozen dead partners. There were certificates on the walls acknowledging major donations by the firm to various hospital fundraising campaigns. I bet they were donations in kind. Billings entered through what appeared to be a panel in the wall with his clients in tow. Everyone exchanged pleasantries and business cards and we took our respective positions on opposite sides of the table.

Harland Jupiter opened the conversation. This man looked like he was born in a pin-striped suit. "Do you know the Lords, Mr. Stain? My family vacationed with the Lords on Lake Michigan every summer in the 1950s. Our fathers were great friends and he did the legal work for the family."

"Actually, it's Stein. And no, I didn't know the Lord family. Our family didn't do much socializing with the Lords or the Bishops and we spent our summers at Winnipeg Beach. But we do belong to a synagogue that has some Blooms." This comment got Bloom's attention.

"We don't have any relatives in Winnipeg so it must be a different Bloom," he turned to face me for the first time.

"You never know, Mr. Bloom. There may be some long-lost relatives of yours here that I've been sitting beside at synagogue. We can check into it if you are curious." Bloom was one of those Jews who tried very hard to be a Jupiter but he was not tall enough, even with the optical illusion of a pin-striped suit. Billings could see that Mr. Bloom was not comfortable with the direction the conversation was taking and he interrupted.

"Excuse me but these two gentlemen did not come all this way to talk about their genealogy. Perhaps we can get down to business."

"Speaking of coming all this way," I said, "did you bring both jets? I trust we won't find a bill charging the expenses of this trip back to the franchisees. You both have a habit of charging your travel to the franchisee group regardless of the purpose for the trip." I wanted them to know right from the start that we had figured out their charge-back scheme for travel expenses.

Billings made the opening defense, blaming some of the misplaced expenses on an accounting department that had gone through significant technological and staff changes. The company was prepared to review these charges to make sure that the franchisees were not improperly charged.

"Look, Ben," Harland Jupiter interrupted, "there may have been some mistakes and, if you show us where these errors are, we can correct them and credit it back to your clients' account. This needn't be contentious."

"As a matter of fact, Harland, I have a summary of these errors with me and it looks like you have a lot of what you call mistakes in your accounting department." I pushed copies of our calculations across the table. "For some reason, every month you have overcharged our client by two to three million dollars. You'd think, if this was a mistake, then there would have been as many errors in our favor as there were in yours. But, all the errors are in your favor. Do you consider that a coincidence or an honest mistake?"

Now it was Bloom's turn. "There may have been some extravagances. Show us the proof of your claim and we will give the franchisee group credits against future advertising and marketing expenses. We should be able to wrap this up quickly. These kinds of accounting errors happen all the time in large businesses. There is nothing sinister about it. It's just part of running the business."

I decided to cut their patronizing comments short. I had had enough. "Gentlemen, these mistakes, as you call them, amount to between two to three million a month and we don't want your credits. We don't think it's a coincidence. We want the money plus interest just like our clients gave you money when you defrauded them. The only issue here is whether we are going to take your stock in Jupiter as security against payment or if we will insist upon irrevocable letters of credit from your banks. Besides, there is also the matter of disclosure to the securities regulators."

Harland could not resist. "Stein, these accusations of yours are slanderous. We're not going to let you treat us like common criminals. As you must know about me, I would not hesitate to initiate a slander action against you and your client. No one has ever successfully defended a slander claim against me. You could pay with your license to practice law."

"First of all, I do not consider you a common criminal, although your motivation is common enough. You have stolen too much to be considered common. And, once we get all the documents from your gambling and so-called companionship disbursements, we'll see about this unblemished litigation record. You know, truth is a complete defense to a claim of slander. By that time, you'll be answering to other people both outside and inside your business and social circles. Once we're finished not even a fat donation will get you an invitation to a Palm Beach charity ball."

That was the statement which triggered it. Rupert's analysis of these two social climbers was dead on target. I could see Harland Jupiter's eyelids start to twitch just like Rupert had said they would. He moved his hands from his lap to grab hold of the leather arms of his chair and his manicured nails left quite a deep indentation in the leather. I wondered if Billings would charge his client for repairs to the boardroom furniture. *No*, I thought, *he'll likely bury the expense in the photocopy bill.* Mr. Bloom started shifting in his seat once he noticed that Harland Jupiter couldn't sit still. Those two were joined at the hip. Nothing was said. Billings broke the silence by asking for a few minutes alone with his clients.

Their consultation lasted ninety minutes. The only thing I had forgotten to bring was a deck of cards. I don't know what they talked about but we had gotten their attention. When they came back, Billings did all the talking. They now realized that trying to impress me with stories about vacationing with the Lords was not going to work and threats had not had the desired impact. They were forced to deal with the merits of the case.

Billings re-opened the meeting by conceding that there might be a valid claim for certain expenses but that I had gone too far in describing it as fraudulent. He insisted that we use more neutral language if we were going to resolve this problem. In response, I took out a securities textbook and read them the definition of fraud under the Securities Act. I explained how it seemed to fit within their so-called accounting errors. Expensing corporate jets for vacations, paying off gambling debts from casinos and bogus consulting fees for their wives and children all fit quite nicely within the definition of fraud. I pointed out that the amount we were talking about amounted to $25 million a year for at least three years plus, interest and costs. This was roughly equivalent to the value of their stock in the company, assuming the price held up. Also, I reminded them that the tax department would be interested in talking to them if some of these Jupiter expenses were generally a disguised form of executive compensation. They would owe back taxes and penalties on these so-called accounting oversights. This comment caused more twitching and armchair grabbing.

To put it mildly, our meeting was not headed toward an amicable settlement. We were not attempting to find a compromise. We were going to win and they were going to lose. That's what we wanted. Given the value of the claim, we told Billings that we were honor-bound to advise the securities regulators in Canada and United States of the claim. We had prepared a draft letter to the regulators and we gave them copies. They wanted another caucus to reconsider their position. I told them they could have all the time they wanted but, we were still going to advise the regulators and, if they were smart, they wouldn't sell any of their shares in the interim because they would be trading on insider information which would lead to a whole bunch of other problems. I could see in their faces that they felt cornered and it was now a matter of how much to squeeze. I knew how much to squeeze. Also, we gave them another letter that we were about to send. It was to their auditors advising them of bogus expenses their clients had been charging to franchisees. We warned them that if they refused to respond, it would be evidence of their complicity. Finally, we gave Jupiter and Bloom a third letter that stated that if their billing practices continued, we would pay the disputed amounts into a trust account until the matter was resolved. We were not going to send money to support their lifestyles at the franchisees' expense. Our strategy was to stop the bleeding, pressure them from all directions and force them to pay attention to our claim.

The meeting was over by eleven and we were on our way. First prize would have been complete capitulation, but that was not realistic. We got second prize. By the end of the meeting, Jupiter and Bloom had come to the harsh realization that they had been caught. Now it was a question of damage control. There would be no more of their name dropping or patronizing remarks. Nothing would deflect us from our goal. It was now a question of how much we would settle for and how long it would take to get the money.

Just as we were leaving, Billings took me aside and asked if we could meet at a convenient time to discuss a settlement amount. I corrected him. We did not intend to discuss terms of settlement but rather we would discuss the terms of capitulation. He laughed nervously, shook my hand and gave me a concessionary nod. A tidal wave of exhilaration and power rushed through my body like nothing I had ever felt before. It was the feeling of victory.

The first thing I did when I got back to the office was call the client committee to give them an update. I told them the meeting had gone well and that Jupiter was taking our claim seriously. There would be another meeting in the near future to discuss the actual amount of a settlement. With the adrenaline gushing from my success, I called Sarah.

43

There was always an element of surprise when I had dinner with my friends but the announcement of my engagement caught everyone off guard, including me.

Murray Wall was the first to break the silence. "Is it Sarah Goldman?"

"Of course. She's the only one I've been seeing."

Gerry Smith, the quintessential bachelor, wanted to know all the details. "When did this happen?"

"Actually, it just happened. I came back to the office from a meeting about the Jupiter case and I called Sarah to say hello. It was one of those calls where we connected on everything. We talked for close to an hour. When I got off the phone, all I could do was think about how good it felt. I called her back and one thing lead to another and . . . we're engaged."

David Kaplan wanted to make sure that he understood correctly that engaged meant engaged to be married. "Is there any chance that you were misunderstood? Sometimes people on the phone talk at cross purposes. It's like asking someone to lie down in the middle of the road but you really don't mean it."

"No chance, I'm roadkill." She was going to call her parents and tell them the news. "There is no doubt that she understood that engaged meant getting married. I meant it."

Paul wanted to know what my parents' reaction was. "I don't know, I haven't told them yet. You're the first to know. After I got off the phone with Sarah, I returned a couple of work calls and then came here for dinner."

Gerry saw the timing as an opportunity. "So you could still get out of this before it's too late. You could call it a big misunderstanding. You meant engaged in the connected sense, not in the going-to-get-married sense."

"I'm not looking for a way out of it. I'm thirty-seven years old. She is more than I could ever have dreamed of. It's not going to get better. It's time I grow up."

"Why grow up?" Gerry pressed. "Has it been so bad not being a grown up?"

"The fact is since age sixteen my social life has been on a steady decline. As I get older there are fewer eligible women. They are mostly divorced and on a ravenous hunt for a husband. I am either chasing young girls or being stalked by older women. Sarah is the first girl in a long time who did not fit either category. And as an added bonus, she's beautiful."

"What about what's-her-name, the nurse? I thought she was the one." Gerry never forgets the beautiful ones.

"Julia. It was a false alarm."

"Have you spoken to Sarah's parents?" Paul inquired.

"No, it only happened an hour ago. I haven't spoken to anyone from her family or mine. I guess I should have called her parents to ask permission, or whatever you do in these circumstances. It just popped into my head to ask her to marry me and she said yes. Anyway I'm not that keen about her parents and I think they feel the same about me. I'm not anxious to talk to them."

Then Murray said what everyone was thinking. "They will be talking about you behind your back. You'll be tagged for marrying rich."

"Look, I know some people will talk about me marrying the Button King's daughter. They will assume the worst. They always do. Otherwise, they wouldn't have anything to talk about. I don't care what anyone says. My friends know the truth and the rest can go to hell."

Paul interrupted, having some experience coming from a rich family. "It's not that simple. Even some people who you think are your friends will look at you differently. Once your lifestyle changes, everything changes. That's just the way it is."

"I'm not going to be one of those trust-account son-in-laws depending on Abe Goldman's table scraps. I make a living. I don't need the Button King's charity or the obligations that come with it."

"I know you don't need it or even want it." David always had the ability to get to the core of the matter. "You're a student at heart who can live on two pair of jeans and a stereo in an attic apartment.

261

But Sarah Goldman likely has twenty pair of jeans, all from fancy designers, a surround-sound stereo system and lives in a real penthouse with a view of English Bay. Of course you'll change. You'll learn how to spend but always buy wholesale."

"I don't know what Sarah has and I don't care. I expect we'll both have to adjust. I don't think this is a big issue and, if the worst thing is that she spends her father's money, then so be it. I'm going to work every day, have my career and come home to my wife and maybe some kids. If that picture works, then the rest will take care of itself."

Murray wanted to know where we were going to live. "I got engaged an hour ago. I don't know where we're going to live. We've talked about me moving to Vancouver after the Jupiter case ends but who knows what will happen."

We were quiet for a moment, all of us realizing that this had become a bit more serious than our usual dinner conversations. Gerry changed the mood with a toast. "To a fallen comrade. May he have a soft landing on a king size bed. *L'Chaim.*"

We spent the rest of the evening catching up on everyone else's life. Paul had sublet the space of his failed singing school for immigrants to a convenience store franchise which was doing huge business selling freezees and peanuts. He had put an upcharge on the sub-lease based on a percentage of sales and he was actually making money. He saw how well this worked and repeated the sublet model a dozen times and now he was becoming the king of convenience store leasing. Murray's Free Willy clinics had continued to expand. He was making a promotional video when the police raided his office and charged the production company and Murray with the production and distribution of pornographic material. This made Murray the poster boy for civil libertarians and it had given him more publicity than he would have generated from the video.

David Kaplan was as steady as always and told us the story about a Bar Mitzvah he went to in a new age synagogue where the rabbi sang the service to the melody of "My Way," and was accompanied by the Bar Mitzvah boy who played the bongos. Gerry told us that he had developed a mathematical formula to determine the perfect age for a female companion. You took the man's age, divided by two and added ten. The adding ten was the flexible part of the equation. To be more precise, no more than ten could be added. This left him the leeway never to turn anyone away because their age was outside the range of the equation. Once he finished his explanation we all sat in awe of his ability to make algebra come alive.

I was home by 9:30 and there were nine messages on my machine, a new record. I expected nothing less under the circumstances. There were three messages from Sarah, two from her father, one from her brother, one from Sarah's aunt in California whose name I could not decipher from the message and two messages from the video store. My copy of *The Last Waltz* was overdue. I love that scene when Bob Dylan comes onstage and everyone takes a step back in recognition of his presence. He is the uncrowned fourth king of Israel.

I called Sarah back to make sure that neither of us had changed our minds. We were still engaged and it was exciting in spite of my apprehension about what was to come. After I spoke to Sarah, I called my parents. I knew I couldn't delay any longer to tell them. I could not take the chance they might hear about my engagement from the dry cleaning delivery person or my mother's hairdresser. My mother answered the phone and I told her that I was coming over to tell them some important news. For a weeknight, this was an unusual time for me to call or visit. My mother's first thought was that I was sick. But I reassured her that I was in perfect health. The other messages would have to wait and I drove directly to their home.

I hadn't told my parents about Sarah so the announcement of our engagement was a real surprise. After going through all the background material about how we met, how long we'd been going out and if I was sure she was the one, my parents were ecstatic almost to the point of speechlessness. They did not realize that Sarah was one of The Goldmans and not just any Goldman. The truth came out when my parents started asking about her family. Both of them were stunned. My father fell silent and my mother saw this as a gold medal performance in Olympic social climbing. Before I could say anything further, my mother got a copy of the funeral contact list her cousin in Washington put together and started calling all over North America with the news. There was no holding her back. We managed to find a few minutes to sit around the kitchen table talking about what was to come and how my life was finally taking shape.

I went home around midnight, called Sarah to tell her about my parents' reactions and went to sleep knowing that tomorrow was going to be the real coming out for Ben Stein. Finally, it was my turn, but for some reason it didn't feel like it.

The next morning I returned the calls from the night before. I called Abe Goldman who conferenced in his wife. They were overjoyed that I was the one. They were relieved that their daughter was marrying within the faith. I admit that it made my life simpler too, but regrettably predictable. In Goldman code, marrying within the faith meant Abe Goldman would not cut off Sarah's inheritance. The Goldmans insisted that I call them Mom and Dad but I felt awkward calling Mr. Goldman Mr. Dad.

By the time I called them back, Abe and Adele Goldman had already called my parents so this eliminated the problem of how I was going to introduce my parents to Sarah's parents. Abe told me that he would host a small party so our respective families could get to know each other. He told me to set aside Saturday night for an informal gathering at the Goldman house. Then I spoke to Sarah's aunt who reminded me how lucky I was to find such a wonderful girl.

I couldn't get any work done with all the calls going back and forth to my office, so I went into hiding for the afternoon. I was tired of telling and retelling the story of how we met and detailing our long-distance romance. I decided to pick up a newspaper from Mr. Cohen and spend the afternoon at the Italian Coffee Bar. No one pays any attention to anyone there while a soccer game is on the satellite feed. I was sure to be left alone.

"Hello, Mr. Cohen. Do you have today's *Globe?*"

"Stein, congratulations! You're very lucky to be marrying a girl from such a fine family. Who would have thought that you would be marrying a Goldman. How did you convince such a family to marry you?"

"Thanks for your kind wishes but I'm not marrying the whole family. One of them is plenty for me. Somehow, I'm not surprised that you know."

"Abe Goldman's driver shows up like clockwork to get his *New York Times*. She was coming from the printer where they are printing the engagement party invitations. She showed me the printer's proofs and there you are: Ben Stein the son of Mr. and Mrs. Nathan Stein.

Well I was speechless. I know the boy who is marrying the daughter of Abe Goldman, I thought to myself."

"If I could get my newspaper, I'll be on my way." This was not a conversation I wanted to pursue.

"Sure. So when are you getting married?"

"We haven't decided but I'm sure you'll hear once we order the invitations."

"Okay, Stein, here is your paper. It's on the house and, don't worry, from now on it will always be today's edition." He leaned over and whispered, "Don't worry about me, I won't mention a word about that girl you were seeing. We all understand. Send my congratulations to your parents. I called my daughter in Toronto to tell her."

I spent the balance of the afternoon hiding in the Italian Coffee Bar, talking to the four Tonys and reading the newspaper. The first thing I checked was the announcement section of the paper and, thank God, my engagement hadn't made it in by press time. I called Three-Quarters Dana who told me Sarah had called to say she was coming in Friday night for the family party on Saturday and that her dad had hired a courier service to deliver the engraved invitations to make sure everyone got them on time for Saturday. Apparently, the printer needed an extra day to do hand engraving of the Goldman crest so the courier had to work fast. The invitations would all be delivered by Wednesday night.

Over the next two days, my private life became public. The announcement appeared in the Toronto, Vancouver, Miami and Winnipeg newspapers and I was getting calls from distant relatives who hadn't spoken to our side of the family for at least fifteen years. At work a steady parade of lawyers and secretaries from the firm were coming into my office to congratulate me. I had this sinking feeling that my engagement would culminate into the wedding of the year. But I didn't want the wedding of the year. I wanted only family and a few friends attending in the rabbi's study. I was uncomfortable with the attention and the impending spectacle of a double-ring circus. Sarah and I had not discussed any wedding plans but it was apparent that my idea of a wedding and the Goldmans' idea of a wedding were not the same. I broached the subject with Sarah and she told me it would be a waste of time to try and convince her parents otherwise. She said I shouldn't fight it because it was going to happen Abe Goldman's way, no matter what I said. It was just a party and not worth fighting over. It was only one night.

Sarah flew in on Friday and we had a passionate reunion. It was our first time together since we had gotten engaged. Now that we were official, Sarah decided she should stay at her parents and not sleep at my apartment. Once she became engaged, her parents insisted on this facade of propriety until we were married. Casual sex at the Fontainbleau with her parents next door was fine but, when it got serious, abstinence had to prevail. The logic escaped me.

The casual Saturday get-together was anything but casual. The little family gathering turned out to be for 100 guests, eighty-nine of whom were friends or relatives of the Goldmans and only eleven from the Stein family. My mother bought a new dress made by some Italian designer and my father got a new suit, shirt and tie. I wore my blue suit and one of my father's red paisley ties. The car valets wore red and gold uniforms and the valet tokens were brass coins with the Goldman family crest stamped on one side and an identification number on the other. This was not the Mogan David valet service. In the foyer of the Goldman house was an ice sculpture of Venus de Milo with champagne cocktails coming out of her cut-off arm. I half expected meat knishes to pop out of her ass. And this was the understated part of the evening.

Both Adele and Abe Goldman dressed the part. Adele wore a winter-white pant suit dripping with beads. It was accented by a gold T-shirt that seemed to glow in the dark. She brought out the family jewels for the evening and, for fake diamonds and emeralds, they looked authentic. Abe Goldman was right. Not one person in the room thought those stones could be fake. As for Abe, he outdid his wife. Although he was only 5'7", he seemed so much taller. He wore a blue cashmere dinner jacket and black tuxedo pants. His jacket had the Goldman crest embossed, in gold, on the chest pocket. He wore black alligator shoes with gold buckles that had the same crest as the jacket engraved on them. He looked like the lead singer of a Motown band, if you didn't count color.

Sarah and Abe Goldman introduced me, one by one, to all the Goldman invitees. Every single one of the eighty-nine guests from the Goldman side showed up and every single one of those eighty-nine guests told me how lucky I was to be marrying Sarah. Abe Goldman had prepared a one-page biography of my academic and working career which he distributed with the invitations so the guests had something to say to me when we met. By the time I got through the group of eighty-nine, it was time for Abe to give a speech. There was no time to introduce Sarah to my family, all eleven of them.

He started his usual way. "At this happy time, we all know that Sarah and Ben's future lies ahead of them." Mr. Dad only had one speech and he adapted it to every occasion. It worked for graduations, engagements, anniversaries, but not for funerals. He was too cheap to commission a new speech. Of course, everyone in attendance applauded since it was Abe's champagne cocktails, knishes and free valet service. I was convinced that Abe put cheap sparkling wine in recycled Dom Perignon bottles, following the Golex principle, and I could picture the staff in the kitchen pouring Portuguese sparkling Rose into those Dom bottles and then serving the swill in champagne cocktails to his guests with their discriminating palettes. As always, for Abe Goldman appearances were everything, and he pulled it off.

At the end of Mr. Goldman's speech, he spoke about my 1972 Datsun 510. He joked that the security guards for the party had checked if someone driving that automobile could be a guest at this party. Everyone laughed and I forced an approving grin. The irony was that my car was the only one in the lot that was paid for in full. The rest were leased on the never-never plan. In typical Goldman style, Abe directed all the guests to look outside where a new, red Porsche 911 wrapped in a big blue ribbon was parked in the driveway. He gave me the keys to the car and told me to drive the Datsun into the nearest farmer's field.

My first reaction was to check if it was a real Porsche or one of those kits with a Korean engine. I could not afford to replace another Goldman gift for the real thing. But not even Abe Goldman could fake one of these cars. I knew there would be a catch. I gave an academy award winning performance about how grateful I was to the Goldmans for their generosity. Then I saw it. The car had a designer license plate with "AGIFT" written on it and the registration was in Abe Goldman's name. This gift was licensed to Abe Goldman and he hadn't transferred title to me or Sarah. It was a variation of the Rolex scam. Instead of giving a fake, he gave the real thing but retained the title.

By the end of the evening, I could see that my parents had very different impressions of the coming-out event. My dad always said that the people who buy the silent toilets often leave the biggest stink. The Goldmans had seven of these toilets in different pastel shades. I expect that the rest of the guests were equally equipped. My mother saw the Goldman clan as a new branch of the family tree which would further secure our roots as Canadians. As for me, I was with my dad on the silent toilet side except that I could still hear what was really going on in the bathroom.

I was uncomfortable the entire evening but noticed that Sarah was completely at ease mingling with the guests. Watching her work the room was impressive although she did have the advantage of knowing eighty-nine of the 100 guests by name. She was hard to figure out. This was the same girl who had told me that she treasured her anonymity and that was why she had moved to Vancouver. I could not reconcile these two images of her. Maybe this engagement had been premature and I didn't know her as well as I thought I did. Maybe my instinct to break away from my ethnic heritage was wrong. I didn't want to confront these contradictions as I sat in the Button King's stone mansion and drank champagne cocktails. But I felt like a stray dog performing dumb tricks in appreciation for a warm floor to sleep on. Still, the party was only one night. And, it is a beautiful car, even if it was a loaner that would remain in Abe Goldman's heated garage for the balance of the winter.

44

February and March were very busy. Sarah came in every weekend but we had very little time alone. There were so many invitations from an endless stream of her relatives. On the few weekends that nothing was scheduled, Abe Goldman insisted that we spend time at his house so he could talk about himself. Every time we were invited over to one of Sarah's relatives, we were given an engagement gift. Those gifts were increasingly becoming a burden. How many sterling silver pickle dishes does one household need? I prefer to eat pickles right out of the jar. How many Swedish crystal pepper-mills could one house absorb? Besides, I don't use pepper. It gives me heartburn. To make matters worse, if that were possible, every time we received one of these gifts I had to give a thank-you speech as if I were thanking the Nobel Society for awarding me the prize in chemistry. To top it all off, this stuff came from a wholesale in Chicago where there were no refunds or exchanges. The gifts were piling up in my apartment to the point where I was tripping over the boxes. These gifts were the last things I saw when I went to bed and the first things I saw when I woke up. The social events and the gifts grated on my nerves to the point where I told Sarah to stay in Vancouver so we could have an excuse to refuse the invitations. The truth was, I needed a break. I was running out of patience and storage space.

Luckily, I always had the ever-reliable excuse of work. March was a pivotal month for the Jupiter case. The Ontario Securities regulators and the U.S. Securities Exchange Commission had decided to look into Jupiter's dealings with their franchisees. Both agencies coordinated their investigations since they were both looking at the same transactions, pooling their manpower to avoid duplication. The securities lawyers told me that such co-operation between the agencies was unprecedented. Neither Bloom nor Jupiter were sympathetic litigants and it was only a matter of time before charges would be laid. These investigations always bore fruit and, in this case, it was of the low-hanging variety. By this time Jupiter's problems were appearing regularly in the newspapers. To think it all started with Mr. Zimmer bringing me two jars of pickles as a retainer. When the newspapers reported on Jupiter, I was usually identified as the emerging franchisee lawyer who had broken the case open, and that made me into a minor celebrity at Lord's and in the media.

Finally, Harland Jupiter and Isaac Bloom came to the conclusion that, if they could settle the franchise case, the rest of their problems would go away. They reasoned that the regulators would lose interest once the franchisees were satisfied. Jupiter and Bloom did not realize that their arrogance had made them the standard of greed by which all others would be measured in the future. The government lawyers would not lose this opportunity to prosecute.

As events unfolded, a meeting was scheduled for April 1 at Billings' office. This meeting was pivotal. Either a settlement would come together in that April meeting or we would be going to court to prove our claim. I had picked the time and place for the meeting. It was my way of telling Jupiter what I thought of their case. Since our February meeting everything had been done by phone. Our relationship with Billings had changed once he grudgingly accepted that his clients were going to pay a substantial sum of money and that we were not backing down. Billings became much less polite and his language became considerably less elegant. He was not a gracious loser. By April 1, we all understood the issues. It would likely be the last time we would attempt to settle the case, regardless of the outcome.

The April Fools meeting was very different from the February meeting at Billings' office. Rupert MacIntosh and two representative franchisees attended with me. Harland Jupiter dispensed with his usual name dropping and patronizing tone while Isaac Bloom sat quietly, having abandoned any attempt to make an ethnic connection with me. Both Jupiter and Bloom now realized it was time to settle up and put their franchise problems behind them. Rupert was sure that Harland Jupiter would settle in spite of his appetite for litigation. His name had taken a beating from the business writers of the major North American newspapers about the extent of his overblown expenses. Rupert had checked the invitation lists of the various charitable balls in Palm Springs and Palm Beach and both Jupiter and Bloom's names were noticeably missing. Rupert was convinced that

Harland Jupiter needed a quick settlement to salvage his reputation. If they settled and put the right spin on it, Jupiter and Bloom could rehabilitate their reputations. With some substantial donations to certain charities they could still make the summer party list at Martha's Vineyard.

Rupert opened the meeting. "We have come here either to settle this litigation or understand the extent of our differences. Do you have a proposal for us to consider?"

"Actually," Billings replied, "we were hoping to see a revised proposal from you. It's only right that your clients should reveal their position since you are chasing us. You must be willing to take less since you came to this meeting."

I was annoyed by this superficial jockeying when we both knew they must have come with a check or why bother. I couldn't tolerate any more of their transparent tactics. "Listen, we're not amateurs here and we're not about to waste our time talking about who takes off their pants first. If we limit the claim to four years, which is a significant concession, you will owe us about one hundred million plus costs and interest. Everyone in this room knows you are going to pay. The only issue is how much and how long it will take to get the money. So our total claim, based on four years liability, is one hundred and twenty-five million dollars plus the other issues we need resolved. Do we have a deal?"

Isaac Bloom couldn't keep quiet any longer. "Stein, you're much more confident since we last met. Either you're putting on a bit of a show for your clients and senior partner or getting engaged to my friend Abe Goldman's daughter has given you some newfound confidence. By the way, congratulations, you've found yourself quite a family."

I couldn't believe Bloom would stoop so low. "Thanks for your kind thoughts. Abe Goldman never mentioned that you were his friend and I didn't see your name on the guest list for the wedding. I imagine you are getting accustomed to being left off guest lists by now. Anyway, my newfound confidence is based on the state of your case. You know the problems better than I do. I don't see any reason why we should take less than what our clients are entitled to. We don't compromise a winner. The compromises have to come from the loser."

Billings could not resist. "So why did you bother coming if you're so sure you'll win?"

Rupert did not like where this conversation was leading. It was getting too personal and he interrupted. "Getting our money early is worth something and resolving this makes good business sense. If you settle with your franchisees there may not be any lasting animosity. I don't have to remind you that we need each other to make money. It's for the good of all concerned to get this case behind us. Mr. Billings, it makes sense for your clients to settle. They don't want an angry franchisee group when the Securities investigators come knocking on the Franchisee Association door. So why don't you stop playing games. How much do you intend to pay our clients? Deal with what you owe them while we outline the other parts of the settlement."

"And what are the other terms of this settlement? Isn't the money enough?" Billings said, trying to keep himself as a necessary player in the meeting.

Rupert listed the terms. "First, we must have a guarantee that you don't implement a new innovative accounting plan which would make us go through this all over again. We want an agreement that says that if there are billing disputes going forward, we will be able to arbitrate such disputes within ninety days of filing an objection."

"I take it there's more," Billings said, not even looking up from his page where he was writing notes as we spoke.

"There is more," Rupert continued. "We want guarantees that no franchisee on the association committee will have their franchise lifted for a minimum of fifteen years and that their supply of tires will not become unreliable."

"What else?" Billings continued to take notes.

"We want representation on the Accounting and Audit Committees of Jupiter and we want those committees to be principally responsible for settling the accounting and audit policy for franchisee related transactions."

Billings put down his pen and said sarcastically, "Is that all of it?"

"No, there is one last item. Until we are confident that your accounting system has been fixed permanently, we want you to give the franchisees a franchisee fee holiday. No bills and no one pays until we are sure the expenses are proper."

"And how do you propose we convince you of that?"

"That's negotiable. We won't be unreasonable. Also, I expect you realize that we won't take the settlement money on the payment plan. We expect to be paid in full and right away, just as you demanded the franchisees to pay for your gambling debts."

"Well that's quite a list," he said. Billings reviewed his notes. "We'll need some time to consider all these issues."

It was my turn again. "You knew these issues were on the table. We've been talking about these conditions for the last month. If we're going to make a deal, I don't expect to be sitting around here all day until you decide to reply. Let's each take one hour to consider our respective positions. If we don't get anywhere by then, it will be obvious that we're wasting each other's time and we'll get out of here. Sitting here looking at pictures of your dead partners doesn't inspire us. So let's get on with it."

We decided to leave Billings' office. We had taken a room at the hotel across from Billings' office because we felt it would not be beyond Harland Jupiter to have the boardroom bugged, even without Billings' knowledge. We gave them our room number and asked them to call us when they were ready or in one hour, whichever came first. For the balance of the day and into the evening, we negotiated back and forth. There was a steady stream of people going between Billings' office and our hotel. By 9:00 P.M. we had settled most of the issues but the deal was not done. Jupiter did not want us involved in their internal affairs and did not want us to sit on their committees. In addition, they insisted that the terms of the settlement be kept confidential. We, on our side, could not give them any assurance about the settlement terms being kept confidential given the large number of franchisees involved and their right to know the terms of any settlement. Also, we did not trust Jupiter or Bloom and we needed some mechanism to keep them honest. Their word had no value to us. Representation on the Audit Committee was our form of insurance to protect the franchisees against any future attempts of fraud.

By 10:00 P.M., it was obvious that these two issues were not going to be resolved that evening. We all needed a break to consider our respective positions and we decided we would get back together the following morning. Neither party could afford to walk away from the deal at this point since the money had already been settled.

We had agreed on $100 million plus legal costs to date to be paid within seventy-two hours of signing any settlement agreement. Before I went home to get some sleep, I stopped for take-out Chinese food from the Jade Dragon. Chinese food tastes better the later you eat it.

When I got home the message light was blinking. I had three messages. Before I had gotten engaged, I would have jumped to retrieve three messages. Now that I was engaged, three messages just didn't give me the same sense of anticipation. The messages were probably about a change to a wedding detail or another unwanted invitation to dinner from one of Sarah's many cousins. I hit the play button unenthusiastically while I ate my lukewarm Chinese food, glanced at the newspaper and turned on the TV for the late-night news.

The first message was from my mother asking me to come over for dinner. She said she hadn't seen enough of me. If I visited my mother three times a day, I'd get the same message from her. She had developed an insatiable appetite to talk to me about the wedding arrangements. She reminded me that it was March and the wedding date was set for August 30.

The second message was from Sarah. She wanted to know if lavender napkins shaped like roses were fine with me. Why would I care? She would decide regardless of what I thought but she still wanted to talk to me about it. Sarah also said she wasn't coming in that weekend and wanted me to visit Mr. Dad and Mrs. Mom.

The third message had been left at 10:15 P.M. "Hi, stranger, it's Mrs. Chicago. At this very moment I'm sitting at the bar where we spent our first evening together and you're not here. It's not polite to stand up a woman, even a married one. I saved you some mixed nuts and ordered you a vodka tonic. They close at one so you better get over here soon."

I found myself at the fork in the road. I could have continued dining on take-out Chinese, watch the news and disregard the message. Or, I could put the take-out Chinese in the fridge, change out of my office clothes and be at the Fort Garry Lounge within twenty minutes.

I spotted Julia as she sat at the bar and all the old feelings came back. Although almost three years had passed since our first evening at this bar, she looked more beautiful than ever. She was dressed in black, accented by an emerald necklace that matched her sparkling eyes. I walked up behind her and sat down on the bar stool next to her.

"How are the mixed nuts in this place?" I asked in a matter-of-fact way.

"Pretty good, as long as you take the ones from the bar. They're fresher." She flashed a smile.

"Where'd you learn that?"

"A lawyer I knew who reminded me of Al Pacino told me." She looked right through me.

"At least he didn't remind you of Clemenza."

"He's a lot cuter than Clemenza." She put out her arms to embrace me.

I kissed her on both cheeks and held her for a moment. "You look better than ever."

"So do you," she responded in kind.

"At least this time I didn't spill my drink. What brings you here? It's still winter, you must be the only tourist in the city."

"I'm here to see my family. After three days of non-stop family, I needed a break. So, I came for a drink. I was hoping to find you sitting here waiting for me. You weren't." She crossed her legs in a seductive way. "So the bartender gave me a phone and I called you. And here you are. I knew you were too much the gentleman to stand me up. Now, are you still a lawyer or did you go back to school for another degree?"

"No, I'm practicing law and I'm still at the same firm I articled with. I don't want to talk about myself. I'd rather hear about you. I've thought about you so often but didn't have the nerve to pick up the phone."

"You should have had more nerve." She said taking a sip from her drink. "I'm still married to Robert and living in Chicago. I'm not working and I really miss that. Mostly what I do is redecorate our apartment, read and go shopping, not necessarily in that order."

The bartender had brought me a vodka tonic and I raised my glass, toasting her for remembering. It's the small memories that bring people closer, particularly when you're searching for that common thread. "Tell me about this husband of yours."

"Robert is a prominent surgeon," she explained. "These surgeons have huge egos. They see themselves as holding life and death in their hands. He knows everything about everything and, on the off chance there is something he admits to not knowing, he assumes it's not worth knowing anyway. He is completely self-absorbed and spends very little time away from work. Our vacations usually double as one of his conferences where I go off on the wives' bus tour while he gives speeches and socializes with his doctor friends."

"You never struck me as someone who would take the wives' tour."

"I'm not. But he does. The truth is I'm completely frustrated with him. But Chicago is terrific so it keeps me stimulated. If I didn't live in a city with so much to do, I don't think I could have lasted." She mixed her drink with the straw as she looked down.

"Should I ask if you have an escape plan?"

"Should you ask? Of course you should ask since you're the only person I would want to tell. I don't have a real friend in Chicago and my family can't see past the things we bought for our apartment. They would never understand how someone with everything could be unhappy.

"So what are you going to do?"

"I am preparing myself mentally to leave but I'm not quite ready. I want to revive my career so I can take care of myself. I've gotten too accustomed to his money and I don't want to feel vulnerable for a monthly maintenance check. When I leave I want to cut all ties with him and his family."

"You don't look any worse for wear. In fact, you are more beautiful than ever."

She smiled and winked at me. "I knew there was a reason I called you. You've always done wonders for my self-esteem. Now it's my turn to ask the questions. What's happened to you?"

"Work has a way of filling up a lot of time and actually, I have a pretty good career. By accident I've become a bit of a franchising expert and I am in the middle of a case which has been attracting a lot of publicity."

"I have to confess that I know something about that. My sister has been sending me newspaper clippings when you've been quoted. It looks like you've done quite well."

"Don't believe everything you read." I was uncomfortable with the notoriety. "But I am thinking of opening my own office. I don't make a very good employee. It's just not in me to ask permission. I find it demeaning." It was time to tell her about Sarah. "The other news is that I'm getting married."

"You call that *other* news! I guess it's your turn to break my heart. Who is she?"

"She's from Winnipeg but now lives in Vancouver." It was time to get to the point. "Julia, why did you sleep around when we were together? You really stuck a knife in me and it hurt for a long time." I had wanted to say that for so long and it felt good to finally say it.

"I didn't mean to hurt you. To me it was just sex. When you work in medicine, sex is just another bodily function. It was a lark that meant nothing. She reached over to hold my hand. "I thought you'd always be there when it counted. I was counting on you to take me away before I walked down the aisle. Just before I said 'I do' at my wedding, I turned around hoping to see you rush in to stop the madness. You weren't there. I was so mad at you. I felt abandoned."

"I don't know how to ride a white horse to the rescue. Looking at you now I feel the same way I did the first time we met."

"Except you haven't spilt a drink, at least not yet."

"I've been practicing drinking at a bar and I'm a lot steadier. Also, I stay away from clamato juice. It really is messy."

"So tell me about this girl you're going to marry?"

"Her name is Sarah and we met at law school. If you remember our graduation ceremony her father gave the convocation speech. Mr. Goldman wrote a check to the university and they gave him a doctorate of something."

"I didn't stay for the convocation speech. As I recall, I went to my graduation so my parents could take the picture of me getting my degree. They got the picture. I left you a note and I got out of there. That was plenty for one day."

"I'll never forget that note. I still have it. Anyway, Mr. Goldman didn't say anything worth staying for. He's one of those guys who talks about himself and makes big donations to get his name on the sides of buildings. If building names were based on personality, the only place you'd find his name is on a proctological research center, The Goldman Center for Assholes."

"When is the wedding date?"

"Right now, it's set for August thirtieth."

"What do you mean 'right now'?"

"What attracted me to Sarah was that she didn't want to lead the same life her parents did. When she finished law school she went off and traveled and then moved to Vancouver. She got a job on her own, even though her father is connected, and she didn't use his money or name to find work. She could have easily been just another trust account kid spending the winters in Florida. I found her independence and energy very seductive and . . . she is quite beautiful."

"It sounds pretty good. Rich, independent and beautiful. What could be wrong?"

Julia was invading my most private thoughts. I'd never shared those feelings with anyone. But for some reason, I let my guard down and was willing to tell her how I felt. This was becoming a very risky conversation. But I'd kept all this inside for too long and it was time to relieve some of the pressure that had been building up. I needed to tell somebody and it might as well be Julia.

"Since we got engaged, I've seen a side of her that did not fit the image I had of her. Now she acts just like her parents and she seems to want their same lifestyle. It's as if our engagement has brought her into their fold and she's comfortable with it. I don't want to have anything to do with her family or their dinner parties or their presents but Sarah seems to be enjoying the whole thing. I haven't talked to her about it, hoping this will all pass once the wedding is over and she'll go back to being the girl I wanted to marry."

"That's quite a chance you're taking." She really seemed concerned for my future.

"Yes, it's a risk, but we've already chosen lavender for the napkin color at the wedding reception and you wouldn't believe how many sterling silver pickle dishes we've received for engagement presents. Did you know that a standard-size pickle dish only holds five pickles sliced in half?"

"I'm not up on my pickle dish statistics. We make quite a pair. I'm married and trying to work my way out of it and you're about to get married and not sure if you should get into it. We must be meant for each other. Does your family have any idea how you feel?"

I shook my head. "You're the only one who knows. You wouldn't believe my parents' reaction to this engagement. My mother is so excited about this marriage it's hard to contain her. Sarah's family is at the top of the social totem pole in the Jewish community.

Everyone knows Abe Goldman. My parents are thrilled to be on the same pole as the Goldmans and relieved that I didn't bring home a Windsor. But, you would have been worth it."

"Even with a Christmas tree in the living room?"

"Even with the tree, as long as you could operate the portable defibrillator once my mother saw those Christmas lights."

"At least I would have been able to keep up my nursing skills."

We sat at the bar and talked as if there were no one else in the place. The bar closed at 1:00 A.M. and, just like on the first date, we were the last to leave. This time, though, Julia had a car. That was my bad luck . . . or was it my good luck. I was not ready to say good night or good-bye. I didn't want the evening to end no matter how exhausted I was from what had turned out to be a very long day. We agreed that she would call me at the office if she had the time. Julia was only in town for two more days and she had family commitments. I didn't feel any bitterness now for what she had done to me. That was behind me. My inner voice told me to be cautious and let her go. Chalk it up to a fond memory and accept the fact that we'd gone our separate ways. But I knew I would never have another chance with her if I walked away now.

I was home by 1:30 A.M. and feasted on my cold Chinese food. Breaded spare ribs and sweet & sour chicken are some of my favorite cold leftovers. They required a double dose of Maalox for dessert but were well worth it. I tried to sleep but, between the Chinese food, Julia and the wedding, I could not relax. The last I remember was the clock radio showing 3:20. At some point exhaustion overcame my active mind.

The phone woke me at seven and I picked it up on the fifth ring.

"Good morning, Ben. Haven't you slept enough?"

"Julia, I didn't expect to hear from you so soon. You gave me another sleepless night."

"Don't be so unsociable and buzz me up."

"You're downstairs."

"Of course I am and it's freezing, so release the door."

I pressed the security door button on the telephone and jumped out of bed. After putting on my bathrobe, I opened the apartment door and went into the bathroom to brush my teeth. When I got out of the bathroom Julia was standing in the front hallway wearing a blood-red sheared beaver coat.

"Julia, you are a constant surprise. How do you look so good so early in the morning? Last night I didn't know if I would ever see you again."

"Oh, I knew you were going to see me." She undid her coat and let it fall to the floor and I stood there in stunned silence. She was wearing nothing underneath. Eight minutes before I had been sound asleep and now the most beautiful girl I had ever known was standing stark naked in my doorway.

We stayed in bed the whole day and woke up in each other's arms sometime around 2:30 in the afternoon. She made no effort to move until she had to leave for a family dinner. It was the best April second I ever had in thirty-seven years.

45

The next day, Friday, I was at work by eight. Margaret and Bill greeted me as if I had been missing in action and was later found walking out of the jungle. They had left six messages at my apartment but I hadn't returned their calls. As a result, everyone on the Jupiter case was in a mild panic. Billings had called our office four times expecting to meet for further negotiations. He had Jupiter and Bloom sitting in his office all day waiting to meet. Margaret and Bill were concerned that we might have squandered our chance to settle the case. But I knew otherwise and calmed everyone down.

I went to see Rupert who was anxious to see me. "Where have you been? We've been looking all over for you. We even called that coffee bar you hang out at but even they hadn't seen you."

I was starting to get worried about the case. "What's going on?"

"Billings was expecting to meet with us. He was furious when we kept putting him off without any explanation. We kept telling him that we'd get back to him later. But by four o'clock we gave up on you. We had to tell him that we weren't meeting."

"How did he take that?"

"He threatened to terminate all negotiations and said his clients would not meet with us again without some unspecified pre-conditions. He told us to call him when we were ready and Harland Jupiter would decide if he was willing to talk."

"Do you think they still want to make a deal?" I was worried I had pushed them too far.

"As long as Jupiter and Bloom believe they can save their precious reputations, they'll settle the case."

"I'll give Billings a call. How did you leave it with the franchisees? Are they mad?"

"Not at all. I told them we were considering our next move and we're in no panic to act. Considering all the time Jupiter took over the document disclosure, they were happy to have Jupiter wait for us. In fact, they were quite pleased at how the day went."

"Thanks, Rupert. You saved me a lot of explaining."

"There can only be one reason that would keep you away from the office yesterday." Rupert smiled as if he understood why I had not been at work.

"See you later, Rupert." I got up and left. I went back to my office to call Billings. Just as I was about to call him the phone rang. "Ben Stein speaking."

"Good morning, Mr. Lawyer."

"Are you going to tell me that you're in the reception area wearing your beaver skin coat?"

"You only wish."

"It would give a whole new meaning to the term reception area."

Julia interrupted my fantasy. "I'm going home tomorrow and called to say good-bye."

"I won't see you again? This day is not turning out as good as I had hoped."

"I'm totally booked up with family and I can't get away."

"The story of my life. Julia, was yesterday just for old times sake?"

"You know as well as I do that there has always been something between us. That's why I kept in touch. Casual sex is not what we're about and we'll have to resolve it no matter where that leads."

"You've always had a way of complicating my life."

"This doesn't make my life any simpler either. You're engaged, but don't forget that I'm married. I don't want to keep hoping that my next love will be the real one. I'm sick of hoping for next time and always wanting you. We'll have to find a way to see each other." She hesitated and then continued, "Does it bother you that you're doing this behind Sarah's back?"

"This is not a casual affair with a girl I met in a bar. Although, we did meet in a bar. We have a right to be happy no matter how bumpy the road is to get there. Anyway, you have seniority over Sarah. But, we are an unlikely couple, don't you think?"

"Mr. Pacino, you went to school too long. Don't think so much. Why must you try to analyze everything that happens to you? Can't it be as simple as there is something between us that won't go away?"

"I still can't believe that a beauty like you would want me."

"Come on. We're not exactly beauty and the beast."

"We're not?"

Neither of us wanted to end the call. It felt good talking to her. Of course we didn't settle anything and speculated on how and where we could meet. Julia's husband was always going off on four-day medical conferences. Even though she usually went with him, next time she'd tell him that she would rather stay home. That wouldn't stop him from going and it would give us four days together. Once I knew when he would be going I'd find some excuse to travel somewhere for work and we'd meet wherever that work took me. While we were talking, the call waiting light kept blinking like a broken street light. Finally, Three-Quarters Dana came into my office and gave me one of those What-the-hell-are-you-still-doing-on-the-phone looks. I folded under the pressure and knew I had to end the call.

"I'll speak to you next week. Meanwhile, I'll dream about your coat lying on the floor of my apartment. Travel safely."

I was sure that no one knew what was going on in my life. I was too boring and average for anyone to suspect that I was having an affair, let alone while I was engaged to another woman. One of the benefits of being engaged was that if I got a lengthy call at the office from a woman everyone assumed it was the girl I was going to marry. Just as I hung up from Julia the phone rang again.

"Ben Stein speaking."

"Ben, I've been holding for twenty minutes."

"Sarah, I'm sorry. You should have left a message and I would have called you back."

"I did leave a message for you but I wanted to hear your voice. I wanted to tell you I was not intending to fly to Winnipeg this weekend unless there is an emergency. I was just calling to see if any emergencies came up."

"No emergencies. Only work this weekend and no distractions." I didn't have to work that weekend but I needed a break from her and her relatives. They had been occupying every minute of every weekend. This was the first time I had ever lied to Sarah so as not to see her. Our conversation was making me uncomfortable and I wanted to get off the phone as soon as possible so I wouldn't have to tell her another lie and complicate my deception even further.

"You can't be working every minute of the weekend. Do you think you'll have time to drop in and say hello to my parents? You can visit our new car."

"I don't think I'll have time to stop by. I'll call to say hello." That was the second lie I had told her in as many minutes. I had plenty of time that weekend. What I didn't have was the desire. The rest of our conversation was taken up by wedding plans. I never realized that a wedding could be so complicated. Sarah told me we had to make an appointment to audition the band. She didn't trust my taste in music to make that decision alone. Next, Sarah announced that she was having five bridesmaids so I had to come up with five ushers to accompany her bridesmaids down the aisle. Also, I needed a best man to accompany the maid of honor and Sarah did not want me to pick Gerry because he was single. The issues were endless. Every time we settled one issue there were two problems which resulted from that one decision. Once she decided we'd have five ushers, then we had to decide what they would wear so it wouldn't clash with the bridesmaids' dresses. After that, we had to decide where to rent the tuxedos and who was going to pay for them. This led to questions about gifts for the bridesmaids and ushers. She didn't like my idea of pickle dishes. After 20 minutes of non-stop problems, I told Sarah that I had to take a conference call and I'd call her later. That was the third lie in the same call. Sarah could sense that I was distracted and she was disappointed that I did not want to talk about the wedding plans. We said good-bye. I was happy to get off the phone but my guilt lasted the whole day.

I had to call Billings. I had meant to call him an hour earlier. Just as I was about to dial his number the phone rang. I asked Dana to take a message. She took the call and then told me that Gerry Smith was on the phone and he needed to talk to me. Friendship runs deeper than clients, so I took the call.

"Hi, Gerry, what's up?"

"Did you get laid?"

"What are you talking about? Sarah is not here and, in fact, she is not coming in."

"I wasn't referring to Sarah."

"Well who are you referring to? I'm engaged."

"I'm referring to the nurse with the green eyes and brown hair that you went out with a few years ago. What was her name?"

"Julia Windsor."

"That's right, Julia. She was spectacular. So, did you get laid?"

"How would you know? No one could possibly know."

"It's a small world, Ben. Murray Wall's sister is a lab technician at St. Boniface Hospital and works in the Children's Ward. Four days ago, she's at work and your Ms. Windsor comes in to visit some of the staff she once worked with. Murray's sister is introduced to her by a doctor who worked with the stunning Ms. Windsor. Now the plot thickens. The day before yesterday, Murray's sister is at a medical meeting at the Ft. Garry Hotel and . . ."

"You can stop there. She's in the hotel bar and she sees me sitting at the bar with Julia. She calls Murray who in turn calls you to find what's with Ben and here we are."

"Basically, you got it right. Ben, do you have any idea what you are doing?"

"Julia showed up unexpectedly. We met for the first time in years when Murray's sister saw us. Nothing happened between us that night. But one thing lead to another and . . . yesterday was the greatest day of my life."

"Isn't she married?"

"She is married but it's grinding down to an unhappy ending. Anyway, we had a day to remember and it has definitely complicated my life."

"Look, I'm single, so I don't give advice about relationships except how to avoid them. But don't confuse lust with love. Lust doesn't last forever, even though this Ms. Windsor is a major lust feast, from what I remember of her."

"I know the difference between lust and love."

"But does she?"

"I'm counting on her."

Gerry promised to get a hold of the boys to arrange a dinner and we said good-bye.

Still holding the phone in my hand, I shook my head in disbelief. Yesterday was the first time I had ever cheated in any relationship. One day later I'd lied to Sarah three times. Then, I was the subject of a third-hand sighting at a bar with the woman I later slept with. I wondered who else might know. It wouldn't have surprised me if Mr. Cohen knew. Maybe I should call Sarah and confess everything before she called to confront me. Luckily or not, I regained my composure and, like all men, I reconciled my sin of omission. If I were confronted, I would deny everything. I just had to be more careful until this was all sorted out. I placed a call to Billings.

"Hello, Mr. Billings. This is Ben Stein."

"The elusive Mr. Stein. I thought we were going to get together yesterday. Why didn't anything happen?"

"I'm to blame. I wasn't ready to say anything definitive. There was a wide range of opinion among our clients and we needed the day to sort ourselves out."

"And have you managed to sort out what it will really take to settle this case?"

"I've had a pretty good idea all along. We just needed to keep everyone on the same side."

"I'm not sure our clients are still interested in what you have to say. Harland Jupiter and Isaac Bloom are very unhappy with the way they were treated and my instructions, as of last night, were not to bother any longer with the franchisees."

"Out of respect for Harland Jupiter, we'll meet him in Toronto. We aren't giving it away but we'll go to him. You know as well as I do the strength of our case and there are no gifts. But, we are willing to go to Toronto to pick up where we left off."

My motive for meeting in Toronto had little or nothing to do with Harland Jupiter. I had no regard for that pompous jerk or his short sidekick. My plan was to find a date to meet in Toronto that fit Julia's timetable so she could come up from Chicago and we could spend four or five days together without the threat of any third-hand sighting. Harland Jupiter and his overblown ego would believe we were coming to Toronto in deference to his self-professed stature. I'd see Julia, not miss any work and we'd stay over the weekend. It was perfect. I just had to coordinate the dates.

"Mr. Billings, why don't you speak to your client and get some alternative dates to meet and we'll do our best to accommodate Mr. Jupiter's calendar. Please don't make it at the beginning of the week so we will have a chance to get organized before we come. Let's try for Wednesday to Friday dates. That would work a lot better for us."

"I'll talk to my client but no promises. I'll get back to you."

As soon as I got off the phone with Billings, there was another call waiting.

"Ben?"

"Hi, Dad, sorry to keep you waiting. How are you?"

"I'm at the emergency ward of the Health Science Center. Your mother had a heart attack."

"I'm on my way."

46

The universal truth about death is that you can't avoid it and you don't know when it will happen. I was not prepared for the loss of my mother. No matter what I did she always supported me. And God knows I tested that loyalty to the limit on many occasions. Her death left me with an overwhelming sense of loneliness. That feeling of security which only a parent can provide could never be replaced.

The reception at my parents' home after the funeral was well attended. Every family has one member who takes on the task of calling everyone in the family to advise them of a death. In our case it was my cousin Ruth from Washington. Ruth kept a funeral contact list and programmed the phone numbers into her speed dial. That list even included relatives no one had talked to in years just to make them feel guilty that they had never settled up with the dearly departed. In nine calls over the course of four hours, Ruth told everyone on the list how overcome with grief she was that she could barely speak. Then she recounted in microscopic detail the final hours of my mother's life with a non-stop twelve-minute monologue.

All the relatives and those friends close enough to my parents to be considered almost relatives attended the funeral and reception. In addition, Sarah's parents came. My mother would have been quite impressed with Mr. and Mrs. Goldman pulling up to the house in their chauffeur-driven car which meant they were going to stay long enough to drink. Mr. Goldman shook my hand and told me that, in such a difficult time, I should remember that my future lay ahead of me and I must move forward. *He really should invest in a second speech,* I thought.

One hundred and twenty people came to the house that day to pay their respects. As I wandered around the house I caught snippets of the various conversations. As at every Jewish event, food, both quality and quantity, was a major theme dominated by the ongoing debate on which is better, Atlantic or Pacific smoked salmon. The second theme had to do with who had recently died or who was terminally ill. And the third theme had to do with convincing Air Canada that one is entitled to a bereavement discount ticket. As I overheard, the discount was only for immediate relatives even though a cousin swore she was like a sister to her.

For the most part, I sat in the living room and watched my dad graciously receive all the guests. It was remarkable how he kept his composure. I watched Sarah work the crowd as if she were already the grieving daughter-in-law. The whole scene made me speculate about who would receive the mourners when I die. I had to make a decision about Julia. My mortality clock was ticking.

As I sat watching this scene as if it were a surreal movie, I looked up to see Arlene standing in front of me. She was dressed from head to toe in black and had a look of genuine concern for me on her face. She smiled and sat down beside me on the piano bench. We talked for a few minutes but I don't remember anything we said. She mentioned something about Sarah but I wasn't paying attention and just nodded as she spoke. Arlene put her arm around me to console me and it felt so warm. It reminded me of the night we actually slept together.

Most of the guests came, ate lunch, paid their respects and left within two hours. All the smoked salmon was eaten, the bagels were gone, the chopped herring was consumed and most of the Scotch was drunk. I sat on the piano bench, just as I had for the High Holidays, expecting my mother to come walking out of the kitchen wearing her grey skirt and blouse and sit down beside me. This was the moment when the reality of her death hit me. The emptiness of that spot on the piano bench beside me was indescribable. I sat there in the private world of my regrets and did not even notice the guests leaving or hear their parting words of support. As the last guest left, my dad sat down beside me, filling the void on the piano bench. He rubbed his hands together as if he was preparing to tell me something.

"Your mother would have enjoyed all these people coming to the house and eating her lunch. It always gave her such pleasure."

"I was thinking the same thing. But I never felt so alone even in a room full of people."

"Ben, now that your mother is gone we should talk about some family business."

288

"Can't this wait?" I said somewhat impatiently. "I am just start-ing to realize that she won't be coming out of the kitchen to sit down with us. I never realized till now the importance she placed in bringing the family together and keeping our history alive. Dad, this is her legacy. We must respect it and keep it alive."

My dad sat there beside me not moving. I noticed his arms were crossed and he seemed very defensive. Something was on his mind. He was breathing heavily and he could not speak for fear of breaking down. He took an envelope out of the inside breast pocket of his jacket and placed it gently on my lap. I picked it up. Suddenly my dad lost his composure and broke down. Crying, he got up from the piano bench and left the room. I sat there staring down at my name written in blue ink on the white of the envelope. It was my mother's handwriting. I could not bring myself to open the envelope. I felt as if I would be violating the dead. But this was her way of speaking to me one last time.

Gathering all my courage, I slid the palms of my hands carefully under the envelope as if I was cradling a priceless manuscript. The envelope felt so heavy and ice cold. In fact, I had never felt anything colder in my entire life and I could barely sustain the weight of it although rationally I knew it weighed only a few ounces. Finally, and with the utmost of caution, I opened the envelope. I took out two folded handwritten pages which I recognized to be my mother's handwriting. The letter was dated May 4, 1984 which, for some unexplainable reason, was the date of my law school convocation. I unfolded the pages with great care, gathered all my inner strength and began to read the contents of what would be the last time my mother would be speaking to me.

My Darling Ben,
    If you are reading this letter, I have died before your father. Although this must be a sad time for both of you, I want you to understand that I have lived a full life and have enjoyed the greatest gifts of a loving husband and a wonderful son. I would have liked to have lived longer but I go to whatever is next knowing that I've had the best that life could offer, the love of my family.
    What I am about to tell you is difficult and embarrassing for me but I hope in time you will come to understand. When your father and I left Europe, we did not come directly to Canada. Immigration

was very difficult and we were not welcome. No country wanted us. We had left our families behind and went to Palestine. Although we had very little, we took nothing with us, not even a picture. Life was very hard there.

Palestine was not the land of milk and honey as it was described in the Bible. We spent eighteen months in Palestine until our immigration papers to Canada came through. During that time, your father went up north to work in the orchards and I took a job as a housekeeper to a wealthy land developer in Jerusalem. It put a great strain on our marriage and we separated.

Ben, please don't be mad at me for what I am about to tell you. I fell in love with my employer and got pregnant. Other than Nathan, no one knew who the father was. I decided to have the baby and I did, a beautiful baby girl named Jaylan.

Once your father returned from the north we renewed our love and commitment for each other. Soon after, the immigration papers came through. Our dream had come true. When we found out that the papers did not include any children we tried everything but the Canadian officials would not permit Jaylan to enter Canada on our papers. We had two choices, leave Jaylan with her father and work to bring her over later or stay in Palestine and let our immigration documents expire. Jaylan was only four months old and her father's family loved her very much. Amazingly they welcomed her as one of their own. It broke my heart but we had to leave Palestine or we might never have had another chance to come to Canada. I held on to my dream that one day I would be able to bring my daughter to Canada. But, as Jaylan grew up, her father did not tell her about me and she assumed that the woman who was raising her was her mother.

Jaylan was a happy child and her family in Palestine loved her very much. We did not want to disrupt her life. I kept in touch with her father over the years to make sure she was well. But, to this day, she has no idea about her real mother and my relationship with her father.

Ben, you must try to understand that a child born out of wedlock at that time was an unspeakable humiliation. I could not tell anyone about it or my feelings of loss. Nathan swore that he would never say a word about this to you without my permission and I have never given him that permission. But I cannot bear to take this secret to my grave.

Forgive me for keeping this from you. With your wisdom I am confident you will use this information wisely. My parting gift to you is to give you the sister you never had.

I love you and hold you close to my heart. I wish for you a life of love and happiness, always.

Your Mother

I sat on the piano bench motionless and in stunned silence, trying to grasp the enormity of what I had just read. I felt betrayed, elated, confused and sad all at the same time. How different my life might have been had I known that I had a sister. I thought about conversations I had with my mother over the years and whether there had ever been some clue she was trying to give me that I had a sibling. I put the letter carefully back in its envelope, placed it in my breast pocket and walked into the den where my dad sat waiting for me. I sat down on the black leather couch facing him.

"Why didn't you tell me?"

"At first you were too young to understand and, as time went on, your mother decided to leave well enough alone. Jaylan has a good a life and so did we." My dad looked down at his hands as he spoke and could not make eye contact with me. "We did not want to disrupt either of you or relive that time in our own lives."

"Dad, once you knew about the baby how did you deal with knowing she had been with another man?" I had to ask.

"Your mother was my best friend. She cared very much for me. But, it was a very hard time and we were both grasping for a better life. When I came back from the north, we discovered we were still in love and that's what was important. I could not dwell on a momentary lapse in our relationship. Memories fade over time and other memories replace them. At first we talked about Jaylan every day but, as time went on and we created a new life for ourselves in Canada, you became the entire focus of our lives. Finally, we stopped talking about it altogether." My father looked up at me and smiled.

"But I could have had a sister."

"I was torn by that decision. But it would have meant a lot of explaining and embarrassment for your mother. Telling the story was going to affect a lot of people and we were not convinced that everyone would be better off for it. In the end, it was your mother's decision."

"Do you know how to reach Jaylan?"

291

"Yes." My dad hesitated. "Her last name is Levine. She lives in Israel. But you must use this information wisely because it could turn her and her family's life upside down."

"All these years, I was an only child and I never knew the truth. It's as if I have lived a lie. I'm not sure what to believe anymore."

"Our family is not the only ones with secrets. We built a new life in Canada and we did not want to look back. It's the immigrants' curse. You always leave something behind when you move on and sometimes it's best left there. When you live in a country as safe as Canada it is hard to appreciate what people will do in more desperate circumstances. Canada was our chance for a new life and we took it."

Suddenly I was angry. "I won't live an immigrant's life and I don't have an immigrant's curse. I don't have to forget that I have a sister. That was your life, not mine. All I know is that I have a sister whom I have never met and she doesn't even know that I exist."

"Don't fool yourself, Ben. Your family history is part of you and it will remain part of you even if you deny it."

"No. Your past is not the burden of my future."

My dad stood up and left the room. There was nothing more left to say.

I cried.

47

For the next seven days my dad and I sat in mourning. Neither of us went to work and I slept at my parents' house. Friends and relatives came over to pay their respects and many of them told me stories about my mother's numerous acts of kindness. I couldn't reconcile these stories with the cruelty of leaving a child behind to start a new life. She tried so hard to keep our family together and yet she had abandoned her own daughter. As the week went by I began to get over the initial shock of her death and the news of my sister. I started to appreciate how very painful living a contradiction for over forty years must have been for her. I wondered how often she thought about the daughter she left behind and why they had never told me, especially because I was an only child. But even with all that baggage, my mother had been a wonderful mother and a loving wife. I realized her silence could not have been a heartless gesture. It was her way of protecting us both. Now, I had to decide what to do with the family secret.

By the seventh and last day of mourning, I was still confused. Sarah had been calling me every day but our conversations were strained. We had little to talk about other than her wedding plan emergencies and I had no interest in the subject. I also had my doubts about Julia. She had betrayed me and now she was doing the same thing to her husband. Where would it end? Everything in my life seemed too complicated and I craved simplicity, certainty and transparency. I just wanted to find a girl who loved me for who I was and to live happily ever after. On the last day of *Shiva*, I got my usual morning call from Sarah while sitting at the kitchen table watching the news.

"Hi Ben. How are you feeling?"

"It's been a week and I still can't accept that she's gone. I expect her to walk in any moment even though I know that's not going to happen."

"The sooner you get back to your daily routine, the sooner things will get back to normal. Have you decided about how many out-of-town guests you want to invite to the wedding? Their invitations have to go out early."

"Sarah, maybe we should scale back on the wedding or even postpone it. I don't feel like celebrating and my mother's absence will be difficult for my family. Perhaps a quiet afternoon ceremony next year with just a few close family and friends."

"You're not in any frame of mind to make that kind of decision. Anyway, your mother would have wanted a celebration where everyone is together and enjoying themselves. We should not postpone our right to get on with our lives. This wedding is about our future and what is ahead for us."

I couldn't believe what I was hearing. Maybe it was genetic that everyone in Sarah's family should sound like Abe Goldman. I hope they don't mutate. I wanted to scream in frustration but I didn't have the energy. Instead I said, "Sarah, you may be right. This is not the time to decide. But I don't feel like celebrating and I can't promise that is going to change by August."

"Wedding plans can't be changed on the spur of the moment." Sarah's voice took on a sharp tone. "Dresses have been ordered, the hotel is already booked and out-of-town guests have to make arrangements. We just can't say, sorry, we changed our minds or see you next year. My parents have spent a lot of time planning their only daughter's wedding and they would be crushed if we told them to cancel the plans. You'll see, it will be a beautiful wedding and your mother would be pleased."

"Look, this is not about how your family feels or what my mother would want or the inconvenience of cancelling a hotel booking. This is about how I feel and I'm telling you that I don't want to go through with some overblown extravaganza courtesy of Abe Goldman so he can show the world how much he can spend on his daughter's wedding." There, I had said it. As soon as the words came out I knew it was a mistake but it was too late to take them back. After a few seconds of silence, which felt like an eternity, Sarah replied.

"Is that what you think this wedding is about? My father putting on a show for his friends? Did you ever stop to think about me? That this was about my celebrating that I met the man I wanted to spend the rest of my life with and our public declaration to this commitment?"

"If this is all about us, then why hasn't anyone asked me what I want? I am being told what to do, where to go and asked to choose a napkin color. Napkins are not about commitment. Napkins are about putting on the perfect show where I play the part of the groom. A wedding just wouldn't be the same without one."

"This is obviously not the time to discuss it." Sarah sounded as if she was holding back the tears. "Once things settle down, we'll deal with it and see how we feel. Let's just forget about this conversation and chalk it up to a bad day."

Sarah was giving me a way out and I took it. But, we could not erase what had been said. Although neither one of us would admit it, this conversation had changed our relationship. I had tried to bury my feelings but, eventually, it had to come out. We both knew something was not right.

After a week at my parents' house I told my dad that I'd talk to him every day and I moved back to my apartment. It felt so good to sleep in my own bed. Nothing feels as good as your own mattress and pillow. There were twelve messages waiting for me; eight from friends offering their condolences, three from Julia wondering where I was and one message from the newspaper offering me a 33 percent discount on a second death announcement if I booked it three days in advance of publishing within the next twelve months.

I wanted to call Julia but I couldn't risk her husband answering the phone. These are the details you have to consider when you're having an affair with a married woman. *But,* I thought, *deception seems to run in my family and now I can blame it on my genetics.* It's the updated immigrant's curse . . . one generation later. Only this time it involved two women and one man and I wasn't sure who would be left behind. Maybe me.

I was looking forward to getting back to my regular routine. Work was predictable, reliable and, for the most part, I was in control. It provided me a certain sense of security. It was common knowledge around the office that my mother had died and that first day back everyone pretty much left me alone to work at my own pace. The first item on the agenda when I got in was to go through the pile of mail. In that pile were nine bereavement cards and at least ten office memos. Normally I don't bother reading those memos but, for some reason, that day I took the time. They were mostly about parking, building hours and interoffice meetings. But, buried in the pile was a memo entitled:

David Black—File Transfer
To: All lawyers . . . April 10
From: Mr. Basil

David Black will be leaving us at the end of this month to go back to the Toronto office. Within the next week, his files will be distributed among the lawyers who will be responsible for their ongoing execution. With each file there will be an accompanying memo explaining the history of the file, what needs to be done and the client contact. I have a master list of all the files and who will be responsible for them. If you have any questions about the work then please speak to David before he moves on.

I couldn't understand what was going on. David had built a house just a few years earlier and he seemed so settled. No one was talking so I called the one person who knew everything that went on in the office, Mr. Basil. Discreet as ever, he did not reveal any details. But he did tell me about the jockeying among some of the partners to claim David's corner office. David hadn't even left, yet the partners were trying out his furniture and checking the view. I knew there was more to this story and I decided to launch a frontal assault and speak to David himself.

"Ben, I heard about your mother. I'm sorry. How is your father dealing with the loss?"

"My dad is a pretty tough guy. But the house is very quiet and everything in it reminds him of their life together. She always took care of him and it won't be easy for him. He doesn't even know how to turn on the microwave oven, so there will be some changes to his lifestyle. Other than that, he's holding up pretty well."

"I like your father, so please send him my regards. I sent a card but I didn't know if he'd even remember me, so I wrote in the note that I was the grateful customer who came to his office on a Saturday wearing a suit. That should jog his memory."

"He remembers you and he paid you his ultimate compliment. He said you were a good boy." I decided to get to the point. "David, why are you moving back to Toronto? I thought you were settled here."

"You mean the gossip machine at Lord & Bishop hasn't reached you?"

"I'm not in the gossip loop. Anyway, I never thought that fifth-hand gossip was reliable."

As David looked down at his hands resting on his desk he explained, "It's time I had a change of scenery. There was an opportunity in the Securities group in Toronto, so I took it." He did not seem excited or anxious for this new adventure.

"I came to Lord's because of you. You interviewed me and offered me my articling job. I consider you a friend in this shark tank and someone I can confide in. Is there anything I can do to help?"

"The last thing you need is to listen to my problems. You created this franchise practise and it is promising. You don't need to confide in me. In a law firm, once you are busy you are in control. When you have to depend on work from others then you are vulnerable and replaceable. Now, you can do what you like wherever you choose to work."

"So, why are you moving? You're busy. You bring in lots of work and you don't depend on others in the firm. You can go wherever you like."

"Sometimes, your personal life will influence your career decisions."

"Your wife is making you move back?"

"Actually," he hesitated, "she is staying here."

"David, I had no idea. I'm so sorry."

"Our marriage looked so perfect from the outside. My wife is beautiful, I have a good career, the kids are terrific and we live in a beautiful home. What could be wrong? But no one really knows what goes on behind closed doors. The fact is that none of these things matter. I had a richer life as a poor student in rural Ontario than I do now."

"What happened?" I asked.

"My wife is . . . only concerned with herself. You don't need a husband if you're completely self-absorbed. All you need is a banker. I've reached my limit and I'm going back to Toronto with the kids."

"How do the kids feel about moving?" His story touched a nerve.

"In their own childish way they know it is for the best. They'll do fine."

I smiled trying to lighten the mood. "You know, this information could upgrade my status in the rumor mill. I have information rights from the horse's mouth. This could be my big chance for a three-window office facing the river if I play my cards right."

"Don't forget the more windows you have looking out, the more windows to look in. It's not one-way glass, no matter what you think. So tell me, how are you and Sarah?"

"Well, it's not perfect. There have been some problems since my mother died. She is the only daughter of a very wealthy man. That doesn't bode well for compassion or companionship. Now I'll offer you some first-hand gossip." I wanted to change the subject from me and Sarah.

"What's that?"

"Your partner John Bishop in Toronto. Let's just say that he puts his bishop in places that you may not find very appealing. He tried with me and I bolted for the elevator."

David waved off my comments "Old news . . . you aren't the first."

The balance of the morning was taken up with calls to Julia, Mr. Billings and our Jupiter clients. I spoke about my mother with Julia and she seemed genuinely concerned about how I was coping with her death. I wanted to tell someone about my newfound sibling but not quite yet. By mid-morning, I had arranged a meeting with Harland Jupiter and the franchisees in Toronto that coincided with Julia's husband's conference schedule. April 19. That would leave Julia and me with five days together, counting the weekend. Julia told me her husband did not mind her traveling as long as she was there when he got back. To complete my plan I called Sarah and told her that in two weeks I was going to Toronto for work and would be staying over the weekend. I didn't feel that guilty about my sin of omission. I *did* have to go to Toronto for work and I *was* staying the weekend. I tried not to think about the one detail that I didn't mention. Even though I felt guilty the sense of accomplishment that I could coordinate all these different schedules to my own end made up for it. It was barely Monday noon and I had already put in a good day's work.

Every day, I stroked off the days on my calendar until I could see Julia. We developed a routine where I would call her at a time when there was no chance her husband would be home. We would talk for hours about how our paths kept crossing and the inevitability of our relationship in spite of the complications. She asked me if I felt that I had betrayed Sarah but I didn't see it that way. This was my chance for happiness.

Sarah came to Winnipeg that weekend and we did our usual round of relative dinner parties. I wanted my dad to come with us but he was not ready for any social outings. He was just as happy to stay at home with his memories. I felt the same way but I had no choice. I could not be the engaging conversationalist at these dinners and everyone took this to be the residual effect of my mother's death. No one came close to sensing my disdain for Sarah's family and the drivel they talked about. Their conversations were always about what they were going to buy, what they had bought or how much they had paid.

We had not made love for what was now her third visit. A month before we could not keep our hands off each other. By the end of the weekend, Sarah could not hold back her feelings. While I was driving her to the airport for her flight back home, she said, "Ben, maybe you should consider grief counseling?"

"No."

"These people can help you cope with the loss of a parent. You seem to be taking it out on me and my family."

"My feelings about you and your family have nothing to do with my mother's death. I have nothing in common with your relatives who all depend on your father for a living. Their conversations bore me."

"Is that what you think of me too?"

"No, or we would not be engaged."

"But you seem so distant."

"I have a lot on my mind."

"What is it?"

"I'm still not sure about this wedding and these elaborate plans. It's out of control and I don't like being the object of a spectacle." It was just my luck that I caught every red light, which prolonged the conversation.

"A lot of people have gone to a lot of trouble to make this a perfect wedding and I don't want to disappoint them because of a passing whim."

"This is not a whim. I'm not going to put aside my feelings to accommodate a wedding planner and their suppliers."

It was easier to play the overdone wedding plans excuse then admit to the other woman. This way all my options remained open. If it didn't work out with Julia before I had to declare myself about the wedding, then I could still make the great gesture and go along with the wedding plans.

48

April 19 finally arrived and I left for Toronto. We met Mr. Billings and Harland Jupiter in Toronto and signed a settlement agreement after three days of negotiations. They had agreed to $100 million and the franchise group was allotted two seats out of the five on the audit committee. This would protect them from any further attempt by Jupiter to pass off any questionable expenses. For reasons which I could not explain at the time, Harland Jupiter was much more motivated to settle than they had been in Winnipeg. I later found out that Harland's bankers and the security analysts told him to get his franchise problems behind him. The market takes a discount for family feuds.

Once the news of the settlement was out, I was interviewed by all the major business publications. Jupiter's stock shot up $2.50, which increased Harland Jupiter's personal wealth by some $25 million. That's a pretty good result for losing a case. The newspapers described me as the young lawyer who had taken a retainer of two jars of pickles and single-handedly brought Harland Jupiter to his knees. I gave Rupert, Bill and Margaret credit for their work but that did not make it into print. Sincere thanks does not make good copy.

The clients were so pleased they arranged a big celebration for June 15 which would be the date the $100 million check would be deposited in the franchisee association's bank account for distribution to each franchisee. We were going to celebrate the settlement with a weekend at Caesar's Palace in Las Vegas. They were going to charter a private jet to take me to Las Vegas for the weekend. I was starting to understand how Harland Jupiter and comrade Bloom could get accustomed to corporate life on someone else's account.

Having Julia with me in Toronto made the euphoria of the settlement that much more special. We had our own private celebration at a small inn about 100 miles northwest of Toronto. Our weekend was a combination of intimacy, intimacy, gourmet dining and more intimacy. We both understood that a weekend getaway would not test our relationship or provide any insight into how we would handle the tensions of day-to-day living. But, we were still confident that our relationship was based on more than a series of weekend flings. Julia came up with a plan for the summer. She was going to tell her husband that she wanted to spend the summer at Gimli Beach near Winnipeg to be closer to her family. That way, we could see each other while her husband worked in Chicago or traveled to his conferences. During the week she could stay at my apartment or I could go out to her cottage.

Julia was taking the first steps in separating herself from her husband. I felt honor-bound to respond in kind. I had put my trust in Julia's commitment to our relationship and her willingness to risk her marriage. Now my talk had to turn into action which meant I had to tell Sarah it was over. I got my courage to confront Sarah from Julia's willingness to take a chance on us. But Julia would not let me use her as my justification for leaving Sarah. She was very stern with me that I make this decision for myself and not for her. She would not take any responsibility or be accountable for breaking up my engagement. It sounded to me a little like lesson three from one of those loathsome self-help books. I assured Julia that she had only hastened my break up with Sarah. She was not the cause of it.

Over the next few weeks, Julia came twice to Winnipeg to find a summer cottage and finally found a small, one-bedroom cottage on the lake. It was only ninety minutes from my office and an easy commute. She rented it from May 15 to September 15, although she did not plan on moving there until June 1st. Her husband, Julia said, didn't seem to mind her leaving Chicago for the summer. He must have sensed the inevitable end of their marriage as much as she did.

While Julia was coming in to settle the cottage arrangements, I was telling Sarah not to come to town because of my work commitments. Deception became the norm in my relationship with Sarah. But she never questioned my work as a priority. Sarah thought work was therapeutic and would get me over my mother's death. She was happy to see me immersed in my work.

On Wednesday, Julia came in to make the final arrangements for the cottage and stayed until Friday. She went home to spend the weekend with her husband. I was relaxing in my apartment after our two-exhausting nights when the security buzzer rang. It was Sarah.

If she had come a few hours earlier she would have run into Julia and it would have been a scene out of a "B" movie. I was stunned.

"Aren't you glad to see me?" Sarah said, sensing my tension.

"Of course, I just didn't expect you. When did you get in?"

"I came straight from the airport. I thought we would spend the weekend catching up, if you know what I mean." She took off her coat and, as it turned out, she was wearing clothes underneath and sat down beside me on the living room couch. "There are no dinner engagements, my family doesn't know I'm here and it's just you, me and Tubby's take-out pizza," she pulled a bottle out of her bag, "with champagne, Dom Perignon. The Gimli Goose of France. You spring for the pizza."

The reference to Gimli made me nervous. *Did she know what was going on?*

She took my arm, led me to bed and proceeded to undress me as I stood there in compliant silence. Deciding whether I should tell her sent shivers down my spine. As usual, my libido beat out chivalry. We spent the weekend in bed. It surprised me how intimate I felt with Sarah and how much I had missed her. I was trying so hard to be bored and uninterested but I wasn't. This unanticipated turn of events added another layer of confusion to my already complicated life. Julia was moving back in a few weeks and now Sarah was lying in my bed, anticipating a wedding with lavender napkins. I had to make a decision. By the end of the weekend I was lost. I couldn't have both of them and I was at risk of losing both of them. My passion for Julia, the forbidden fruit, was undeniable, or was it . . .

While my personal life was a cauldron of confusion, the Jupiter settlement catapulted my career as a franchise lawyer. I was getting calls from both fanchisee associations and corporate clients. I was retained by an oil company to give them advice on the franchise relations with their 700 franchised gas stations across Canada. I was retained by a Japanese automotive company to deal with a dispute with their franchise car dealers. These two files alone raised my profile in the firm well beyond my years of practice. Quickly, I was becoming a three-window lawyer.

The firm held me up as the paradigm of how to create your own practice and sent me to the other Lord offices to set up a national franchise practice group with me at the helm. This was unconventional because I was not a partner and was leading a practice group which included partners, associates and students. Some of the partners and senior associates were opposed to my leadership but I kept David Black's advice in mind. As long as I didn't depend on anyone for work and created work for others, I was untouchable. My entire practice was now franchising and I generated all the work. It had all started from my dad asking me to help a friend and Abe Zimmer putting his trust in an articling student. Now the issue became how much was I willing to share my practice with the firm.

In the middle of all this, Abe Goldman came to see me about his idea of putting retail carts in shopping malls. I tried to discourage him and told him that he would be better off hiring a stranger so it would not strain our personal relationship. He would hear nothing of it and was insistent.

"Ben, I want you to handle the franchise issues and I won't take no for an answer."

"Look, Mr. Goldman, you deal with lots of law firms. You could find someone who is able to take on your project."

"Ben, I've watched how you handle yourself. You showed a lot of diplomacy when you found out that I had you followed in Miami and I liked the way you kept quiet with that little watch incident. You handle yourself well beyond your years and I need someone with that kind of judgment."

"Mr. Goldman, thank you for your confidence."

"Please, call me Abe."

"I rely on my clients to make a living but, I am not prepared to have you as a client and rely on my father-in-law to make a living." Being a fully occupied lawyer made me feel quite assertive.

"This has nothing to do with you marrying my daughter. Even if that doesn't work out it wouldn't affect our business relationship. This is a great opportunity for both of us and don't let family get in the way of a profitable business relationship." He learned forward across my desk as his way of drawing me in.

"It's already gotten in the way. Your money can't buy my services and, by the way, when am I getting that Porsche out of your garage that I noticed was registered in your name? It's spring and there is no salt on the roads." I wanted him to know that he was not going to pull another Rolex scam on me.

"You can come and get it anytime." He fidgeted in his pocket for a cigar.

"Mr. Goldman, I spent thousands of dollars on a watch I didn't need and I am not about to do the same thing on a car that I can't afford. Transfer the registration into Sarah's or my name, I don't care which, and we'll come and pick it up. Don't tell me what you're going to do. Just let me know when it's done."

"I'll transfer the registration when Sarah next comes to town." I noticed him rolling his cigar between his thumb and forefinger. "Please, call me Abe."

"You are one of a kind. You trust me to represent you in a business with millions of dollars at stake but you don't trust your future son-in-law enough to register a car in my name."

"Ben, let's just say that you're not my son-in-law quite yet and this is a very small city, no matter how discreet you think you are." He winked at me. I couldn't believe what I was hearing. He knew about Julia and he was using it to pressure me to take on his franchise work. "Abe Goldman carries a lot of clubs in his bag. I had you followed in Florida so there is no reason why I couldn't do the same thing here."

But he had made a mistake by showing his hand. Now I would never take him on as a client and he knew about Julia. I would not let him dangle this over my head like the Sword of Damocles. If I gave in to him, it would never end. I couldn't leave myself vulnerable to the likes of Abe Goldman. My decision about Sarah and Julia was becoming easier.

"Mr. Goldman, you don't really understand what's going on in my life, no matter what you may think."

"Please Ben, don't make excuses for my benefit. You don't have to explain yourself to me. You're not the first person something like this has ever happened to. But, I hope you're smart enough to know the difference between getting laid and being in love. For Sarah's sake, don't get the two confused and you and I will get along just fine. Now, let's get back to business. You don't have to give me an answer right now. But, consider your position in every aspect and, hopefully, you can be my lawyer in this new venture of mine. I'd like to get started right away. By the way, as an extra incentive, if you take on the work I'll give you a bonus of three percent of the stock in this venture with an option to buy another seven percent at a favorable price."

"Mr. Goldman have you ever seen the movie *The Godfather?*"

"Of course. It's just business, it's not personal. By the way, call me Abe."

49

By May 15, the wedding preparations were in full swing. The invitations, set to be mailed out on June 15, were being printed and addressed to 800 of the Goldmans' closest friends and relatives and 150 guests from the Stein family. There was no overlap on the two lists. Security bracelets were being mailed to each guest with their invitation to identify those invited. The wedding had evolved into the socio-political event of the year and the security procedures were reviewed by the RCMP because of the number of expected dignitaries. I took on the self-appointed task of counting the number of Golexes worn among the invited guests.

The wedding menu was created by the head chef of the Fontainebleu. It included tri-colored tomato salad, vegetarian ravioli, onion tart, flaming chateaubriand and a candy boat floating in chocolate with strawberry cheesecake as the cargo. Four chefs from the Fontainebleu were flying in from Miami to supervise the food preparation. There were weekly logistics meetings to review all the wedding plans to which I was not invited nor which I wanted to attend. But, there was one issue that neither the high-priced wedding planner from Montreal nor the chefs from the Fontainbleau could control. There can't be a wedding without a groom even if there was a five-colored tomato salad. It's really that simple. No groom, no wedding. If I didn't go through with this wedding, it was off, even if that caused a minor recession in the North American hospitality industry.

In sixteen days, Julia was set to move into her cottage at Gimli and I was more confused than ever about what to do. I considered talking to my dad about the wedding but I decided not to. I could not bring myself to tell him about Julia. I did not have a sibling, at least not one I knew personally, to confide in so I did the next best thing. I arranged a dinner with my friends. As usual, Gerry was the clearing house for the dinner arrangements. The Old Bailey gave us our usual corner table. It was still the best place to be seen and not heard.

Like most of our dinners the conversation began with the latest vacation stories and anecdotes from work. We heard about Paul's latest business venture which was neon-lit gravestones. The dearly departed or next of kin could buy or lease to own a gravestone that had "Mom" or another designated relative lit up in neon against a contrasting granite gravestone with a flashing arrow pointing down. It was solar-powered for marketing to the families of environmentalists. We all listened in amazed astonishment to Paul's latest sure-fire way to down-size the family trust account.

Eventually, the dinner conversation got around to my wedding. My friends were all in the wedding party and they wanted to know if they were getting a gift for participating, all except Gerry who was more interested if Sarah's cousin had a boyfriend. He was hoping she did because then, if they went out, he would know that they were both after the same thing, captivating conversation.

"Does Abe Goldman call you son?" Murray asked as we were waiting between courses.

"He calls me Ben and I call him Mr. Goldman. I want nothing to do with him. But, strangely, I like the man in an odd way. The problem is he can't be trusted."

"Does Sarah realize what you really think of her father?" David asked.

"She doesn't have a clue. She thinks he is a pillar of society that everyone admires. She has no idea." I caught the waiter's attention and ordered another round of drinks.

"Are you going to tell her?" David pressed on while taking the last piece of cheese toast from the wicker basket.

"Well, that's the big question. I have serious concerns about Sarah's judgment when it comes to her family. She wants to be the next matriarch of the Goldman dynasty. To me, this would be a curse and the cause of a great deal of friction between us."

"You mean you're not getting laid?" Gerry had this ability to interpret code phrases. To him, friction in a relationship means not getting laid and he was right. Gerry had missed his calling. He should have worked at deciphering enemy code.

"Actually, I am getting laid . . . but it's not Sarah."

There was sudden silence around the table. Everyone grabbed for their respective drinks and looked around to see who would speak first. Since they had all attended Sir Edmund Hillary Secondary they hadn't been taught to take turns. They all spoke at once.

"Details . . . we want details. What do you mean not Sarah? Who is she?" My friends sounded like a synagogue board meeting.

"You remember Julia Windsor, the nurse I went out with a few years ago? She ended up marrying a doctor from Chicago and moved away."

"You mean the drop dead gorgeous girl who none of us could figure out what she saw in you?" Gerry asked just before knocking back a vodka on ice.

"That's the one. I've been seeing her and she's moving here for the summer to be closer to her family . . . and me." I was relieved to finally be talking about my situation.

"What about her husband?"

"He's staying in Chicago. He may come up for some weekends."

Murray took over the questioning. "Are you confusing getting laid with being in love?"

"You're the third person who's asked me that. Just because Julia is married, it can still be love."

"Isn't this just another way of describing an affair?" The drink server returned with the next round of alcohol and allowed us a moment of silent reflection.

"No, it's more serious than that."

"So what are you going to do?" Everyone let Murray do the questioning.

"I don't know but I've got to do it soon. Any suggestions?"

"You can't trust this woman," Murray said, offering the collective advice for the group.

"She left you and now she's leaving her husband. This is not a good track record."

"As they say in horse racing circles, she has bad form," David butted in.

"The road to happiness can be rocky," I said defending our relationship. "It's not always straight or smooth."

Gerry, after staying uncharacteristically quiet, interrupted to tell us that he had the answer. "Look, it's obvious. Dump them both and start again. You tried Miss Rich Bitch and she's boring, egocentric and her father is an asshole. You had an affair with Mrs. Gentile and she can't be trusted. Neither work, so dump them both, wipe the slate clean and start again. Maybe open a restaurant . . . Jewish/ Malaysian fusion."

"I'm not that confused." I was annoyed by the humor but somehow he did make sense.

"Yes you are. How much more confused can you be than sitting in a restaurant with your bridal party and talking about having an affair with a married woman who is about to leave her husband to be closer to you? I call that the definition of confusion. What am I missing?"

Paul, ever the pragmatist, had a question. "If you don't go through with it does that mean, we don't get the wedding party gift? Anyway, what did you get us?"

"I think it is some Italian designer golf head covers and two dozen golf balls."

"I say go through with the wedding. I could use the balls and, from the sounds of it you could use some too."

"I'm losing my patience with this conversation," I said sharply. "You aren't taking this seriously." Everyone broke out in spontaneous laughter and so did I.

We spent the rest of the evening exchanging gossip, retelling old stories and planning our next trip to Las Vegas. By the end of dinner, I was comforted by the security of my lifelong friends. No matter what happened, my friends would be there accepting me for who I was and reminding me not to take myself too seriously.

There were two messages on the answering machine when I got home. Both were from Sarah and they were an hour apart.

"Hi, Sarah. I just got your messages. What's doing?"

"I've been on the phone with my mother half the night about wedding plans. The details are overwhelming. She's worried about the morning-after brunch for the out-of-town guests and whether it should be at their house or the golf club. What do you think?"

"By the time we get to the Sunday brunch, I'll be so sick of these people that I'll be by myself at the Italian Coffee Bar having a cappuccino. You can tell the guests I died from an overdose of insincere gratitude."

"That's cruel. For weeks you've been quite distant and sarcastic every time the wedding plans are mentioned. What's really going on?" Sarah was mad.

"You're right, I have been distant and I am annoyed about having a bit part in an Abe Goldman extravaganza. Why do we need all these parties and plans? This isn't for us. This is about your parents giving yet another demonstration of their ability to spend." I was impatient about all of it.

"Can't you take any joy in the fact that my parents want to do this for their only daughter?" Sarah was sick of my attitude.

"This is what makes you happy? Garish overspending so hundreds of people who owe their livelihood to Abe Goldman can pay homage to his wealth?"

Sarah was livid. "You've had a distorted view of this wedding from the start. All my parents want is to celebrate with their friends and relatives. These guests admire and respect my parents for what they have accomplished and for their generosity."

"Don't kid yourself. They don't care about your parents or us. Abe Goldman has summoned them to attend. The only thing missing is conduct money. They are doing what they are told with the payback of being seen at the social event of the year. This has nothing to do with respect or generosity. It's all about obligation and debt."

"If that's how you really feel about this wedding, maybe we should just call it off." She was crying.

Here was my chance. She had said it. Now I either step up to the plate and seize the opportunity or blurt out some mushy, insincere, backtracking statement to salvage the relationship. If I said nothing, I would be missing my chance to get out of this wedding without having to reveal anything about Julia. This was the moment to make a life-altering decision. "I told you when my mother died that I had reservations about this wedding, and nothing has changed. I want to call it off. I can't be any clearer than that."

"So do you want to cancel the wedding?" a chill had crept into her voice.

"Since my mother died, I've had this magnified sense of my own mortality. The thought of deciding what I'll do the rest of my life is scary. There is too much to see and experience for me to promise till death do us part for anything. A year ago I was ready to get married but I'm not ready now. I'm not ready to make that kind of commitment."

"Why didn't you say this before we made all these wedding plans?"

"I told you this months ago but you were so pre-occupied with lavender napkins that you didn't listen to what I had to say."

"You know, I've been reading a book about relationships and, when one person says they aren't ready, it often means they're seeing someone else. Is there another woman?" She asked the right question and caught me off guard.

"Just because I don't want to get married and be the social spectacle of the year doesn't mean there is another woman." I had to think fast for my response.

"Well, are you? You aren't answering the question."

"Our problem is not speculating on whether I'm having an affair. Our problem is that you expect a lifestyle which is typified by this wedding. I don't want it. There is a great deal I love about you but I don't want a life like your parents."

"You're not answering my question. Is there another woman? A simple yes or no will suffice."

I did what every red-blooded male would do. I avoided the question. I can live with committing sins of omission but I just couldn't bring myself to outright lie to her, even if it was over the phone. "Sarah . . . there is no point continuing this conversation. I'm not going through with this wedding. You can take from that what you want but I'm telling you that I won't be there."

"Ben, if you don't give me a straight answer to my question you'll never hear from me again. Not only will there not be a wedding this summer, there will never be a wedding and this will be our last conversation. Is there another woman?"

I said nothing and she hung up.

I didn't know what caused me to end our engagement there and then but it just came out. I didn't realize it at the time but that would be the last time I ever spoke to Sarah. I tried calling her back three times but she wouldn't pick up the phone and she didn't return my messages. Sarah's notion of self-worth was too great to tolerate being dumped and she wouldn't take the first step or second to salvage any relationship. Her ego-driven nature was, for me, a blessing in disguise. I didn't have to resort to one of those "It's me not you" speeches. A burden had been lifted from my shoulders. Still, I was overwhelmed with doubt if I had done the right thing. I could not separate my decision to call off the wedding from my feelings for

Julia. I was counting on Julia to confirm that I had not made a life-altering mistake.

That night, I replayed in my mind the conversation with Sarah and how I was going to break the news to my dad and friends. I couldn't sleep at all. So I got out of bed, packed up all those sterling silver pickle dishes and crystal salt and pepper shakers and piled them up in the outer hallway. By seven the next morning I had called a courier and arranged for them all to be picked up and delivered to the Goldmans. Now we'd see if all those Goldman relatives could return pickle dishes to the discount wholesale supplier. It may be a bargain to buy from a wholesaler but not such a bargain if you try to give the stuff back.

That morning I called my dad and arranged to meet him for breakfast. Next, I called Julia to tell her the news. I felt relieved that I could stop all the lies. But Julia did not sound as enthusiastic or relieved as I had hoped. She was cautious and emphasized that canceling the wedding was my decision and said I had to take responsibility for what I had done. I assured her that this would have happened anyway but I was hoping that she would have said something positive about us being together or how this was a positive step in our relationship. But that was not what I heard. She had not told her husband that she was leaving him but I had told Sarah it was over. Down deep, I knew something was not right. I felt vulnerable.

I met my dad at one of those original Fifties diners that you find in any wholesale supply district of any city. We sat at a booth in the back corner where no one could overhear our conversation. I tried some initial small talk but almost immediately I broke the news to him that the wedding was off.

"Dad, I just couldn't go through with it. It didn't feel right. Sarah expected me to adopt her family's ethic and it wasn't for me. The simple truth is her family should learn some manners. It was difficult to be civil to them. For some reason, her family thought that being related to Abe Goldman made them smarter than everyone else and that they were entitled to live a life of privilege." Nervously, I played with the cutlery.

"Ben, I never cared for Abe Goldman or the rest of Sarah's family. I never said anything but Sarah was not for you."

"Why didn't you ever tell me?" We were momentarily interrupted as the server came for our order, two breakfast specials and hold the bacon.

"How do you tell your son that he's marrying the wrong girl? You can't give advice about such things, especially to your own child. Anyway, your mother was so thrilled that you were getting married and to such a prominent family. Maybe I should have said something but I thought that, somehow, you'd do the right thing. And you did."

"Why didn't you think I should marry Sarah?"

"Sarah is beautiful, smart and comes from an established family. But, she never seemed at ease or comfortable laughing. It always seemed contrived. She smiled when it was appropriate to smile and laughed at the right time but it was never spontaneous. People who don't genuinely laugh can never be trusted. A Jewish boy with a degree in animal husbandry better have a wife with a sense of humor. She's going to need it and this one didn't have it."

"She didn't have much of a sense of humor, that's true, but there was something between us?"

"Don't confuse being in love and being in bed."

"You're the fourth person who's given me that advice. You're not upset that I called off the wedding?"

My father shrugged and lowered his voice. "I'm relieved for both of us. Let's eat our breakfast specials as our private celebration, with white paper napkins."

I arrived at the office about 9:30. There were three messages from Abe Goldman, each one telling me to call him right away and tell his secretary to interrupt whatever he was doing. Although I was not looking forward to the conversation, I had to call him back.

"Ben, I spoke to Sarah this morning. She told me to cancel the wedding because you want nothing to do with her or our family."

"I'm not sure I'd put it that way, but the wedding plans should be cancelled. We are not getting married. It's better we decided this before rather than after the ceremony."

"This only happened last night. There is still time to save this if you act quickly. I can help if you want to talk to Sarah."

"I don't want your help and I don't want to save our relationship."

"I told you not to confuse getting laid and being in love."

"I took your advice."

This was the first time I heard Abe Goldman raise his voice. "To hell with you. You can't treat a Goldman like this. You can't

314

have your way with my daughter, have an affair on the side and then drop my little girl as if nothing happened."

"Mr. Goldman, I'm not one of your cavalcade of admirers and I don't want to do your legal work. Also, I'm not one of your relatives who depend on you for a living. I don't want the crumbs off your table. Your threats are as phony as your gifts. Good-bye, Abe." He had always wanted me to call him Abe.

50

The news of my aborted engagement spread quickly. I avoided places where people I knew congregated. I did not want to face any questions about my private life. But, in spite of my best efforts, I kept running into people I knew who asked me in one way or another what had happened. Everyone sounded so concerned for me because they assumed that Sarah had dumped me. No one could seriously believe that Ben Stein would call off a wedding with Sarah Goldman. The story going around was that she had left me for another man and I'm sure Abe started the rumor. He could not bear the thought of someone like me rejecting a Goldman. Even Mr. Cohen offered his condolences for my loss. In a moment of compassion, he gave me a free newspaper which turned out to be yesterday's edition. I played the role of the jilted lover with Olivierian dignity, understated, quiet, but with a deep sense of loss. Playing the victim worked well in the circumstances as it diverted attention away from my relationship with Julia.

Julia moved to Gimli a week earlier than I expected. Her husband was away and not returning to Chicago until June 4 so there was no reason for Julia to wait. By May 25, we were living together in my apartment. She bought a telephone switch that could forward her calls from the cottage to my apartment and we installed it on a separate phone line. Anyone who called her thought she was answering from the cottage. It was apparent to me that no one in Chicago knew about us and Julia intended to keep it that way. At the time, I forced myself not to think anything of it.

Our first week together was a honeymoon. I took time off work and we spent the days shopping for household appliances, like a toaster. As a bachelor I had no need for such items but co-habitation prompted the acquisition of small appliances. We made meals for each other, talked for hours at a time and went for long walks. She settled into the apartment and our living together took on an inevitable routine. But, with the advent of a routine something changed in our relationship. The reality of day-to-day living took hold and we actually slept at night. I was going to work at 6:30 in the morning and she would go about her day doing domestic chores such as grocery shopping, laundry and visiting her family. I didn't know how she explained her living situation to her family but I did not press the point. She never wanted me to meet her family, regardless of the pretense.

We started to notice each other's annoying habits and that too caused some friction. I couldn't understand why she would buy a 24-roll pack of toilet paper for two people living in a one bathroom apartment or a 15-liter box of laundry detergent which, by my calculation, would last the better part of eighteen months. There was no room in our apartment for such quantities. She couldn't understand why a grown man would keep five different varieties of popsicles in the freezer which left little room for anything else. Also, she had not developed much of a palate for pickled herring in wine brine. When the jar went mysteriously missing from the fridge, I promptly replaced it only to have it go missing again. The one positive change was that she was no longer a vegetarian. As a consequence of living in Chicago, she started eating a little delicatessen.

We had our first real fight on June 6. I was late coming home from work and did not call to tell her that I was going to be late. Julia, who was not comfortable in the kitchen, had prepared a meal and it sat there on the table getting cold and increasingly unappetizing. When I came home, she told me that I had no regard for the work that goes into preparing a meal and that, if I respected her effort, I would have called. I tried to explain that I was in a meeting and did not have a chance to excuse myself to call her. All of the other small separate annoyances came together that night like nuclear fission. You could see the mushroom cloud rising from the apartment. When the fight ended we didn't apologize to each other and we reached an uneasy truce with no one declaring victory or conceding defeat. From that point on, our conversations were more guarded and took on an edge of civility.

Our relationship lost a certain spontaneity and Julia started to go out more on her own without telling me where she was going. I admit it crossed my mind that she might be having an affair. If she was with another man then she would be having two affairs at the same time. I discarded that possibility because the logistics of keeping

317

three stories straight between three men seemed a practical impossibility.

I was worried about the direction our relationship was heading. Daily life was tense for both us. We stopped talking about our relationship for fear of where the conversation might lead. I had no contact with my friends and I did not tell my dad anything about Julia. I had no one to talk to about my troubled personal life. On two occasions, I went over to my dad's house to visit but we did not talk about my private life. He didn't want to know. Since calling off the wedding, everyone thought I was in mourning. No one asked me if I was going out with anyone because they felt it was like poking at an open wound. My cousin John sent me the latest innovation in athletic shoes as his way of telling me to keep up the chase and never give up. Little did anyone know I was so removed from Sarah and her family that I barely remembered that I had been engaged.

June 15, when I would be going to Las Vegas to celebrate the Jupiter settlement, was fast approaching. I had planned that Julia would come along as our coming out as a couple. I was excited to be going by private jet and to enjoy an all-expense-paid weekend. It seemed like fortuitous timing because our relationship was rocky and I thought that a weekend away might ease some of the domestic pressure.

Julia was not excited about the trip. She had been to Las Vegas many times and she had traveled by private jet with her husband when pharmaceutical companies had flown them to speaking engagements or promotion trips. I tried to be nonchalant about the whole experience but, in truth, I was excited beyond belief. The plane would leave whenever we wanted, there were no metal detectors or rude ticket agents and the food was pre-ordered from a gourmet menu. We would land at the private terminal in Las Vegas where all the high rollers are flown in on the casinos' private jets and a limousine from Caesar's Palace would be there waiting to take us to the hotel and then to the reception where the check for $100 million would be put on display. I was the guest of honor.

During the reception, members of the franchise committee expressed their gratitude for my work, not only for getting the $100 million settlement, but also for solving the ongoing accounting issues. Mr. Zimmer spoke about how we had met and how generous I had been with my time when the case had only involved his store. In truth, it was Mr. Zimmer's generosity which gave me this opportunity because he had put his faith in an articling student with no track record. I reminded him that in just a few months I would be expecting my annual payment of two jars of pickles. It was a great night. Julia played the role perfectly but she did not seem genuinely happy for my success. It was as if my success deprived her of the limelight, although every man in the room was taken by her beauty and her smile. She charmed the crowd and laughed in all the right spots. None of it was genuine.

We had no commitments the day after the reception. Julia and I went our separate ways for the morning but arranged to meet at 1:30 for lunch at the Stage Delicatessen in Caesar's Emporium. Julia went to the spa for a hot rock massage and body moisturizer treatments where they cover your entire body with vegetables. I imagined her lying there like a tossed salad dressed in oil and vinegar. I arranged to meet Mr. Zimmer at the craps tables where I would teach him how to play. He was a thoughtful and enthusiastic student of the game. As it turned out, luck was with us as we stood alongside a woman who hit twelve consecutive points and held the dice for over thirty minutes. Mr. Zimmer and I each made $2,800. I went directly to the jewelry store just off the casino floor where I bought Julia a gold rope chain with a "J" attached to it. I planned to give it to her at lunch.

The Stage Deli was much like the one in New York. It had the same menu, same size portions, same style of waitress and the same prices. The interior design was a combination of arborite tables and New York posters. For a food hound like me, the Stage Deli was the Wailing Wall of delicatessen.

We were seated right away and, before I could ask, there was a small pail of half-sour pickles on the table. I could have eaten every meal there but I exercised restraint and restricted it to one lunch. After limited deliberation, we decided to stick with classic deli sandwiches. Julia was not familiar with most of the ethnic dishes such as verenikes or chicken in a pot. Happily, there was no brown rice or tofu on the menu. We decided to split two sandwiches, one brisket and one medium lean smoked meat, both on russian rye with hot mustard and a side of cole slaw. The waiter asked us what we wanted to drink.

"I'll have a Dr. Brown black cherry." It was my favorite deli refreshment.

"I'd like a large skim milk," replied Julia.

"Julia, I don't think you should have milk," I said somewhat amused by her lack of protocol.

"Why not?" she asked innocently.

"It's just not done."

"Why not?" Julia asked as she looked at the waiter for help.

"No one has milk with a smoked meat sandwich in a delicatessen. It's not . . . done," I explained. But I didn't say milk with smoked meat was like wearing a neon sign which flashes "Gentile."

"But that's what I want," she repeated, not understanding the issue.

"Look around. Do you see anyone here having a sandwich with milk?"

"I don't care. Please bring me a large skim milk and put it in a brown paper bag so I won't embarrass my friend here." The waiter sensed a problem and made a hasty retreat.

"Julia, in a Jewish deli you don't have meat and milk. It's against the dietary Kosher laws."

"The what?" She sounded irritated.

"You don't eat meat and dairy. You can't eat crustaceans or animals with split hoofs either."

"Who made up these rules?"

"I don't know who made up the rules but they are about three thousand years old."

"You mean to tell me that three thousand years ago, someone made up some rules about what you can eat and now I can't have a smoked meat sandwich with a glass of milk sitting at the Stage Deli in Las Vegas?"

"Three thousand years ago these rules made good dietary sense. It's not just that some person who decided arbitrarily what we should or shouldn't eat for lunch. At the time, it was the healthy way to eat."

"But haven't you ever had a cheeseburger or a lobster?"

"Sure I have."

"So why is it wrong that I have a glass of milk with a smoked meat sandwich and it's not wrong if you have a cheeseburger?"

"Because I don't have a cheeseburger in a Jewish delicatessen. I eat it at a burger restaurant."

"So, it's not the fact that I'm having meat and milk, but where I'm having it. And you call that a rule? That's hypocritical and, anyway, these dietary rules made three thousand years ago don't make sense anymore. There is no reason to live by these antiquated rules and there is no reason to make me feel out of place. If I'm not supposed to have milk then it shouldn't be on the menu."

"It's just a tradition. It's done out of respect for our forefathers. Some Catholics have ceremonies in Latin and no one at the service understands a word they're saying. It's still done and people still go to church."

"But at least you can translate the Latin into something that makes some sense. These kosher rules of yours make no sense in any language and you only follow them in certain restaurants."

"There is no right kind of restaurant for a smoked meat sandwich with milk. It's wrong anywhere in the world. It is a bad combination." It was my turn to be irritated.

"How bad is this combination? Is it the combination of the food or the combination of the Jewish lawyer with the Gentile girlfriend who embarrassed you in a delicatessen? It's only odd because it makes you feel out of place. I'm perfectly comfortable with what I ordered."

The conversation had degenerated into a very bad argument. I had never intended it to become a debate over the relevance of Jewish tradition or mixed-race relationships. I had never before spoken about her being Catholic, if she was Catholic, and this was the second time she had brought up the fact that I was Jewish. I had to be careful not to overreact for fear that I could lose Julia right there at the Stage Deli in Las Vegas.

"Julia, this has gotten way out of proportion. I was just trying to help. I didn't mean to ridicule. These restaurants have certain unstated practices and ordering milk with a smoked meat sandwich is not what's done. It is bad form."

"The waiter thought it was fine."

"He was just being polite."

"So, everybody patronizes Gentiles in these places and this is where you feel comfortable?"

"It's not patronizing and all I was trying to do was give you some advice."

"Advice. I don't need any advice about three-thousand-year-old rules that no longer make sense. It seems to me that if you blindly follow stupid rules than you're the one out of place and you need some advice, not me."

She had gone too far. "Respect for history if not stupid. That's one of the things about Judaism that makes it special. We respect the past and the wisdom of our forefathers. We don't simply discard our history because someone has a new way to eat or a new style of conduct. Judaism is not a smorg where you pick the parts you choose to respect and throw out the rest."

"It all sounds so righteous and then you order a cheeseburger. If you mindlessly cling to three-thousand-year-rules then you're wasting your time."

"I never considered it a waste of time being Jewish. I admit that I don't follow every Jewish rule on how to conduct my life but, if you want to talk about clinging to historical nonsense, tell me how can you believe that a virgin gave birth to a child. At least in the rules of Kosher, it was relevant at one time. Even two thousand years ago no one could conceive without getting laid."

"Well, it's obvious that my kind aren't welcome here and you feel out of place with me, so enjoy lunch, send back the milk and I'll see you later."

With a single theatrical motion, Julia got up and walked out of the restaurant. I didn't feel up for the chase or scene two in the shopping mall. I stayed in my seat, ate lunch and tried not to think about what had occurred. The smoked meat sandwich was terrific. I asked the waiter to take the milk away. As I reached into my pocket, I felt the weight of the gold chain. It reminded me that, less than an hour before, I was picking out my first gift of fine jewelry for Julia and now she had walked out on me over a glass of milk. I had no idea how this had happened and the irony of my defending three thousand years of Jewish tradition was not lost on me.

I spent the afternoon avoiding our hotel room. I did not want another confrontation like the one at lunch. I wasn't that good at handling conflict in my personal life. I walked up the Vegas strip, looked in the various hotels and inevitably found my way back to the crap tables at Caesar's. I didn't do as well as I had in the morning session but I still made a few hundred dollars for my afternoon's effort. When I got back to the room, Julia was watching television

322

and eating an order of spare ribs and shrimp cocktail snack from room service. Crustaceans and pork ribs were not going to get a reaction out of me. There was an empty glass of milk on the tray which I am sure was her way of poking me in the eye. I was not going to take the bait.

"Where have you been?" Julia asked as I walked into the room.

"I've been in the casino." I had my hand in my pocket, feeling the gold chain, but I did not take it out.

"Did you win?"

"I won a few dollars. Julia you just can't walk out on me if you disagree with something I say. A relationship is hard work and you have to fight for it. Getting up and leaving is not the answer."

"I wasn't going to sit there and be insulted. I don't ask you to respect what I believe so why do you ridicule me because I don't observe your rules?"

"I wasn't trying to convert you. I was just trying to help so you wouldn't look conspicuous."

"The only reason you care about me being conspicuous is how it looks for you. Don't try to turn me into something I'm not. It will never happen."

"Please, this is only about a glass of milk. I'm not trying to turn you into anything. I don't want you to be different than what you are. Your difference is what I find so appealing. You are exaggerating this whole issue beyond anything I ever intended."

"It's not an exaggeration when you're the one being ridiculed."

One of us had to concede. This problem was not going to go away unless we had some type of closure and that meant someone had to be wrong. Julia was not in the mood to admit anything so it was up to me to wave the white flag or we were in serious trouble.

"Look Julia, I can see why you would feel this way. I'm sorry I made your food order an issue. It's my mistake. It will never happen again."

"That's okay. I'm happy to put this behind us." She got up, kissed me on the cheek and went back to watching her television show. In spite of what she had said, we both knew it was not behind us. I debated if I should give her the gold chain to seal our reconciliation but decided to leave it in my pocket, at least for now.

There were no other incidents during our trip. We both avoided any topic that could become controversial and it was all very civil.

Needless to say, we didn't go back to the Stage Deli, in spite of my craving for a hard salami sandwich and Dr. Brown. We went to two Las Vegas shows where there was very little opportunity to talk while we ate dinner. For the balance of the trip, Julia went to the spa and I gambled unsuccessfully at the craps table. We had the good sense to buy books for the trip home which gave us excuses not to have any lengthy conversation in the close quarters of an eight-seater private jet. Who would have thought that I would have rather flown commercial?

We came home in the early evening. Julia decided to stay out at the beach but I did not go with her. Instead, I went to the office and checked on what had gone on while I was away. In fact, for the balance of June, Julia stayed at the cottage and I only went there every few days to have dinner and sometimes spend the night. She made friends with some of her neighbors and we had most of our meals with people in the adjacent cottages. These group dinners were enjoyable and it took up the majority of our time together. There always seemed to be other people around. We slept together only a few times and it felt like she was doing it more out of obligation than love.

At the beginning of July, Julia told me that she had certain obligations back in Chicago and she was going home for ten days. I took her to the airport, helped her check in and watched her walk away as she went through security. I wasn't sure if I would ever see her again in spite of her assurances that she'd be back in ten days. She didn't call me until the tenth day of her trip and then only to tell me the flight number and time of her arrival. I wanted to believe we were still together but I could not reconcile how we could be together and her not calling for ten days. I asked her why she hadn't called and she said simply she'd been too busy. I didn't accept her terse explanation and she got angry as I questioned her further. She wanted to know if I would still pick her up from the airport and I told her that I would. I was there when she got off the plane just like I had been there when she left. Neither of us said another word about our call. For the next two weeks, she commuted between the cottage and my apartment. When we were together in the city, our social schedule amounted to walks down Wellington Crescent and stopping to get an iced latte. We never talked about the future or anything potentially controversial. More to the point, we talked as if we didn't have a future. We both knew that within the next month Julia would have to decide if she was going to stay or go back to Chicago. I knew things weren't perfect but I was confident we could work it out if she were willing to try. What I didn't know was whether Julia had ever committed to anything other than herself.

51

Something happened to Julia while she was in Chicago. I speculated there had been some sort of reconciliation with her husband but I didn't want to ask, fearing the answer. Although it was only the beginning of August, the leaves were already starting to change color and this was nature's reminder that we had to deal with our relationship. I knew that we were in trouble but my feelings for her were still strong and I did not want to face the prospect of her leaving. Somehow, I hoped she would find a way to make it all work. I had relied on her for that from the first night we had met.

On August 19, Julia was driving in from the beach and we arranged to meet at my apartment. I told her that I'd be late but she had keys to the apartment to let herself in. I arrived home about 9:30 expecting to be greeted by her. Nothing felt as good as finding Julia in my apartment after a long day at work. But Julia was nowhere to be seen when I got home. The apartment felt different and I could not identify exactly what had changed. It seemed empty. Perhaps Julia had driven in early, organized the place and had then gone out, knowing that I would be late. I opened the fridge door to get a drink and then I saw it, the milk carton, in the center of the center shelf of the fridge. Taped to the front of the carton was a picture of Julia and below it a typed line "LOST . . . BUT DO NOT FIND." As I took the carton out of the fridge there was a folded piece of paper underneath it with "B.S." written on it. I took out the note and read.

> I am on my way back to Chicago. I really do love you but it was not meant to be. My life is too complicated. You were right, smoked meat and milk don't go together.
> Love always . . .
>
> Julia

52

Again, I felt no sense of closure with Julia but I was not surprised that it had come to an end. I wasn't even surprised at how it had ended. Julia was not the type to face her problems. She preferred to walk away from them. Regardless, I didn't love her any less. She always managed to leave open the possibility for revisiting the relationship at some later time. But for me it was over because I swore never to leave myself that vulnerable again. It's all too much. The saving grace was that so few people knew about our relationship that I did not have much explaining to do. And those who knew about us thought she was going home after her summer at the beach. Still I needed to talk to somebody about it.

"Gerry, it's Ben."

"Where have you been hiding all summer? You just disappeared."

"I called to say you were right."

"Of course I was right. What exactly was I right about this time?"

"Julia."

"What was I right about Julia?"

"I spent the summer with her and she walked out on me and went back to Chicago. Remember at our dinner you told me to dump her before she gets the chance to dump me?"

"I don't remember saying that but I'll take credit for it as long as I was right."

"You were right."

"You see, I told you so. You should have listened to me."

"You're right. I should have listened."

"So, let's go celebrate the second dump by the same woman. Not everyone can achieve such status. Or would you like to wait until she does it a third time?"

"There won't be a third time."

"We'll see. I'll let the boys know you're sitting double *Shiva*. We'll all come over, eat deli and talk about how you blew it with rich Goldman's daughter and twice with the married Gentile from Chicago."

"Okay."

"Okay, you get the deli and the Chivas and we'll pay you a surprise visit."

"I'll look forward to the surprise. See you later."

There was a real sense of emptiness in the apartment without Julia. I looked forward to finding her there at the end of the day. It's a lot better than coming home to an empty apartment and hoping to find the message light flashing. After Julia left, I didn't feel very sociable and I had no desire to go out. I wasn't ready. I spent my evenings working, eating take-out Chinese with my dad, going for a walk in the neighborhood or some combination of the above.

By the middle of September, most of the leaves had turned color and had fallen off the trees. I enjoyed walking in the evening so I could hear the rustling of leaves under my feet. On one particular Tuesday night, I took such a walk with no particular destination in mind. I was standing at a crosswalk waiting for the oncoming cars to pass when a set of headlights came to an abrupt halt at the pedestrian crosswalk. I was about to step off the curb when I noticed Sarah driving our Porsche with someone in the passenger seat. That could have been me in the passenger seat of that car, instead of walking in front of it. It was fitting that she was doing the driving. I looked directly at her as I crossed the street but she was too busy talking to the passenger to notice me. When I looked through the front windshield, I saw that the passenger was Barry Altman. There was a certain irony to all of this and in some twisted way I felt vindicated. As she sped off, all the old memories came flooding back of my two failed relationships. Maybe I had been too judgmental of Sarah. But, looking at my Rolex brought me back to reality.

Although I had not intended it, my walk took me to the Italian Coffee Bar. I said hello to the four Tonys and took my regular seat at the round table. I took a newspaper that had been left on another table and sat reading it, occupying my time as I drank a double espresso.

Suddenly I heard, "Hello, stranger." It was a familiar voice. "Is this seat taken?"

I put down the paper. "Arlene, what a great surprise. You're just the person I've been waiting for. Please sit down."

She smiled and kissed me on both cheeks. "You always were a smooth talker. The sure way to a woman's heart."

"Lately it hasn't worked that well."

"It sounds like a story. Tell me about it."

At first I avoided talking about myself and asked Arlene about her social life. She updated me about Rubin, the bicycle racer with the flat tire. His surgery did not take. He had taken up self-propelled lawnmower racing and was captain of the Toro racing team on the South Dakota racing circuit. She was not cut out to be a self-propelled lawnmower groupie, touring the plains of South Dakota, particularly with Rubin's flat tire. Eventually, the conversation got around to me. For some reason, I wanted to tell Arlene everything. We were old friends. This familiarity made it easy to speak candidly. I updated her about Sarah and Julia and tried to be truthful and explain what really happened. It was difficult because I wasn't exactly sure what had happened.

"You know, this assimilation business is a lot harder than it first appears." I confessed.

"What do you mean?" Arlene inquired.

"Well, I didn't want the life my parents had. I wanted more. My parents' world felt so claustrophobic. But, for some reason I didn't want to abandon my upbringing either."

"The fact is you can't count on anyone outside your own."

I pointed my finger at her. "That is the paranoia of an ethnic minority speaking. We always feel under siege. There isn't an anti-Semite lurking under every rock and behind every tree. I don't accept that way of looking at life. I wanted to be a citizen of the world and I thought Julia was my chaperone and soulmate into that world."

"But it didn't work?" Arlene had stated what was painfully obvious.

"No, it sure didn't. And at the same time that I was trying to be worldly, I still wanted to hold on to what I was. It felt secure. I could not abandon all the generations who preceded me and belittle all the pain our forefathers suffered to maintain their identity. But I still want more than a life in a cloistered community, quivering at the outside world. I want to experience everything life has to offer."

"So what's the answer?"

329

"I don't know." I got the barista's attention and ordered two more espressos. This time with alcohol. "I learned from my relationship with Julia that, to my astonishment, assimilation does not suit me. For whatever reason, I could not abandon or dismiss my heritage. It's not someone else's problem. It is part of me. Now I understand those stories of Jews who were brought up as non-believers and then forty years later discovered this need to know about their religion and become raving Orthodox lunactics. I can't explain what drives it but now I know it's real. I know that halfway assimilation is not the answer. You partially lose your identity but the void is filled with confusion. You're not sure what you are or what you should become."

"What do you mean?"

"Look at those Reform Jews."

"You mean the ones with those stupid bushes at Chanukah who wear turtleneck sweaters to synagogue?"

I laughed at her description. "Yeah, that bunch. If a traditional law is inconvenient or does not fit their assimilated lifestyle, they change the rules so they can consider themselves observant. If it's boring to attend a long religious service then make the service shorter. If the rules of Kosher are inconvenient, then change the rules. You can always be devout if you change the rules to fit your lifestyle. It's just another way to justify convenience. It complicates and confuses our understanding of what we really are about and how to conduct our lives."

"Maybe the problem is that we aren't Jewish enough."

"I don't know. I was brought up in a semi-assimilated lifestyle and that felt too confining. I tried full assimilation with Julia and I failed at that. I never considered what it would be like to be truly observant." As I talked it was as if there was no one else in the coffee bar but Arlene. Or, at least no one else that mattered.

Arlene and I sat and talked for two hours in the coffee bar. Although she had her own failed relationships, we both had this same confusion of not really knowing the kind of life we should live. In spite of outward appearances, she was not sure that aspiring to her parents' lifestyle was the answer for her either. We understood the necessity of earning a living and how much energy that takes up. But, we didn't have a clue how to conduct our lives other than not violating the Criminal Code of Canada. It dawned on me that I might never meet the right woman if I didn't know the kind of life I want to lead. I needed a road map, but not the kind from the Automobile Association. Instead of directions, Arlene came back to my place for the night. Being lost has its unique privileges.

53

The first thing I did when I got up the next morning was call Mr. Basil. As office manager I had to tell him that I was going away and not to expect me back for a while. I wasn't sure how long I'd be gone. I told him I'd call once my plans were settled. Mr. Basil told me they would have to convene a management committee meeting to consider my request for a leave. I corrected him. It was not a request. I was going and, by the time they got the management committee together, I would be gone and there would be no point in having a meeting. He wished me luck.

After speaking to Mr. Basil, I had my call transferred to Margaret and Bill. I told them to take over all the files and meet with the clients. It was now their practice. They were nervous at the prospect of having their own practice but I assured them they could easily handle the work because they were already doing most of it anyway. I reminded them that the lawyers who control the work are untouchable so they should not be reluctant to seize the opportunity. In any event, Rupert was there to help if they got in over their heads.

The third item on the agenda was the bank. I took out the key that had been sitting in my medicine cabinet for the last three years and went to the bank. I gave it to the bank attendant to open my safety deposit box. They put me through a detailed security check and the bank official asked for multiple identification cards. Finally, he conceded that I was likely who I said I was and retrieved the security box. I emptied the box of the Israeli bonds that my parents had given me for my graduation, including their note telling me how proud they were of me. Also, I took out a loan for $10,000 with security of my stock in that Seattle software company. As it turned out, that $10,000 investment was now worth $200,000 and climbing. The bank was happy to extend me credit. I arranged to have an automatic transfer of funds to cover the rent and utilities.

Next, I went to the El Al airline office to book business class seating for a flight to Tel Aviv. They let me pay with State of Israel bonds which was considered the currency of Bar Mitzvahs, graduations and wedding gifts. Next, I drove to my dad's office to tell him that I was going away that afternoon. He did not seem surprised by my sudden decision. I asked for and he gave me Jaylan's, my half-sister's, address. He warned me to be careful, whatever I decided to do. The story of her real mother would be a big shock for her not to mention finding out she had a brother. I decided to call Jaylan first to introduce myself rather than appearing unannounced at her doorstep. The overseas operator put through the call. Despite all the latest technology in Israel, overseas calls still used operators. I was advised that it was a security issue to monitor all calls going in or out of the country. With the eight-hour time difference it was early evening in Israel.

She answered the phone. "Hello, this is Jaylan Levine."

"Ms. Levine, you don't know me. My name is Ben Stein and I am calling you from Canada."

"Canada is a big country. Where exactly are you calling from?"

"I am calling from Winnipeg."

"Is that close to Montreal?"

"It's two thousand miles away from Montreal so I would not describe it as close."

"In the Middle East you could cross ten countries in two thousand miles. Why are you calling, Mr. Stein?"

"Please, call me Ben. I recently found out that we were related. I am leaving for Israel today and I wanted to meet you."

"And how are we related? I thought all my family lived in Israel. I never knew of any relatives in Canada."

"Ms. Levine, you have some close relatives in Canada and I was hoping that I could explain it to you in person. It is a rather complicated family history."

"It all sounds very mysterious."

"It is a bit of a mystery but I can assure you it's real, if you give me a chance to explain. Given the time change and the flight time, I am hoping we could meet the day after tomorrow. We can meet at any time and any place you choose. You may want to tell your father. I have never met him but he will likely know the family name Stein from Canada."

"I should be more cautious but you have an honest voice. Call me when you get settled and we will arrange to meet."

"I look forward to meeting you in two days."

"Travel safely."

I went directly to the airport after my call to Jaylan. We met at the ticket counter where we checked in and went through security together. I emptied my pockets to go through the metal detector and put the gold rope chain with the letter "J" into the plastic container. Then we sat in the business class lounge waiting for our flight to be called.

"What's that for?" she asked.

"It's a gift for my sister."

"I didn't know you had a sister."

"Neither did I. It's a long flight and I'll explain later."

El Al 112 lifted off on time and we settled in for the flight. The flight attendant came around to take our lunch order. It was a choice of meat, fish or vegan. We both opted for the smoked meat platter.

"Would you like a glass of milk with lunch?" I asked Arlene.

"Are you crazy? I'll have a Pepsi."

After Arlene fell asleep I had a chance to think about what I was doing. although it was a spur-of-the-moment decision, I had prepared for this trip a very long time. I put my hand in my pocket, felt the chain and thought about meeting the sister I never had. This was my last gift to my mother. She spent her life trying to keep the family together and now I was the link between her past and whatever is to come. My future does lie ahead of me.